Transforming Pandora

Transforming Pandora

Carolyn Mathews

ROUNDFIRE BOOKS

Winchester, UK
Washington, USA

First published by Roundfire Books, 2013
Roundfire Books is an imprint of John Hunt Publishing Ltd., Laurel House, Station Approach,
Alresford, Hants, SO24 9JH, UK
office1@jhpbooks.net
www.johnhuntpublishing.com
www.roundfire-books.com

For distributor details and how to order please visit the 'Ordering' section on our website.

ISBN: 978 1 78099 745 2

A CIP catalogue record for this book is available from the British Library.

Design: Stuart Davies

Printed and bound by CPI Group (UK) Ltd, Croydon, CR0 4YY

CONTENTS

In a dark time, the eye begins to see.
Theodore Roethke

I dedicate this book to you, dear readers.
May you be well.
May you be happy.

Chapter 1 – SPRING 2003

'It'll do you good,' Margery said, as she dusted round me. 'You can't just lie there moping all day. You never know, you might hear something that'll perk you up.'

'It's not really my sort of thing.' I sniffed, wishing she'd go away and leave me in peace. I had no desire to witness anyone's Uncle Arthur hailing them from the great beyond. I was quite bereaved enough without wallowing in other people's misery, thank you very much.

Margery's nose twitched. 'For someone who's got all them wotsname books—' She nodded towards the bookcase.

'Mind, Body and Spirit,' I muttered.

'—I would've thought an Evening of Clairvoyance would be just your cup of tea.'

'I haven't opened those books in ages,' I said, feeling something approaching shame that I still had them. 'Most of them came from my mother. She's into all that.'

Margery shook her head and came closer, giving me a piercing look, just as my grandmother had when I was developing measles or some other infant inconvenience.

'You still on them funny pills?'

She was referring to the medication I'd been prescribed for the fear that had gripped me when my husband had become ill. But once he'd died I needed to know where I really was on the grieving scale, so I'd flushed them all away.

'No. And I might be sad but I'm not mad. At least not mad enough to believe that he'll be popping back from beyond the grave for a chat.'

My tormenter thrust her duster into the pouch in her apron and sat down opposite me on Mike's armchair. The lady was not for turning.

'There's no harm in it, you know. We sing a couple of hymns, the medium gives a little talk, then a demonstration.' She leaned forward, seeking to mesmerise me with her bulbous eyes. 'Come on. I was only saying to Bob the other day, you've hardly been out since the funeral.'

The thought of Mr and Mrs Grove discussing my every move induced a mild attack of paranoia, so I made my escape to the kitchen sink, with her following close on my heels, like a terrier.

'Thing is, my friend Joyce – who I usually go with – she's away at her sister's. So you'd be doing me a favour. It's only £4. Won't break the bank.'

'Okay Margery,' I sighed, knowing when I was beaten. 'But if I come with you, you've got to promise me something.'

'Course, love. What is it?'

'You've got to stop doing my cleaning. I'm perfectly capable of doing it myself.'

Seeing her face fall, I put my arm around her, clumsily patting her back, which was both plump and solid at the same time.

'I really appreciate it, Margery, but I can't let you do it any more—'

I paused, not sure how to continue. I knew why she'd been coming. It was displacement activity for what she really wanted to do.

'—I know how much you miss working at The Cedars.'

She rallied at this, sensing an opportunity.

'So do you think you'll be taking some bookings? Now that you're...on your own?'

That was a question that had been troubling me a lot recently. I'd suspended operations six months before Mike had died, which was when I'd laid her off. But since the funeral, Margery had been turning up unannounced at my cottage, brandishing her Brasso. At first I'd been glad of the company. And the hoovering. But it couldn't go on, as I was in no position to pay a cleaner. Not with my reduced income, and The Cedars in need of a new roof.

She was waiting for an answer.

'I'm not sure whether I'll revive the business. In the meantime, we'll leave it that Bob still does the gardening and I'll call on you if I do decide to reopen the house.'

Despite being in her late sixties, Margery looked more than a little piqued that her husband still had a job and she didn't.

She shrugged. 'Well I hope you make the right decision, for your sake. They always say new widders shouldn't do anything hasty. And you'll need something to occupy yourself, specially now he's gone...'

She was interrupted by Oscar cannoning through the dog flap, spattering the newly washed kitchen floor with soil from a flower bed he'd just excavated. Margery pursed her lips, grabbed her coat and bag, and made for the front door.

'I'll leave you to it, then. See you at seven. You don't mind picking me up do you?'

Oscar looked perplexed at her rapid departure, cocking his right ear appealingly. Blessed with good looks – his fur a silky pale grey, except for white paws and moustache – he'd grown used to people cooing over him, not retreating from him.

I bent and kissed his handsome head. 'Thank you, darling. I thought she'd never go.'

* * *

So there I was, at Margery's insistence, perched on a hard wooden chair, bang in the front row of a musty old spiritualist chapel, devoid of the riches and ritual once familiar to a lapsed Catholic like me. She, eager to witness the communion of living and dead, and I, dreading being singled out for psychic attention. The last thing I wanted was to burst into tears in front of forty or so perfect strangers.

The room we occupied was the size of a small hall. At the further end stood a table covered with a white lace-edged cloth, too short to conceal its chipped legs. A plain, brass cross sat in the centre, flanked by a vase of tired flowers and a large candle in a glass container.

Facing this makeshift altar were ten rows of eight chairs, divided by an aisle. The wall behind the altar was scattered with pictures and posters, the rest of its surface displaying traces of Blu Tack and yellowing Sellotape. Among the pictures were some colourful, framed portraits of attractive subjects, bathed in light.

'Who are those pictures of?' I whispered to Margery.

'A couple of them are angels and the others they call ascended masters. They've got funny names like Lord Khutumi and St Germain.'

She pointed to a portrait of a tall, blond, curly-haired youth in a white pleated robe, his muscular upper body surrounded by an aura of blue, white and gold contained within the upper curve of his wings. In his right hand he held aloft a shining sword.

'That's my favourite, Archangel Michael. They usually ask for his protection before a session. Course, I'm C of E really. Me and Joyce are more spectators, if you get my drift.' She winked. 'It makes a change from the telly.'

We'd already had the hymns, sung *a cappella* in the absence of an organ. Not recognising any of them, I'd just opened my mouth like a goldfish. The chapel chairwoman, who was overseeing this evening's meeting, had then led us in the Lord's Prayer, after which she'd introduced the medium, a man called Reg, who was almost as antiquated as the chapel. He'd been sitting behind a lectern, to the right of the table, and now rose to his feet and launched into his preamble.

'Good evening, ladies and gentlemen. A few of you will know me already. I'd like to welcome anyone here for the first time.' I deliberately lowered my eyes so he couldn't read that I was one of those. 'And, for your benefit, I'll give you my little spiel and I'm sure our regulars will bear with me.'

He beamed at his fan base and they responded with knowing smiles.

'So for those of you unfamiliar with the process of communicating with spirit, I am, to put it simply, a channel to the astral plane.' He paused for effect. 'But I don't have any control over who comes through, so if you've come here to contact somebody in particular, there's no guarantee they'll appear. Then again, Great Aunt Maud, who passed over before you were even born, very well might.'

There were some murmurs of agreement in the ranks. 'But,' he continued, rubbing his hands and beaming at us, 'with the help of my Cherokee spirit guide, Tooantuh, I'll do my best to transmit what comes through, in the hope that it will not only show evidence of life after death, but also give some guidance along the way.'

So saying, he bowed as far as his ancient joints would allow, and began slowly pacing from side to side, his right hand clutching his temple. His first targets were a middle-aged couple across the aisle from us, and he approached them, announcing, 'I've got a Ron here for you. Can you place that name?' They looked baffled, and he added, 'Or maybe it's Don. He's wearing a trilby hat and he's showing me a train. I can feel a pain in my leg.' But they shook their heads. Reg opened it up to the room, with no response.

After that he walked up and down the aisle throwing out names and giving descriptions of the dead persons who were making contact, but only getting an occasional reaction from the audience. While waiting for some spectral recognition to take place, I found myself fantasising about what these departed spirits might be able to communicate to the still-alive and kicking. Even if nobody recognised them, Reg could still ask them some searching questions. Could they explain crop circles, for example? The Bermuda Triangle? Or, on a more terrestrial note, provide the key to unsolved crimes. Like the identity of Jack the Ripper.

Reg paused beside a man and began to describe a red-haired girl who had died young, asking if he knew who she could be. The man said he didn't, but Reg continued anyway.

'This little girl. She's saying you've been having trouble with a battery of some kind?'

The man looked puzzled, until he remembered something. 'I had to get a new back light for my bike last week.'

Reg nodded. 'That's it. She's sending you a message to check your inner tubes as well. She's fading now.' And on he moved up the rows.

I had an irresistible urge to laugh, but managed to control myself by concentrating on the picture of the delectable Archangel Michael. An explosive sneeze from Margery, however, brought me back to the medium's voice. He was telling a woman that her dead mother needed 'healing thoughts'.

I couldn't resist whispering to Margery, 'It's a bit late for healing thoughts now she's croaked. Is this as good as it gets?'

Margery smirked behind her hand. 'He's not having much luck, is he? Poor old devil. His mate Tooantuh's not adding up tonight...'

'Or maybe he's legged it back to the Happy Hunting Ground,' I giggled.

But almost before the words were out of my mouth, Reg's voice rang out from the back of the room.

'Tooantuh is bringing me Mike. I feel he's passed over recently.'

An old woman piped up, 'Is it my Spike?'

'It's Mike, dear, Mike,' Reg said, raising his eyes to heaven.

Margery elbowed me in the ribs. 'Put your hand up.'

'But it might not be *my* Mike,' I hissed back.

'Oh, don't be so daft,' she retorted and raised her own hand, whereupon Reg strode down the aisle and planted himself in front of us, a palpable look of relief on his face.

Margery swiftly presented Reg with the facts of the matter, either because she'd taken pity on him or because she was getting bored.

'Her husband's name was Mike. He died of a heart attack three weeks ago.'

Reg's beady eyes lit up. I could see what he was thinking. This could be his chance of salvaging the evening and keeping his reputation intact. As they say in football – you're only as good as your last game.

'...As I said, passed over recently,' he intoned. 'Yes. He's saying it was a shock.'

I nodded, to encourage him to go on. Although actually it hadn't been such a shock. He'd had his first attack a few months before.

'May I ask your name?' said Reg, addressing me.

I hesitated because I hated answering that question. People usually said something like, 'You don't look like a...'

'Pandora,' I answered, and someone in the room sniggered.

Reg cocked his head as if straining to hear. 'That's not the name I'm getting. Did he call you something else? Something like Sandy?'

My spine started to tingle slightly, all the way up to my neck.

'He called me Suzy.'

Reg touched his forehead and looked into the middle distance. 'That's right. He's saying that's what he preferred to call you. I'm getting a picture of you and him with your children.'

He glanced at me enquiringly, expecting confirmation, but, without thinking, I gave my stock reply: 'I haven't got any children.'

Bemused, Reg began tapping his forehead for further inspiration. It was at that point that the chairwoman pointed to her watch and raised an outspread hand to signify that he had five minutes left. As a result, Reg decided to quit while he was, just about, ahead.

'He sends you his love, my dear. He says he didn't suffer and he's always with you.'

And then he moved on to a woman the other side of the aisle and began describing her dog. It was too late to call him back, but I was kicking myself for not answering yes to his last question, because although I didn't have any offspring, Mike did. I felt a nudge.

'He got the name thing right, didn't he?' whispered Margery.

'Not really,' I protested.

'Well, as near as makes no difference. And he gave you a nice message. I told you it'd be worth coming.'

I smiled weakly, and dug my nails into the palms of my hands as all my grief at losing Mike flooded back. Coming here had made me feel worse, but I couldn't tell Margery that. She was enjoying herself too much.

Becoming aware of Reg talking to a giant poodle called Spike, I started to worry about Oscar being on his own, especially as he was missing Mike so much himself. I had an overwhelming desire to get out of the place and race home, but I couldn't because of Margery and her lift.

While this was running through my head, I heard the chairwoman announcing that this reading would have to be Reg's last. Spike's owner was now sobbing and being comforted by her friend, so it was with obvious relief that Reg returned to the lectern. He was just reaching the end of his valedictory speech, however, when he stopped dead, pointed towards us and declared, 'Hold on. We haven't quite finished yet.'

Margery and I regarded each other, unsure who was being addressed. To my embarrassment he announced, in a sepulchral voice, 'Pandora. I have a High One here, whom you have called in. He says contact between you is not possible yet, but if you meditate every day, your vibration will rise and you will eventually be able to connect with him.'

Reg paused, scanning my features for a sign of comprehension. But I sat immobile, still taking it in. So he continued, 'He says try to bring to mind your previous practice. Do you remember how to meditate?'

My brain creaked into life again, enough to remind me of an attempt I'd made years earlier.

'Yes. But...'

'Good,' said Reg, then slumped down in his chair, mopping his brow.

'That was powerful,' he puffed, as he swallowed half a glass of water.

I stood up, with the intention of approaching him for more details. Sensing this, Margery took my arm, gesturing towards the chairwoman who was rattling her keys.

'She gives him a lift home, so I wouldn't hold him up with questions if I was you.'

As we made our way out of the building with the rest of the congregation, it dawned on me that my message – to me so mystifying and portentous – to them would probably have seemed par for the course. Margery's words confirmed it.

'I shouldn't worry too much about that last bit, dear,' she said, in the tones of an old hand at the game. 'If the evening hasn't gone so well, they often do something like that at the end. For effect. You know, a bit of a show so's people won't be disappointed.'

After dropping her off, I put my foot down and got home in record time. As I pulled into the drive, passing The Cedars and turning right on to the small road leading to my cottage, I wondered if what Reg had said really had been all hot air – something to impress the punters so the evening ended on a high note.

I let myself in, expecting Oscar's usual exuberant greeting, but there was no sign of him. I eventually found him upstairs, on my bed. He'd only started doing this since Mike had died – maybe there was still a trace of Mike's scent in the room. He raised his head when he saw me and looked mournful, but wagged his tail weakly and followed me down to the kitchen where I made some tea for both of us.

Later, as I lay in bed, I went over the evening in my mind. Had Mike really communicated with Reg? If so, why hadn't he chosen to talk about something more meaningful than my name? Maybe it was my fault for stalling at the word 'children'. If I'd kept quiet, Mike might have dropped some pearls of wisdom from the astral plane. Like how I could go on living without him.

I had a little weep on my pillow and considered what else Reg had said about Mike. I wasn't too happy with the promise that he was always with me. Not in the bathroom, surely?

As if in response to this thought, an image of Mike's amused blue eyes popped into my head. There was a certain expression he would wear when he thought a situation or person was ridiculous, usually accompanied by a pithy comment. I could almost hear him say, 'Don't forget to check your inner tubes, Suze.'

My heart seemed to squeeze in on itself, it missed him so much. I closed my eyes and flicked back through my internal photo album, to the very first print of him.

Chapter 2 – SPRING 1970

Mike and I first set eyes on each other at the Green Oak Rhythm and Blues Club, held in a hall attached to a pub called The Woodman's Arms. My friend Cecilia and I had been planning to go to the Mecca Palais, where the DJ played records with a good beat – easier to dance to than some of the music at the Green Oak. But it had one drawback. The other girls tended to have jobs, whereas we were still at school doing A-levels. Our experience in the past had been that the boys who patronised the Palais thought themselves too cool for schoolgirls.

The Palais was aptly named, as it was truly palatial. An impressive revolving stage dwarfed the DJ on the nights when no live bands played. The dance floor was vast, and surrounded on three sides by gold-legged burgundy velvet chairs and glass-topped tables. At the back of the ballroom was a sweeping staircase which led to a wonderful powder room, with rows of mirrors where we could back-comb our hair and freshen up our eyeliner and pale pink lipstick to our hearts' content.

In contrast, the Green Oak R & B club was as basic as could be, with plain stackable chairs along the walls, dingy wood-panelling and bleak toilets. It too, had a stage, but this one was framed by cheap cotton curtains, usually closed on weekdays, their grand opening being reserved for the bigger groups who played at the weekends.

The acts tended to set up on ground level in the week, so they were flanked by the crowd, who either stood tapping their feet on the wooden boards or danced in couples to the music. The club owner had laid a curve of carpet in the corner, to the right of the stage, to mark the musicians' territory. As the evening progressed, the foot tappers were displaced by the dancers. But since it moved them nearer to the bar, they didn't seem to mind.

The Green Oak may have been shabby, but it was in a more salubrious neighbourhood than the Palais. The admission was cheaper as well, which was why we finally decided on the Green Oak. We had just enough money for the entrance fee, bus fare and one drink – Cecilia because she earned a bit babysitting her younger sisters, and me courtesy of my Saturday job at Roy's Fashions.

We were in the final weeks of our seven long years at St Thérèse de Lisieux Convent High School for Girls. Cecilia's sights were set on teaching, while I was desperate to go to work, so I could afford to extend my meagre wardrobe of two tops and two miniskirts – even though, as Cecilia the mathematician pointed out, that did make up four outfits.

Cecilia, who preferred to be called Cece – as in two letter Cs (or yes-yes in Spanish) was always kitted out in new gear because her mother was a dressmaker and would use up spare bits of material to make her skirts and dresses. They were about the same size, and Cece even wore some of her mother's stuff occasionally.

There was no danger of me borrowing my mother's clothes, because she was no longer around – having failed to come home from a music festival the summer before. But even if the contents of her wardrobe had been available, I wasn't really into the flower power look. Anyway, she was a pocket Venus whereas I was more Olive Oyl – skinny with big feet.

* * *

So we were standing in the Green Oak, this Wednesday night, trying to get into the groove with James Jay and the Blue Jays, at the same time avoiding eye contact with anyone we didn't fancy in case they asked us to dance, when I felt a tap on the shoulder.

'Excuse me. Do you mind if I ask you a question?'

A gap-toothed smile scanned both of us. Its owner was tall and gangly with unusually blond hair, giving him the appearance of an attenuated cherub. Sensing that there was a punch line looming, I assumed my sardonic face, which involved focusing on the end of my nose.

'What?'

'Are you wearing a wig?'

At which point he leaned towards me and gave my long dark hair a sharp tug, to the raucous amusement of three boys standing a few feet away. I noticed he didn't so much as tweak Cece's chestnut pageboy.

'Course I am,' I retorted, gathering up my hair as if to pull it from my scalp. 'It's my Cleopatra wig.'

The blond boy grinned from ear to ear, but before he could say anything, one of the others spoke.

'Don't take any notice of Ray. He's being a prat.'

The speaker was standing quite close to me and he added softly, 'You've got lovely hair...' but trailed off when he realised his friends had moved closer and were listening in. I responded to his compliment by waggling my head and touching my hair like a model in a shampoo advert and we both laughed.

Ray looked a bit miffed at this and turned his attention to Cece, who I could tell was more than pleased, from the way she was widening her eyes and pushing her shoulders back to display her sizeable bust to its best advantage.

The boy who'd spoken to me was shorter and beefier than Ray. He was wearing jeans, a checked shirt and a brown suede jacket – a bit like a cowboy. He had piercing blue eyes which held an expression of interest. He wasn't trying to disguise it, either. As for me, I liked what I saw too.

'I'm Mike. What's your name?'

'Ann.' I didn't want to say what it really was.

He asked us if we'd like a drink and while he was at the bar getting our Cinzano and lemonades, Ray and the other two, a boy called Brian and his brother Rick, told us how they'd been having a bet to see whether I was wearing a wig. This is not as bizarre as it sounds – it was the fashion to wear wigs and hairpieces in those days.

'Who won?' I enquired.

'Mike. He was the only one who said it was natural.'

'He must have been having a good look, then,' chimed in Cece.

'How much did he win?' I asked.

Brian and Rick smiled slyly at each other.

'He won you.'

Cece gave me a meaningful glance and opened her mouth to speak, but I shook my head slightly, as he was approaching with our drinks.

The boys clustered round, including us in their group. It turned out they were members of a cycling club and their conversation largely consisted of drinking and cycling stories, shamelessly exaggerating quantities and distances in view of there being girls present. They were good company and at ease with each other and with us.

We had to leave by 10.30 to be in before the 11.15 curfew our parents had imposed, and when we left, Cece and Ray had already fixed up a date for Saturday. But Mike had just squeezed my hand and whispered, 'See you next Wednesday? I'll be here.'

On the bus home, Cece was highly excited about seeing Ray again.

'I can't wait for the weekend. What about Mike? Are you seeing him?'

Upset that he hadn't made a proper date or asked for my telephone number, but having too much pride to admit it, I just said, 'No. But he said something about being there next week.'

Cece looked surprised.'You looked as if you were really getting on. Are you disappointed?'

The answer was yes on both counts, but I decided not to tell her that in case she told Ray. I knew in my bones that Mike fancied me, so why hadn't he made a date? Maybe he was too cool to go out with a schoolgirl, even though I was eighteen. Anyway, if he was in the process of making up his mind, it was better for me not to blow too hot. One thing I did know was that the male of the species would rather chase than be chased.

Trying to sound detached, I said, 'Maybe I'll see him there again,' and left it at that.

* * *

I couldn't wait for Monday morning to find out how Cece's date with Ray had gone, because I'd been hoping that Mike had asked for my phone number. She looked tired but happy. She said the weekend had been great. Ray was great. Everyone she'd met was great.

They'd gone to a party, at the house of someone called Phil, where there were loads of boys from the cycling club. His parents were away and apparently all the lads with girlfriends had been trying to take advantage of the – um – shall we say, bedroom facilities. Cece went into detail about the cut and thrust of her romantic skirmishes with Ray. More cut than thrust – we were good Catholic girls still at that point.

There being only one partygoer I was remotely interested in, I finally exploited one of her rare pauses.

'Was Mike there?' And, as an afterthought, 'And Brian and Rick?'

'Yes, they were all there. Brian and Rick were both chatting up the same girl but she wasn't interested, so they went for a curry. A few of us went with them. My parents went mad at me for being late, but Ray came round on Sunday and they liked him, so it's all right.'

I couldn't have given a tinker's cuss whether Mr and Mrs Byrne had turned double cartwheels at Ray's arrival, killed a fatted calf or danced naked on the red carpet. I had to know.

'Did Mike go with you?'

'No, he'd already left.' She paused, '...With his girlfriend. They're getting engaged. She was telling me they've been going out for two years—'

That's when my heart froze and I was transported back to the day last year when my dad told me my mother wasn't coming home. It was as if all the good had been sucked out of everything and life had turned a miserable grey.

'—She's a hairdresser and she's quite pretty. Small with long, blonde hair.'

In my relatively short life I'd had quite a lot of practice faking unconcern but I wasn't sure I was up to it this time.

'Are they all lovey-dovey?' I gulped, trying to keep the misery out of my voice.

By now some atavistic instinct had alerted Cece's antennae. It was dawning on her that I wasn't quite as interested in her love story as I should have been, and she had no compunction in quashing any hope I had.

'Not really. But she knows all the other girls and I heard her talking about Mike's mother. She's a widow and she gets on really well with her. Goes round and does her hair.' Cece must have taken pity on me then because she added, gently, 'I suppose that's why he didn't make a date with you.'

My heart was still encased in ice but my brain had begun to unfreeze enough to examine this revelation. He might have a girlfriend, but I was sure the attraction between us had been as genuine on his side as it was on mine. And I certainly hadn't imagined the way he'd stood next to me all the time we were in the Green Oak. Like a centurion, protecting me from unwanted attention.

Cece continued. 'Your name *was* mentioned, though.'

I caught my breath.'Who by?'

'Well Ray was telling some of the others how he really thought your hair was a wig and he'd pulled it. And I said, "Pandora didn't mind," and Mike said, "Who?" and I said, "Pandora", and he said, "I thought her name was Ann". Then I said, "That's what she tells people because otherwise they think she's posh." And then he looked annoyed and...'

She broke off, looking unsure whether to continue.

'And what?' I demanded.

'Oh, something about you being lady muck.'

A wave of humiliation flooded my veins and I felt my cheeks

blaze.

'Oh flippin' heck.'

'So then he took his girlfriend home. She wanted to stay but he said he was tired.'

* * *

Cece was my best friend but when it comes to boys, teenage girls can lose all sense of loyalty, you know what I mean? And now she had a proper boyfriend, she was relishing her superior position. In the days and weeks that followed, she'd occasionally feed me morsels of gossip about seeing Mike at this party, or that restaurant – Indian or Chinese and always lateish in the evening after the pubs had closed. Sometimes he was with the boys and sometimes with his girlfriend, who was called Val.

When I finally saw Mike again it wasn't in the Green Oak – I hadn't ventured back there since Cece and Ray had been dating. So I hadn't seen him at all, until I bumped into him outside Campbell's grocery store one afternoon on my way home from school. He was carrying a tray full of canned goods, which he dropped when he saw me. We both stared at each other in deep, blushing embarrassment. Him in his crumpled white delivery outfit and me in my school uniform. Cece had told me he had some sort of driving job, but I had no idea it would bring him so close to home.

'How you doing?' he mumbled.

'All right,' I said, wishing I could think of something fascinating to say. Something that would make him want to go out with me. And ditch his girlfriend. (What did I say about teenage girls?)

To cover our embarrassment, we both began frantically rescuing fifty-seven varieties of canned soup from the pavement.

'Haven't seen you at the Green Oak lately,' he said, his tone veering towards reproachful.

I had toyed with the idea of asking Anna, one of the girls from school, to go with me, but the memory of what he'd said to Cece had put me off.

'I haven't been for ages,' I answered. 'Not since we met you...and the others.'

Our hands brushed as we piled the cans into the delivery tray. His blue eyes were level with my green ones and he held my gaze.

'Why not?'

'Because Cece told me you called me lady muck.' My voice dipped at the last two words, I disliked that expression so much, but I wanted him to know it had hurt me.

He looked uncomfortable. 'Well why didn't you tell me your real name?'

My voice got higher without my wanting it to. 'Because people usually laugh and make jokes.'

Like the boys at junior school who'd christened me Pansy Potter. Or, worst of all, frying-pan. Had my mother had such a deficiency of imagination that she was unable to work out how my first name would combine with my surname, Fry? It was almost as bad as Eileen Dover.

His eyes had softened in sympathy. 'It's not that bad.'

'I hate it. My mum named me after some film she saw when she was pregnant, *Pandora and the Flying Dutchman*.'

'Could have been worse,' he grinned. 'It could have been *Lassie*.'

This failed to amuse me. And coupled with the fact that mentioning my mother had triggered a great surge of missing her, my eyes misted up with tears. He began to look worried.

'What do your friends call you?'

'Pan.'

We'd returned all the cans to the tray and Mike lifted it easily off the pavement. He was strong and healthy and good-looking. And I didn't mind a bit that he was a delivery man, which surprised me somewhat.

'Where do you live?' he asked.

'Just around the corner. Nightingale Road.'

At that moment Mr Campbell appeared in a flurry, to see why his delivery was taking so long. Mr Campbell knew my father, so I didn't hang around.

I waved goodbye to Mike, leaving him red-faced and irritated at this interruption. I almost skipped home, my longing to have my mother back being rapidly replaced by a yearning to see Mike again.

I was sure he was still interested, but I kept telling myself to let him do the chasing. After all, he could contact me via Cece if he really wanted to.

Chapter 3 – 2003

It had been a couple of weeks since I'd received my message from above – that I had to meditate if I wanted to contact a 'high one' – whoever that might be – but not much had happened on the meditation front. The fact was, although theoretically I knew how to do it, I wasn't very good at it.

I went through a phase in my thirties, heavily influenced by my mother, of spiritual exploration. She bought me books on self-improvement and took me to Mind, Body and Spirit exhibitions. I even braved the odd healing workshop, where we placed our hands in prescribed positions on one another, with the promise that if we wanted to do it for money, we could sign up for the next certificate. And the one after that. I never sought professional status, but my mother accumulated quite a few diplomas, which she displays to this day on the wall of her healing room in Glastonbury.

In fact, my dear mother Frances is now a typical Glastonbury native – she and her partner Charles happily running a crystal shop cum healing centre. My poor dad Francis, on the other hand, died when he was only fifty-two. Mum used to joke about Dad having the same name: Frankie Fry, saying it sounded like fast food. That'll be two frankie-fries please and hold the mustard. But I was always embarrassed by it.

Come to think of it, my whole life I've been embarrassed by names one way or another. Maybe it was genetic. After all, hadn't my Irish granny had her name anglicised from the softly vowelled Doireann to the more emphatic Doreen. As one of her brothers had put it, 'God, Doireann, the way the English say your name sounds like they're impersonating a donkey.'

Getting back to meditation matters, years earlier, Frankie had persuaded me to do a Transcendental Meditation course with her, because she'd been told that meditating regularly had an anti-ageing effect.

Our trainer, a young man with a tweed jacket and a knitted tie, was not quite what we'd expected. Pleasant enough, he struck us as more Geography teacher than guru, disinclined to deviate from his lesson plan.

He started with a coloured poster, pasted on to card and balanced on an old easel, which symbolised the mind's activity. There were rising and falling waves and many bubbles, representing persistent thoughts. Our goal was to empty our minds and let the bubble thoughts evaporate.

Then the 'after' picture was revealed with a shallow line and just a few bubbles, signifying our calm, receptive state during meditation, having transcended the chatter of our minds and altered our brain waves to alpha, or even theta, waves.

'This state,' he said, 'will bring enormous benefits to your mental, physical and spiritual health if you practise regularly.'

We were told to focus on our breathing, lower the chin, and think of nothing else for a minimum of twenty minutes. Try it, and trust me, you'll find it the longest twenty minutes of your life.

The next time the class met, we had to give a report on how our practice had gone at home. Most people had found it hard, and there were tales of interruptions from phones, doorbells, and curious family members. I didn't have that problem, living alone in my flat in Fulham.

One young woman looked mournful as she described her difficulties.

'I've got a four-year-old and he just wouldn't give me any peace. In the end, I had to lock myself in the loo.'

There were murmurs of sympathy but I felt sorrier for the little boy. If I had a four-year-old, I thought, I'd far rather be with him, than meditating behind a locked door.

When it was my turn to speak, I revealed that I'd felt a sort of tingling in the middle of my forehead.

'That's good,' the trainer said encouragingly. 'That's your third eye waking up.'

'Third eye?' I queried.

'Also known as the brow chakra,' he replied, pointing to a space in the middle of his forehead.

The room that he'd hired happened to have a wall chart showing the chakras, which were portrayed as coloured 'stars' superimposed on the body, starting with red at the base of the torso and working up through the colours of the rainbow to violet just above the head. He moved closer to the chart and read out the list of qualities to be gained from a healthy relationship with one's third eye. 'Intuition, soul realisation, insight, imagination, clairvoyance, peace of mind, wisdom.'

A man put up his hand. 'What is a chakra exactly?'

The trainer looked at the clock, consulted his notes, and answered briefly, 'The word is Sanskrit for "wheel" and it's the Hindu name for the seven main energy centres of the body which correspond roughly to our physical glandular system. These endocrine glands are the portals between the physical and the etheric body. The third eye relates to the pineal and pituitary glands.'

'Why a wheel?' asked the same man.

'It's a wheel in the sense of rotating motion. Healthy chakras have a pure colour and good movement.' Shuffling his papers, he said firmly, 'Okay, so back to the question. Anybody else have any other sensations? Or experiences?'

Frankie put up her hand. 'I felt my eyes move back in my head, as if they were trying to turn over. It felt quite weird.'

A couple of other people said they'd experienced the same thing, and the teacher beamed.

'That's good. It means the third eye is opening and your brain's going into a meditative state.' Seeing no more raised hands, he continued swiftly, 'So if you'd like to close your eyes, slow your breath...let's make it happen.'

The highlight of the course was when we individually received a personal mantra to focus on, in addition to the breathing. On the day it was given to us, we had to take a flower and a piece of white cloth.

I took an embroidered handkerchief, which I've still got somewhere, the dried flower pressed inside its folds. The teacher spoke some words in Sanskrit, then whispered my personal mantra which was 'hiring' pronounced to rhyme with 'earring'. I got this really fantastic feeling when he gave me my mantra, almost of bliss.

Afterwards, he addressed the whole group.

'Think of your mantra when you meditate. Remember, never speak it out loud, never write it down and never tell anyone else what it is.'

Of course, on the way home, my mother couldn't resist checking we hadn't been given the same one. 'My third letter is an "a",' she said, and I shook my head, unwilling to divulge more in case I was visited by the mystic wrath of the Maharishi, founder of the movement and close buddy of the Beatles. As you can see, I have no qualms now.

Inspired by the course, I was initially quite keen on practising regularly, but after a couple of weeks there didn't seem enough time first thing in the morning, and I was too tired at night. In the end, like most pursuits which don't yield quick results, my interest in it waned. My mother kept it up for longer than I did – but then, she was more in need of the anti-ageing benefits than I was.

* * *

So when I sat down to meditate, the morning after my outing to the spiritualist chapel, I knew what I had to do – close my eyes and focus on my breathing. After about five minutes I felt my eyes roll back behind my lids, which I knew to be a sign that things were on the right track, so I didn't bother with the mantra. I'd set the kitchen timer to thirty minutes in the hope that the longer I did it, the quicker I'd see results. But I soon started to fidget. And then the post came, Oscar went barmy, and I had to concede defeat. I suppose Oscar was being the equivalent of a four-year-old child.

But I finally did have a supernatural experience, one evening while I was idly meditating, eyes half closed, when I perceived a flash, like a spark, in the middle distance. At first, I thought nothing of it, just that it was the light catching one of the crystal pendants adorning the table lamp, so I closed my eyes completely and continued focusing on my breath, struggling to empty my mind.

After ten minutes or so, I opened my eyes to see a flickering tongue of light the size of a candle flame about eighteen inches in front of me, level with my gaze. I found that when I moved my head, it moved with me, so I started circling and turning my head left and right to see if it would follow. But the flame soon tired of this dance, and began to blur – diminishing in size until no trace of it remained.

That night I had a dream. In it there was an old man clad in a simple linen shift, with a beard and long, white hair which rolled under at clavicle level. I am sitting at a desk and he is standing by my right shoulder. There is a blank sheet of paper in front of me and a pen lying beside it. He seems to be urging me to listen but he has no voice. Or perhaps it's me – I have no ears yet. I feel he wants me to transcribe what he says but I have no idea what or why.

The morning after the dream, I woke up feeling unusually cheerful. As I applied my war paint in front of the bathroom mirror, I decided my hair had been neglected for long enough. A few random white hairs were visible and it needed cutting, so I made an appointment at my usual place. I left home a little early to browse the village shops and found myself enticed into the Cool Cake Boutique, a wonderful cake emporium a couple of doors down from the hairdresser's.

While trying to decide between the pistachio macaroons and the lemon and lavender fairy cakes, I spied a notice on the wall behind the counter, announcing there was a part-time job available.

I dug my glasses out of my bag, to see the details.

Part-time Admin. Assistant wanted, to process orders and liaise with baking staff. Position also necessitates advising customers on their product choices.

My reading was interrupted by Christine, the counter assistant, asking what I would like. I plumped for half a dozen macaroons, still eyeing the job description.

Giving me my change, she said, smiling, 'Would you like an application form?'

She smiled because we knew each other slightly from when I'd occasionally placed orders for the groups using The Cedars. So I suppose, in her eyes, I was an unlikely candidate, to say the least.

I don't know what possessed me but I found myself saying yes. So she handed me an application form and turned her attention to the next customer. I still had ten minutes before my appointment, so I filled out the form in double quick time and gave it back to her. By then there were no other customers in the shop, so she said, 'Could you hang on a moment? Olivier asked me to show him the application forms as they came in.'

A couple of minutes later she returned.

'He asked if you had time for an interview today.'

Calculating how long my hair would take, I found myself saying, 'I can be back here at twelve o'clock.'

I arrived back on the dot and Christine showed me into a sort of waiting room, with easy chairs and a long, low table scattered with albums containing pages and pages of beautifully crafted cakes and desserts for all occasions. I was intrigued by the pole-dancer cake – for a stag night, presumably. I would have thought one in the shape of a kebab would have been more appropriate. But I hated the cake in the shape of a sleeping baby. How could people bring themselves to cut into it?

'Hello. My name's Olivier Dubois.'

A tall, dark man, in his thirties, I would say, with a strong French accent and twinkling blue eyes, stood in front of me holding out his hand. I got up and shook it, relieved that he seemed like a person I could easily win over.

'Hello. I'm Pandora Armstrong. I've just been looking at your couture cakes. They're amazing. Do you make them all yourself?'

'Ha!' he almost shouted, following it with a hearty laugh. 'No, we 'ave a small team of *pâtissiers* working 'ere, in the bakery. I supervise the finishing. I spend some time taking the orders and advising clients but I need 'elp with that. So I want to train someone to assist me.'

We sat down and he told me that the job also involved stock control, and checking that the bills had been paid. It all sounded pretty straightforward. I told him that I was recently widowed and would welcome a part-time job to get me out of the house and take my mind off losing my husband. He nodded sympathetically and consulted my application form.

'I see you run a meetings venue.' He paused, no doubt waiting for me to say why I couldn't have used that to take my mind off Mike.

'It's not active at the moment. I'm not sure I want to revive it.'

Then it struck me that he might be testing my commitment to his job, so I quickly added, 'If I restricted it to weekends, I could manage both, of course.'

Olivier looked thoughtful, then got up and offered to give me a little tour around the place. Down the corridor was the office where I'd be based if I got the job. The bakery itself comprised most of the rest of the property.

When we said goodbye, he gave me a kiss on the cheek. But I put that down to Gallic charm, rather than proof of any success. I had a feeling that, like his counter assistant, he thought I didn't really need the job.

But, to my surprise, the next day he called to say I'd got it. And the following Monday I started work. At the end of the morning, Christine asked me if I'd enjoyed my training with Olivier.

'Yes,' I said brightly, 'I think I've got the hang of the basics.'

'So you'll be back on Wednesday, then?'

'Definitely,' I replied. Olivier was handsome, French and funny. What was not to like?

* * *

Soon after I'd started work, Olivier asked if he could come round to see me one afternoon 'to discuss a proposition'. I had no girlish flutterings at this, as by that time Christine had confided that Olivier was doing very nicely thank you with his boyfriend Justin, with whom he shared a luxury penthouse flat. Justin had a separate catering business, specialising in weddings, for which the Cool Cake Boutique supplied the cakes and desserts.

'I've been thinking about running a cupcake-decorating class,' Olivier twinkled, once he was ensconced on the sofa with a cup of tea. 'I assume your venue is the big house I just passed?'

A vision of Margery's doleful face tiptoed into my mind. I suppose it wouldn't hurt to revive The Cedars in a small way. I could give her the task of making sure all was spick and span before and after the event, to cheer her up a bit. So I took Olivier over there to inspect the kitchen.

'This is wonderful, Pandora,' he'd enthused. '*Superbe*. It's big enough for minimum twenty people. Although...' He paused, looking round. 'We'll start off smaller, till we get the 'ang of it.' He beamed at me, rubbing his hands. 'Let's say Saturday afternoon – in two weeks – and if it goes well, maybe a more advanced course over an 'ole weekend? Residential, perhaps?'

A vision of the leaking roof made me doubtful we could manage that, but I didn't want to rain on his parade, so I kept my misgivings to myself.

By the time I arrived at work the following Monday, Olivier had printed posters and handbills for the cupcake-decorating workshop, which he distributed to shops in the village and in the nearest town, about five miles away.

When the day came, it all went swimmingly. Margery had cleaned the kitchen to within an inch of its life, so all I'd had to do was provide enough tables and chairs for fourteen people and set them with the icing materials that Olivier brought with him. He also supplied the cakes, as there wasn't time for baking as well as decorating.

I stayed in the kitchen, to be on hand if anyone wanted anything. Olivier started with a demonstration of how to form sugar paste figures of animals, teddies, butterflies, and the like. And how to paint and glitter them with special edible fairy dust. He then gave the workshoppers some time to produce a little heap of them.

The second part of the demonstration saw him wielding a plastic bag with exquisite precision to produce perfect piping. He revealed how to colour the fondant icing, cram it into a plastic bag, and squeeze it like toothpaste in concentric circles and curlicues on to the cakes.

Olivier than gave his audience *carte blanche* to create their own little masterpieces, which brought varying degrees of success. It seemed to me that the figures they'd made were the wrong scale for the dainty cupcakes, leading to erratic slopes with jumbo teddies and fairies sliding drunkenly downhill. But I observed that when he conducted his final inspection, Olivier made no criticism, even of the ropiest attempts. In fact, he was charm itself, both to the women and to the two hapless husbands who'd been dragged along.

At the end of the afternoon, all the participants were in high spirits. After photos had been taken and cakes boxed up, the happy punters were treated to a glass of champagne. Olivier raised his glass and gave the toast, his eyes sparkling.

'Long time live the cupcakes.'

Chapter 4 – 1970

Mike's delivery job entailed him getting up early and, on the bonus side, finishing halfway through the afternoon. So who knows how long he'd been sitting at the end of my road when I came home from school the day after the falling tray incident. All I know is, when he emerged from a battered blue Ford Cortina, he had the look of someone putting his neck on the block. He could hardly pretend he'd just been driving past, could he? He was patently lying in wait for me, knowing I lived in Nightingale Road.

I thought I'd better put him out of his misery.

'Fancy seeing you here.'

And then I dried up. Completely ran out of merry quips. Me, the girl who always had plenty to say for herself. Mike looked pained, as if he was regretting the whole thing. He smelled faintly of aftershave and was wearing what looked like a new pair of jeans and a black shirt with white buttons. He studied his shoes.

'Do you want to come to the pictures tonight?'

'Okay. That'd be great.' The words had come out more eagerly than I'd intended. We stood smiling shyly at each other.

'I'll pick you up at seven, then. What number's your house?'

The movie played in my head of how my father would react if Mike knocked on the door. He'd sit him down and interrogate him. He'd ask where he lived, where we'd met, what his job was. He'd definitely disapprove of his job. While I couldn't see him stopping me from going out, he'd probably be waiting up, and I'd get a pep talk on no boyfriends until I'd taken my exams. And strong hints about boys with no prospects. No. Mike couldn't knock for me. Not yet.

'Do you mind if we meet here?' I said, 'It's just that you can never get away from my dad once he starts talking.'

I was sorry to slander my poor father in this way because as a rule he was a man of few words. Mike's smile had tightened slightly.

'Is anyone in now?'

'No. Why?'

'How about making me a coffee?'

Mrs Browning next door had eyes in the back of her head and I didn't want her reporting any unusual callers to my dad. I couldn't risk anything that might jeopardise our evening. So I came clean.

'Sorry. Better not risk it. I've got a nosy neighbour.'

I made a face to take the sting out of what he might take as a rebuff. Mike relaxed. He seemed to understand.

'Okay. How about a drive to Jubilee Park?'

This was a good suggestion, it being an unusually warm day in May and the park only ten minutes away. Throwing my blazer and school bag into the back of the car, I jumped in the front seat. Luckily, my summer uniform of white dress with navy blue stripes and short sleeves, was less obvious than the winter one, which involved a tie. With a bit of luck it wouldn't stand out too much.

I hadn't been to Jubilee Park for ages. As soon as I walked through the entrance, flanked by two massive iron gates, I was back there with my mother, playing hide and seek with my friends, while she sat on a green park bench with the other mums, chatting and handing out sandwiches. Once, a big boy had pushed me off a swing and made me cry, causing the park keeper to be summoned. I still have the scar on my knee to this day. I was telling Mike this fascinating piece of information while we made our way through an avenue of pink cherry blossom to the café in the middle of the park.

His childhood memories were of a different, more impressive park, Oak Green where he lived being a cut above Manor Wood. I held no particular allegiance to Manor Wood, what with the Irish ancestry on my dad's side and my mum a rolling stone, and I quite envied him his superior neighbourhood.

'So you're slumming it, then,' I said, getting my own back for the "lady muck" remark, 'Coming to a park with no bandstand or boating lake.'

He grinned. We'd reached the park café and I sat down outside while he fetched ice lollies for both of us. Then he got talking about the cycling club and I couldn't resist asking him about Ray and Cece.

'Is he keen on her?' I asked.

'Yeah. He seems quite keen. She certainly keeps her eye on him. We call her No-no.'

'Why?'

He chuckled. 'Why do you think?'

I smiled and tried to look faintly disapproving at the same time. We virgins had to stick together. I wondered whether it had occurred to him that Cece might have told me about his girlfriend Val. But now wasn't the time to confront him with that. I decided to sidestep the No-no comment.

'She really likes him. And so do her mum and dad. Which is a miracle. I can't believe they're letting her go out with him while she's doing her A-levels.'

He looked thoughtful.

'Are you glad they're together?'

I didn't really understand the question.

'Yes. Why not? She's my best friend.'

'So you're not interested in Ray, then?'

I was so surprised that I dropped the lolly on my dress.

'Give over. I've only ever been interested ...' I stopped because I didn't want to frighten him off. '...He's not my type.'

'Well he wasn't too happy when he didn't pull you. You know, that first night at the club.'

Mike lent me his hankie and I dabbed at the bright orange stain, wondering what his mother would think when she fished it out of the laundry basket. His eyes were questioning, waiting for me to comment.

'How do you know he wasn't happy?' I asked.

'Just something he said.'

Putting two and two together, I guessed that Ray had made a crack about Mike being out of the running, him already having a steady girlfriend.

'So what would he say if he knew we were going out tonight?'

Mike shrugged. 'I don't give a toss.'

I got up to deposit the remains of my lolly in the bin. When I came back I took Mike's hand and said, 'Neither do I.'

We walked a bit further into the park and stretched out side by side on the grass, savouring the remains of the weakening sun.

He clasped my hand and started talking again. I loved his take on the world. The wry way he found other people amusing. Not to mention his dimples, his mouth, and most of all his lovely crinkly blue eyes. The eyes themselves weren't crinkly, of course, just the skin surrounding them. One of the things he talked about was how much he loved cycling. As he spoke, he stroked my hand.

'We go out all day at the weekends. My first time out I couldn't do the last fifteen miles. Our trainer had to come and pick me up in his car. But you get used to it. I love it. It's a fantastic feeling of freedom. Last year me and Ray took our bikes up to the Lake District. Best holiday I've ever had. And we're planning to tour France with Brian and Rick.' He added, 'Maybe Phil too, if his girlfriend'll let him.'

At the mention of the 'g' word, a nagging little voice inside my head whispered: and what about *your* girlfriend, will she let *you* go?

I looked at my watch and realised I needed to get home to get the evening meal going before my dad got in from work. But I didn't want to say that. So I just said, 'I'd better get back.'

Before we got up, I turned towards him, expecting him to do the same. But instead he pulled me on top of him. My body moulded into his as we kissed. To begin with he explored my mouth very softly with his tongue and, by degrees, more solidly and insistently. I was captivated by this process, and my body moved as of its own accord, until the sharp edge of his belt buckle brought me back to reality and I rolled off on to the grass.

'Ouch. Your buckle's just stabbed me.'

He stretched lazily. 'You won't report me to the park keeper, will you?'

'It depends whether it's drawn blood or not.'

He laughed and got to his feet, pulling me up with ease.

Hand in hand, we made our way to the car. I felt protected. And warm. And loved.

* * *

Back home, peeling potatoes and wrestling with two enormous pork chops (most of my cooking was a combination of guesswork and asking Mrs Browning next door), my joy at seeing Mike was beginning to be diluted by the humiliation I felt at still being at school and having to wear school uniform, rather than out earning money like him and his girlfriend. Added to that was the embarrassment of having a father who disapproved of boyfriends unless they were at grammar school, or did something safe but boring in an office.

In theory, I'd been longing for a proper boyfriend, rather than the juvenile inter-school pairings that involved mild snogging with boys from St Vincent's, who you might meet in the Wimpy Bar a couple of times until it all fizzled out due to lack of funds, transport and anywhere else to go.

But in practice – what with homework, exams coming up, only two tops and two skirts – a proper relationship with a proper boyfriend had so far been an impossibility. Cece didn't know how lucky she was, with her extensive wardrobe and steady cyclist. Roll on the summer when I'd be able to leave school. And give up the Saturday job in Roy's Fashions where the manageress talked non-stop about her sex life. And most of the customers were over forty.

When we'd finished eating, I told my dad, as casually as I could, that I was going to the pictures with Anna that evening. He looked pleased. I think he sometimes felt sorry for me slaving over hot textbooks, although I doubt I did anywhere near as much homework as he thought I did.

'I'll pick you up if you like, love.'

My heartbeat paused for a moment. This wasn't in the script.

What do I say now?

'It's okay, Dad, we'll be fine on the bus. And there's two of us.'

Can he see I'm lying? I hate this, I thought. Why can't I say I'm going out with a boy?

'It's no trouble. It'll save you walking from the bus stop. What time does the film end?'

Never mind what time it ended, I didn't even know which film I was going to see.

'I'm not sure... '

My father took a ten-shilling note from his wallet and handed it to me. His mouth was trembling a little, his eyes watery.

'Here, love, treat your friend. Give me a ring if you change your mind.'

So now it was money by deception added to the roll of dishonour. I took the money and kissed my dad's cheek to avoid eye contact – in case he read the relief in my eyes.

* * *

Later, sitting in the cinema, with Mike's arm around me, watching Ali McGraw get sicker and sicker in Love Story, I kept returning to the stricken look on my father's face when I'd refused his offer of a lift.

I tried to put it out of my mind by concentrating on being close to Mike, but it wasn't working. I'd been looking forward to the evening so much...until I'd had to lie to my dad, which had triggered the anxiety that had been the subtext of my life ever since my mother had left. How I hated all this subterfuge. And being out with a boy, illicitly, was added pressure. Particularly when that boy already had a girlfriend. It was all too much and I began to weep silently.

Mike leaned across for a kiss, and laughed when he felt my face all damp.

'Aah. What is it with girls and sad films?'

I sighed. Even my tears were untrustworthy. But I could hardly tell him that it wasn't Ali MacGraw's fault, could I?

'Won't be a minute.' He disappeared and I assumed he'd gone to powder his nose. Left alone, I continued to snivel.

'This'll make you feel better.'

He reached behind my ear and pretended to magically produce an ice cream. And at that, I cheered up. I was with someone I loved being with. Someone who wanted to make me happy. I had mint-choc ice cream. Who could ask for anything more? When the Ali MacGraw character died, I cried again, but this time it was for her, not for me. And so for that short time I felt authentic.

When the lights went up, we found we just had time for half an hour in the pub opposite the cinema before he had to drop me at the bottom of my road. Our lovely spring day had disgraced itself and the road we had to cross was now awash with rain. I wasn't dressed for it, so Mike took off his jacket and put it round my shoulders until we reached the doors of the pub. Once inside, he scanned the place. He was supposedly looking for somewhere I could sit while he went for the drinks, but I suspected he was making sure there wasn't anyone in there he knew.

As I sat waiting for him to come back from the bar, I thought about what I would say to him. There was so much I wanted to say, but was it too early to mention his girlfriend? Would he think it pushy of me comparing our one date to their two years? But I couldn't ignore it. I didn't want my boyfriend to be a two-timer.

Mike appeared with our drinks. He'd bought me a Cinzano and lemonade.

'See. I remembered,' he smiled.

'Thanks.'

I raised my glass to him, pulled the cherry off the stick with my teeth, and took several sips. I offered him a ciggie, my hand shaking slightly as I lit it for him.

'The film was all right, wasn't it?' he grinned. 'Sad enough for you?'

I nodded, took a gulp of my drink, and galloped in where no angels would dare to tread.

'Mike, that wasn't the only thing I was upset about.' I paused, but the rush of alcohol spurred me on. 'Cece said you had a steady girlfriend called Val.'

At the mention of a girlfriend, his complexion had darkened. He gulped his beer and lowered his voice, eyes glinting angrily.

'What the fuck business is it of hers? What does she know about me?'

The force of his anger alarmed me, but I couldn't stop now.

'So is that a yes, then?'

He didn't answer, but just tightened his grasp on his glass. I pressed on.

'I don't like everything being so secretive. I don't like you having to worry in case someone sees us.'

He raised his eyes and stared accusingly into mine. 'Yeah, you're so honest you couldn't even tell me your proper name.'

Riled, I snapped back, 'I've already explained why I did that.'

'And what about picking you up from the bottom of your road? You're the one who wouldn't tell your mum and dad we were going out. I suppose I'm not good enough.'

His tone was harsh and getting louder. The couple at the next table had stopped talking and were listening in on our argument. I needed to calm things down. I'd have to tell him what I rarely told anyone – because the more I said it out loud, the more real it became, and I didn't want it to be true. I lowered my voice.

'My mum doesn't live with us. She left home last year. It's just me and my dad and he doesn't want me to...see anyone until after my exams.'

I couldn't tell him the real truth. That my dad, who assembled tables and sideboards at the furniture factory, wanted an 'educated' boy for me. Someone with prospects who would wear a suit to work.

'Anyway,' I went on, 'what's that compared to not mentioning that you're getting engaged?'

He stubbed out his cigarette forcefully and when he looked up, his eyes were full of anguish. 'I'm not getting engaged. I've decided. I'm breaking up with Val this weekend.'

Chapter 5 – 2003

I was four weeks into my new job and while I got on well with Olivier and the other staff, I still felt very much the new girl who knew nothing. I still couldn't quite believe I'd taken a job as a baker's dogsbody. I couldn't think what had come over me. Although in a way, it was consistent with a lifetime of occupational flirtations with various establishments as and when I felt like it.

For you see, in both sporting and working terms I am not a long-distance runner. Always been more of a sprinter. One of nature's temps. No job ever interesting enough to dedicate myself to entirely or induce me to stay for very long. Whenever I'd taken a permanent job, one look at the annual leave rota with my name at the bottom was enough for me to suffer the almost physical pain of my wings being clipped.

I think my record was eighteen months in one workplace until Fiona, one of my fellow management trainees, made it known she was looking for a travelling companion on a tour of Australia, and that was that. Cue swift exit from oil company under the baleful glare of Mrs Drake, our training supervisor.

'You've wasted your education,' my father would say. But my mother approved of me not wanting the BIG career.

'Do your own thing, Pan. Be happy. Be free.'

I was with her in spirit. Although as it turned out, her version of 'happy and free' had involved an awful lot of trailing around after footloose boyfriends – whether it led to Marrakesh or the Mull of Kintyre.

* * *

At the Cool Cake Boutique that morning I resumed my foray into the jungle that was the filing system. Olivier had asked me to find some invoices that his accountant had requested, but as he'd been in the habit of shoving them into any one of several large lever-arch files, I was having my work cut out tracking them down.

Olivier wandered into the office and found me sitting on the floor surrounded by the bulging files.

'Pandora. I think you need a little rest from this...' he struggled for a word and settled on 'chaos'.

I hauled myself to my feet, wondering if Christine needed help in the shop.

'I have a Mr Willoughby coming at eleven and I was hoping you would masquerade as my Personal Assistant.'

My laughter stopped him in his tracks. I had a vision of me dressed in a power suit and high heels, taking notes of their meeting.

'I'm serious, Pandora. I just want you to greet him, sit him in the reception room, ask him if he wants something to drink. Generally keep him happy.' He looked at me almost pleadingly. 'Would you do that?'

'Of course I will.' I waved my hands at my clothing. 'As long as you think jeans and trainers will convince him.'

'Pandora, whatever you wear, you look lovely.'

Compliments will get you everywhere, I thought. If only Olivier were straight, he'd be the perfect man for me.

He sat down and became conspiratorial.

'I've applied to be a chef on a new television series and he's from the production company. I want to make a good impression. Can I count on you?'

'Of course, *M'sieu Dubois,*' I grinned.

And so it was that half an hour later I showed a distinguished, white-haired gentleman into the reception room, following which I extracted Olivier from the bakery and conducted him into the presence of the big cheese, for their formal introduction.

'Can I get you tea, coffee?' I asked, after pleasantries had been exchanged. Mr Willoughby said he'd love some coffee. This came as a great relief, as, in anticipation, Olivier and I had selected a plate of the prettiest *pâtisserie* as an accompaniment.

About forty minutes later, Olivier appeared at my desk.

'Pandora. Mr Willoughby is looking at some of our designs. Would you help him while I make a call? He asked for you.'

I felt like demanding why he couldn't look at the pictures himself, but I remained in role and did my master's bidding, while he stayed in the office to ring a customer who'd wanted to speak to him urgently.

In the reception room, our visitor patted the seat beside him and I sat down. It was a two-seater chesterfield and he was fairly corpulent, so I shrank as close to the side as possible. He already had an album on his lap and I was wondering what exactly I was expected to bring to the proceedings, when I felt his leg travel eastwards so it was nudging mine. He turned the page and pointed to the lap-dancing cake.

'You didn't model for that by any chance, did you?' he wheezed, guffawing as he leaned in towards me, his right arm pressing my left breast, his hand grasping my thigh.

A mixture of rage and humiliation made my face burn. I longed to stamp one of my size sevens hard on the old devil's foot – a ploy which had got me out of danger in the past, especially when stiletto heels had been involved. But I didn't want to jeopardise my boss's opportunity to be on telly.

To my relief, Olivier appeared at that moment, and Mr Willoughby briskly closed the album and got to his feet, cool as a cucumber, as if nothing had happened.

'Well, it's been good to see you, old chap. Very useful. We'll be in touch.'

Olivier, oblivious to what he'd interrupted, escorted him to the shop door, beaming his goodbyes. When he reappeared, he exhaled in relief.

'I'm content that's over. But I expected a media type – linen jacket, chinos. A man in a suit like a lawyer, *non*. But 'e was very agreeable. We keep the fingers crossed.'

I didn't have the heart to cast a shadow on his good humour, so I just said, 'Well done, Olivier. I hope you get the job. Who could match you? You're a true artist.'

He looked like the cat who'd got the cream.'*Merci,* Pandora. And please call me Olly.'

Fascinated, I observed a tiny flame of light executing a cheeky cha-cha-cha over the crown of his head. It was the same terpsichorean display I'd observed a few weeks ago – the night before I'd seen the job ad. The thrill of delight that accompanied it lifted my heart. I even began to feel better about my encounter with the lubricious Willoughby.

The flame gradually disappeared and Olivier with it, taking himself off to the bakery, whistling as he went.

* * *

Later, as I drove home, I looked forward to the afternoon ahead, when I was planning to settle down with a good book and a rejuvenating face pack, after taking Oscar out for his walk. Finishing at two o'clock was one of the reasons I'd taken the job, because he didn't like me being out for too long.

And I should really start meditating again this evening. The surprise appearance of the dancing flame had reminded me I'd been neglecting it lately. I'd allowed myself to be distracted by confectionery, what with the excitement of the cupcake-decorating workshop, and my attempts to familiarise myself with the seemingly endless selection of cakes and desserts by bringing the albums home and studying them in the evening.

I called Oscar's name as I let myself in, but he didn't come to welcome me, so I assumed he was upstairs on my bed. But he wasn't there. I finally found him in the living room, lying listlessly on the sofa. Dotted round the room was Technicolor evidence of a gastric disturbance. I stroked his head tentatively and he licked his dry lips in a feeble greeting. My chest felt an ache of fear.

'Darling. Poor little boy. What's wrong?' But he couldn't even manage to lift his head.

An hour later, he was in the vet's and on a drip, having to be kept in overnight for observation. He was dehydrated and had a temperature, so they were going to run some tests. They told me to ring for an update on his condition the next day.

Driving home from the surgery I dreaded the coming hours when, for the first time since the funeral, I would be alone in the house at night. The dog kept the house alive. Now when I closed the front door the lack of movement within it was stifling. That and the aroma of Oscar's accidental deposits.

Carpet cleaning was first on the agenda. But why stop there? Oscar hated the noise of the vacuum cleaner so now was my chance. Hoover every room. Wash the kitchen floor, clean the windows, scrub the loos, change the sheets unnecessarily. Anything to keep my mind off the possibility of losing him as well.

A veterinary nurse once told me how sensitive dogs are to the emotions of the people they live with. If someone in the house is depressed, it can affect them too. Had my grief in some way contributed to Oscar's condition?

I sat in Mike's armchair and tried to slip into meditation, in an attempt to quieten those persistent, unwelcome thoughts. Instead, weary from my cleaning frenzy, I sank into sleep. When I woke up, the room was in darkness. I'd been dreaming about Oscar. In the dream, he was a tiny grey and white puppy again – running like the wind in a lush green meadow strewn with buttercups, poppies and white daisies. I was at one side of the meadow and Mike was at the farther side. Oscar was running back and forth between the two of us, but towards the end of the dream he was exhausted and gasping for breath.

As I roused myself, I felt a sensation in the middle of my brow and wondered if the dancing flame would appear again. But what I saw this time was far more spectacular. In the darkness I could distinguish the outline of a figure of about my own height. He seemed to be made up of shadows, like a da Vinci sketch. Chiaroscuro. Light and shade. The image increased in contrast, to reveal long white hair and beard, and a floor-length robe tied about the middle with a cord – all of which seemed familiar. It was the figure in the dream who'd been standing by my shoulder.

And then the figure spoke, although I don't know if I could describe it as speech. It was more like words playing in my head.

I am pleased to meet you at last. I have been trying to communicate with you but our frequencies were not attuned sufficiently. Now we have established contact you can get in touch with me whenever you want. Just sit quietly, focus on the middle of your brow. Think of me, say my name, and I will be with you. Now rest. Breathe slowly. I am with you. You may ask me some questions now or on another occasion when you are more rested. As you wish.

I lay back in my armchair and basked in the comfort of his message. It was a welcome respite from the gloom and anxiety that had enveloped me since Mike's death, and I savoured every moment. A few minutes later, my logical mind intervened, prompting me to ask why he was here. At one stage he instructed me to get some paper and make notes in case I forgot what he was telling me.

After twenty minutes or so, his form grew fainter and our connection began to fade. He had warned me earlier that when this happened it would be because I was tired, and that I should then go straight to bed, where I would have a good sleep and awake refreshed.

As predicted, I slept like a baby and woke with a light heart. He had told me his name was Enoch and I could look him up if I liked.

Chapter 6 – 1970

Mike knew I had to get home by eleven, so we left the pub quickly – but not quickly enough to stop us both getting soaked, as it was raining more heavily now. We arrived at the bottom of my road with fifteen minutes to spare. He turned off the car headlights and adopted snogging position, pulling me towards him – as much as he could with a gearstick in the equation. I was as eager as he was, but after our first long kiss, I drew away. I needed to get something straight.

'Mike. What did you mean when you said you'd be breaking up with...' I was unable to say her name so I just said, 'your girlfriend?'

I couldn't see his face very clearly because it was dark. Boys don't park near street lights on these occasions. He needn't have bothered, actually, as by that time the combination of our damp clothes and his ardour, had sufficiently steamed up the windows for any privacy required. He dug his fingers into his temples, as if trying to erase the thought of what he had to do.

'As soon as she started talking about getting engaged I knew I didn't want to go through with it. I don't love her. I should have said something months ago but I thought if I didn't seem keen she'd take the hint.'

He brought his hand down hard on the steering wheel.

'She's not what I want. She's pretty, but—' he sounded embarrassed, as if he felt disloyal saying it, '—sometimes I find her boring.'

And then he kissed me again, his lips exploring mine and descending to my neck. I allowed myself to enjoy it for a couple of minutes but I wasn't going to be silenced. And I couldn't risk getting a love bite, so I broke free.

'But why did you let her go on thinking you were getting engaged? Cece said she was talking about rings. She said you'd been looking in jewellers.'

He leant back and let out a groan.

'Look, it's complicated. My mum's all on her own. My dad died when I was ten and my sister got married and emigrated last year. My mum really misses her. And Val...Val's good to my mum. She makes up for Linda not being there. She does her hair, they go shopping. They get on well.' His voice broke and I felt as if a knife had pierced my heart. 'When I tell them, they'll both be really upset.'

He rubbed his eyes hard with his fist. But I couldn't share his compassion for them. He was the only one I cared about and all I could think of was my own need for him, so I said, 'Isn't it better to tell them now? The longer you leave it...'

He was trying to control his tears, so when he spoke he took a deep breath after every two or three words.

'I've been too much of a coward. What's wrong with me?'

I cradled him clumsily, instinctively stroking his hair, as you would a baby. Gradually his body relaxed and he lay his head on my chest and sighed. Our breathing synchronised and we both closed our eyes. We clung to each other, and as I held him, I thought over what he'd said.

There was a risk that being the sort of person he was, he'd never pack his girlfriend up, and I'd never have him. But that didn't stop me liking the way he was. He was decent and not by nature a two-timer at all. And I loved him for that. I whispered 'I love you' to comfort him – and because it was how I felt – and he whispered 'I love you too' back.

He sat up and pulled me closer. This kiss was harder than before, his tongue snaking into my mouth as it had in the park. He cupped my breast and lay his other hand over my pubic bone. He took my hand and placed it in the same place, over his jeans. Things were just about to get even steamier when a passing Alsatian started barking when he saw movement in the car. The couple walking him began shouting at him to be quiet, resulting in Mike and I reluctantly resuming driver and passenger positions.

It had been a dramatic evening for both of us. What with the girl in the film dying young, all the tears we'd shed between us, and the rain beating on the car, I felt the pathetic fallacy to be alive and thriving in my neck of the woods. (My English Literature studies were at the forefront of my mind at the time.)

We left it that he'd be waiting for me at the bottom of my road on Monday afternoon. At the weekend he'd break the news to Val and his mother. We agreed not to say anything to anyone else until he'd told them first. Slightly to my surprise, he said he wanted to meet my father as soon as possible to put us on a proper footing. He said that if my dad didn't want me going out too much before my exams, that was okay. We could see each other at the weekends.

I said I'd ask if he could come round one evening after tea – we called it tea but it was dinner really. I mentally determined I'd tell the truth, that I'd met him at the Green Oak club. And I'd emphasise that he was a keen cyclist – that would impress my dad, who liked anything sporty. After arranging all this, it felt as if it was already a reality, and we were both on a high. Mike seemed to have mastered his misery and sounded like his old self when he said goodbye. 'I'll be here at four o'clock on Monday. Wish me luck.'

I dashed out of the car and home, only just making it before curfew. On the doorstep, I looked back down the road and he was still there. I waved to my centurion. Still on watch.

* * *

That weekend nothing upset my apple cart. Even when Doris, the manageress of Roy's Fashions, made me clean the shop windows, I just smiled sweetly and thought of Mike, and dreamt about the future. I imagined my dad getting on well with him, and how Mike and I would go out in a foursome with Cece and Ray. In fact, I was glad it was a Saturday because if I'd been going to school I might have ended up blurting out to Cece that I'd been on a date with Mike and how he was going to pack Val up. I don't think I could have contained myself. I was so excited and thrilled by the way it was all turning out.

On Sunday afternoon, when my dad was at the snooker club with his brothers Dave and Anthony, I even rang my mother – something I'd only done once since she'd left. She was living in Chelsea with a psychedelic artist she'd met at last year's Isle of Wight music festival.

It was all Bob Dylan's fault. She loved him but my dad couldn't stand him, and when she found out he was performing at the Isle of Wight instead of Woodstock, New York, she decided to go with a friend. It was there that she'd met Toby, who was with his then girlfriend. Frankie and Toby came back as a couple and went straight to his house. The girlfriend didn't seem to mind much. She'd even lived with them for a little while, until she'd found another boyfriend.

But, naturally, my poor dad went mad. My mum phoned him to explain she'd fallen in love and she couldn't help it, and he'd threatened to kill Toby.

Luckily, he didn't know where they lived. When I'd phoned her before, my mother had asked me to visit her and meet Toby, but I said I'd better not because of Dad. I was thinking that if he became suspicious and followed me, I could have my mum's boyfriend's death on my conscience. Nice position for an eighteen-year-old to be in. I don't think.

So I dialled the number and she answered. When she heard my voice she started crying, saying she missed me and she was sorry. I told her I really missed her too, but because I was so happy about Mike, I was able to say this without bursting into tears myself. She asked how my dad was. What could I say? That he moped around the place. Did as much overtime as he could. Occasionally got drunk in the Marlborough Arms. That when we went to any family gatherings the usual suspects would shake their heads and tut in sympathy when they saw us – the cuckold and the motherless child. So I settled for telling her that Mrs Browning helped out and we were managing okay.

'By the way, Pandora,' she went on, 'you haven't seen my passport anywhere, have you?'

I thought back to the evening last year when Mum's sister Maggie had knocked on the door. I'd been upstairs in my room, playing records, but had still been able to hear the raised voices, even though I turned up the volume. At first my dad refused, then Aunt Maggie threatened to call the police if he didn't let her fill a suitcase with Mum's clothes and things she needed, like her National Insurance card, so he had to give in. He wouldn't let Aunt Maggie take any of the family photos that my mother had asked for, though, so he got his own back in the end.

'Didn't Aunt Maggie get it when she came, Mummy?'

I don't know why I slipped back into calling her this, but it just seemed natural.

'She did, but it turned out to be an old, out-of-date one.'

'Can't you get a new one?'

'Yes, love, but I'd have to say I lost it and it would all take ages. And Toby wants me to go to Spain with him next weekend and I've only just realised myself that I haven't got it. He has to go because he's got a commission to paint the inside of a night club.'

I had an image of an arty-farty man with a waxed moustache and beret, in painter's overalls, slapping emulsion on to Spanish walls.

'They're letting him choose the name and he's thinking of calling it the Inner Beast. I was going to help him with some of the easy bits of painting. Never mind. I've always got The Unicorn to fall back on.'

The Unicorn was the Chelsea pub where she'd been working as a barmaid since her change of accommodation. My mother had told me that Richard, the tenant of the pub, was an old contact of hers from the days when they worked for the same brewery chain. Luckily my dad never travelled further south than Kilburn, so he was unlikely to ever spot her.

Although she was working as a barmaid, she and my father had started married life as trainee pub managers. I was born a couple of years after they'd been given their own pub, but the long hours had proved difficult with a small child. My dad stuck it until I was four, and one day went out and found a job at the furniture factory, before handing in his notice. My mum had to go too, as they only employed married couples, but she chose to stay in the business as a barmaid because she liked the work. Between them, they had just enough to afford a mortgage on our little house in Nightingale Road. But I think it was probably then that my mum had looked anew at Frank Fry and decided that life wasn't going in quite the direction she'd envisaged.

'Where do you think the passport is, Mum? I can look for it if you like.'

I knew that if I found her passport she would have to give me her address or meet me somewhere, but I was prepared to do that, as it was a sort of emergency. She told me it used to be in one of the sideboard drawers so I put down the phone and rummaged around. It wasn't hard to find. I slipped it into my bag and tidied the drawer so my dad wouldn't suspect anything.

She was overjoyed when I told her I'd found it. She gave me the address of The Unicorn and told me where it was on the King's Road. I was to deliver it to her any evening this coming week, but on no account to tell Dad. I agreed and, against my expectations, felt light hearted rather than guilty – full of the anticipation of seeing my mum after nearly a year. It was going to be a busy week. Mike on Monday, then arranging for him to come and meet Dad, then going to see Mum. Maybe Mike could come with me to meet her. She'd love him.

Chapter 7 – 2003

The day after properly meeting Enoch for the first time I awoke feeling refreshed and upbeat. It was a non-working day, so after going for a quick jog, I rang the vet's to see how Oscar was. They said his temperature was down but he still wasn't eating so they would keep him in until he was taking solid food. The tests had revealed he was suffering from an inflamed pancreas which can be quite dangerous – in humans as well as dogs. Oscar was now on painkillers and anti-sickness medicine, as well as the drip.

I vaguely remembered writing some notes when Enoch had been "speaking" to me, the evening before, and it occurred to me that I should go and read them. I had scant recollection of what I'd written, so it was almost like reading someone else's writing. What I found there was all about Oscar, and I recalled that I'd been dreaming about him just before I'd slipped into meditation.

My notes outlined the reasons that Oscar had got ill in the first place and the measures to be taken to restore him to health.

Reasons for onset of dog's illness:

- *His grief at Mike's death.*
- *The strain of being exposed to the discordant energy you are producing because of your grief.*
- *Loneliness, which resulted in the release of harmful hormones.*
- *Too rich a diet.*
- *All these stresses and pressures resulted in a physical imbalance.*

Ways to alleviate his condition:

- *Put him on the special diet that the vet recommends.*
- *Don't give him harmful treats because you feel guilty when you leave him.*
- *Make sure he's in the company of other dogs (and people) as much as possible.*
- *Don't use him as a 'prop' to support your emotional need.*

- *Be happy around him.*
- *Give him lots of walks in the fresh air.*
- *See that he avoids stressful situations.*

And the best part was the next five words.

He will be all right. You nearly lost him but he has a strong spirit. Now it has been explained to you just how much you have been draining his energy, you will have to nurture him back to health with love. This should be given freely and unconditionally. The more love you radiate to him, the stronger he will become and the less likely the disorder will become permanent. Tell him often that you love and appreciate what he does. Apologise for the hurt you have unwittingly caused him and ask his forgiveness.

Everything in the transcription rang true and resonated with my earlier gut feeling that his illness had been linked to my sadness. Yet part of me still felt totally ridiculous for believing it.

Nevertheless, I found myself drawn to a photograph of Oscar which I kept on a table in the living room. In the absence of the real thing, this would have to do. So I focused on this image and self-consciously spoke the words Enoch had told me to.

'Oscar. Thank you for being such a loving companion. I'm so sorry if anything I've done has contributed to your suffering in any way. Please forgive me. I want you to be strong and healthy again. I love you. Please come back home safe and sound.'

To my surprise, I managed to do this without weeping uncontrollably like the wimp I had become in the last few months.

About an hour later, the phone rang.

'Hello, it's Dove Lane Veterinary Centre here. Just to let you know that Oscar's managed to eat a few pieces of chicken, so you can come and pick him up any time.'

Blimey, I thought – is that a quick result or what? My sceptical head presumed coincidence, but my heart was hoping like mad it was the Enoch effect at work.

I hurried off to collect him. He was so pleased to see me, he almost licked all my blusher off, but as soon as we got home and he tottered weakly into his basket, I realised just how poorly he still was. With him had come several tins of low fat food, his medication, and a diet sheet, which specified absolutely no fatty treats like his favourite pigs' ears. Poor Oscar. Life was going to be hard when his appetite returned and he found that overnight he'd become a weight watcher.

A little later on I took him out to stretch his legs. He was on limited exercise for a few days, so it was only a gentle stroll down the lane. We bumped into a fellow dog walker so we walked along together, chatting – mainly about Oscar's sudden attack. The two dogs sniffed and nuzzled each other; Oscar appearing almost vivacious. It made me reflect on what Enoch had said about dogs needing company for the good of their health. In fact, when I sat down later and took another look at my notes, it came home to me that all the things that referred to Oscar getting ill, could also apply to any human.

He was very quiet and ate little for the next three days, barely lifting his head when I came in from work or shopping. But when I took him back for his check-up, the vet felt his abdomen and declared the swelling and tenderness greatly reduced. She said she was pretty sure he was on the road to recovery and there was no need for a return visit unless he had a relapse.

Buoyed up by this positive prognosis, I was tempted to go to the library on Friday afternoon to do some research on Enoch, but when I put on my jacket and opened the front door, I found Oscar by my side, so I took him for a good walk in the woods instead, to celebrate his revival.

* * *

Mike's laptop would have come in handy for the research on Enoch

I wanted to do, but I'd given it away to his son Danny along with various other belongings shortly after he'd died. Danny hadn't wanted to remove the stack of possessions I'd asked him to take off my hands – Mike's bike and rowing machine among them. But I couldn't bear to have his things around as a constant reminder that he'd never use them again. The rest, mostly clothes, I'd taken to charity shops. I kept some other stuff stored over in the cellar at The Cedars, but it was out of sight, so safely out of mind.

In my grief, I'd hidden all the photographs of him away. Even our wedding photo. In fact, I'd made such a good job of obliterating any trace of him that you'd hardly have known he'd ever lived here. All that remained of his clothes was one lilac cashmere sweater I'd bought last Christmas which he'd said was too good to wear. I think what he was trying to say was too gay to wear. But I made him put it on for Boxing Day when Danny, Mei, and their children came over.

The best photograph I took of them that day is in a frame, nestling at the bottom of a bedroom drawer. They're at the dining table, wearing party hats at odd angles. Mei and William are in the act of pulling a cracker. Hannah is wearing Groucho glasses with fake moustache and bushy eyebrows, and Mike and Danny are holding up their gifts in pretend delight – Mike's got a luxury handbag mirror and Dan a set of mini screwdrivers. I'm glad it's such a happy picture, but it made me so sad, I couldn't bear to look at it.

In the last few weeks I had occasionally got the lilac sweater out of the wardrobe and put it on, imagining it still smelled faintly of him. Which is impossible because it had been washed and put away in January, so any scent could only have been fabric softener.

With the absence of a computer, I therefore decided to delve into some of the books I'd acquired in my New Age interlude, to see if there was any mention of an Enoch. I hadn't opened any of them in years. In fact, when we moved here, I'd denied them an open bookcase and incarcerated them behind glass doors, along with rarely consulted maps and reference books. It was a bit like being a lapsed Catholic, only without the guilt.

I was struggling to recollect why I'd stopped reading spiritual development stuff and then I remembered the workshop with Harmony St Clair, author of several books on angels. I went on my own to this workshop – I think Frankie was abroad with one of her succession of boyfriends – and it had been a way of passing an empty Sunday.

Harmony was petite and vivacious with short, dark hair, red lipstick and carefully plucked eyebrows – beautifully dressed, and festooned with a flowing scarf. There were tables full of her books, CDs and angel trinkets on sale at the back of the room, along with scarves similar to her own in all colours of the rainbow.

At the beginning of the day she explained that Harmony St Clair was not her birth name, but one her special guide had given her. This statement had irritated me slightly. I felt she'd sent out a message: I'm special, but you lot aren't.

She asked us to place our chairs in a large circle and then led us in a visualisation. This involved her describing a scenario, (in this instance, a trip to a crystal temple on top of a mountain), where we would find our guardian angel. Upon meeting him, we were instructed to ask his name. This guided visualisation was accompanied by background music, reaching a crescendo when we scaled the mountain, dwindling to diminuendo as we descended some time later, bearing a loving message and a gift from whatever his name was.

As Harmony spoke the words, 'And now you are back in this space. Keep your eyes closed for a minute or so. Then wiggle your toes, slowly open your eyes, take a sip of water, ground yourself,' the realisation hit me that although I could vaguely remember her giving the instructions, I hadn't followed any of them. I'd just sort of chilled out and nodded off.

Harmony's next move was to ask each person in turn what their guardian angel's name was, and what they'd been given. Their answers featured an assortment of biblical-sounding names, vivid colours, gifts of precious stones and messages to live in the present, follow the light, etc. When she came to me, I was too embarrassed to admit that I'd zoned out, so I stole an angel name from a previous speaker and a message from another. But I saw her eyes harden at my answer. I think she saw right through me.

After that, she opened the floor for questions about all things angelic. One of the questions was about feathers.

'Can you tell me please, Harmony,' asked a woman with a mop of frizzy red hair, crushed velvet trousers of chartreuse green, and a rustic smock, 'why I often see white feathers?'

Harmony looked smug. This was an easy one. 'They're a sign that the angels are around and they're watching over you.'

I really wanted to say – 'Er, don't birds have white feathers?' But there had been so many murmurs of agreement on feather sightings from the circle, that I held my tongue.

The day cranked on, and the other course participants got more irritating. Five o'clock came at last, and Harmony led the group in sending healing to various countries and causes. She'd given us each a flower, which we'd placed in the middle of the circle, and on which we were to focus as we sent healing thoughts. Finally, she told us to direct healing to a person, country, or constellation of our choice. I chose a neighbour of mine who was recovering from a stroke.

When the meeting broke up, I walked into the circle space and bent down to pick up my flower to take home to Mr Stein, assuming it was mine to take. But she called out curtly, 'Please leave the flowers where they are. They're not for taking away.'

I stopped in my tracks, not sure I'd heard correctly. 'But this is the flower you gave me.'

She paused momentarily but then continued, 'No, I'm sorry. I'm going to use them in a ceremony at home this evening.'

A couple of women had moved towards her, wanting her to sign a book they'd bought at lunchtime, so I looked pointedly at them and back to her when I said, 'I want to give it to my neighbour. He's very ill.'

But she still wouldn't budge, shaking her head impatiently and avoiding my gaze by directing a rictus grin at the women. So I shrugged my shoulders and said sarcastically, 'Well good luck with the book, because I won't be buying it.'

Maybe it was petulant pique on my part, but after that I stopped going to similar meetings or talks, and I asked Frankie not to give me any more of those sort of books.

* * *

Back at the bookcase, I found there was a preponderance of works by two authors my mother had been keen to pass on to me – an American, called Magda Laney and good old Harmony St Clair. The American was a prolific writer and wife, for she had been married several times. In her work there was usually a section on how to find a soul mate, but her record of four husbands at the last count indicated that she'd performed the ceremony a little too often.

Both authors claimed they had channelled their writing, which gave their books a bona fide stamp of authenticity better than any PhD.

This channelling lark means that people can get their books written for them by getting directly in touch with higher beings from the supernatural realms like archangels and ascended masters. I'd been reminded of this group by the pictures on the wall of the spiritualist chapel. Ascended masters are very evolved individuals who have incarnated on Earth, often more than once, and who are ready and willing to give 'downloads' of wisdom and advice to those who are able to receive. I suppose it's a bit like a radio being tuned in to the right waveband. According to their blurbs, these authors had been lucky enough to have had their books dictated by one or more of these higher beings.

This brings to mind that old Romantic, Samuel Taylor Coleridge, who fell into a trance and woke with two or three hundred lines of poetry in his head. He'd managed to jot down fifty-four of them when someone knocked at the door. But in contrast to the likes of

Harmony and Magda, poor old Samuel lacked the knack of tuning back in. So *Kubla Khan,* magnificent as it stands, is just a shadow of the self it could have been if its author hadn't been so rudely interrupted.

I'd been wondering if Enoch was an angel. I hadn't seen any wings when he'd appeared to me, but just because angels have them in old paintings, is it necessarily true? After all, Enoch had brought me a message, hadn't he? And angels are known to be messengers of God – wasn't it the Angel Gabriel who told Mary that the Son of God would be born to her? Okay, Enoch's message wasn't on quite the same scale as a virgin birth, but dear old Oscar had done well out of it.

I worked my way through the indexes of the angel books and was disappointed to find no trace of him. Looking around for any other books that might help, I finally found one on saints which I'd been given as a school prize. But there was no mention of an Enoch.

Idly leafing through it, I stopped to read the chapter on St Thérèse, the patron saint of my school. It said that her motto had been 'what matters in life is not great deeds but great love'. My thoughts wandered back to a school pilgrimage to Lourdes, when I overheard Sister Joseph picking on dear old Sister Veronica, the school secretary, and a couple of the other nuns bickering as well. Maybe they were overheated in their long black habits, or even menopausal, but I didn't feel any great love on that trip.

I was beginning to tire of this fruitless search, so I closed the bookcase and went to make some dinner. Later on, I sat down to read the paper in the living room, after which Oscar jumped on to my lap and we ended up watching three whole hours of telly before going to bed.

But my failure to discover anything about my apparition kept me awake. Skimming through my books had brought back memories of the past – when I'd been curious about the supernatural and drawn to the esoteric. It had whetted my appetite for more research and I determined to find out more as soon as I could.

Chapter 8 – 1970

At 3.45 on Monday I left school and started the ten-minute walk home. Before that, I quickly rolled the waist of my school-uniform summer dress over a white belt which I'd taken with me especially for that purpose. This by no means rendered it a mini but at least it didn't look quite so frumpy. As soon as I was out of sight of the school, I disposed of my awful, potty-shaped straw hat, which buckled obediently into the confines of my bag. I reached the end of my road at about 3.57 and stood a little way from the spot where Mike had parked before, trying to look as if I had a purpose, which is difficult in the absence of a bus stop.

At 4.30 he still hadn't turned up and a little devil inside my head kept whispering, *he's not coming, he's not coming*. Thank goodness I hadn't mentioned anything to Cece when we'd met at lunchtime. Instead, I'd told her about my mum and how I'd be going to see her one evening that week – but I had to keep it from my dad.

'So can I say I'll be going round your house, Ce?'

'Course you can. Give her my love. I miss her too.'

Cece was fond of Frankie because up until her disappearing act, the three of us would often go out together. She'd take us to central London at weekends to see the sights and the shops. A couple of times a year we'd go to the British Museum or one of the South Kensington museums: Science or Natural History to please Cece, and the Victoria and Albert to please me. And, more frequently as we got older, shopping in Oxford Street.

The paucity of my present wardrobe owed a lot to Frankie's absence. She had been generous, both with pocket money and clothes, but now she wasn't around I couldn't keep asking my dad for cash, as he was famous for being careful with money. It would be, 'switch off the light if you're not in the room', 'don't talk on the phone for too long', 'turn the gas fire down'.

As far as he was concerned, my Saturday wage of three pounds ten shillings should have been sufficient for all my expenses.

Whenever I asked him for a little extra to buy a pair of shoes or something, he'd always say the same thing.

'Five pounds?' (I'd learned to ask for a little more than the item cost for obvious reasons). 'For God's sake, Dora—' (This was the closest he could get to his mum's name, Doreann, which I'd been supposed to have.) '—I'm not made of money. Your school uniform cost me a packet. What's wrong with your black school shoes?'

But give him his due, he always stumped up in the end.

* * *

I was still waiting at the end of my road at five o'clock when Mrs Browning passed by with two bags of shopping, by which time I was chilled through and had a thumping headache. I was under strict instructions from my dad always to help Mrs B with her shopping if I saw her in the street, because the odds were that a good half of it consisted of provisions she was buying on our behalf. So I offered to carry one of her bags and she accepted. She chattered about her cat, and asked about school and I answered her on all points. There I was, heart breaking, faking unconcern. We said goodbye at the door. She said she'd bring the shopping in later, when my dad was home.

Once inside I stared at the phone, in too much anguish even to cry. It was an emotion past tears – as if a chasm had opened where my heart had been and I couldn't allow myself to fall into it or I'd never come out. I was contemplating the phone because although Mike and I hadn't exchanged numbers, he knew my surname was Fry and the road I lived in, so he could easily have found it. Equally, if I wanted to look up Armstrong, even though I didn't know his exact address, I would probably find him eventually.

So I opened the directory and found four Armstrongs living in Oak Green, one of them with the initial M and another listed as Mrs B. Armstrong. I jotted down both numbers and put the piece of paper in my pocket. I would wait to see if he rang me. But of course I didn't really think he would, in case my dad answered. And I hated the idea of ringing him and his mother answering. What would I say? She'd ask who was speaking and be wondering who the girl was. And then he wouldn't be able to talk privately without her hearing. And it'd be the same if he rang here.

So where was he? Delayed at work? Car breakdown? Worse still, car accident? What could have stopped him from coming? Had he gone off me? At that moment, God forgive me, I'd rather he'd been involved in an accident than decided to choose his girlfriend over me.

At that point, Dad came in from work and I said I had a headache, wasn't hungry and was going for a lie-down. He looked embarrassed as he always did when he thought 'female trouble' might be involved. An hour or so later, I heard Mrs Browning's voice downstairs and after a while she came up and tapped on my door.

'Are you all right, Pandora? I've got a cup of tea and a sandwich. Your dad 's a bit worried about you.'

I opened the door and gladly took the tray from her, on which there was also some Disprin. She was kind and I'd noticed my dad didn't mind her coming into the house and chatting. Uncharacteristically, he seemed happy to pay her to do our shopping and a bit of cleaning, even though he was able-bodied and had a car so he could just as easily have done it himself. I think he just thought it was woman's work. For a variety of reasons he never asked me, thank goodness. I was his daughter, the grammar-school girl, whose job it was to study and get a good job.

Mrs B sat on my bed and felt my forehead. 'If you don't feel any better tomorrow, why don't you have a day off school? You're probably worrying about your exams.'

'Yes, I might. I don't feel very well.'

Now this wasn't strictly true in the physical sense, but most certainly true of mind and spirit. That, however, was a truth I couldn't confide in anyone.

* * *

I awoke on Tuesday morning to a persistent knocking on the front door. Pulling a dressing-gown over my nightdress, I scrambled downstairs to find Mrs Browning on the doorstep, who bustled past me into the kitchen waving a piece of paper. For one mad moment I thought she was delivering a message from Mike, but when she put it down on the kitchen table I saw it was just a ticket for my dad's dry cleaning. I don't know why she bothered bringing it in, as he was bound to ask her to pick it up for him anyway.

I was beginning to wonder why there was so much coming and going lately. Always in and out of each other's houses. They didn't stay very long. Wouldn't want the neighbours talking. Mrs Browning was a widow, Mr Browning having been knocked off his bike some years earlier, meeting his end under a bus. But my dad was still married to my mum, even though she was absent without leave, making it not quite proper for them to be seen consorting.

Surely he and Mrs B couldn't be interested in each other. Mrs B was fat. Well, maybe not fat exactly, but buxom. She had a plump, unlined face. And she always wore her hair in a French pleat; her wavy, reddish mane tortured into submission with vast numbers of invisible hairpins.

My dad was tall and slim with dark hair turning grey at the temples. He was a bit gangly and untidy, but could look all right when he spruced himself up – usually for a wedding or a funeral. He used to put on his Sunday best every week for mass, but had stopped attending when Granny Doireann had died. Said he'd only been going for her sake anyhow.

Mrs B nodded towards the ticket.

'Tell your dad his suit'll be ready tomorrow.'

We stood in the kitchen, trying to read each other's eyes. I don't know what she saw in mine but it prompted her to grasp me to her ample bosom in an awkward hug.

'Sorry if I woke you up, Pandora. Only your dad asked me to look in on you. You know, to see if you wanted anything. I can go to the chemist for you if you like...if you've run out of anything.'

'No, I'm fine thanks, Mrs Browning.'

I surprised myself by hugging her back. I found her concern touching and reassuring. She was a mother herself, but didn't get much chance to practise it. Her daughters had both married soldiers, and were stationed somewhere Jean Metcalfe was dedicating records to on a Sunday morning on *Two-Way Family Favourites.*

Encouraged by the physical contact, Mrs B continued trying to be of service to me. 'Would you like me to bring you in some soup later on? And, Pandora, I think you're old enough now to start calling me Joan.'

I knew Mrs B meant well, but I'd started to rerun yesterday's events in my head and desperately wanted to be alone. And what was this first-name business all about?

'Oh, that's really kind of you, Mrs...Joan. But I need to hand in an essay.'

I could tell she thought I had my period, but I was too embarrassed to say it wasn't that. So I smiled as brightly as I could and said, 'I'd better get dressed.' It was nine o'clock. Crumbs. Until then I really hadn't realised I'd slept so late.

As soon as she'd gone, my white-mouse mind started wheeling. Mike wouldn't get home till some time after three, so there was no point in trying the phone numbers until then. I really did have a History essay to finish and hand in, so I decided to go in at lunchtime, stay for the afternoon, then come back home and make the call. That would be better than sitting at home all day waiting until it was time to phone him.

I got dressed and sat down to write the conclusion to my essay. At the top of every page, we'd been taught, from the age of eleven, to write the initials AMD which stood for Ave Mater Dolorosa – Hail Mother of Sorrows. Feeling so full of sorrow myself, I wished my school had chosen a more cheerful invocation to Our Lady, like Ave Mater Felicitatis – Hail Mother of Happiness. And then it might have rubbed off on me.

* * *

At school, I found Cece in our usual corner of the library. She asked why I hadn't been around in the morning and, trying to look nonchalant about it, I told her I'd overslept. She seemed subdued and I noticed her eyes were swollen.

'You all right, Cece? You haven't been crying, have you?'

'I had a bit of a row with my mum and dad last night. They say I've got to stop seeing Ray.'

'Why?' I couldn't believe it. Up to now, they'd thought he was the best thing since sliced bread.

Cece's eyes welled up. 'My dad was in The Woodman's yesterday. He meets my uncle there sometimes for a game of darts, and he heard a couple of the boys from the cycling club talking. They were saying that one of them's got his girlfriend pregnant. And other stuff. Like they were lucky it wasn't them. So now my dad thinks they're all like that and Ray might get me pregnant.'

At that, Cece burst into deep sobs, prompting some lower-sixth-formers to stare, so we left the library before anyone in authority was alerted. We went to the toilets and Cece splashed her face with cold water. It wasn't break time so we were the only two in there. I gave her a cuddle because I felt her dad was really out of order banning her from seeing her boyfriend. I knew Cece. She wouldn't be daft enough to get into trouble. Why couldn't her dad trust her? Her hands were shaking as she reached into her bag.

'Pan, can I ask you a big favour? My dad said he was going to Ray's house tonight to tell him not to contact me any more. Can you post this letter through his door to warn him? I've explained everything – I couldn't bear it if he thought it was my idea.'

I took the letter, which had Ray's address in Oak Green written on the envelope. I really didn't want to do this. After all, I had plans of my own – which I couldn't confide to Cece. How could I get out of it?

'Couldn't you ring him at work?' Ray was a photographer's

assistant so it was a possibility.

'No. He's not allowed to have private calls. And he's out some of the time anyway.'

'When does he get in from work?'

'About six o'clock. But they've banned me from using the phone because they know I'd ring him.'

'How about a phone box?'

I could see that Cece was getting impatient.

'Where could I say I was going? We'll be having our tea then, anyway. I said I'd cover for *you* when you go to see your mum this week. I know it's short notice, but it is an emergency. I'll pay your bus fare. Please, Pan.'

What could I say? I'd forgotten all about seeing Mum this week and Cece being my alibi. At the moment everything felt up in the air. And Cece's troubles had rattled me even further. I wasn't in the mood for anything other than finding out why Mike hadn't turned up. Worst of all, I couldn't confide in anyone.

After a meagre lunch in the dining hall – neither of us was very hungry – we proceeded to our respective groups. I'd made up my mind to go home before delivering the letter. And this I did as soon as I could, excusing myself early from my History class for a mythical dental appointment. Once I'd changed out of my school uniform, I found the piece of paper with the telephone numbers on, and decided to dial the number for M. Armstrong. My heart had started to race by then, so I went to the cabinet in the living room and poured myself some Advocaat which usually calmed my nerves. This was a Frankie tip and one I was quite grateful for.

I let the number ring for quite some time but there was no reply. The other option was Mrs B. Armstrong. Another few sips and I dialled again. This time the phone was picked up almost immediately. The voice of a middle-aged woman recited the number. I swallowed hard and realised that, what with Cece's drama, I'd never got round to formulating a suitable reply if Mike's mother answered. But I couldn't back out now.

'Hello. Could I speak to Mike, please?'

'He's not here. Who's calling?'

And therein lay the dilemma. Do I give her my name? And if I did, being under strict orders to deliver Cece's flipping letter meant I might not be in when he called back. And if he decided to ring another evening, you can bet your bottom dollar it'd be the one when I was delivering my mother's passport. Damn. Damn. Damn. My brain went numb and I couldn't think.

'Um. Um. Well I've got to go out now. But perhaps you could...'

Something in my tone must have branded me a scheming minx – or whatever expression she'd have used to describe any girl who'd ring a boy who was already promised to someone else.

There was a sharp click and the line went dead. She'd put the phone down on me.

Chapter 9 – 2003

I finally made it to the library on Saturday morning and searched the book finder for the word 'Enoch'. But nothing relevant showed up. So I paid for a couple of hours on a computer connected to the internet, and typed his name in again. What I found wasn't quite what I expected.

The Old Testament shows Enoch as a pious teacher, prophet, scribe, builder of cities, law maker and leader of his people. He was well-versed in the ancient arts and sciences and received divine instruction in the laws of the universe. He's chronicled in the Book of Genesis as being the seventh generation from Adam and great grandfather of Noah. When Enoch ruled, there was peace and justice, and worshipping of idols was forbidden. He lived for three hundred and sixty-five years but, unlike the other patriarchs, he isn't listed as dying at that age. Instead, it says in Genesis that, 'God took him' which is taken to mean that at God's behest, his body was 'translated' into heaven instead of dying a natural death on Earth.

According to a source called *The Book of Enoch* this was not, however, his only visit to celestial realms. On the first occasion, two angels had conducted him from Earth to show him the seven 'heavens' which were not by any means all of them pleasant places. The first was a sort of observatory of the stars, home to astronomer angels; the second one was a place where sinners and fallen angels were kept, awaiting Judgment Day; the third was the beautiful Garden of Eden. In between this and the fourth heaven lay a hellish place where sinners were severely punished. In the fourth heaven he studied astronomical activity including the movement of the sun and the moon, and in the fifth he came upon some rebellious fallen angels known as Watcher angels, who had been incarcerated for their misdemeanours on Earth.

Their transgressions were very serious. The legend goes that two hundred of the Watcher angels descended to Earth, mated *en masse* with human women, and released classified information on topics such as astronomy and magic. Their leader, Azazel, taught the men how to make metal weapons and the women to titivate themselves and to enjoy sex. Which, when you think about it, are pretty unusual areas for an angel to get involved in. In the meantime, the human women began to give birth to the Watcher progeny, called Nephilim, who grew into giant teenagers from hell with cannibalistic tendencies.

Seeing the corruption the Watchers and their offspring had caused on Earth, archangels Michael and Gabriel reported this to their superior. Their God on High naturally disapproved of these goings-on and demanded retribution, so a gang of angels ambushed Azazel, duffed him up, trussed him up and imprisoned him for eternity in a dark place with a coating of sharp rocks for good measure. These Old Testament angels certainly didn't muck about. God's henchmen then forced the rebel Watchers to witness the slaughter of their delinquent children after which they were thrown into a fiery place which is where Enoch observed them on his tour.

The humans who participated in the sinfulness didn't get off scot free either, as, so the story goes, God sent a Great Flood to teach them a lesson. Enoch's great grandson, Noah, was chosen to build the Ark and ensure the survival of the human race – as well as the birds, bees, lions, tigers, fleas, bedbugs, etc.

Enoch the astronaut's journey into space continued onward and upward to the sixth heaven where he saw seven phoenixes and many shining archangels, whose job was to keep records of what occurred on Earth. From there, finally, he travelled to the seventh heaven, where he encountered the higher angels who are positioned close to the throne of God where God Himself sits – so glorious and powerful that not even the angels can look on Him.

Despite the stated inaccessibility of God's ineffable presence, the story goes that Enoch was allowed to sit next to Him, whereupon God revealed great secrets to him which Enoch wrote down in the form of three hundred and sixty-six books. These secrets are said to include how the world was created, how long it will survive, and what will happen after the end of the world. Enoch then returned to Earth for thirty days, after which he was taken back to headquarters on the back of a great horse to be transformed into an angel.

One of the descriptions of this transformation speaks of his body consumed by celestial fire and sparks emanating from him. (Hm, sparks, I thought, visualising the tiny flame I'd seen. That sounds familiar.) A glorious coronation then followed, an angelic herald decreeing that from that moment on he would no longer be known as Enoch, but as Archangel Metatron, and that all angels had to obey Metatron, as he was second in command to God.

For some reason this name had me imagining a sort of enormous tin robot – a science-fiction Jeeves who would take orders and carry them out to the best of his lumbering ability.

So far so fantastic. I was very impressed with Enoch's history – if, indeed, he was the same Enoch as my apparition. At that point I decided to look at the images for the name and there were one or two artists' impressions which certainly bore a resemblance to my bearded friend.

While I was at it, I typed in 'Metatron', and was presented with an image far removed from the robotic creature I had imagined. He was depicted as an attractively luminous figure, reminiscent of the artwork I'd seen on the walls of the spiritualist chapel, radiating rainbow beams of light. A fitting figure to be second in command to the head honcho.

I'd also collected a couple of other odd stories from my rummage around the worldwide web. There was a reference to Enoch being the ruler of Phoenicia, the land of the phoenix, also known as Atlantis. He was therefore also identified as Atlas – he who held heaven and Earth apart, and the universe in balance. Was there no end to this old chap's skills set?

Secondly, Enoch described two angels who visited him as 'tall and wearing coats covered with bird feathers'. Aha. Angels without wings. I was quite cheered to read this as it coincided with my theory.

Despite all the apocryphal razzmatazz, I left the library with a positive impression of who Enoch had been. He seemed to have been a good guy. But whether or not he'd been transformed into an angel remained a bit of a mystery. The morning's research had both answered and raised a few questions. Questions I was planning to pose him at the first opportunity.

* * *

On my return from the library, I found Bob Grove hard at work motor-mowing the grounds of The Cedars with Oscar in hot pursuit, almost back to his old self. Margery was happily cleaning the eight guest bedrooms in preparation for the visitors I was expecting the coming weekend.

The Cedars, which Mike and I had bought just over three years ago, had been chosen for its suitability for courses and workshops, with accommodation if required. The bedrooms were sizeable enough to be fitted with *en suite* bathrooms and we'd got a builder straight on to it. Downstairs there was an enormous room which could be adapted for lectures, or cleared as a studio for yoga, pilates or dance workshops. Mike and I had kept the heavy green silk curtains which the previous owners had left, but had never considered furnishing it for ourselves, because right from the start, we'd decided to live in the cottage.

When Mike had suggested buying the joint properties, I'd said the price was too high because I could only make a minor contribution in comparison to his, but he'd been adamant that he wanted to give me something I'd be interested in; something that would occupy me while he was at work. A little enterprise that would keep me in touch with people, so I wouldn't be lonely.

Marketing The Cedars had been easy. There was a lot of demand for residential venues not too far from London, with plenty of parking. The clients organised their own courses and paid me a set fee. Margery and I were able to handle coffee and tea breaks, employing agency staff for more extensive catering. And I still made a healthy profit.

We'd had everything from team-building courses to Indian head massage. And sometimes I'd been lucky enough to be roped in as a guinea pig for aromatherapy and other complementary treatments. I even let my mother run a crystal-healing workshop once, from which she made a tidy sum, what with her crystal sales and distance healing deals. Even though I waived the hire fee, she let me pay for the food provided. Behold the Frankie paradox – she'd give you her last penny if she thought you needed it, but rob you blind if she felt you didn't.

It was after Mike had his first heart attack, that I stopped taking bookings for The Cedars. He protested that it wasn't necessary but, for me, the visitors had become a distraction. Once he'd cut down on his work commitments and was at home more, I just wanted to concentrate on him. It was during this time, following a particularly bad storm, that Margery noticed that the roof was leaking. But as we were hardly using the house anyway, I just pushed it to the back of my mind, and did nothing.

After the success of the cupcake decorating day, Olivier had decided to go ahead with the more lucrative weekend residential event, entitled Cakes For All Occasions, and it was this that Mr and Mrs Grove were helping prepare the house for.

Olivier had previously been contacted by a *Daily Messenger* journalist, for an item about food fads. She had a theory that cupcakes were addictive which was why they, more than any other confection, had an enduring appeal. She'd mentioned the coming workshop in her article, and the response had been overwhelming.

All the places had been taken, but at the moment, we weren't sure how many people would be staying overnight. So to be on the safe side, all the bedrooms were being prepared, even the attic rooms – whose ceilings Bob had sealed and painted in an effort to conceal the damp patches. As long as it didn't rain this weekend, we should get away with it.

* * *

Later that day, I got out the notes I'd made that morning in the library, and formulated a few questions for you-know-who, and they went like this:

- *Are you Enoch, great grandfather of Noah?*
- *Did you visit God in heaven?*
- *Did you ascend into heaven rather than dying a human death?*
- *Did God send the Great Flood as a punishment?*
- *Did you see Hell?*
- *Do you know when the world will end?*
- *Were you the Phoenix King? Did the phoenix bird really exist or is it a myth?*
- *Are you now the angel Metatron? If so, why have you appeared to me as Enoch?*
- *Do angels have wings?*
- *Can you tell me again why you appeared to me? I know you told me this the first time you spoke to me but I didn't write it down and all I can remember is – something about me needing you? Can you elaborate please?*
- *P.S. Thanks for your help with Oscar.*

After I'd written these questions, I concentrated on my third eye, in the centre of my forehead, and spoke Enoch's name. Then my hand began to fly across the page, the pen twisting and turning of its own volition.

Chapter 10 – 1970

Hearing the click of Mrs Armstrong's telephone being replaced in its cradle, I felt hot with anger and humiliation. But disastrous as the attempt to make contact had been, in a funny sort of way this was just what I needed, because it shook away the fog of anxiety which had clouded my thinking, and which had left me unprepared and vulnerable. Who did they think they were? Both Mike and his mother had now made it into my bad books. I was offended, and wasn't going to waste any more of my time worrying about either of them. I had a mission to complete – Cece's letter to deliver. They could both go to hell.

Clutching Cece's directions, I hit the road. Turning left, I cut through the alleyway and waited for the bus on the main road. It was quite straightforward – the bus journey was about twenty minutes; after that, it would be a five-minute walk from the bus stop.

I found Ray's road quite easily and hurried down it, wishing it had been winter and the street dark. The houses were solid semi-detached properties, built in the 1930s. Privet hedges and wrought iron gates stood guard, along with impenetrable net curtains. The houses were mostly in good repair with impressive front doors embellished with stained glass.

It crossed my mind that when Cece's father paid his visit later that day to drop his bombshell on Ray, he'd be quite impressed – Ray's family home being quite a cut above the rented flat in Manor Wood that the Byrnes occupied. Perhaps he'd end up relenting. Though knowing Mr Byrne, he'd probably demand a signed undertaking from Ray that Cece's maidenhead would remain intact until the wedding night, under pain of death.

As I walked along, I noticed that some of the houses had warning notices screwed to the front gates: *No Hawkers or Circulars.* This made the idea of pushing a letter through a strange letterbox even more unnerving. Suppose when I got to the house there was one of these notices repelling all gatecrashers except a bona fide postman? And if so, would I have the guts to breach their ramparts?

I played out the scene in my mind. The front door would open, just as I approached it, to reveal Ray's irate mother, who would seize the letter from the harlot who wasn't her son's regular girlfriend.

'Well, no, you've got it wrong Mrs...' (What was Ray's last name?) 'Mrs Roberts. Cecilia's my best friend. I'm just delivering this letter on her behalf.'

At which the old trout would signal her disbelief by tearing it into tiny pieces and slamming the door in my face.

It was such a relief when I finally reached Ray's house to find that no notice forbade me, and no one responded to the creak of the front gate by flinging the front door open and demanding to know what business I had invading their front porch.

The envelope slid easily through the slot. It was that simple. I almost skipped across the road as I made my way back to the bus stop, which was deserted, suggesting I'd just missed a bus.

To pass the time, I began thinking about when I was going to see my mum. Why not the next evening? I would tell my dad I was going round to Cece's when I got home. I had entered a world of subterfuge, which, to my surprise, held a certain allure. I was getting hooked on the high that comes from getting away with something.

At that moment, a car drew up and stopped. It was a dark blue Cortina. Mike leaned across and opened the passenger door.

'Get in. I'll give you a lift home.'

So in I got. And on the way home, as he drove through the rush-hour traffic, he told me the following.

Last weekend, before he was able to tell Val it was over between them, she told him she was pregnant. But it wasn't the end of the world, was it, she said, because they were about to get engaged anyway. It just meant the wedding would have to be brought forward. And it would have to be a register-office quickie rather than a big church wedding. Her mum had already suspected, because she'd been sick a couple of times in the morning. Her dad wasn't very pleased about it, but she reckoned he was relieved because it saved him having to shell out for a big wedding. And he knew Mike would stand by her. She wanted Mike to tell his mum either then or the next day, so they could set a date and decide where they were going to live. Maybe with Mike's mum to begin with – she'd be glad of the company, wouldn't she?

There was other stuff about her being on the pill but forgetting to take it just the once. Even a girl of my limited experience smelt a rat with that one.

'So what did your mum say?' I whispered.

'She wasn't very happy. I got upset when I told her. She could see it wasn't what I wanted.'

He brushed his eyes with the back of his hand. A muscle in his cheek jerked uncontrollably. It was all incredibly clear to me now. It was Mike that Mr Byrne had overheard the lads talking about in the pub. Mike was the one who'd got a girl pregnant. The one who'd caused Mr Byrne to ban Cece from having anything to do with Ray. Which had led to me delivering the letter. And Mike was still oblivious to this particular sequence of events. I wondered whether I should tell him, but he'd started speaking again.

'I'd already dropped a couple of hints to my mum that I was too young to settle down, so she couldn't understand how I'd let it happen. It was so embarrassing – had to tell her about Val missing the pill. She asked me if there was anyone else and I said there was someone I liked. I think she was worried that I wouldn't do the right thing by Val. It's such a bloody mess. I don't want any of this. I'm only twenty-one, for Christ's sake.'

His voice broke as he was speaking, but he carried on driving. I was in such despair that I couldn't even comfort him. I needed comforting myself. But for the life of me I couldn't think of anyone I could safely turn to.

'That's why I didn't turn up yesterday. I'm sorry. I found your number in the book but I didn't know how to tell you, after what we'd said...planned. I'm such a bloody coward.'

By now, we'd reached my road and the car had come to rest. As he turned off the engine, his whole body seemed to sag as if all his strength had seeped out of it.

'Val's itching to tell the girls, so Cece'll get to hear about it soon enough,' he said wearily. 'I didn't want you to hear it from her, so I waited for you today. But you didn't come past at the usual time. Then I drove to your school. Then I came back. I even knocked on your door, but there was no one in.'

I thought of how I'd left my class ten minutes early for a fictitious dental appointment so I could ring his number. We must have just missed each other. So maybe subterfuge didn't suit me after all.

'How did you find me at the bus stop?'

'I live the other side of the street from Ray. We went to school together. Our families have known each other for years.'

By now it was 5.30 and my dad would be on his way home. If I wasn't there when he arrived he'd be worried. Mike continued, but his voice had a hard edge to it.

'I was in the front room and I couldn't believe it when I saw you posting something through his door.' He turned and glared at me, expecting an explanation.

I had the distinct impression for the second time that afternoon, that there was an implied floozy accusation in the air. First from his mother putting down the phone on me, and now from him. I was about to explain when I saw my dad's car approaching from the opposite direction. And besides, what was the point of Mike's jealousy in view of the situation he'd landed himself in?

I shrugged my shoulders.

'I've got to go. My dad's just come home.'

There was no point in saying any more. He'd got a girl in trouble and he had to do the right thing. Even if he refused to marry her, my dad wouldn't let me go out with someone who'd fathered an illegitimate baby. It was a hopeless situation and I was out of my depth. I felt as if life had taken its revenge on us for daring to be happy when it meant making someone else unhappy. Mike sat like stone, without speaking.

I put my hand on the car door but he turned on the engine, as if to move off with me in the car.

'What were you doing writing to Ray?'

He was shouting now. I was both frightened and angry at the same time. How could he believe I'd tell him I loved him one week, and write a love letter to his best friend the next?

I yelled back, 'It wasn't *from* me. And anyway, what difference does it make now you've gone and spoiled everything. Just let me out.'

He reached across me and opened the door without saying a word. I jumped out and slammed the car door shut. But almost before it had closed, he started up the engine and roared away, tyres screeching.

And that's how Mike drove out of my life. It was more than thirty years before I saw him again.

Chapter 11 – 2003

When my hand stopped moving I avidly read the answers to the questions I'd asked Enoch, written like magic by my pen on the pad of file paper.

Greetings, scribe.

He hadn't called me this before but I quite liked it.

Yes, I answer to Enoch, which means 'initiate' or 'anointed one'. I am known by many other appellations – among them Thoth, by the Egyptians, Hermes by the Greeks, Mercury by the Romans and Merlin by the Celts. Noah was, indeed, my descendant.

You ask if I visited heaven. My physical body did not travel to other dimensions, but my spiritual lightbody did. This only became possible after many years of meditation.

You ask if my physical body ascended into heaven at death. The answer is no. It was left behind when my soul ascended. My soul went straight to God because I had achieved the highest state of enlightenment by completing all the initiations on the human path of evolution. My mission is to help other souls achieve the same. Others who attained enlightenment were the Buddha and the Christ Jesus. But this state can be achieved by anyone who is willing to walk the right path.

You ask if God sent the Great Flood as a punishment for the misdeeds of humankind. The God of the Old Testament has as many facets as he has names – angry and jealous, all-loving and forgiving, bloodthirsty and punitive. In this case, he was being depicted as a vengeful God.

Look at it a different way, dear one. The flood was the result of wrongful actions. Wrong actions create bad consequences, just as right actions create good consequences. It is the Law of Cause and Effect – known by some as Karma. Therefore, the Great Flood was not sent by God, but conjured up by the deeds of Humankind. Despite what the Bible says, there has NEVER been a separate, patriarchal, judgmental God who had to be appeased with sacrifice, who sent punishments for His children instead of loving them. This idea of a merciless God was a projection of human fear. The souls of

Humankind were low on the scale of evolution at that time, so the God figure they held in their psyches, reflected this. Christ's gift was the truth that God is merciful and forgiving. A God of Love, not hate.

The report of me witnessing the torment of the fallen angels and beholding the fires of hell, is false. I did not describe those places because I did not see them. They did not and do not exist. How could a God who is all that is good, torture souls in a burning hell? As I said, God does not punish anyone nor does He send anyone to hell to keep them out of heaven. It is Humankind who keep themselves out by not living by the Spiritual Laws, the most important of which are Honour Thyself and Know Thyself.

To honour oneself is to love oneself. Men and women have to love and honour themselves so that they can love and honour others. If they feel shame or self-loathing, then they will loathe their neighbours, and there will never be peace on Earth.

By looking back with compassion on your life and forgiving yourself and others for all the incidents you regret, you transfer your focus from the mask of Ego, allowing Grace and Light to take its place. Once people love themselves they get to know their true God nature and become one with God. And recognise this God nature in others. It is through loving yourself unconditionally that you can transmute into your true form. By honouring (loving) and knowing (recognising) yourself, you step into the Light. You become en-light-ened.

You ask if the phoenix bird was a myth. The answer is that the phoenix existed in another dimension, at times coming into contact with the dimension of planet Earth. Which is why there are so many myths with common themes in different cultures – the gods and the human protagonists having similar experiences but different names. The phoenix goes by the name of Chol, Vena and the Bennu bird, among others. At the end of its long life cycle, the phoenix bird is consumed by flames and reborn more beautiful than it was before, symbolising resurrection, rebirth, and transformation.

One of my personae was the Phoenix King. The Greek word 'phoenix' from the Egyptian Pa-Hanok, translates as 'the House of Enoch'. In ancient times, I ruled over Phoenicia, also known as Atlantis. Through your research, you have discovered that my life was long and my soul was reborn in heaven more beautiful than before, as Metatron, so the phoenix can be seen as a symbol of me. And of anyone whose soul has evolved and ascended a little higher up the scale.

You ask if I am now the angel Metatron. The answer is yes and no. Just as different civilisations have adapted aspects of me as part of their own culture, (as I said before, I am known by many different names), so Metatron is a facet of me. He represents my perfected immortal soul. And he shares the same responsibility – to prepare souls for enlightenment.

You ask if angels have wings and the answer is no. They are neither of the physical plane nor are they birds, so why would they have feathers? If any clairvoyant sees 'wings' as part of an angelic vision, it is because of the energy vibration and light such beings emit, which gives the appearance of huge wings. However, do not take this answer as indicating that those who speak of white feathers as a sign of angels, are mistaken. You on Earth are right to look for signs and portents of the spirit world and if the collective consciousness believes that the sighting of a white feather indicates the presence of an angel, it can be so.

You ask again why I am appearing to you. It is because something in your psyche called me up. You will have to examine your own soul to find out why you 'called' me. Meditate on the information I am giving you now and see if anything resonates with you. I will be here as long as you need me.

P.S. Don't mention it.

The last line threw me until I looked at my original questions and realised he was responding to my thanks for his help with Oscar. As for the rest, apart from making me feel a bit guilty about doubting the feather spotters, it all rang incredibly true to me.

Despite having a pretty impressive celestial pedigree, Enoch seemed like quite a down-to-earth old gent. I'm glad he ignored my end of the world question. I didn't really want to know how nigh it was was anyway.

The only bit I wasn't sure about, was him placing the ball firmly in my court as regards his appearance in my life. Come to think of it, he wasn't actually appearing now – not even a little spark, let alone a full-body manifestation.

So I wrote another question.

Why am I not seeing you today?

The pen in my hand moved swiftly across the page.

Now that you believe I am here, there is no need.

This made sense. But there was something else that was different.

Why am I not hearing you as I did at first? When you told me about Oscar, I heard your voice in my head and it was like a dictation, whereas now I'm not seeing or hearing anything. Just writing.

My pen recorded his answer without pause.

You have discovered your individual strength. With some it is clairvoyance – but seeing images is not easy for you. With some it is clairaudience, hearing words. This was better, but the strain of listening was sapping your strength. With some it is clairsentience, sensing and feeling, but your emotions are so raw that you are protecting yourself against too much feeling at the moment.

The pen paused long enough for me to feel a slight disappointment at not being fully possessed of these occult powers. I'd always thought how handy it would be to have a bird's-eye view of the world. It would save a lot of time and effort if one knew which job not to apply for, which potential love interest not to pursue, and, especially, which plane not to board. But if I wasn't adept at those things he'd listed, what had I developed, exactly? In any event, I hoped whatever it was would be strong enough to keep him around a bit longer, as I was enjoying our conversations. The pen became agitated again so I re-established contact with the page.

Your gift is more subtle and is called claircognisance, or inner knowing. This is what enables you to produce psychography, also known as automatic writing. You have the ability to get your conscious mind out of the way. To leave it to one side, and let yourself be a channel to the knowledge coming through. You have become my amanuensis, child.

I'd never come across that word before and paused to consult the dictionary which was always close to my desk. The definition of 'amanuensis' read: 'A person employed to take dictation or copy manuscripts. From the Latin *servus a manu* – slave at hand (i.e. handwriting).'

The pen had paused with me, and then continued: *Do you notice a development in our communication today?*

As the words appeared to me I realised that, during the latter part of this session, I'd been able to absorb immediately what my hand had written, rather than having to read it afterwards to make sense of it.

My understanding of what you are communicating is becoming more immediate, I wrote. (Mentally adding – as long as you haven't swallowed a dictionary and use words I can understand.)

Good. Now you are fully receptive to me, we will communicate in this way, as it puts the least strain on you.

How sweet of him to care about my wellbeing, I thought. But me a channel? Wasn't that what I'd disapproved of in the authors of the New Age books, thinking it was a lazy way of writing, and half-doubting it was true anyway.

So I scrawled: *Is it possible to channel a whole book?*

Yes, people do write books with the aid of channelling. The higher beings use writers as a conduit if they have important messages to impart. But they cannot control everything the channeller writes, because humans have free will to write what they please.

Ha, I thought. That may explain why I kept reading about ways of divining the future with cards, pendulums, etc, in some of these so-called 'channelled' books. I'd tried the methods a few times and found them completely unreliable.

So are we right to question some of the methods written about in these books?

Enoch was again quick to respond.

Some authors examine what others have written and include that in their books, which is how false practices are perpetuated. They are often not open to receiving the authentic view. Look how inauthentic The Books of

Enoch have become. I wish my name were not attached to them. So much of what is printed is full of half-truths or half-understood truths. As for divining the future, it is very difficult, due to humans having the free will to change their plans.

The best action to take is to meditate regularly, which will increase your powers of intuition, and thus help you make the right decisions in life. But remember, intuition does not predict, it simply points the way.

At his mention of meditating regularly, I felt guilty, as it wasn't exactly high on my list of favourite pursuits. But Enoch's concluding words were encouraging.

Meditation is not a complicated process, dear one. Just sit in contemplation and allow in the guidance, which will help you to recognise the purpose you came to Earth to accomplish.

I was intrigued at the idea that I might actually have a purpose in life, and could have happily continued this Q & A session, but at that moment Oscar jumped down from his favourite chair, sidled past me and disappeared through the dog flap. This visit to the garden to sprinkle the lawn was his signal that it was bedtime.

Since Mike's death, Oscar had taken to sleeping in my bedroom instead of downstairs in the kitchen as he used to, and he liked both of us to retire together. It was eleven o'clock and I needed to get up fairly early the next day, because Danny and his family were coming to lunch, so I put my hands in prayer position, bowed my head in thanks to Enoch and made my way up to bed. Oscar bounded upstairs after me – his figure a little more defined now, thanks to his reduced-fat diet – and lay back on his doggy snuggle bed, legs akimbo, happy to snore gently all through the night.

Chapter 12 – 1970

With the screech of Mike's tyres still reverberating in my ears, I sprinted the short distance to my house. As it turned out, I needn't have worried about my dad wondering why I was coming in at 5.30. He seemed distracted and didn't even question it. My pallor didn't go unnoticed, but he put that down to whatever it was that had given me a headache the day before. And he wasn't wrong in that respect, was he?

He cooked us both a quick meal of bacon and eggs since I hadn't had time to get anything else ready. As we ate, I told him about Mrs B coming in that morning and leaving the dry-cleaning ticket, at which he looked uncomfortable. He said he had to go out to see someone the next afternoon and would come home early from work to change first.

He seemed relieved when I said I'd be going round to Cece's, and even gave me some money, telling me to take her somewhere – bowling, maybe. It was the second time in a week he'd shelled out. Strange behaviour indeed. I felt guilty because I was actually going to see my mum, but I took it anyway.

Picking up the cleaning ticket, my dad predictably excused himself at about eight o'clock to 'pop next door for a quick word with Mrs Browning'. This suited me, as the strain of faking indifference about the day's events was killing me.

I hadn't got to sleep last night until the early hours and I knew an even more dreadful night lay ahead unless I could get to sleep quickly. So I took all the necessary steps. A long warm bath, followed by one of my dad's sleeping tablets (prescribed shortly after my mum left home) washed down with a navvy-sized mug of Horlicks, laced with brandy.

My head hit the pillow at 9.30. I felt deceptively drowsy at first, until the toxic thoughts showed up, like manic gnats bombarding my brain. I alternately loved and hated. I hated Mike for sleeping with his girlfriend, getting her pregnant, and for being the reason Cece's dad had turned against Ray. I loved Mike with all my heart and felt so sorry for the mess he was in. I hated my mum for not being here. I loved her and missed her. I wanted her to come back and for us to all be together as a family again.

And then all the what-ifs joined in. What if I'd gone back to the club the week after I'd first met him as he'd wanted me to? What if he'd split with his girlfriend a few weeks earlier? Maybe she wouldn't have got pregnant then. On and on until I was sick to death of the whole thing.

It must have been approaching dawn before I finally succumbed to exhaustion. When the alarm sounded at eight o'clock, I switched it off and fell back to sleep. The next thing I knew it was past midday and the phone was ringing. I stumbled downstairs and managed to get to the phone before whoever it was rang off.

'Hello.'

My head felt muzzy from the delayed effect of the sleeping pill.

'Pan, it's Cece.'

I struggled to gather my wits. Now why would Cece ring me at this time? She should be at school.

'I'm ringing from the office. Sister Veronica said I could use the phone to check you're all right, as you haven't been there for registration two mornings running.'

I knew this wasn't usual school policy. At least, not after two measly days' absence. Was I to assume I was on some special register for girls-with-no-mothers-around? As with most displays of compassion or concern, I had to fight off the urge to blub. And the horrendous night I'd had wasn't helping either.

'Oh. Um. Thanks, Ce. Tell them I've been having headaches. No, say stomach aches. But I should be in tomorrow.'

It occurred to me that Cece might also be ringing to find out if my go-between mission had been accomplished successfully.

'And don't worry, I delivered the letter.'

I found myself wishing I could still be there in that moment, having just posted the letter, innocent of all the bad news, until Mike had turned up. Instead of here and now, experiencing the aftermath. Cece muttered her thanks and my mind cleared enough to be curious about the outcome.

'Did your dad go round to Ray's last night?'

Cece lowered her voice, 'Yes. I'll tell you quickly. I haven't got long, Sister will be back any minute.'

'What did your dad say to Ray?'

'Ray wasn't in. He'd gone out for a drink with Mike. My dad spoke to Ray's parents and they said Ray wasn't like that. My dad said they were respectable people with a nice house. He's calmed right down and he says I can see him on Saturday.'

'That's good,' I responded, trying to sound as if I cared, but Cece was still talking.

' ... But then something awful happened. When they were in the pub, Mike told Ray he saw you deliver the letter.'

Flipping heck. He hadn't wasted much time bringing that up, had he?

'I know. He gave me a lift home. But I didn't tell him who it was from or what it was about.'

I thought it best to leave out the bit about him following me and more or less accusing me of trying to seduce Ray. It was bad enough being in a love triangle with Mike and Val, let alone sharing an isosceles with Ray and Cece as well.

'Yeah, I know,' said Cece, speaking even more quickly. 'He told Ray all that. Look, it turns out the person my dad heard them talking about was Mike. Val's pregnant.'

Cece paused and, woolly-headed as I was, I remembered that I wasn't supposed to already know this, and I should react accordingly.

'That's bad luck.'

This seemed to satisfy her and she rattled on.

'Mike got really drunk last night and he did something stupid.'

'What? What do you mean?'

The permutations of what Mike could have done stretched

endlessly before me. One night of chattering-monkey brain was enough, the prospect of another day of it was unbearable. I began to pray that any passing nun would stay clear of the office long enough for Cece to spill the beans.

'He didn't believe Ray at first – thought the letter was from you for some reason. Then when Ray showed it to him to prove it was from me, and he read what was in it – that my dad was trying to split us up because he'd heard that one of the lads had got a girl pregnant, he went mad. He picked a fight with Brian, because he thought that's who'd blabbed, and he was thrown out of The Woodman's. To top it all, he crashed his car on the way home and he's in hospital with bruises and a broken arm.'

Again I made some noises of sympathy and surprise. But I wasn't surprised at all. Considering the mood I'd last seen him in, it all sounded horribly plausible.

'And worst of all, Pan, the police asked for a blood sample. If it's positive, he'll lose his job. Even if it isn't, he won't be able to drive for weeks.'

I was beginning to wonder about the source of Cece's intelligence. Considering there'd been a Ray embargo in the Byrne household, an awful lot of information had managed to filter through.

'That's terrible. How do you know all this, Ce?'

'Ray called in sick at work because he wanted to visit Mike in hospital. He met me on the way to school and told me all about it. He's pretty shaken up himself. Couldn't believe that Mike thought there was something going on between him and you. Visiting time's at two o'clock – he's taking Mike's mum to the hospital. Val's going in the evening.'

At the mention of that name, I closed down. Cece continued with the gossip, but I broke in, 'Cece, I'll definitely be in school tomorrow. We can talk then.'

'It's okay. Sister Veronica's not back yet.'

There's never a nun around when you need one, is there, I

thought.

'Sorry, Ce – there's someone at the door. I'd better go. See you tomorrow. Glad things are all right with you and Ray. Bye.'

There was no one at the door of course, but I needed to regroup my thoughts with the help of a cup of coffee, a chocolate biscuit, and a Rothman's. And my mum. In fact, as I was home alone, there was no reason not to ring her and tell her I was coming to see her now instead of waiting for the evening.

When she heard I wasn't at school – no need to lie about my non-attendance, Frankie was nothing if not tolerant of the occasional peccadillo – she told me to come over as soon as I could. She would meet me at South Kensington tube station and take me back to their place for something to eat, which was surprising considering that up to now she hadn't revealed her address because of my dad's threats to kill her lover.

'Are you sure, mum? I don't mind meeting somewhere else.'

'No, darling, there's been a development which I need to talk to you about. Don't forget the passport. See you at two o'clock.'

I rushed around getting dressed and checked my bag to make sure the passport was still there. But there was something else I wanted to do. Under the bed in the spare room was an old brown suitcase full of black-and-white photographs and odds and ends that we'd all accumulated – newspaper clippings, holy medals, certificates for swimming and licensed victualling – that sort of thing. I opened the suitcase and chose a photo my mum had always liked. It was of the two of us when I was about three years old. She had dressed me in one of those toddler suits fashionable at the time, consisting of a coat and leggings to match. I still remembered it because of the thick black elastic attached to the bottom of the legs which was pulled over my black patent shoes. The outfit was red but of course you couldn't tell that from the photo. We were sitting on a park bench, me with my legs dangling in space and her all dolled up in a fitted suit. We were both laughing at Dad, who was taking the picture.

While I was rummaging in the case for the photo, I came across an old paperback which looked interesting, so I took it with me to read on the tube to keep my mind off Mike. It would make a change from the A-level English set texts, my usual reading matter at the time.

It turned out to be the story of a Tibetan lama. It was written simply, with a lot of fascinating detail about his early life, the customs of the country and how he came to be a priest. When the train reached South Kensington, I was sorry to close the pages.

Mum was standing outside the station looking pretty in flared trousers and a pink crinkly top. Her hair was even longer than mine. We kissed awkwardly – not having actually seen each other for almost a year. She looked me up and down.

'You've grown, you know. You're taller. Your legs are longer. You could do with fattening up a bit, though.'

We both laughed. I'd been a puny child, and granny Doireann had been forever saying, 'she could do with fattening up a bit'. My mother saw the book in my hand and looked puzzled.

'Where did you get that? Haven't seen it in years.'

I explained that I'd found it while I was looking for the photo, which I pressed into her hand along with the passport, so I wouldn't forget. I put the book in my bag to continue reading later.

She beamed at the photo and told me that it had been taken on their day off. She and Dad often used to take me for a walk in Hyde Park and then on to Maison Lyons at Marble Arch, where granny Doireann was a nippy, which is what they used to call the waitresses.

We chatted easily as she walked me to Toby's house. She wanted to know all about what I'd been doing in the past year. Toby's place in Mulberry Walk turned out to be much grander than I'd expected. My idea of an artist involved easels, brushes and palettes strewn around an attic room with cobwebbed windows. But this was a large town house, tastefully furnished and expensively carpeted. There were antique cabinets, an enormous grandfather clock and impressive oil paintings. Mum saw my reaction to this grandeur and smiled. She explained that Toby had inherited the house from his father, but it was expensive to keep up. As a result, he'd converted the top floor into studios, where he worked and other artists rented space. The majority of his recent commissions had been murals in night clubs, so he was working outside of his studio most of the time at the moment.

Mum led me from the wide hall into a long dining room, the table already set with various salads, and expensive-looking cold meats. She poured us some wine – a medium glass for her and a smaller one for me. I couldn't help thinking that all we needed was a big glass for Daddy Bear to complete the picture. We sat down and started eating. I loved the bone-china plates and crystal glasses. I felt maybe my mother had got the best stuff out to impress me. To show me how her life had improved.

Mum was in reminiscing mood and we talked about the outings we used to have, like the time she'd taken Cece and me to the Beatles' Apple Boutique in Baker Street to show us the beautiful psychedelic mural of what looked like a giant red Indian, completely covering the building.

'Well, believe it or not, Toby was one of the art students who helped paint it. Of course, that was well before we met...'

At that moment the door opened and a tall young man in his twenties with floppy dark hair, wearing Levis and a striped granddad shirt, came in.

He stretched out his hand.

'Hi, I'm Toby. You must be Pandora. What's all this about your dad wanting a divorce, then?'

Chapter 13 – 2003

It was Sunday morning and I was looking forward to seeing Danny and his family. I loved Danny. He was so like his father, except he had his mother's fair hair. He was now thirty-two, a little taller than Mike had been, but with the same muscular frame that needed regular exercise.

Since I'd completely missed watching Mike change throughout his twenties, thirties and forties, I'd consoled myself with the thought that as Danny's features matured, I'd be able to fill in the missing years. That is, if we kept in touch.

The joint was in the oven and everything else prepared and under control, so I headed for the conservatory with the intention of tackling the Sunday papers. Oscar and I settled ourselves down, basking in the autumn sun. I tried to focus on the news, but my thoughts kept turning to the past.

* * *

After that terrible day when he told me about Val being pregnant, I never thought I'd see Mike again. Never thought I'd unlock the box with his name on it. Whenever he accidentally came to mind – a sports item on cyclists, say, or a mention of the film we'd seen, I did my utmost to suppress the memory. Yet, hard as I tried not to dwell on him, I always felt a pang of sympathy for that twenty-one-year-old whose future had been wrecked. I always pictured him the way I'd seen him at our last meeting – full of rage and railing against the rotten hand life had dealt him.

Then out of the blue Cece got in touch with me. It turned out that she and Ray had moved to Brighton to run a hotel and she wrote asking me if I'd like to visit them.

I'd deliberately lost touch with Cece after we left school. Having no desire to hear about Mike – it would have been torture – I reluctantly decided to cut the ties. Joining Frankie and Toby in Spain straight after my exams, gave me the excuse I needed to let our friendship fizzle out. In fact, I never contacted any of my old school friends after I came back from Spain. There had been no point, as Frankie and Toby had said I could move in with them, so I wasn't even going to be around.

I picked up Cece's letter from the mat that morning in the spring of the millennium year and read it with mixed feelings.

Dear Pandora,
You must be surprised to hear from me after all this time. (My mother got your address from Joan – they both send their love, by the way.) Ray and I have been thinking about the old days – must be our age – and wondered if you'd like to meet up.

We moved to Brighton last year and are now the proud owners of The Glasshouse Hotel. If you'd like to see it (and us) we'd love to have you. In fact, we've already reserved you a room. And if you have anyone you want to bring, please let us know.

There followed details of where the place was and a telephone number to contact her.

I put the letter behind the clock and sat down for a think. Cece and Ray had always been associated in my mind with Mike and Val, who for me had been associated with heartache and pain. So if I got back in touch with them, could I bear the moment when the subject of Mike came up? Which it was bound to, because Ray would never have lost touch with him, even if it was only through their mothers.

I picked up the phone and summoned Peter (the dear old thing who lived in the basement flat) for lunch, hinting that I had something to talk through with him. A retired psychotherapist, he was always ready to listen to my problems and guide me towards the best decisions. On the occasions when I went my own way, despite having had the potential pitfalls pointed out, I usually lived to regret it. But the old darling never said I told you so.

Peter arrived, as always, accompanied by a good bottle of red 'to oil the wheels'. I served lunch quickly, talking about everything except the topic uppermost in my mind – aware that I had to be patient, given his preference for counselling on a full stomach.

Wiping his mouth after his second helping of steak and kidney pie, he gave a contented sigh and motioned his head towards the easy chairs.

'Shall we?'

We settled ourselves opposite each other and Peter asked me to talk about what was on my mind. I thought it best to read out the letter and proceed from there. On I rattled for about five minutes until a moment of aural clarity stopped me in mid-sentence.

'Sorry, Peter. I'm whining, aren't I?'

Peter smiled.

'Take a few deep breaths and come back to a calm state, Pandora.'

And he breathed with me to slow my respiration rate down.

'I'm going to ask you a few questions and I want you to answer as quickly as possible. Try to keep your answers short. Then I might ask you to imagine certain scenarios.'

He paused to wait for my agreement, and continued.

'Do you have warm feelings for your friend Cecilia?'

'Yes. Well, warm memories. But maybe not so much once Ray and Mike came on the scene.'

'Visualise yourself reunited with her and her husband. Is it a friendly occasion?'

'Yes. I think it would be. From her letter she clearly wants us to meet up again.'

'Now visualise yourself asking if they know what happened to Mike?'

'I wouldn't ask the question. I'd avoid any mention of him.'

'Ask it anyway.'

After a minute or so, seeing my difficulty, he instructed me to go back to my breathing and forget the question for the time being.

'Can you imagine yourself bumping into Mike in person? What

do you think he would say to you?

'He'd probably say, didn't you use to be Pandora Fry?'

Peter suppressed a giggle, and the tension within me evaporated. He quickly seized his advantage. 'What would you say to him?'

'I suppose I'd ask him how he was, how many children he had, what he was doing for a living – all the usual stuff.'

'And how are you feeling when you're asking him?'

'Fine. I'm really interested and hoping he's had a good life. I don't want him to have been unhappy or stuck in a dead-end job or an unhappy marriage.'

'And what do you think he'd say to you?'

'He'd ask me the same sort of questions, I suppose.'

'And how do you think he'd be feeling at that time?'

'I'm not sure. He might wish that my life had gone wrong like his.'

I tried to picture Mike's face looking mean, but all I could see now were his dimpled cheeks and sparkling eyes. I felt such a rush of love that my heart hurt with it.

'No. He wouldn't...couldn't...feel like that. He'd want the best for me. As I would always want the best for him.'

And then the floodgates opened, and it felt like all the tears I'd previously suppressed decided to make a break for it. It was like being a child again, when you sob so much that you can no longer take a breath without your whole upper body convulsing.

Peter appeared next to me with some tissues. He fetched me a glass of water, and then gently patted my hand.

'I recommend some rest. You'll feel better after that. I'll come back about six o'clock for coffee and dessert. And to check you're all right.'

I smiled weakly and managed to shudder, 'Th-th-th-thanks.'

As he left he called over his shoulder, 'I think you'll find you did some good releasing today.'

* * *

My reverie was interrupted by Oscar barking and scratching at the conservatory door. William, a pink-cheeked, dark-haired version of Danny, was chasing his older sister Hannah round the garden.

Danny and Mei were peering at me through the glass. I opened the door and Oscar sprinted out to join them.

Danny kissed my cheek. 'We tried the front but you didn't hear us. Hope we didn't wake you.

This remark made me feel about a hundred.

'Hello Dan. I wasn't asleep, I was just thinking about...'

The children tumbled in from the garden.

'Hi Nana-panda.' Nana made me feel old but they had to call me something. As for panda – it took me right back to having my plaits pulled at primary school.

We all gravitated towards the kitchen and the smell of roast beef. My cooking had improved a lot since the days of the burnt offerings inflicted on my poor old dad.

After lunch, I hit a bit of a low. Maybe it was the memories that surfaced from being with Mike's family, but the familiar dark clouds were beginning to accumulate. Sitting here with them, being called 'Nana', I felt like a fake.

If only Mike could have been here. It shouldn't be me. I was the imposter. My eyes grew damp and I turned my attention to the dishwasher so they wouldn't see.

'Can we go into the big house to play, Nana?' lisped four-year-old William.'

His sister elbowed him and whispered, 'You mustn't ask that.' She had long, glossy hair and dark brown, almond-shaped eyes like her mother.

Danny and Mei studied my expression for clues to my feelings on the matter. We all knew why William wanted to go. And where. Certainly not to the ground floor – its only furnishings being chairs, tables and an old dresser. It was the cellar that called to William – an

Aladdin's cave of sports memorabilia Mike had collected over the years.

On their last visit, when they'd come to pick up Mike's things, the children had gravitated, as usual, towards the cellar. I'd found the sight of the signed cricket bats, baseballs, footballs, and other treasures that Mike had loved, a little overwhelming, and had disappeared and left them to it. But today I wanted to share their fun, so we made the expedition into the magic cellar and one of the autographed footballs was taken into the garden for a game.

We had a goal net which Mike had installed as soon as William could walk, and trainers in various sizes so no one would have an excuse not to play. We all took turns as goalie and Oscar easily won the competition for the highest scorer. He could weave past the best of us.

During the game, I noticed Danny glancing up at the roof. When we stopped for a breather, he observed, 'Looks like you've got a few tiles missing, have you got any spares?'

Bob Grove had asked me the same question when his wife had first noticed the damp patches on the bedroom ceilings. We'd searched the garage, the basement and the shed, to no avail.

'Afraid not, Dan,' I answered glumly, 'We couldn't find any spare tiles anywhere. Bob took one to a local supplier, but he said they were hard to find these days.'

Danny wanted to see the damage, so we went inside the house, to the upper bedrooms, where Bob had tried to conceal the water stains. But their outline was still visible through the paint.

Danny shook his head, 'It's a finger in the dyke job. Let me take a look at the roof.'

We got the ladder out of the garage and Danny shinned up the rungs. He was up there for ages, repositioning it several times so he could see as much as possible.

Mei was on the pitch and I joined her. 'I'm sorry, Mei, It was his idea to go up there. I'm frightened he might fall off.'

Mei smiled, 'Don't worry, Pandora, he loves it. He can't resist ladders. I think he's a builder at heart.'

'Or a window cleaner,' I laughed. But I wasn't laughing when he finally came down and gave me the news I'd been dreading.

'It's not too good, I'm afraid. Too many damaged tiles to leave it much longer. If I were you I'd get a couple of quotes for a new roof.' My face must have fallen, because he went on, gently, ' You'll need to get it done before the winter sets in.'

I thanked him for the warning, saying nothing about having no money for a new roof. Danny was under the impression I was comfortably off because I'd always insisted that I didn't need any of Mike's money; that having The Cedars and the cottage was enough. So I put on a bright smile and said I would get some quotes.

As a finale to the day, we spent an hour in the garden of my local, the Lamb and Flag, just down the road – which had swings and a climbing frame the children loved. The landlord recognised Danny when he went in for drinks, and came out and chatted to us, reminiscing about Mike and his skill at darts which had led the pub team to victory the year before.

They left when it started to get dark. Kissing them goodbye, I bit my lip hard so as not to cry. Not so many months ago, Mike had been standing with me, joking with the children, hugging Mei and patting Danny on the back.

As they pulled away, I heard William ask, 'When's grandpa coming back?' and his mother shushing him in case I heard.

Oscar and I repaired to the living room to put our feet up. This time I really did get down to the Sunday supplements. I always bought one broadsheet and one tabloid and the tabloid magazine had a special feature on psychics and esoterica. As I leafed through it, I spotted an advertisement for something called The Enoch Society. There were no details other than a telephone number. I pulled out the page, carried it into the study and placed it on the top of my bureau, under a glass paperweight.

I wasn't sure whether I would take it any further. I'd see how I felt the next day.

Chapter 14 – 1970

Frankie's face when Toby dropped the bombshell about my dad wanting a divorce, was a study. Her cheeks were flushed bright scarlet – with anger at Toby, I guessed, for being so crass. Her eyes were alternately flashing at him, and discharging compassion at me, her mouth pulled to one side in distress. Who wouldn't be distressed at the failure of something that had once been precious?

It took Toby a while to decode Frankie's facial gymnastics, but my ashen cheeks may have given him a clue. When it finally dawned on him that I hadn't had any idea that such a thing was on the cards, he mumbled an apology and backed out of the room. Frankie was about to follow him, still with fire in her eyes, but I managed to distract her by asking for a tissue.

She took a hankie from her bag and, kneeling on the floor beside me, dried my tears as if I were the three-year-old in the photo I'd brought with me. I could see streaks of mascara on the handkerchief and dreaded to think what my eyes looked like.

'Don't cry, Pan. Never think that when I left home, it was you I was leaving. And it wasn't that I was desperate to leave your dad, either. It was more about what and who I was going to.'

She stroked my face and I inhaled her familiar essence – a mix of powdery perfume and her natural body scent. She seemed desperate to justify herself but I needed no explanation, as I was more than aware of the limitations of life in Manor Wood. She continued in her own defence.

'Meeting Toby and seeing how exciting life could be, I just couldn't go back. I never dreamt your dad would go off the deep end the way he did and make it impossible to see you...'

I interrupted her before she had a chance to rerun her movie of the past year. I'd screened my own version too many times already.

'Mum, it's okay. I understand what you mean. You and Dad live apart. But he never said anything about a divorce, that's all. So it's come as a bit of a shock.'

She led me out of the dining room into what she called the drawing room, where we sat down on a large chintz settee, and she cradled me as she used to when I was little. We were both crying now. Every so often I caught a glimpse of Toby out of the corner of my eye, hovering in the hall to monitor the level of hysteria.

Gradually the tear-fest abated and Toby sheepishly appeared with some coffee and chocolate brownies. He set these down on a low table and took his place next to Frankie, who smiled and said, 'I'll be mother,' while she poured the tea.

Toby's large brown eyes wore the expression of a depressed bloodhound.

'Sorry if I upset you both. Didn't mean to. Foot in mouth, I'm afraid.'

We told him everything was okay and Frankie stroked his hair, which seemed to soothe him. After tea, Frankie started fiddling with her wedding ring, which I'd noticed she was still wearing, and resumed her divorce story.

'Darling. Your dad rang me yesterday. To say he'd been to a solicitor about a divorce—' she looked embarrassed, '—on the grounds of adultery. But he told the solicitor he didn't know where I was, only that I was living with an artist called Toby with a double-barrelled surname, somewhere in London. The solicitor put him in contact with a private detective who found Toby's address and phone number in no time, as his work's quite fashionable and in demand—.' Toby's chest visibly swelled at this. '—I suppose the man watched the house and saw me coming in and out.' My mother must have read my startled expression.

'Don't worry. There was no shouting or threatening to kill Toby, like before.'

Toby tried to look tough, but his cup rattled against its saucer as he placed them on the table. Mum squeezed his hand. He took hers eagerly, like a forgiven child, and kissed it. After a few moments Frankie tore her eyes away from Toby's and fixed her gaze on me.

'Your dad's quite friendly with Joan Browning, isn't he?' she said.

I wondered what Mrs Browning had to do with this.

'Well, she helps with the shopping and sometimes he goes into hers for a chat.'

'Do you get on all right with her, Pan?'

Once again, the penetrating look as if seeking clues to my state of mind.

'Not too bad.'

I could hardly say that we were worlds apart and that a middle-aged neighbour hardly registered on my teenage scale at all. Mum's voice grew solemn as if she were breaking some bad news. 'When I asked your dad what the hurry was, he said they're thinking of moving in together. But they wouldn't do it without getting married first.'

It was difficult to know what to say next. I'd always hoped that Frank and Frankie would get together again and we'd be back to being the three Frys – all for one and one for all. But it was crystal clear to me now that this was never going to happen. And I couldn't express that forlorn hope in front of Toby, anyway, him obviously being on the sensitive side. So if Dad had made up his mind to marry Mrs B, maybe that was a good thing. At least I wouldn't have to worry about him being lonely.

I jumped up from the sofa and went to the window. I could feel them both watching my back intently for signs of distress. I gathered myself and turned to face them.

'Mum. I just want you and Dad to be happy. If he wants to marry Mrs Browning and you want to be with Toby...' I swallowed hard at the finality of it all, '...then do what you have to do. Now can you point me to the bathroom, please, because I need to repair the damage.'

* * *

I got home about eight and found my dad and Mrs B sitting at the kitchen table. He was drinking Guinness and she was sipping what looked like a shandy. The aroma of pigs' trotters still hung in the air – a delicacy withheld from my father by my mother on the grounds of taste and decency, but obviously tolerated by Mrs B. My father's eyes turned towards the clock.

'You're early. Weren't you going bowling with Cecilia tonight, love?'

Damn. I'd forgotten that was my cover story – but what with getting to Mum's early, and finding out my parents were getting divorced, my timing was all to pot.

'Hello Mrs Browning,' I said, adopting a diversionary tactic. She smiled nervously in reply.

But my dad was still looking at me quizzically.

'No, we didn't go bowling in the end, Dad, we just played records in Cece's room. I've got a bit of a headache, so I came home early.'

Mrs B looked sympathetic, 'Still got that headache, dear? How about some brandy and hot milk?'

This was not such a surprising suggestion, as I'd been on the receiving end of hot toddies since quite an early age, to treat anything from a cold to a toothache.

My dad was wearing his best suit and Mrs B was quite dolled up, in what she called a 'costume' which was a matching skirt and jacket in a shiny brown material. Her French pleat had been carefully engineered at its pinnacle into a beehive, and lacquered to within an inch of its life. Given the festive atmosphere of best clothes, Guinness and trotters, I was wondering whether they were going to break the news of their wedding plans to me. I thought I'd throw them a line and see if they took it.

'You both look nice. Are you celebrating?

They each looked a little shocked, as up to then they'd always assumed the roles of friendly neighbours, and here I was exploding the myth by placing them together as a *couple* with something to celebrate. My dad took a swig of his drink and gave Mrs B an eloquent glance.

'Pandora.' He rarely called me this so I knew something important was coming. 'I went to see a solicitor today. Mrs Browning came with me.'

Ah. The business of the dry cleaning of the suit became clear. He studied the contents of his glass, his facial muscles working overtime.

'You see, it's like this. I managed to trace your mother...through a friend.'

Little does *he* know, I thought, that *I* know it was a private detective.

'And I spoke to her on the phone yesterday.'

He wrung his hands as he always did when he was anxious or upset and my heart went out to him, but I still kept my expression impassive so he didn't suspect that I already knew it all.

'The long and the short of it is, that we're going to get divorced. I started the proceedings today, now I know her address.' He paused, 'And that she agrees to being the guilty party.'

He stopped there, waiting for a response. The moment was a bizarre imitation of earlier in the afternoon with Toby and Frankie. But I was more composed this time. No more histrionics. So I hugged him. And Mrs B as well. She was so relieved, she reacted with a bear hug which squeezed every last breath out of me. 'You're a brave girl, a brave girl.'

Then, realising that they hadn't actually told me the full plan, she nodded at my dad to continue. He was beginning to resemble a condemned man, but he managed to get the words out.

'Mrs Browning and I – Joan and I – we're thinking of getting married. As long as your mother doesn't change...'

Mrs B looked flustered. Maybe my dad, like me, had also harboured secret thoughts of a possible reunion. I broke in, to prevent him from saying something he might regret.

'That's lovely, Dad. I think it's a good idea.'

And I found myself smiling at their obvious relief, and at the truth of it. It *was* a good idea for both of them. And it left me free to do what I wanted after I'd got my exams out of the way. And what I wanted was what had been suggested earlier by Frankie and Toby – to join them in Spain, painting the night club. What better way to forget Mike? Wasn't that what they used to do with broken-hearted girls – pack them off abroad to recover and forget?

I would leave to some future date the breaking of this news to my dad, when I'd had a chance to shape it into an acceptable proposition. In the meantime, I joined the two of them at the kitchen table for a hot toddy, and after a little while, wished them goodnight.

Despite feeling tired, I worried that sleep might be elusive because of all that had gone on, so I tiptoed downstairs to my bag, handily looped over the banister, and fished out the book written by the Tibetan. It was quite a slim volume and it didn't take me long to reach the last page. Reading it had calmed me, and as I drifted into sleep I thought perhaps I could mention some of the lama's beliefs to Sister Joseph in our next Religious Education class.

Chapter 15 – 2003

It was Monday, the day after Danny and his family had come to visit, and I'd arranged to see Olivier in the office that morning. He wanted to give me the finalised timetable for the coming weekend's Cakes For All Occasions course and the list of participants.

Since he'd been interviewed in connection with the new television programme, Olivier hadn't been around so much. There was to be a book accompanying the series and he was busy testing out new recipes in the hope that he'd be given a contract. He was convinced that one of the reasons he was in line for the job was the publicity generated for the workshops, and I felt pleased that The Cedars and I had been able to help him.

'And Jason 'ad a brainwave, Pandora,' he confided. 'To keep down costs, he suggested to use some students from the catering college in town. They're preparing and serving lunch on Saturday and Sunday, and an evening meal on Friday and Saturday. It counts towards their portfolio of work experience. Naturally, we pay them a small fee as well. But much cheaper than hiring professionals.'

This sounded too good to be true.

'Yes, but who's going to be supervising them, Olly? And who's buying the food?'

I considered I had enough on my plate supplying continental breakfasts and drinks at break times without having to haul industrial quantities of ingredients from the supermarket to the kitchen. Or supervise potentially feckless teenagers.

Olivier giggled. 'Don't panic, *mignonne*. I bring the food and, Jason, he supervise. There are nineteen boarders, by the way.'

The six main bedrooms slept fifteen between them. The two attic rooms which we'd prepared, as Olivier put it, 'for the snorers', had four single beds. So we were, indeed, already fully booked. But I found myself feeling apologetic on hearing this.

'Maybe you should have gone for a larger venue, Olly. I hope you don't regret choosing us.'

I mentally kicked myself when I said that. There was no longer any 'us'. Just me.

'Of course not, *chérie*. We also 'ave seven day guests. This number is perfect.'

His eyes twinkled as he patted my hand, 'Unless you want to accommodate a couple more in your cottage – 'ow many bedrooms have you got?'

I laughed, assuming he was joking.

'Three, actually. But I think they'd be more comfortable at your place. You could charge them more for a penthouse experience.'

He looked serious for a moment but then one of the *pâtissiers* approached with an order query, so we parted with him saying, 'I'll be there on Friday at four.'

* * *

There wasn't much for me to do that afternoon, Margery having readied The Cedars to a high degree of excellence, so happy was she to be back in harness. So I took Oscar for a leisurely walk, to reflect on my relationship with Mike's son and his family.

Despite some past lapses of judgement which seemed to point to the contrary, I had quite a logical brain, and it was this that questioned how my connection with Mike's son Danny and his family – with whom I had no blood ties – would continue. If it continued at all.

I'd seen them three times since Mike's death. First at the funeral in Southampton, then when I'd given Danny Mike's computer and other personal effects, and then when they came yesterday. Mike had been buried in Southampton because I was such a wreck after he died, that I'd been more than happy for Danny to arrange everything. And I thought that their little unit of four tipped the balance in favour of location selection, Oscar and I being his only relations in Chace Standen. At the back of my mind there had also been the uncertainty of how much longer we could afford to live here.

Val, Mike's ex, hadn't attended his funeral, so I never did meet her. But she sounded as if she'd been a good mother to Danny and a high profile grandmother to William and Hannah. Mei's parents were alive and well and part of the family circle, so what was my function? I was just a spare part. A sort of pity-nana. Someone who wasn't necessarily in the photograph.

Fond as I was of them all, did I really have any right to expect them to include me in their busy lives? The eighty miles or so that separated us ruled out any babysitting – so what practical use was I to them? I wondered what Mike would have wanted me to do. I re-examined my selfish intention of keeping in touch with Danny because I could see Mike in him, and felt ashamed.

Calling Oscar to heel, I bent down to put his lead on before crossing the road between the woods and the house, kissing his head as I did so.

'Can't let anything happen to you, can we, boy? You're the closest thing I've got to family now.'

His eyes softened and he smiled – opening his mouth and panting in response. And on we both trotted, making our way past The Cedars and home to Phoenix Cottage.

* * *

Later in the afternoon I decided to re-read Enoch's answers to the questions I'd asked him. The question of why he came to me had still to be resolved. I opened the file and looked at his words.

You ask again why I am appearing to you. It is because something in your psyche called me up. You will have to examine your own soul to find out why you called me. Meditate on the information I am giving you now and see if anything resonates with you. I will be here as long as you need me.

So I sat down to meditate and after twenty minutes or so, wrote down which pieces of information had stayed in my mind.

Enoch's mission is to help souls achieve enlightenment.

One has to love and know oneself in order to love and know others.

God does not punish.

Phoenix = the house of Enoch.

The word 'enlightenment' made me think of a book by a Tibetan Buddhist that I'd read when I was a teenager. Some years after that, I'd been to a couple of lectures on Buddhism where we were told that enlightenment can't really be explained, but in general terms it's being at one with the universe. I had some notes somewhere, probably buried under a stack of handouts from other talks and workshops I'd attended.

Another thing that had stuck in my mind was the Buddhist goal of escaping from the cycle of karma and reincarnation and reaching a state of nirvana. It sounded pretty hard to achieve – not something the common-or-garden devotee could pull off very easily.

The Buddhists say that human suffering is caused by our cravings and desires which are, by their very nature, transient and changing. When you think about it, most people spend their lives in a state of craving. Setting their sights on the next must-have. Boarding the Big Wheel for the next pleasure ride. Whether it's for the perfect man, woman, car, job, drug – it's all craving. And once we've got what we thought we wanted, are we happy? Not usually. Or, at least, not as completely as we thought we'd be. Like King Midas, who turned everything to gold including his breakfast, it's often a case of be careful what you wish for.

Having been told in my Religious Education class at school that Buddhists don't believe in God, I'd double-checked this with the speaker at one of the Buddhism lectures, and he'd confirmed that they don't actually have to believe in a god, the idea being that spirituality comes from within, not from some outer source.

But, surely, I thought, considering Enoch's prominence in the Old Testament, his view of enlightenment would bring God into the picture, wouldn't it? I decided to leave that for the moment and moved on to the next point on the list, about loving oneself. Enoch's message seemed to be: God is love and if we show love to ourselves and others, so we become more like Him. I immediately determined to love myself a bit more. I wasn't quite sure how, but I wrote LOVE YOURSELF on a post-it note and stuck it on the fridge, as a start.

One thing I certainly did love was the message that God doesn't punish, feeling validated in my instinct against the teachings about hell and damnation that I'd received at school. So I wrote GOD DOES NOT PUNISH on a post-it note, but put it in a less public place. Finally, I exulted in the coincidence of living in Phoenix Cottage. Who'd have thought it translated, more or less, as Enoch's Place? The main house was called The Cedars when we bought it, but the smaller one next to it, had not been named. It was Mike who'd given the place its title. We were browsing at a country fair one day, when we came across a stall selling house plaques. One of them had a picture of a beautiful purple-breasted phoenix with gold and scarlet plumage, astride a flaming nest.

'Hey, look Suze, it's the hot bird.'

I couldn't help laughing. I had a Chinese-style dress with a similar pattern and he persisted in calling it the hot bird dress. When I'd first worn it he'd nicknamed me Suzy after the Chinese prostitute in a novel called *The World of Suzy Wong*. Nice.

Then he had a rare serious moment.

'The phoenix rises again, doesn't it?'

The stallholder nodded in agreement, sensing a sale. Mike lowered his voice.

'That's us, really. Don't you think, kiddo?'

I squeezed his hand in reply. So we rolled with the metaphor and got the stall holder to paint 'Phoenix Cottage' around the edge of the picture of the hot bird.

* * *

You may have noticed that this time I hadn't involved Enoch himself in my musings, the reason being that he'd asked me to work out for myself why I'd called him up, like a genie. But I wasn't convinced that I'd actually figured that out yet. Could it be as simple as needing guidance over Oscar's illness? But did it really need an antediluvian patriarch of mythological magnitude for that? The words sledgehammer, crack and nut came to mind.

What about the biggest problem looming in my life – the loss of Mike? Yet how could Enoch solve that? Unless he could raise the dead. For now, I'd be content with trying to love myself. And with revising my opinion of God Almighty. No longer would he be a bearded old man sitting on a cloud in judgement on all of us sinners, but a jovial figure – a bit like Father Christmas, showering us with gifts and *bonhomie*.

Sensing I'd finished my cogitations, Oscar jumped down from the sofa and ran towards the door, making little whimpery sounds. I followed him, thinking we were both headed for the kitchen but instead he veered off in the direction of the study. I continued on my way, filled his bowl, and called him to come and get his low fat din-dins. But he wouldn't come so I went to see why. He was in the study scrabbling at the base of the bureau and looking upward. I told him sharply to stop scratching the wood, and followed his gaze. He seemed to have his eyes fixed on the glass paperweight, underneath which was the folded page I'd removed from the Sunday magazine supplement.

As soon as I picked it up, he ran into the kitchen and scoffed his dinner, leaving me scanning the page for the ad which had caught my eye the day before. There it was. The Enoch Society and a telephone number – nothing else. I was beginning to get used to recognising 'signs' and 'portents', so I trusted that this would be the right thing to do, and dialled the number.

The voice that answered was hard to identify as male or female. I pressed on.

'Hello, I'm ringing about your advertisement for The Enoch Society. Could you give me a few details please?'

'Certainly. We are an organisation which exists to show people how to improve their lives. We find that those who answer our advertisements have often experienced uncertain times and are in need of a course of study to focus their thoughts. This takes the form of distance learning. Would you like me to send you some details?'

'Um—' My brain was struggling to digest all this. I don't know what I'd expected, but it wasn't a correspondence course. '—Do you have any classes? I could get to London, if you run any there.'

'We don't do those. It's just the postal course.'

Written down in black and white, the tone of this statement may sound brusque, but in fact it was delivered in the same neutral manner as all that had gone before. I say neutral, but it was the kinder side of neutral.

'Okay. Well if that's all you do, that's what I'll have.'

'Excellent. We'll get the first one off to you right away. Name and address please.'

I gave him, or her, my name and address but I still hadn't any idea of the course content. Or how long it would take. Or how much it would cost. So I attempted to prolong the conversation.

'Will you want any money beforehand? ...Er, I'm sorry, I don't know your name.'

'My name is Cass. And there's no charge. We operate as a charity. For those in need.'

I suddenly felt embarrassed. Short of funds I might be, but I was hardly a charity case.

'No, that's okay. Really, I want to pay.'

But it was too late. Cass had already ended the call. I put down the phone, and instantly my discomfort lifted, to be replaced by excited anticipation of what would soon be winging its way to me. Whoever and whatever Cass and The Enoch Society were, I was willing to give their correspondence course a try.

Chapter 16 – 1970

The day after the divorce revelation from both my parents, I handed Sister Joseph a forged letter from my father, excusing my absence of the previous two days. She read it quickly and asked pointedly if I was all right now, to which I replied that I was feeling much better.

After taking the register, she gave us a pep talk on the coming A-level exams. How we should be revising every minute we could, so as not to let the school, our parents, and God down. And how we should pray to Him, and to Our Lady, and the school's namesake – St Thérèse de Lisieux – for a successful outcome.

It was Thursday, and the first class was Religious Education, which everyone in the upper sixth was required to attend. I had a lot to tell Cece, but we all knew better than to try to chat in Sister Joseph's class.

Every lesson was preceded by a prayer. It was Sister Joseph's habit to include a little extra request, and this morning it must have seemed to her appropriate to add, 'Dear God, please bless our studies and support us in the coming examinations.'

We sat down and she read out the Gospel for the day, which happened to be the parable of the talents. She then delivered a short homily on it – probably a complete steal from the priest who'd said mass at the convent that morning.

As I'm sure you know, the talents in the story refer to money that the master gave to three of his servants to invest for him. Two of them succeeded in increasing theirs but the third had dug a hole and buried his, so he got a clip round the ear and was kicked out. Sister Joseph obviously identified with the master, urging us not to hide our lights under any bushels.

'You are the cream of the crop. Only the girls with the best eleven-plus scholarship grades are admitted to this school. So make sure that's reflected in your results.'

When she'd finished, I raised my hand and asked if I could tell her about something I'd read in a book written by a Tibetan lama.

Sister Joseph composed her face into what passed for a tolerant expression and nodded half-heartedly.

'Sister, when he was describing the Buddhist philosophy, he said that they never pray for favours. They believe that God doesn't answer such prayers, because that would mean giving preference to one person over another. If He practised favouritism, he wouldn't be a just God.'

Sister Joseph's plump face assumed a ruddy flush at this point and she began tugging at the white pleated wimple which encased her neck. I should have recognised the danger signals but I blindly pressed on to the next part, which concerned reincarnation – the belief that the soul is constantly reborn in different circumstances, incurring karmic debt for any misdemeanours, which can be carried over into the next life.

I was in full flow, my eyes lowered to quote another passage, this time on the subject of stepping off the wheel of reincarnation and achieving nirvana, when the book was snatched from my hand. Sister Joseph was standing next to me, her quivering jowls flecked with spittle.

'Where did you get this from, Pandora?'

I was taken aback. Sister Joseph was treating me as if I'd been caught reading *Lady Chatterley's Lover* on school premises.

'I found it at home, sister.'

She raised her eyes to heaven as if to say – what can you expect in a household that's produced a fallen woman.

'My girl, if you're questioning the power of prayer, I don't know what you're doing in a Catholic school.'

The heat of her scorn was like the sting of a slap, without the physical contact. Some girls whispered uneasily. My instinct told me to backtrack.

'But, sister. I just wanted to ask you what you thought about it. For a class discussion.'

In answer, Sister Joseph marched back to her desk, threw my book in the desk drawer, and locked it.

'Pandora Fry, there is no discussion to be had. I'm confiscating this because it's a sham. Buddhists don't believe in God, so why would this so-called lama pontificate on whether or not God answers prayers? Whoever wrote this book wasn't a Tibetan or a Buddhist. If you want the class to take what you say seriously, I suggest you refer to a legitimate source book, not a hippy fantasy.'

I could hardly believe my ears. How could it have been published if it was a fake? I consulted some notes I'd made.

'I think he was writing about his form of Buddhism...'

Sister Joseph silenced me with a wave of her hand.

'If you want this trash back you'll have to get your parents—' She bestowed on me a look of distaste. '—In your case, your father, to write a letter requesting it. If there's no request by the end of term, it will be disposed of.'

My heart started pounding and I felt a rush of blood to my head. I'd always suspected Sister Joseph had it in for me because I didn't come from a devout family, like the Byrnes, who had a high profile in the local church. Just you wait, Sister, I thought. The moment I leave this place, I'm lapsed. I refuse to be in any club you're a member of.

At break, Cece and the other girls sympathised with me. We'd all been shocked at the ferocity of Sister Joseph's reaction to the book. I told them how it had been really interesting and felt completely authentic.

'You should ask your mum what she thought of it,' said Cece. 'She might know more about who wrote it.'

I felt quite singed by the heat of Sister Joseph's disapproval but at least discussing it with Cece had deferred the moment for the topic of Mike's accident to arise. Part of me wanted to hear how he was, and the other part wanted to stick my fingers in my ears and forget all about him. As far as I could tell, Cece had no idea how deeply I'd fallen for Mike. And no idea that we'd been planning to become an item. But he was Ray's best friend, so I'd have to endure some discussion about his accident some time.

Break over, we went to our separate classes, Cece and I arranging to meet for lunch as usual.

It was a sunny day so we decided to eat our sandwiches outside in the courtyard, where there was a patch of grass with some benches for the exclusive use of the sixth form. No one else was around so we took a bench each and stretched out in comfort, while Cece filled me in on what had happened in our favourite soap opera the night before. I'd missed it because I'd been to see my mother, who Cece was eager to hear about.

'What was it like, seeing her after so long?'

'It was...good.'

I wondered whether to mention the divorce but it was still quite painful to think about, so I said nothing. 'She sent you her love, by the way. And her boyfriend's really nice.'

'Is he good-looking?' asked Cece, with interest.

I thought it best not to mention how young he was, as this would go straight back to Mrs Byrne and be broadcast to the neighbourhood by this time tomorrow. She wasn't known as 'the News of the World' for nothing.

'Yeah, tall and dark. They're driving to Spain this weekend.'

I hesitated, not sure if Cece was ready for what was coming next.

'They want me to join them after the exams.'

Her face crumpled.

'But I thought we said we'd go away for a week to celebrate.'

Cece's aunt had a caravan in Margate which she lent to members of the family, some of whom weren't scrupulous in cleaning up when they left. I'd been there once before and had no inclination to return.

'You could always go there with Ray.'

We both smirked at the prospect of her parents allowing such a thing. It was about as likely as Sister Joseph handing me the key to her desk. Then I had an idea.

'Why don't you come out to Spain?'

I wasn't sure if this was feasible but I wanted the hurt look on Cece's face to go away.

She brightened up immediately. 'That'd be great.'

'Okay,' I said, glad that she'd cheered up. 'I'll ask my mum and see what she says.'

We chatted on about my mother and what she and Toby were going to be doing in Spain, until I felt that, as the conversation had mostly been focused on me, perhaps it was time to ask about Ray and Mike. So, perversely, I found myself introducing the unmentionable just to get it out of the way.

'What about yesterday, Ce? Did Ray visit Mike?'

Cece screwed up her eyes, as if trying to remember what she'd already told me.

'Oh yeah. He took Mike's mum to the hospital. Mike's right arm's quite badly broken. And he's really down in the dumps, worrying about losing his job. Ray said he was really quiet.'

She stopped and I felt I should contribute something. Sometimes silence can be interpreted as lack of interest, sometimes as too much.

'When's he going home?'

'Not sure. He hit his head on the steering wheel so they kept him in, in case he had concussion. Ray said he looks terrible – he's got a black eye but no one knows if that's from the steering wheel or the fight.'

'Did any of the other boys go to see him?'

I was trying to suppress my interest but it was getting the better of me.

'I don't think so. It's just been Ray, his mum and Val, I think.'

At the mention of Val I felt the same sense of desolation as I had yesterday.

Keen, now, to change the subject, I got up and brushed the crumbs from my dress. We had fifteen minutes before our next lessons. The school chapel was a two-minute walk away, up a flight of stairs in the main building.

'Come on,' I said, linking arms with my friend. 'We've just got enough time to say a prayer for our exams. To keep Sister Joseph happy.'

Cece thought I was joking but I pulled her along with me, up the stairs and into the small chapel.

We genuflected in front of the altar, making the sign of the cross. Cece took sixpence from her purse and lit a votive candle for her intention. The statue of Our Lady, robed in blue and white with a golden halo of stars circling her head, silently received Cece's prayers for success in her exams.

On the other side of the chapel stood a statue of Jesus, his sacred heart visible and pierced by thorns. I had no intention of following Sister Joseph's wishes and praying for good exam results, after she'd been so horrible to me, but I still lit a candle.

I lit it for Mike. I didn't really know how to frame my prayer, apart from wishing his injuries better. I had a feeling that if I prayed for his happiness it wouldn't be a true prayer because deep down I didn't want him to be happy without me. And I couldn't bear for him to be happy with her. So I concentrated on his health because that was all I could manage in the circumstances.

After we'd finished, we sat quietly for a few minutes because it was so peaceful in there. That was when I put Mike and his world in a box that I locked as firmly as Sister Joseph's desk, and sent far away.

* * *

When I got home I quickly rang my mum to ask her about the book.

'I'm glad you liked it, Pan. A customer in one of the pubs lent it to me and never came back for it. It's quite spiritual, isn't it?'

'Yes. It's the story of a Tibetan priest. But Sister Joseph didn't approve.'

'Why, because he wasn't a Catholic?'

I laughed. My mother's words had been dripping with scorn.

'Probably. But it was more than that. She went ballistic when I read out some bits of it in class.'

'Why did you take it to school, love?'

'Well, there was something in it I thought we could talk about in RE.'

'What, exactly?'

I felt a bit embarrassed talking religious philosophy with my mother.

'Oh, something about the way God answers prayers. Or doesn't. It's just that Sister Joseph said it was trash. And it wasn't written by a real Tibetan.'

My mother immediately bridled.

'Sister Joseph is a narrow-minded old battle-axe.' She paused a moment and continued, 'I seem to remember something about it being channelled, but I can't recall anything in that book that could be described as trash. Do you want me to report her to Sister Agatha?'

The thought of Frankie, living in sin, having abandoned her husband and daughter, engaging in a conversation with the headmistress about the behaviour of one of the religious teaching staff, gave me my second adrenalin rush of the day.

'No, really. It's okay, Mum. I just wanted to ask you if it was genuine or not.'

'Well I've still got a good mind to ring the school and complain.'

'I felt it was time to change the subject before things got out of hand.

'I'll be leaving soon anyway. I can't wait. Then it's Spain, here I come.'

My mother's voice became animated at the mention of abroad.

'I'm getting so excited. So have you decided when you're joining us, Pan?'

'Probably the end of June. Oh, and do you think Cece might be able to come for a couple of weeks?'

'Of course she can. The nightclub's underneath an apartment block. We're being given a two-bedroom apartment, so you can share. We'll pick you up from Girona airport. Have you told your dad yet?'

'Um, no. I think I'll leave it a little bit, if that's all right. Mrs B was there when I got home last night and they told me about the divorce. I didn't let on I already knew.'

There was a slight edge to my mother's voice when she answered.

'Did Joan say anything about getting married?'

'No, but Dad did. That's why I'll have to choose the right moment to tell him about Spain. In case he thinks I'm going because...you know, because of Mrs B.'

There was a pause before she spoke.

'That's very sensitive of you, Pan. You take after your dad. He never liked hurting anyone's feelings. Although sometimes he did without meaning to. Give him...' Her voice trailed away for a few seconds and then revived. 'Never mind. I'd better go, darling. Mustn't be late for my last shift. Especially as Richard's promised there'll always be a job for me when I get back.'

'Okay, Mum. By the way, how long do you think we'll be over there for?'

'We're not really sure. Toby won't know until he sees how big the place is. Bye now, darling. I'll be in touch when we get there.'

* * *

Dad came in at his usual time and we sat down to one of my semi-burnt offerings. After picking at it for a few minutes, he pushed his half-eaten meal to one side, rolled a cigarette and asked me to make him a cup of tea.

'Thanks, love. Now, Dora. Sit down a minute.' His expression was a little anxious, as it had been last night. 'Are you sure you're okay with Joan and me getting together?'

I nodded, but was tempted to ask if *he* was okay with it.

'Look, it's going to be a bit of time before this divorce is official and, what with your exams, and you going to work eventually, you shouldn't have to do the cooking. So we were thinking, maybe Joan could come in and do it.'

He looked pleadingly at me. Mrs B had probably suggested it and who was I to disagree? I smiled at him.

'That'd be great, Daddy.'

How long since I'd called him that? Maybe now was the right time to mention Spain. I should strike while the iron was hot.

'Dad. About getting a job. Is it all right if I wait until after I get my results in August?'

'Of course it is, love. Maybe Roy could give you a few weeks at the shop to keep you busy. Until you start applying for a proper job.'

That wasn't in my summer schedule at all. In fact, one of the things I'd been looking forward to most of all was handing in my notice, and never again having to serve middle-aged women unfashionable clothes and pretend they looked the bee's knees in them.

'Actually, I've got the chance of a working holiday. But I wanted to ask you first.'

I'd decided I was going to Spain whatever happened. The trick would be to go with his blessing.

'Mum said that I could spend the summer with her in Spain.'

At the mention of my mother his face darkened.

'Doing what exactly? You're not working in some sleazy bar. I won't have it.'

'No, Dad. It'd be more like...interior decorating and design.'

I didn't want to mention Toby, so I had to improvise.

'It's in a new apartment block, helping to get the apartments ready for the tourists.'

My dad's comprehension of what sort of work was available in a Spanish resort was nil, so he didn't put up much of a fight. He took a drag of his roll-up.

'And who's paying for your fare?'

'Don't worry. Mum said she would. You know, to make up for not seeing her for so long.'

Reading his suspicious look, I fibbed fluently.

'She phoned me today to tell me about the divorce—' I assumed a sad expression.'—And she thought this would cheer me up.'

It was probably guilt that prompted his next move. He got out his wallet, peeled off several notes, and slapped them down on the table.

'Here you are, love. Get yourself a couple of nice dresses for your holiday.'

I took the money, got up, and kissed his stubbly cheek. He smelled of sawdust and Old Holborn. As he worked in a furniture factory and smoked a good many roll-ups a day, it wasn't surprising.

'Thanks, Dad.'

We didn't say things like 'I love you', but I did love him. And I hoped he knew I did.

* * *

As I lay in bed that night I thought about Sister Joseph. I suppose it was understandable that she'd rejected the idea that it's not God's job to fix things for us. But I'd expected some debate on the subject, not just a tirade.

We'd been taught at primary school to say a morning and evening prayer. It was something along the lines of a Hail Mary, followed by asking God to bless our family and friends and anyone we knew who was sick. This practice of wishing people well, felt right to me.

On the other hand, praying to God to help me pass my exams struck a false note. I definitely agreed with the author of the book, whoever he was, on that one. Surely it was up to me to be well-prepared, rather than doing the minimum and hoping for a miracle. So I resisted the temptation to request divine intercession to boost my grades, and instead offered up a prayer of thanks for having my eyes opened about what sort of prayer is worth saying.

Chapter 17 – 2003

The next day I didn't have to go in to work. Mine was the perfect working week for a dog-owning, recovering widow – a part-time job with Tuesdays and Thursdays free, ensuring no consecutive early starts. After a few household chores and a bit of shopping, I took Oscar for a walk through the coppery woodland. There was no one else about, no other dog walkers to chat to, and my mind drifted back to the day before, and of my sketchy memories of the Buddhist teachings. When we got home, I decided to unearth my notes to satisfy my curiosity, and eventually found what I was looking for in a dusty cardboard box in the loft.

The lecture handout listed the four Noble Truths: 1. Life is suffering. 2. Suffering is caused by desire and greed. 3. Liberation from suffering, can be attained. 4. Following The Eightfold Path is how to extinguish desire and greed and be liberated from suffering.

These eight ways were listed with a brief description.

Right Understanding – a true understanding of the world as it is, without delusion.

Right Thought – a true desire to change and to free oneself from attachment and ignorance.

Right Speech – telling no lies, speaking no slander, all communication non-harmful and kind.

Right Action – the ethics of not exploiting or harming others or oneself.

Right Livelihood – earning a living honestly without exploiting others, including animals.

Right Effort – conscious direction of one's mind energy to focus on good qualities.

Right Mindfulness – being totally aware of our thoughts, words and deeds.

Right Concentration – the practice of one-pointedness of mind in meditation.

There was a fuller explanation of each of the practices, but I had enough to go on, so I sat down at my desk and ran my eye down the list, trying to absorb the wisdom of the teaching.

When I got to the last one, I felt my pupils move back and up into my eye sockets. I decided to go with the flow, so I concentrated on the centre of my brow and tried to clear my mind. I sat like this for about twenty minutes, lost in the meditation. I didn't call Enoch's name but when the image of a small flame appeared behind my closed eyelids, I knew he was there.

I reached into my desk drawer and took out the pen and pad of paper I used for our sessions.

Soon, his first words appeared on the page.

How can I help you, scribe?

I just let my hand do the talking.

Is your definition of enlightenment different from the Buddhist one, master?

I was somewhat taken aback by the title I had addressed him by. 'Master' sounded a touch archaic. Arcane, even. Was I turning into a sorcerer's apprentice? The reply came quickly.

There is no shame in addressing me in such a way. For you are, indeed, a novice. Our communication is filtered through your mind. Therefore the mode in which I speak to you is your translation of my diction. So, in effect, I send the message and you choose my words. To you I sound like a 'master' so that is how your psyche writes me.

This explanation was both credible and slightly unsettling. How foolish of me to have assumed I was his only correspondent.

Are you saying, Enoch, that you speak the way you do because that's how I'm channelling you? And someone else may receive you in a different voice?

It is common sense, my friend. When I inhabited Earth I spoke an ancient antediluvian language in an idiom long since lost. You are channelling me in your own tongue. How else would you understand my words? But if someone received me as speaking Spanish, or Hindi, or any other language, in a style familiar to them, that would be effective too. My perceived mode of speech would be dependent upon their education and expectation.

I scanned the possibilities of this revelation and imagined Enoch being channelled as a cockney.

'Well, me old cock sparrer. 'Ow's it goin? Fancy taking a schlep up the apples and pears to enlightenment? But you'd better knock the boozing and the birds on the 'ead first. The Guvnor don't take too kindly to sins of the flesh. Know wha' I mean?'

The pen began to tap impatiently on the page, suggesting that Enoch had had enough of my flights of fancy.

Back to business, scribe. An enlightened being, like the Buddha, is one who is awakened to God. The word Buddha means 'awakened one'. God is Light. And Love. God is everything, everywhere, all the time. Each of us is God. Those who open their hearts to the God within and fully recognise their own divinity, truly walk with God all the days of their lives. God has many names and yet no name, in the sense that He is indescribable. Ineffable. Gautama Buddha simply chose not to describe God.

I contemplated the beauty of this answer for a few minutes until another question came to mind.

How is the phoenix important for me?

The answer flowed eloquently across the page.

You have been thinking about the phoenix lately. Of the sign you and your loved one chose for this house. Of the link with my name. Of your love for each other that was revived after many years Have you thought of another way the phoenix can relate to your life?

As I was pondering this, the pen took over, so I shoved my conscious thoughts out of the way and gave it full throttle.

Each phase of my life where I have made a decision to leave a person or situation has been a sort of death. Often the circumstances of leaving have been painful, equivalent to the fire of the phoenix's destruction. I have reached a point in my life when I don't want to continue with this pattern.

On receiving this last sentence, my conscious mind put the brake on. What was I saying, stop the world I want to get off? Was my higher self encouraging me to commit suicide? Enoch broke in quickly.

Think not of such things. Remember, the death of the phoenix is also her rebirth. What other ways can you think of to break out of this pattern?

What appeared next was a conundrum. I read the words but didn't grasp the meaning.

I can break out of this paradigm and choose my own reality...

At that moment the phone rang and my hand went limp, the pen dropping from my grasp on to the page beneath. Damn. That was why it was safest doing this sort of thing in the late evening, when the likelihood of unexpected phone calls or visitors was minimal.

It turned out to be Olivier, who had an unexpected request.

'Ello, Pandora,' I loved the way he pronounced my name, with the accent on the last syllable. I could almost forgive him for disrupting my contact with Enoch. 'I want to make a little request, but please don't feel you 'ave to. One of the producers from Oven Ready Productions want to come and see me in action this weekend. And we need to put up him.'

'Put what up him?' I could never resist a gentle gibe when he forgot to split his phrasal verbs.

'Eh?' He laughed half-heartedly and ploughed on. 'Pandora, darling, will you come to the rescue of two poor chefs who need this producer to be in the best possible mood all weekend?'

He meant himself and his boyfriend Justin but I was still puzzled as to why they couldn't wine him, dine him, and butter him up in their penthouse apartment. The Cedars was already full, so he couldn't stay there. I wasn't too pleased at the prospect of an unexpected house guest. There was only one *en suite* bathroom in Phoenix Cottage which meant I'd have to give my bedroom to the guest and sleep in one of the smaller rooms. Oscar wouldn't be too pleased about that, as he was fond of his special spot in the corner of our usual bedroom. And then a dreadful thought occurred to me.

'It's not Mr Willoughby, is it?'

There was a significant pause during which my heart sank.

'I'm not sure. There are three names on the letterhead. One of them is Willoughby. Why? You didn't like him?'

I thought quickly. I hadn't said anything at the time, so how would Olly know he was a randy old goat? I couldn't let Olly down. If necessary, I'd have to barricade myself in my room.

So taking pity on my French friend I said, 'Okay. I suppose if it means that much to you. But you'd better tell him there's a dog in the house – in case he's allergic or doesn't like them.'

'Don't worry. I checked with the office. Dogs are no problem.'

It sounded as if Olivier had pretty much clinched the deal already.

'As long as he doesn't expect four-star treatment. Why can't he stay with you and Justin, by the way?'

'Impossible, *chérie.* Justin's using both spare rooms at the moment. One as an office and one as a store room. He's looking for bigger premises, but in the meantime our spare bedrooms are *hors de service*.' His voice trembled slightly. '*Entre nous*, Pandora, I don't know how much more I can take. I like to leave my work at the door but now when I get home all I see is kitchen equipment and invoices.'

I felt something approaching sympathy. Maybe I'd misjudged him in assuming he was fobbing the producer off on me.

'I'm sorry to hear that, Olly. Of course he can stay. What time is he coming?'

'He's travelling down from London on Friday evening and leaving on Sunday. He wants to get a feel of the workshop and the kind of people attending. And to see how a similar scenario might work on TV. Thanks, darling. Big kisses. *Ciao*.'

* * *

I was glad when Friday came at last. And especially glad, for the roof's sake, that no rain was forecast for that weekend. The first workshop had been an experiment and had felt more like a fun event. But there was so much more hinging on this one – Olivier's budding television career being the most important, followed by the expectations of the punters after even more hype from The Daily Messenger's food correspondent. It was a long time since I'd had so many overnight guests. I just hoped they behaved themselves, were not incontinent and didn't sleepwalk. Thank goodness I'd be well away from them in the cottage. The downside of that, was that I was going to be alone in the house with a strange, potentially lecherous man. And Oscar would be as much use as a chocolate teapot, more likely to be offering up his nether quarters for frottage than defending his mistress.

Just to be on the safe side, I called Bob Grove to have him fit a lock on the door of the bedroom I was to occupy. He mulled over my explanation that I had an unexpected male guest who was coming for the workshop, and adopted a lugubrious expression.

'Take your mobile phone up with you as well, Mrs A. Can't be too careful. Don't want to be murdered in your bed, eh? Or worse. You can always dial 999 if you hear him moving about outside, trying the door handle.'

I paid him and showed him out. No way was he getting his customary tea and biscuits after scaring seven shades of living daylights out of me.

Friday afternoon went by in a bit of a blur in the end. Olivier arrived in a fluster, muttering in French under his breath.

'Justin's tied up. One of his staff went sick, so he can't 'elp until tomorrow. *Zut*! 'Ow am I going to cope *tout seule*?'

Swallowing an urge to make a crack about bondage, I offered to lend Olly a hand unloading his van, and was manhandling my first box of vegetables when a minibus drew up, out of which piled the catering students, to whom we immediately consigned the fetching and carrying.

They were followed by a trickle of guests who all seemed remarkably good-natured and in full control of all their faculties. I showed them to their rooms, telling them that dinner would be at seven. Olivier was now busy in the kitchen, assigning the students their tasks, so I excused myself and made for the cottage.

Oscar was delighted to see me. And even more delighted to see his dinner. I settled down with a book, thinking my job was done for the day. And then the phone rang. It was Olly. What sounded like a riot seemed to be taking place in the background and he had to shout to make himself heard above the noise.

'Pandora. Could you possibly come over. Willoughby 'as just arrived and I need someone to tell our guests that dinner is a little bit delayed.'

Oh flip. I'd been so busy counting off the workshoppers that I'd forgotten about the producer. Then my brain registered the dreaded word 'Willoughby' and a different 'f' word sprang to mind. But I had to keep Olly calm so I feigned composure.

'Sure I will. Sorry. I just popped back to feed the dog. It's a bit raucous your end – are the hungry diners revolting?'

Olly was not in the mood for humour. 'Pandora, be serious. This is an SOS. Get over here now.'

So I flew like Superwoman to poor Olly's rescue, letting myself in the back door and making straight for the dining room, where I found the guests all seated expectantly. It was seven o'clock and no sign of food or wine anywhere on the table.

'Hi,' I said cheerily. 'Sorry about the slight hold-up. I'll get one of the waiters to bring you some wine.'

They exchanged expressive glances, as if sharing a special insight into the workshop experience and its failings.

I crossed the hall on my way to the kitchen, expecting to see the overweight, white-haired individual who'd come to the Cool Cake Boutique, and instead beheld the most gorgeous man emerging from the cloakroom. Tall, with Scandinavian colouring, he had an aquiline nose and a faintly patrician air. The vision smiled and offered his hand. He looked about forty and reminded me of someone I used to know. Until, that is, he spoke.

'Hello. I'm Zac Willoughby.' He mistook my semi-paralysis for incomprehension and raised his voice slightly. 'From Oven Ready Productions? Sorry I'm a bit late, but Friday evening traffic – you know what it's like. Everyone escaping to the country.'

'Hello. I'm Pandora.' I said, in my best accent. Glad for the first time in my life that I had a rare and singular name. He held out his hand and I returned his firm handshake. His palms were smooth and dry.

'Have you met Olivier? I'm not sure what's going on in the kitchen. Shall we find out?'

Phew, that was a close one. For sixty seconds or so I'd broken my lifetime rule of treating attractive men as if they weren't. Attractive, that is. A lack of female swooning usually presented a challenge to them, which had often worked to my advantage.

He smiled. 'Yes, we met briefly. It was hard to hear what he was saying over the rumpus.'

We entered the kitchen together to find Olly, normally the most even-tempered of men, remonstrating loudly but ineffectively with the rookie cooks and waiters who were pelting each other with bread rolls. Zac Willoughby and I stood watching the chaos in dismay, until the half dozen teenage boys and girls slowly became aware of us and subsided into semi silence, whereupon I seized the advantage. I didn't screech. Instead I lowered my voice and tried to sound like Al Pacino.

'Stop fucking about or I'll kick your asses out of here. Next, I'll report you to the principal and charge the college for the agency staff we'll replace you with.' I glared at them each in turn. 'So what's it to be?'

Needless to say, this was all hot air, but I had to scare the crap out of them somehow. Otherwise it was going to be impossible to get any hot dinners out of the kitchen and down the gullets of our guests.

Catching Zac's startled eye at this point, I feared he'd probably marked me down as a vulgar fishwife, but his answering wink gave me hope that he hadn't.

To my intense relief, the rioters lay down their bread rolls, and shuffled mumbling to their work stations, returning meekly to the tasks that Olivier had given them.

Having commandeered one of the girls to serve wine to the waiting diners, I escorted her to the dining room and stood in the corner while she filled their glasses to the brim, so they'd be full of good cheer and forget about the delay.

Back in the kitchen, I found Olivier chatting animatedly to Zac. On the long table, was a row of goats' cheese tartines ready and waiting to be served. Catching Olivier's eye, I motioned my head towards the door. He got the message and stopped in mid-flow.

'Ah, Pandora. We're ready to serve the first course. Would you show Zac to the dining room, please?'

I almost felt like curtseying. If only I'd had on a short black dress, black stockings and suspenders, little white frilly pinny, it would have completed the farce that the evening had been so far. But why was I fantasising about bobbing a curtsey to Zac in a maid's outfit? I shook my head to erase this image, and led him to the remaining empty chair at the head of the table.

The guests were by now chattering away, and it occurred to me that with Olly supervising the food, Zac was in danger of having no one to talk to, tonight's guests all having come in pairs or even larger groups. As I left him, I remembered something. 'Is that your bag in the hall? I'm afraid the house is full, so you'll be staying in the cottage. I'm going there now, so I'll take it if you like.'

Zac didn't look at all surprised. 'Thanks. I was told I'd be staying with you. I'm looking forward to meeting your dog.'

The way he looked at me made me wish I really was wearing a saucy maid's get-up.

'Okay,' I blushed. 'See you later.'

I waved self-consciously and hurried from the room and into the kitchen to check on Olly and the catering crew. What I saw warmed my heart. They were now beavering away enthusiastically, joking and laughing, but getting on with it at the same time. I began to feel quite proud of our bunch of zippy kids.

While I was there, I asked Olivier if he was going to stay on and talk some more with Zac, because if so, they could come over to the cottage, away from the guests.

'That would be wonderful, Pandora.' He lowered his voice so the teenagers wouldn't hear. 'And are you 'appy with your 'ouse guest?'

I felt myself blush. The more I blushed, the more his blue eyes twinkled.

'Knowing my luck, he'll probably turn out to be gay.'

'Oh no,' Olly giggled, blue eyes sparkling. 'He's certainly not that.'

'Why, have you already tried it on with him, Olly?'

He tutted. 'Pandora, you're very naughty. I'm effectively a married man. Let's just say my gaydar says most emphatically not.'

I mimed excitement by rubbing my hands and licking my lips. But the word 'married' had stalled me.

'He's probably already taken.'

'I didn't see a ring.'

'Well *you* don't wear one. Does Justin?'

'No, but we work with our hands – it's not hygienic. And, anyway, it's not official.'

At that moment, one of the teenagers called him over, so I made a quick exit. I still had one more task to complete, which was to check on Zac.

As I approached the dining room I could plainly hear Zac's rich public school vowels, holding forth in no small measure. Whatever the tale he was regaling them with, his audience was spellbound. Unlike Olly, Zac was definitely a male who had no need of a Superwoman to rescue him.

Chapter 18 – 2003

Zac knocked on the door of Phoenix Cottage some time after nine. I'd expected to see Olivier with him and asked where he was.

'Still supervising the delinquents. Last I saw of him, he was issuing rubber gloves and scouring powder. Thought I'd make myself scarce in case he roped me in.

He followed me into the living room and slumped down in Mike's armchair.

'It's been a long day. Nice to be able to relax at last.'

He looked like a man slightly the worse for drink.

'Can I get you a coffee?' I asked. He eyed the drinks cabinet longingly.

'Wouldn't say no to a whisky if you have it.'

I found a bottle of Mike's single malt and two glasses and poured us each a shot.

'Ice? Water? Soda?'

He shook his head. 'No. This is perfect.' But he wasn't looking at the drink in his hand, he was looking at me. And then he raised his glass and said, 'To life and love.' And we clinked glasses.

Olivier turned up about an hour later by which time Zac and I had put away half the bottle between us. Oscar had added to the conviviality of the evening by demonstrating his limited repertoire of tricks. The first was sitting up in begging position holding one of his front paws out at the command, 'Shake, Oscar, shake'. The second was the same pose but this time moving both front paws up and down at great speed, which might have seemed like a different trick, but was actually a demonstration of his impatience at not getting a reward quickly enough in the first place. As treats had been in limited supply since he'd been ill, this second trick was becoming quite a habit.

After a couple of slugs of whisky, Zac had decided Oscar needed to learn a third trick, and was on the floor demonstrating how to roll over and die for the queen. The dog was standing over him, head on one side, trying to work out how to elicit something edible from the situation. I had just turned up the volume of a Snow Patrol track at Zac's request, so I didn't hear Olivier's knock at first. He had to tap at the window to attract my attention. I led him into the living room, where the scent of Laphroaig laced the air. At the sight of Zac wrestling with Oscar, who had wrongly deduced that this was what was required of him, Olivier threw his arms in the air, his voice descending to a stage whisper.

'*Oh la la*. How am I going to get any sense out of him now, Pandora? What 'ave you done to 'im? He's rolling all over the floor.'

'Well you shouldn't have been so long, Olly. Chill out. Have a drink.'

I waved the bottle of whisky at him and his face wrinkled in disgust.

'Pandora. How can you offer me alcohol, when you know I'm driving? First I had to supervise the cleaning, and then I had to wait for the minibus to take the monsters home, to make sure they didn't get up to any more mischief.' He put his hand to his head. 'My God. I'll be glad when this weekend's over. Never again will I work with *amateurs*.'

I hoped he was talking about the teenagers and not me.

Zac, by this time, had distracted Oscar by throwing his squeaky hippo to the other end of the room, and was sitting upright. He surveyed Olly sympathetically.

'Things not going so well on the kitchen front, old bean? Sorry to hear that. Thought the meal very good. Didn't you want to talk to me about something?'

Olivier looked surprised that Zac was *compos mentis* and had possibly heard every word he'd said. He laughed vivaciously, as if he'd been joking.

'Oh, these trainees. They can be 'ard work. But we 'ave to do our bit training up them.'

Thinking it wise to forego any language correction on this occasion, I sat down and patted the sofa cushion next to me, but

Olivier remained on his feet.

'No thanks, I won't stay. It's getting late. I just wanted to leave Zac the programme for the weekend.'

He swept us both a slightly accusing glance.

'I get to bed if I were you. We all need clear heads tomorrow.'

As I let him out, I patted his back and whispered, 'Don't worry, I won't let him have any more to drink. And I'll make sure he's ready for duty at 9.30 sharp.'

Olly kissed me on the cheek and whispered back, 'Enjoy yourself. But not too much. I want him to have his mind on the job tomorrow. Remember, it's me he's come to see perform. And my delights he's come to taste.'

I gave him a hefty shove out the door and he waved goodbye, grinning.

Back in the house, I found Zac at the kitchen sink, washing the glasses. He turned to me and smiled. 'He didn't stay long, did he?'

'He's worried you'll have a hangover tomorrow and won't be able to assess his performance adequately. And he wants your taste buds clean to fully appreciate some of his new creations.'

Zac moved towards me.

'There's something here in this kitchen that's stimulating my taste buds, that's for sure.'

I slid easily into his arms, my breasts snuggling nicely into his expensive shirt. He kissed me long and softly. The whisky had slowed us both down, so the urgency I'd normally have expected was deliciously diluted into something more tantric. I was the first to pull away in the end, recalling my responsibilities as mistress of the house.

'I'd better show you your room.'

He took my hand and we went upstairs. Oscar followed us, having already sprinkled the lawn in readiness for bedtime. I opened the door of Zac's bedroom, indicating where I'd left his overnight bag.

'Very nice. What's your room like?'

This was accompanied by a mock innocent expression which made us both giggle.

'You're looking at it,' I said. 'Like a good hostess I gave up my room to you. And my *en suite* bathroom.'

'I can't have that,' he said, picking me up and carrying me over the threshold. 'No gentleman could ever allow a lady to suffer the distress of an inferior room.'

He placed me carefully on the bed. The bed which Mike and I had shared. As he closed in on me I prayed he'd live up to the bed's reputation. It should be all right. So far, he'd shown great promise.

Some time later I was woken by a scratching at the bedroom door. I opened it to find Oscar sitting on the landing with his doggy bed beside him, which he must have dragged from the smaller bedroom we'd both been intending to sleep in. The one whose door I'd had the lock put on.

Behind me, Zac was snoring steadily the way drinkers do, his throat muscles having relaxed in ratio to the volume of alcohol he'd consumed. This, plus the potential awkwardness of landlady and lodger waking up in the same bed, inspired me to lead Oscar back to our designated quarters, where we both got into our respective beds and fell promptly asleep.

My alarm went off at six and I whipped Oscar out for a quick walk before driving to the village for a newspaper, and picking up a special order of *croissants, pain au chocolat,* and other breakfast pastries from the Cool Cake Boutique, which I dropped off at the main house.

I could hear the shower gushing when I got in, so I set the table in the kitchen for Zac's breakfast. When he appeared, much more casually dressed than the day before, in jeans and a polo top, his hair still damp, it was almost like meeting a different man. He looked a little hung over. And a little older than yesterday. Which, from my point of view, was a good thing.

'Good morning Mr Willoughby. Did you sleep well?'

I hoped he'd realise where my tongue was (firmly in my cheek).

To my relief he responded in kind.

'Good morning Miss... ?'

'Mrs. Mrs Armstrong.'

'Oh dear.' He looked around in mock alarm. 'Mr Armstrong isn't going to appear with a shotgun at any moment, is he? I assumed you weren't attached.'

'I'm not. Mr Armstrong is deceased.'

Normally I choked up when I had to explain about Mike, but this time I was all right. It felt like a breakthrough, because I didn't want to spend the rest of my life a weeping widow. Zac seemed reassured.

'Oh, that's a relief.' He paused, realising what he'd said. 'No. Sorry. That's not at all what I meant.'

To my annoyance, I started to cry. Must have been delayed reaction. When Zac saw the tears he sat me down at the kitchen table and made us both a cup of tea. In fact, he boiled eggs, toasted bread and reversed our roles completely. I gave him a potted history of Mike and he listened with apparent interest. All too soon it was time to bestow breakfast on the workshoppers.

'The workshop starts at 9.30.' I grinned. 'Olly wants you there on the dot, in the best possible state to assess his performance.'

'Speaking of which,' he drawled, narrowing his eyes and expanding his chest, 'I hope you assessed *my* performance positively.'

I laughed nervously. 'You mean which box would I tick. Good, bad or indifferent?'

He pushed me gently against the fridge, stooping slightly and leaning his forehead against mine. 'Well, it certainly wasn't indifferent.'

'Not sure,' I teased. 'Probably need to have another go. But sober this time. I might remember more.'

He started tickling me until I begged for mercy, which set off Oscar, who proceeded to nip Zac's ankles. When the dog had calmed down, Zac settled himself at the kitchen table with the paper and said casually, 'Can I take you out for dinner tonight?'

This sounded lovely but I didn't want to tread on Olly's toes.

'I think Olly's plan was for you to go out with him and Justin.'

The hands of the kitchen clock on the wall behind Zac seemed to be racing round.

'I must go. Don't be late for the workshop today. Promise?'

'Promise.' He reached down and picked up a square of yellow paper that had fallen from the fridge door and read out what was written on it. LOVE YOURSELF. He looked mystified. 'My fridge note says, buy more eggs.'

I answered almost without thinking. 'Well, it's kind of the same thing, isn't it? It just means look after yourself.'

As I said goodbye to Zac, out of the corner of my eye, I saw a tiny spark.

* * *

I felt a bit of cabin fever that day, being tied to providing drinks at the morning and afternoon breaks, keeping the workshop kitchen dishwasher loaded, and supervising the production and serving of lunch by the catering trainees. I hadn't been contracted to get involved with lunch, but it meant that Olly and Justin got the chance to talk business with Zac. And I figured that if they talked at lunch, they wouldn't need to talk at dinner.

As it turned out, that's just what happened. When I served the afternoon refreshments, Zac took the cup of tea I offered him and said softly, 'All systems go. Book anywhere you like. It's just you and me, babe.'

I sighed with relief, having been dreading the prospect of a whole evening waiting for Zac to come back from his dinner date. The longer I could spend with him tonight, the better. Tomorrow he'd be observing the workshop again and was due to leave for home straight after that. There were things I wanted to get to the bottom of, like if he was spoken for. How old he was. And, as always, my personal preoccupation – how many children, if any, he had.

I cleared the tea things away at top speed and sped back home for a hasty beauty session involving a face pack, deep-conditioning hair treatment, a ton of body moisturiser, followed by make-up and a couple of coats of nail varnish. Zac hadn't said what food he liked but in the end it didn't make any difference because by the time my nails were dry enough to tackle the phone, every one of my favourite restaurants was already booked up.

When he arrived back, I was still in my dressing-gown. Not only was I incapable of deciding what to wear, but I wasn't even sure we'd go out at all, there being no decent restaurant available within a twenty-mile radius.

'What a lovely gown,' he said, as he hugged me. 'Allow me to take it off.'

So upstairs we went. And on the way I counted my blessings that he was a featherbed man, rather than an aficionado of cold, hard, kitchen surfaces.

After he'd smudged my make-up and well and truly dishevelled my carefully coiffed hair, Zac declared he was hungry. I should have told him earlier, but my mind had been elsewhere.

'Bit of a disaster, I'm afraid. Nowhere's free. It's the Saturday night thing. I suppose I could find something in the freezer...'

I yawned as I delivered this line, hoping he'd get my too-tired-to-cook signal.

'Well, my sweet, we could always get a takeaway—'

Great, I thought, he's read my mind.

'—And afterwards, we could maybe walk to the pub down the road?'

The pub suggestion was not such a welcome one. Mike and I had been regulars there and I was imagining the look on some of the faces if I went in with another man so soon after...

'What do you think?' said Zac.

'Fine. Indian or Chinese?'

A couple of hours later, replete with rice, monosodium glutamate, and Tiger Beer, we lay together on my large, comfortable sofa watching a sitcom with the sound turned down, subtitles on, to block out the canned laughter.

'It's the only way to watch 'em,' yawned Zac. 'By the way, if you want to go to the pub, you'd better get dressed. I assume you do have some clothes other than kitchen whites and jeans? Otherwise we're scuppered.'

I had to play for time, so I extracted a *cliché* from my mental lexicon.

'I don't know what to wear.'

Cliché it might have been, but there was more than a hint of truth. My wardrobes were tightly crammed, but that didn't mean I had anything suitable. What did you wear when you wanted to look sexy for the man you were with, but prim and proper in keeping with your status as grieving widow – in case anyone asked after Mike. Like the landlord, for example. Or any of the regulars. Mike had been very popular in the Lamb and Flag.

Zac got up and ambled out to the hall, his footsteps disappearing up the stairs. After a few minutes, he called me. I found him in the main bedroom with the wardrobe door wide open. On the bed, he'd placed one ensemble of black trousers, white blouse and pearl grey silk jacket, and another consisting of a peachy floral dress and a pastel pashmina. He'd even chosen the right shoes for both outfits. He was sitting on the bed staring at something on the inside of the wardrobe door.

'You clever old thing,' I said, not in the least minding his raid on my wardrobe. 'Which set are you wearing?'

He laughed. 'I think we're a different season.'

Aha. So he knew about colour analysis, and grouping clients into seasons of the year. Most men of my acquaintance wouldn't have had a clue. He was my first metrosexual.

'Yeah. I'm Autumn and you're probably Summer,' I said, hoping this would give him a clue to what was on my mind – the age difference thing. But he didn't reply.

I sat down next to him on the bed and followed his gaze. There, sticking to the inside of the wardrobe was the yellow post-it note with the words GOD DOES NOT PUNISH emblazoned on it.

'You're not some kind of a religious nut, are you, Mrs Armstrong? Because if so, I have to warn you that I come from a long line of atheists.'

My heart sank when I saw the message. How could I have known, when I put it there a week ago, that anyone else would ever see it?

There was an urgent need for diversionary tactics, both to take his mind off the post-it notes, and to head him off going to the pub. So I led him into the other bedroom (to save crumpling the clothes he'd so cleverly selected) and made love to him, during which I whispered, 'I sometimes commune with a friendly ghost and he leaves me messages. You don't mind sleeping in a haunted house, do you?' He seemed to think this was funny, so I left it at that.

Some time later, I got up to make some coffee and Zac appeared downstairs to join me, so we returned to the sofa to drink it. Whereas I was still in my robe, he was fully dressed, indicating that he was still angling for a trip to the pub.

Perhaps now would be a good time to distract him with an interrogation or revelation. The revelation being the sensitive subject of my age. Even though I was still in good shape, I was a woman of fifty-one. And this man looked closer to forty than fifty. But maybe I was making assumptions about how he viewed our 'relationship'. Was it just a casual shag or could it be more? If it was the former, my age was immaterial. But if it was the latter...

'So are we going out or not, babe?' he said, stretching his limbs in readiness to do something more interesting than watching the box.

I felt a sudden desire to flaunt my younger, handsome lover in the Lamb and Flag, wearing floral dress, high heels and an almond green pashmina. But that image was rapidly replaced by the memory of Danny's children playing on the swings in the pub garden, barely a week ago. On reflection, it was probably wise to maintain my reputation as an upstanding widow of the parish.

'Not sure if I can be bothered now. Anyway, it'd take me ages to repair hair and make-up after all the hurly burly...'

He chuckled, and settled back into a supine position on the sofa.

'Okay, hon, you're the boss.'

I cuddled into him and casually dealt him the killer question.

'There's something I should have asked you earlier.' I nibbled his ear to soften him up. 'Do you have a partner?'

'Yeah. Two, in fact.'

He adopted a serious expression and shifted himself on to his side so he could loom over me, staring into my eyes.

'There's three of us at Oven Ready. But I've got the biggest desk.'

After I'd bashed his head with a cushion for a few seconds, he came clean.

'All right, all right. The answer is, not at the moment. No ties of any kind.'

I waited a while but nothing else was forthcoming. I opened my mouth to ask for more details but he obviously wasn't in the mood for disclosure, his response being to cover my lips with his. But I did manage to get to the bottom of old Mr Willoughby, not literally, thank heaven – who turned out to be his uncle. He'd founded the business but was now retired, and he liked to be given the odd assignment just to feel useful. Zac pulled a face when I said I'd thought he was going to be my house guest.

'Absolutely not. The old bugger's not safe in taxis, let alone lodgings with access to a lady's boudoir.'

I thought it prudent not to reveal that I knew this from personal experience, bearing in mind that people can say what they like about their own kith and kin, but rarely welcome testimony of it from others.

We ended up falling asleep on the sofa with Oscar repeating his performance of the night before, by waking me up at midnight and asking to be put to bed. This was how the dog and I ended up, for the second night running, in our temporary bedroom. My lover was dead to the world so I covered him with a duvet and left him where he was.

Zac was very sweet at breakfast the next day, apologising for falling asleep and us not going out. He said he'd have to get back to London straight after the workshop, and probably wouldn't have a chance to see me properly before he left, so he gave me his number and took mine.

'I'll be in touch, Pandora,' he promised, adding, 'I mean it.'

The workshoppers were an amiable lot and as I said goodbye to them, and to Olly, Justin and Zac, on Sunday afternoon, I felt several pangs of regret. Everyone was leaving and there'd be just me and the familiar loneliness when they'd gone. Thank God for Oscar. Or maybe I should say thank Enoch for Oscar, since it had been his advice which had pulled him through.

The post-it notes hadn't been such a good idea, though. Maybe I'd confine my *aides-mémoire* to the inside cover of my writing pad in future. Hope Zac didn't think I was completely loony.

* * *

At work the next day Olly told me Zac was very pleased with how the weekend had gone and he'd be getting in touch with both of us. He looked and sounded a little mysterious.

'I can't say too much at the moment, but shall we say, you might be in for a nice surprise,' he beamed, kissing me on both cheeks. 'Thank you, darling. Thanks for all your hard work.'

His eyes sparkled. 'I 'ope it wasn't all work and no play.' He was getting excited now, as he always did when demonstrating his command of English idiom. 'But something tells me it didn't make Zac a dull boy!' He flung back his head and laughed so loudly that Christine popped her head round the door to see what all the fuss was about.

When I got home from work I found an envelope had arrived from The Enoch Society. In it was the first part of the correspondence course. It was a simple task – I had to write about a time in my life when I was happy, and there was no word limit. The address to send it to was a P.O. Box in Reading.

That evening I sat down and began to write.

Chapter 19 – SPRING 2000

The Enoch Society Correspondence Course – Level One
The Happiest Time of My Life by Pandora Armstrong

It was the spring of the year 2000 and I'd been invited to stay with Cece and Ray, some old friends I'd last seen in 1970 when I'd fallen in love with Ray's friend Mike. It had all ended badly and we'd lost contact, but Cece had tracked me down and seemed keen to meet up in the hotel in Brighton they'd recently acquired.

I decided to go by train, rather than my ancient Mini. My flat was just a ten-minute walk from a tube station, which meant the old girl often sat unused for days on end, doing her innards no good at all. This meant that I had to be frugal with my packing. Suitcases may have developed their own integrated wheels, but try getting in and out of trains and up and down escalators – it's then that every kilo counts.

I'd been invited for the Easter weekend, which I thought was a bit strange as that was surely a hotelier's busy time. When I rang Cece to say I'd be coming, one of the first things she asked was if I was bringing anybody with me. After I said no, she dug a bit more.

'I wasn't sure if you were living with anyone. Or had a boyfriend?'

'No. I'm quite happy living alone. But I could bring my girlfriend if you like.'

'Pandora,' she squeaked, 'you're not...you haven't...'

'Joke. Joke. I've turned into an old maid but I haven't *turned*. Although as it happens, I haven't had any action for ages. My last boyfriend wanted to move in and the thought of it...ugh.'

Cece's laugh sounded pleased. Maybe she felt a man would get in the way of our reunion.

'Good. So you're free to come down on Maundy Thursday and stay until Monday?'

I was in one of my resting periods at the time so it made no difference. None of the agencies I was registered with had any PR work for me, so I'd been spring cleaning the flat – which I'd quite enjoyed.

'Yes. Free as a bird. Waiting for the right job to come along – the story of my life.' If you substituted 'man' for 'job', I thought, that would sum it up as well.

Cece rattled on, 'We've got so much to catch up on, Pan. Hell, it's thirty years. We'll be up all night probably.'

I wondered if Cece and Ray might be thinking I lived on amphetamines, and would take them some speed as a gift, instead of chocolates. The truth was, that since the Jay years, I'd swallowed nothing stronger than an aspirin, apart from inhaling the odd spliff.

'Up all night? I doubt it, Ce. I'll probably be nodding off over a cup of cocoa about ten o'clock. By the way, what's the clientele like in your swish boutique hotel? I'm wondering what to pack.'

'We get all types here. Smart, artsy, brassy.' She added, a little tartly, 'You'll fit into one of those categories, I expect.'

Then she was silent for a second or two.

'It might be an idea to bring something a bit dressy for Saturday. Our chef always comes up with a Saturday night special. It'll have an Easter theme so probably lamb, but he'll finagle it into something cheffy. It'll be fabulous. You know, nothing like you'd ever produce at home.'

Speak for yourself, I thought. Some of us have been on *cordon bleu* courses. We made arrangements for the pick-up from Brighton station and said goodbye. The trip was only a few days away so I needed to decide what clothes to take. At least I had something in mind to wear on Saturday night.

I opened my large, fitted wardrobe and shuffled through the closely packed garments until my search revealed the red and gold silk dress. It was patterned with cherry blossom and what looked like dragons and exotic birds. I'd got it in a designer sale but it'd still cost quite a lot. Its one and only outing had been to a friend's wedding. Well, she was more of an acquaintance, really. A ship that passed in the night. She worked at the headquarters of a fashion chain where I was temping, and I'm sure she only invited me because I'd once been married to someone famous.

Anyway, I wrapped it in tissue paper and packed it carefully, along with the red and black chequered sling-backs I'd bought in New York, which had cost almost as much as the flight. I hoped that Saturday night in Brighton would be an improvement on the outfit's one and only airing – a register office in Bermondsey followed by a pub lunch.

* * *

To pass the time on the train down to Brighton, I made a list of the important things that had (or hadn't) happened in the thirty years since I'd last seen Cece.

Number One on the list was: *Losing virginity in Spain*. Although, I thought, it might be better not to mention that on the grounds of too much information. So I struck that one out.

Two: *Hadn't established any professional career when I should have.* Unlike Cece, who'd stuck to her master plan and become a maths teacher.

Three: *Married James Jay in 1975 and for a few years lived it up.* This surely would come as no surprise to Cece who must have seen our pictures in the tabloids, some of them when we were both 'tired and emotional' lurching bleary-eyed out of a club or party.

Looking back, Jay and I had what would now be called a 'co-dependent relationship', but what we thought of at the time as being madly in love. Whatever it was, we were always entwined like chimpanzees and wildly jealous if the other spent too long in conversation with a member of the opposite sex.

Four: *No children – but not for want of wanting them.* She'd probably worked out by now that I couldn't have kids. Or heard it from her mum, who would have got it from Joan.

Five: *Divorce from Jay, 1985.* See above.

Six: *Started taking on free-lance PR jobs.* I had experience of that helping Alvie, the band's PR guy. I learned a lot from him.

I pondered on what else I could tell Cece and Ray. It was fifteen years since my divorce – but no significant achievements came to mind. I'd travelled a bit, visited Frankie wherever she happened to be – which could be a caravan in Devon with a penniless sculptor, or the Chelsea Hotel in New York, with a happening hippy writer.

I'd taken numerous correspondence courses and some residential ones as well. You name it, I'd fallen for it – interior design, sketching, painting, cooking, hypnotherapy. But in the end nothing had led to anything of note.

I'd once had the idea of putting my *cordon bleu* qualification to good use by cooking for other people's dinner parties, until the man I employed as the waiter stole some silver candlesticks. And that was that.

Jay had been generous and the divorce settlement had included the flat in Fulham, so money hadn't been a problem. Actually, with hindsight, maybe money had been the problem – if I hadn't had it, maybe I'd have made more effort to forge a fulfilling career.

As for boyfriends, in the words of the mighty Mick – I couldn't get no satisfaction. And neither could they. Any initial attraction always petered out eventually. Men thought I was playing hard to get, but it masked an indifference, a lack of wanting to make the effort. I read somewhere that 90% of men find most women slightly attractive while 90% of women find most men slightly repellent. So maybe I wasn't so unusual after all. Though the participants in that survey sound suspiciously like nuns and building-site workers to me.

I was glad I'd given my past some forethought, as it made it clear in my mind what I'd be telling Cece and what I'd be glossing over.

* * *

Pretty soon, the train reached its terminus and it was time to negotiate my case through the ticket barrier. I scanned the crowd for familiar faces but could see none. In the distance, two strangers were waving at me. The woman was shortish and plump with a lacquered helmet of dyed auburn hair, her fingers, neck and ears adorned with high carat gold jewellery. The man was tall, and a little stooped, his once platinum hair now an unruly grey. He sported a striped cotton blazer and jeans which contrasted oddly with his wife's square shouldered jacket and beige trousers.

It was indeed, Ray and Cece. But whereas in youth their looks had been in step, the years had taken their features and figures along separate roads. Cece was unrecognisable as the girl I'd known, but there was still more than a hint of the old Ray. Especially when he revealed his gap-toothed smile.

We kissed and stared at each other. Cece was studying me and glancing sideways to make sure that Ray wasn't.

'How do you do it, Pan?' There was an accusatory tone to her voice. 'You must be almost the same size you used to be.'

I decided to play the barren card to defuse any possible resentment. Being a guest for a long weekend would be tricky if my hostess was feeling out-glamoured.

'It's because I never had any children.' And just to make sure, I added, 'Sadly.'

This seemed to satisfy Cece. She linked her arm in mine and started telling me about the hotel as we walked to their SUV. Less than ten minutes later we pulled up outside a Regency town house situated in an elegant square. Ornate railings disguised steps which led down to the lower ground floor. The main steps led up to a large black front door, gleaming with brass fittings, and flanked by two potted bay trees. On the next level, matching black railings enclosed a canopied terrace, behind which sheltered full-length windows. Above that was yet another floor with three smaller windows. Finally, at the very top of the building, perched two attic windows, giving an impression that the house narrowed, almost stupa-like, as it rose to the sky.

We climbed the steps to the front door which opened on to a reception area in *art deco* style. The desk was of walnut and the walls were silver grey with black dado rails. The hotel gave the impression that every last cup, saucer and doorknob had been designed to co-ordinate. I couldn't help thinking that Ray and Cece must have needed a substantial mortgage to afford this property, and all the renovations they'd hinted at on our journey there.

Cece and Ray were due at a staff meeting, so we arranged to meet up later. They told me to wait at Reception and a porter would show me to my room. To pass the time, I walked a few steps forward to peer behind a half-open door. Inside, a squiggly pink neon sign, suspended above an extensive bar, spelled out the words, 'Fallen Angel'.

As my eyes swept the room, they distinguished some display cases containing manacles and wanted posters. There was even an ancient, tattered, convict uniform and sepia photographs of chain gangs. Ray was certainly penal in his choice of memorabilia.

The porter eventually appeared and took me up in the lift to my room. At first glance, I thought it had escaped the penitential theme. The bed was dressed with snow-white linen sheets and spread with a claret red cover, on top of which a medley of plush cushions were positioned artistically. The walls were a slightly lighter shade of red and the ceiling a few tones lighter. A crystal carafe of water sat on one bedside table, an arrangement of pale pink peonies on the other. A stack of books lay on a side table next to a black velvet chaise longue and from the ceiling hung a black chandelier.

The tiles and floor of the bathroom were a checkerboard of black and white so it was difficult to know where the wall ended and the floor began. I was admiring the fluffiness of the towels, the scented candles, the roll-top bath, the hydro massage shower, when I heard the porter cough politely. I'd forgotten to tip him.

Walking back into the bedroom to get my bag, I caught sight of a recessed, glass-fronted cabinet above the fireplace, in which there reposed a pair of handcuffs and a small riding crop. The porter followed my startled gaze, pocketed the tip and winked at me.

'Don't worry. It ain't that sorta joint. It's only Mr Roberts' little joke. Not sure Mrs Roberts is too keen, though. She told me to take 'em out and put a pearl necklace in there instead – which I did. Then he comes up, sees it, and on the quiet, puts 'em back in again. I dunno.'

Shaking his head and sniggering, the porter ambled off.

Oh well, it was Ray's hotel. His prerogative. I just hoped he didn't think I'd gone completely to the dogs – indulging in sado-masochistic practices while high on illegal substances.

Looking for distraction from this thought, I immediately set about unpacking my case, experiencing that little pang of illogical homesickness I always got on the first day away. We'd arranged to meet in the bar at seven, for dinner at eight. Ray and Cece had explained that their private quarters were just a couple of rooms at the very top of the building, where they could cook a simple meal or reheat one from the kitchen. This evening, because I was here, we were all going to eat downstairs in the restaurant.

It was five o'clock. Time for a soak in the bath and one last look at my list before I got dressed and went downstairs.

* * *

We spent the first evening catching up. It turned out that Cece had tired of teaching, which prompted Ray to sell his photographic business and buy a hotel. Neither of them had trained in the hospitality business but luckily had taken to it like ducks to water. All those years of pleasing brides and cajoling bashful children had equipped Ray to be the host with the most. And Cece's head for figures ensured the books balanced.

Ray proudly told me how he'd converted the The Glasshouse from a guest house called Quarters, so named because the square was built on the site of a military camp. Ray had got a job lot of prison memorabilia cheap at a local auction, and installed a sizeable orangery at the back of the building which he'd fitted out as a restaurant, engaging a bright young chef to run it.

Cece then moved on to the subject of their two daughters – what good jobs they had, how well the older one had married. It was the usual proud parent stuff requiring the listener to simply nod and smile every so often. I let them do most of the talking while I concentrated on savouring the pigeon pie. This was served with a pastry pigeon atop – far too much for one person, so Cece and I shared one while Ray feasted on a complete bird.

When he'd finished the last spoonful of dessert, he wiped his lips and grinned at me.

'That's enough about us. Your turn now.'

Cece broke in and suggested continuing over coffee in the bar, so we adjourned to the Fallen Angel, which was pleasantly quiet compared to the restaurant.

Ray stayed to hear my news headlines but fatigue soon got the better of him. Or it may have been Cece's eye signals. I suspected she was eager for some girl talk. Anyway, he took the hint.

As he left, he kissed Cece and ruffled her hair – this was the first time I'd seen it move. She giggled like a teenager and said she'd be up soon. Cece was lucky. She might have lost her looks, but not her husband. Ray turned to me and executed a mock bow.

'Goodnight milady. Hope your room is satisfactory. If there's anything you want, just ring for it. It's a twenty-four hour concierge service. They'll get you anything your heart desires.'

Was it my imagination or did his tone have a nudge nudge, wink wink quality? Was this some hotel code for sex? Did Ray think I needed to order up a rampant male? My lips did that involuntary pursing thing of disapproval but I decided to tough it out.

'The room's great. Love the decor. Not so sure about the whip and handcuffs, though.'

Cece frowned at Ray.

'For goodness' sake. You didn't leave them in there, did you? Pan'll think we're running a brothel. I told Bert to take them out.'

Ray chucked Cece under the chin.

'My eyes are everywhere, my little dumpling, nothing gets past me. And I'm in charge of room design, never forget that. Who's the one who did the course?'

Cece clucked a bit more, but was enjoying Ray in playful mood too much to press the point. Ray's eyes turned to mine again.

'Bert told me that you freaked out a bit. Don't worry, it's all part of the theme. Quite harmless. Being Brighton, the clients expect something a bit different. You should see some of the places in Kemptown.'

He put his arm around me and gave my cheek a peck. It was like being swooped on by a giant seagull. Giant but friendly.

'You convent schoolgirls. You think you're broad-minded but at heart you're all prim and proper.'

I hoped Cece wasn't in a jealous mood. Luckily, the several glasses of wine she'd drunk at dinner had mellowed her.

'Go on, you idiot,' she slurred. 'Pan and I have got things to talk about. Skedaddle.'

And off he sauntered.

When we were on our own, Cece started quizzing me about life with Jay. I was so used to being asked about this, I could now talk about it without getting upset. Then she started on about the old days when we were at school together. And about our parents and how hard it had been to get out in the evenings. And once out, the difficulty of staying out to a decent hour. Remembering those days took me back to my deliberate loss of contact with her, and I began to feel ashamed. Something of this must have shown in my face.

'What's wrong, Pan? Does it make you sad talking about your mum and dad?'

'Yes, it does a bit. But I wish it hadn't ended the way it did. One minute I was living at home with my dad and the next it all changed. It was never the same again. And I wish it could have been different.'

I hoped she would see that as some sort of oblique apology.

'Why didn't you come back to Manor Wood? Your dad said he thought it was because he'd remarried.'

'I suppose in a way it was. Not because I didn't like Joan – she was always nice to me. More because I knew he wouldn't be lonely if I left home. I got on so well with my mum and Toby in Spain, it just seemed natural to move in with them when I came back. And I could come and go as I pleased.'

But Cece wasn't falling for my version of events completely.

'Was it just that, or was it partly because of Mike getting married?'

I was shocked to hear his name and tried, without success, to stifle the old feelings of pain which came rushing to the surface.

'Why do you say that, Ce?'

Cece looked uncomfortable, as if she'd spoken out of turn.

'It was just that on the day of his accident, Mike got so upset when he thought there was something between you and Ray. And it certainly wasn't because he was angry on my behalf.'

Thanks to Peter, my kindly psychotherapist and neighbour, I had done some clearing on my Mike neurosis, but obviously not enough, because tears were soon coursing down my cheeks. It was too public a place for a comforting session, so Cece handed me a small pack of tissues from her bag and continued. She was determined to get the information she wanted.

'Was it him, Pan? Was he the reason you couldn't face coming back to Manor Wood?'

'I suppose so,' I gulped.

Cece smiled, and adopted a knowing look which led me to believe there was more to tell.

'Do you know what happened to him, Ce? Did he marry his girlfriend?'

Cece leaned forward and grinned.

'So you are interested, then?'

What could I say?

'Of course I am. Come on, if you know anything, tell me. Don't torment me.'

I hoped she wasn't going to relapse into Cece mode of old when she wouldn't give you any details you wanted if she knew you wanted them. I think my accusation of tormenting struck home, or maybe it was the wine, but she proceeded to sing like a canary.

'Mike did marry Val and the baby was a little boy. They called him Daniel after Mike's dad. He lost his driving licence after the accident, and got sacked, so his uncle gave him a job in his cycle shop. Mike built it up, and it was left to him when his uncle died a couple of years later.'

I couldn't really see him working in a shop. He'd been too restless. Cycling to him had been all about freedom. The exhilaration of an open road.

'Did Mike carry on cycling?'

I wanted to know what his state of mind had been. He'd loved being with his mates. If he'd had that he would have been partly happy, at least.

'No, he never went back to the club. His mum said it was because Val didn't want to be left alone with the baby at weekends. But Ray thinks it was because of the fight with Brian in The Woodman's.'

'So he never went to France with Ray?'

I thought back to that day in the park when he'd talked about his plans. Listening to him and being with him, had to rank among the happiest times of my life. And the most short-lived.

She snorted. 'Fat chance of that. No, Ray went with some of the others. Mike made some excuse. Val wouldn't have let him even if he'd wanted to.'

'Didn't he ever go back to the Green Oak club or The Woodman's? To see Ray. Or any of the crowd?'

'I don't think so. But things were changing anyway. Ray and I got engaged and so did some of the others. Then we got married and moved nearer to where I worked, so Ray lost touch with most of them. But he knew what was going on with Mike, because their mums were friends.'

'So how many children did Mike have in the end?'

Being unable to procreate myself. I was always fascinated by the extent of other people's fertility.

'Just the one. He's clever. Like his dad.'

Clever like his dad? I'd only known Mike as a van driver. When did he get clever? I thought I'd been the clever one, with my exams and homework. Cece could see I was struggling with the concept.

'Mike's done really well for himself. He bought more cycle shops...'

'Did he have a chain?' I quipped. Quite rightly, she ignored me and continued.

'He sold them and went into the gym business. You must have heard of Armstrong Gyms.'

Of course I had, but had never associated them with Mike. Why would I?

'You're joking.'

'No. And there's more. He sold the gyms and went into leisure centres. Local authorities pay him to provide the administration, equipment, staff. Everything except the building. He's worth a fortune, Pan. You've no idea.'

I imagined Mike and Val sipping champagne in the back of a chauffeur driven Bentley. Well, actually it was two indistinct figures, because I'd never clapped eyes on Val and couldn't picture Mike as a fifty-one-year-old man.

'So do you and Ray ever see them?

'See *them*? No. We never did, really.'

She took a swig of her Irish coffee which left a narrow cream moustache gleaming on her top lip. The alcohol had definitely loosened her tongue, which was a good thing for me and my need to know. But she hadn't finished yet. There was a punch line yet to be delivered.

'When Mike started doing well they moved away. They ended up in Southampton,' she paused for effect, 'and they divorced as soon as Daniel left university.'

My brain went into overdrive. If the son had been twenty-one when he graduated, that would have been 1992 – eight years ago. I started to imagine magnate Mike in astrakhan-collared coat, puffing a cigar, an entourage of busty beauties in tow, deciding which one to make wife number two.

'Why did they get divorced?'

'Believe it or not, Val left him. Mike told Ray she felt neglected. Apparently the Golf Pro giving her golf lessons didn't neglect her, and she took off with him.'

'Was Mike devastated?'

I asked the expected question, but I already knew the answer because of what he'd told me all those years ago. About being trapped at the age of twenty-one. And loving me, not her.

'No, not at all. He travelled around on business a lot. He was hardly at home, especially after their son went to university. So nobody blamed her.'

At this point I stared hard at Cece, almost daring her not to reveal the most vital disclosure of all. But she avoided my eyes. She was doing it again – withholding the most important piece of information. For pity's sake, had he remarried or not? I was darned if I was going to ask outright, so I kept eyeballing her until she cracked.

'I suppose you're wondering what he did then. Well he hasn't married again. He's still living in Southampton, in a huge house which doubles up as business premises. Daniel and his wife live there too. They both work for the company.'

Cece downed the dregs of her Irish coffee and stood up. She looked like a woman whose job was done.

'I think it's time to get some sleep,' she said. I got to my feet and she tottered over to kiss my cheek. 'Night night. I'm free all day tomorrow so I'll meet you at ten by Reception and I'll show you Brighton.'

* * *

Needless to say, with so much to take in, it was a good while before I got to sleep that night. My happiness at Mike's success was mingled with annoyance for the times I'd mourned his fate, assuming him to be enduring a boring, loveless existence. I'd written him off as a loser, living an unfulfilled life that only I could have saved him from. How arrogant I'd been.

But I was forty-eight now, old enough to know better. I should know by now that people's lives are always their own responsibility and it's no one else's job to fix things for them or, indeed, to fix *them*. It seems Mike had done very well on his own and hadn't needed any help from me.

And while his Dick Whittington-like accumulation of riches was a lovely surprise, more intriguing to me was his single status. Cece had only said that he hadn't married again, not that he wasn't living with a woman. My policy with Cece when we were young had been to avoid letting her know how much I was interested in something or someone, because then some contrary little cluster of brain cells in her head would do its utmost to thwart me. It was friendship gone too far; a desire to be everything to another person so they didn't seek anything or anyone else.

I could see it in the possessiveness of her relationship with Ray. Maybe she'd been jealous of his friendship with Mike. And maybe that was why they hadn't seen much of each other over the years. I decided to tread carefully and not to broach the subject of Mike's relationship status.

Cece was as good as her word the next day. We shopped and lunched in the Lanes, had a laugh at the kitsch splendour of the Royal Pavilion, took in a couple of art galleries and finished off with a bracing cliff walk a bit further afield. Cece didn't mention Mike at all. Perhaps she'd been drunker than I thought and had alcoholic amnesia.

Ray was free in the evening and I treated them both to a meal in a bistro they knew and liked. Over dinner, it was Ray's turn to assess my reaction to the news.

'So Cece told you about Mike, then?'

I jumped at the chance for more Mike talk.

'Yes. Unbelievable. Glad for him, though. That he's done so well.'

Ray nodded eagerly and I remembered that he'd loved Mike too. I wondered if he ever regretted becoming Cece's 'best friend' at the expense of the freedom of the open road.

'Do you ever hear from him, Ray?'

I asked because I wasn't quite sure whether he and Mike were still in contact. Ray glanced at Cece before answering. I just caught a slight frown but she said nothing.

'Not much. We used to hook up sometimes when I went to see my folks. Go for a drink. And I'd occasionally see him at an Arsenal game. His mum's dead now, though. But we email sometimes. He knows about the hotel.'

I felt thoroughly ashamed of myself for the leap of relief I felt that Mike's mother was dead. Must have been quite a grudge I'd been holding against her – for putting the phone down on me thirty years ago. I wanted to keep talking about Mike to Ray, but Cece cut in with updates on some of our classmates that she'd seen at a school reunion the year before, so I went with the flow.

* * *

The next day, Easter Saturday, their younger daughter Joanne arrived, bringing her bouncy golden retriever with her. While Ray stayed back to cover staff breaks at Reception, Cece, Joanne, Brody and I drove out to the South Downs and walked for miles over the Seven Sisters cliffs, stopping off for lunch at a farmhouse restaurant and dodging a heavy shower in the process. When we got back, slightly damp and pink-cheeked from the April breeze, Ray greeted us at the door with a towel for Brody's muddy bits. Seeing this, Joanne raised her eyes in mock despair.

'Dad, I've already dried him. Your carpet's quite safe.'

Ray and Brody were by now having a tug of war with the towel.

'Come on up to the penthouse for a cup of tea before you go,' said Ray to Joanne as he tugged Brody towards the stairs. 'He can do what he likes up there, and you can tell your old dad what you've been up to.'

Cece smiled. 'It's more of a bedsit. But you're welcome to join us, Pan.'

It was a kind thought but I sensed this was family time and I would be surplus to requirements. We were all walking up the stairs, as Brody had an aversion to the lift, and I'd reached my floor. I was feeling quite tired after the walk and at some stage needed to address the problem of my rain-bedraggled hair, so I had a good excuse to decline the invitation.

'Thanks, but I think I might have a lie-down.'

'Okay,' said Ray with a tired smile. 'But don't oversleep. We'll see you in the bar at seven for dinner at eight.'

As I said goodbye to Joanne and Brody, it occurred to me that Cece and Ray were dining in the restaurant this evening just for my benefit, when they probably would have preferred a meal on a tray and an early night.

'But you've had a busy day.' I fretted. 'Why don't we eat earlier? I think you could both do with an early night.'

Cece shot Ray an anxious glance, and I realised I'd completely misread the signals.

Handing the towel with Brody attached to Cece, Ray placed his hands on my shoulders and looked deep into my eyes.

'Look, young lady. We love having you here. First of all, you can't possibly miss Grant's Easter special, and it's not served before eight. Secondly, this hotel's our big production and we need someone to show it off to. And that person's you. So see you in the bar in your glad rags at seven. That's an order.'

And that was how I happened to be sitting in the Fallen Angel bar in The Glasshouse Hotel at 7.15 on Easter Saturday, decked out in silk and satin, clutching an Alcatraz cocktail, wondering where the hell the others were, when Mike Armstrong walked in, and made straight for my table.

And at the sight of him striding towards me, my whole body flooded with jets of incredible, warm, bubbly, happiness.

* * *

Having finished my essay on The Happiest Time of My Life for Level One of the Enoch Society Correspondence Course, I paused for a few moments to savour the completion of the task. My satisfaction slightly evaporated, however, when I reread the last line. It made me sound like a human jacuzzi. Dismissing this thought, I sealed it up in an envelope, so I wouldn't be tempted to fiddle with it, resolving to post if off first thing the following day.

Chapter 20 – SPRING 2000

It had taken me more than two hours to finish Level One of The Enoch Society Correspondence Course. I still hadn't bought a computer, so it was all in longhand. I'd decided to finish the essay when I got to the scene in the Fallen Angel bar, judging our first experience of having sex to be neither necessary, nor suitable, for the eyes of the mysterious Cass.

I went to bed but couldn't sleep. My mouth was parched, so I tiptoed past Oscar and went downstairs to make tea, which I knew would keep me awake, but by that time I was past caring. I sat in the comfortable armchair in the living room – the one which had been Mike's favourite – and thought about what had happened next.

* * *

When Mike joined me at my table in the Fallen Angel, all I managed to say to him was, 'Fancy seeing you here.' How corny was that? I'd recognised him immediately even though his hair was quite grey. In reply, he just placed his gin and tonic on the table, and smiled.

He looked older in a healthy way. He must have been somewhere hot recently, as he was bronzed and lined by the sun, but it suited him. The contrast of his grey hair and tan made his eyes even bluer. He'd been well-built when I'd known him and his features had thickened with age, but he didn't appear to be overweight. Although with a blouson jacket you couldn't always tell.

I looked behind me, half expecting Ray and Cece to materialise, shouting, 'Surprise! Surprise!'

'Did Ray and Cece set this up?' I tried to keep my voice neutral, not wanting to reveal how hard my heart was beating.

He shook his head.

'No. It was me. I asked them to get you here if they could.'

His voice sounded almost the same, a little deeper perhaps. The intonation was unchanged, and his eyes still held that intensity which seemed to give his words a deeper significance.

'You mean you managed to persuade Cece to get in touch with me? How much did you have to pay her?'

His gaze wavered for an instant. I wondered if he'd expected me to fling myself at him with cries of, 'my hero!'

'*She* suggested writing to you, as it happens. Why did you lose touch with her, by the way?'

'I went to live with my mother.' He nodded, like an adult willing a child to continue their tale. 'And I couldn't bear the idea of Cece telling me about you. Not knowing...'

He took my hand and I hoped he wouldn't feel it shaking. He pressed the palm softly.

'Not knowing what?'

'Not knowing that we'd been out together. And if things had been different...'

Mike decided to finish my sentence.

'We'd have got together and lived happily ever after.'

For a couple of seconds we were both under the spell of those words, and then, as one, we burst out laughing – maybe to relieve the tension, maybe because we'd both grown cynical in our old age. Whatever it was, I used the moment to release my hand from his in readiness for my big reveal. I had to get this confession out of the way so we could start off on an honest footing.

'If we had got together, it might not have ended happily ever after.'

Mike was still smiling.

'Why not?'

'Because it turned out I couldn't have children. That's why my marriage broke up.'

I waited for some reaction, but he didn't look in the least surprised, which told me that Cece had probably already passed this titbit of information on to him. He took my hand again, which had stopped shaking at last. He stared down at the table and then looked up and blasted me with that scorching blue gaze.

'That wouldn't have bothered me. I wasn't a great father.'

'But Cece said you and your son get on really well.'

'Yeah, now we do. But it wasn't like that early on. I just couldn't get used to being a dad so young. So I kept out of the way and let Val and my mum get on with it. I was at work most of the time. To tell the truth, when the business took off, he only saw me at weekends. That's why we didn't have any more kids.'

I felt a momentary sympathy for his son, quickly superseded by an enormous sense of relief that, as it turned out, I wouldn't have been such a disappointing wife after all.

I became aware of my eyes widening, the way they'd used to when I was attracted to someone. I'd only been with him for five minutes and here I was, behaving like a teenager with a crush all over again. I felt I should say something, rather than just staring at him.

'Well if you have any more kids you don't want, I suppose I could always adopt them.'

He looked at me as if I was mad. Maybe humour wasn't quite in keeping with the turn the conversation had taken. I had a bad habit of keeping deep feelings at bay with flippant remarks. He made an effort, and laughed weakly. There were a few beads of sweat on his brow.

'Before we go on. I want to ask you something.'

Surely he wasn't about to go down on one knee while producing a diamond ring from the pocket of his finest Italian leather jacket. I tried to look desirable and composed.

'Fire away.'

'It's something we never got round to.'

My mistake. He must be talking about sex. Oh dear, much as I wanted to tear his clothes off, I hoped he wasn't going to whisk me upstairs on an empty stomach. I was starving.

'How about a second date?'

I laughed. Half in relief and half in disappointment.

'Well, we're on one now, aren't we?'

'If that's what you want. I didn't want to assume...'

I leaned across the table, kissing my fingers and placing them lightly on his lips.

'Yes we're on a date. And I'm hungry.'

He grinned, downed his drink in one go, and got out his mobile phone.

'Excuse me a minute. Just got to report back to the troops.'

A few minutes later we were joined by troopers Cece and Ray, bearing a bottle of champagne in a silver bucket. They seemed excited – almost more excited than we were. Mike had moved his seat to be next to me and we'd settled into a sort of dazed contentment. The plan was, that we would all go ahead and have Grant's special Easter feast as a foursome, which we did at the appointed hour. After that, once our appetites were satisfied, I hoped our love would be consummated. In a twosome, of course.

During the meal, Cece admired my dress and when the waiter, who was Chinese, came to clear our plates, he heard her asking me where I'd bought it.

'You know the meaning of pattern on dress, ma'am?'

I shook my head.

'It shows dragon and feng huang. Feng huang, female. Dragon, male. Yin and yang.'

Cece asked me to stand up so she could get a full-length view of it. Ray, being the arty one, put on his round specs and also had a good look.

'That's clearly a dragon. The other one looks like a bird. It's beautiful. Look at the tail plumage. I'm thinking of converting one of the rooms to *style chinois*.'

Mike grinned slyly.

'How'd that fit in with your prison theme, Ray? Reckon you'd find any Chinese instruments of torture in the Lanes?'

Ray frowned slightly.

'I've been getting a bit of stick lately from Cece. She reckons we might attract the S and M crowd if we're not careful. So I might have to tone it down a bit.'

Cece was too busy inspecting my embroidered silk cheongsam to take any notice.

'It looks a bit like a phoenix, Cheung,' said Cece, addressing the waiter.

'Yes, yes. Feng huang phoenix. Chinese phoenix. Phoenix graceful. Dragon powerful. And bring good luck. Together they mean,' he paused to search for the right words, '...brissful, happy marriage.'

By now I was sitting down, and Mike had extended his arm across the back of my chair in order to stroke my neck. Cheung smiled at us and gave us a thumbs-up.

'Good to wear for wedding.'

I giggled in embarrassment. Mike had begun tracing a more floral element of the pattern across my upper back.

'What about the cherry blossom?' he said. And to me, under his breath, 'You remember that afternoon, in the park?'

I certainly did and was touched that he did too. Cheung thought for a moment. 'In China, cherry blossom refer to beauty of woman. And passion.' His face grew more serious. 'In Japan, cherry blossom like life. Beautiful but fragile. When fall from tree, blossoms can mean early death of warrior. Symbol of sadness.'

'We'll go for the Chinese one, then,' said Mike, and Cheung bowed and retired to the kitchen, wishing us good fortune as he went.

Later, at the end of the meal, Cece must have morse-coded Ray, because they both got up together.

'We'll leave you guys to it,' said Ray, winking at Mike, who responded with the Buddha smile he'd been wearing all evening and which had grown wider with each glass of wine.

Cece gave me a satisfied look. The look of someone who'd pulled something off and was happy to bask in the success of her strategy.

'I expect you'll do your own thing tomorrow morning. Give us a ring if you fancy doing anything in the afternoon.' She smiled at

Mike. 'Okay then?'

He nodded. Ray patted his shoulder. 'Goodnight, mate. Let me know what's happening before you go.'

Mike was staying in the hotel but it was my room that we went straight to. He chuckled when he saw the handcuffs and took them out of their display case, attaching them to the bedpost for a laugh. He said when the maid cleaned the room she'd see them and it'd get back to Ray and Cece.

'It might enhance your reputation, but it won't do mine much good,' I told him. 'I think they've got some idea of me being a sex-crazed junkie, just because I was married to Jay.'

'I don't mind the first bit,' he breathed, as he relieved me of my cheongsam.

I lay on the bed and watched him undress. He was in very good shape, probably due to all those years of gym ownership. He was certainly a good advertisement for his trade. He'd been a strong, handsome lad when I'd last seen him, and was still strong and handsome for his age, but with deep lines around his eyes and forehead. He must have had similar thoughts about me. I still had dark hair but it was shorter and not so sleek and silky. So no danger of anyone mistaking it for a Cleopatra wig, as Ray had, all those years ago.

I asked him to turn off the light, but he said he wanted to look at me.

Too much sunbathing and too many cigarettes had taken their toll on my skin, but luckily I'd stopped doing both early enough to limit the damage. Frankie always said that after thirty-five everything starts to go downhill, and she was right. But I hadn't suffered as much subsidence as my married friends, who claimed that I'd kept my figure because I'd never had children.

For a few minutes, his hands and lips traced the contours of my body, making me wish he could have seen me in my prime – as I'd been when I was with Jay. Wanting to divert his attention from my fault lines, I opened my arms for him to embrace me. We kissed and held each other, then he whispered in my ear.

'You're beautiful.' Then, laughing, 'Not bad for your age. Fancy a shag?'

Observing a certain part of his anatomy, I was glad to see that all the liquor he'd put away hadn't diminished his ardour. I was also fired with stirrings of my own. Mike's pheromones were having the desired effect, and I was getting impatient for the off. He seemed to expect a reply before he went any further.

'What else would we be doing stark naked in bed together? Let's get on with it.'

The resulting love-shag, as Mike so succinctly put it, was as intense as it was loving. Feelings I'd thought had gone into fatal decline, miraculously revived. Like Lazarus, they got up and got going at the touch of a special man.

Finally, the storm subsided and we lay still for a little while.

We took turns in the bathroom. I felt it was a bit soon for shared showering.

When we were both back in bed, Mike took my hand and said, 'I was just thinking about what you said earlier.' He hesitated, then went on, 'Did you do drugs, Suze?' (He'd decided earlier in the evening to call me this because he didn't like Pandora or Pan, and he said I looked like Suzy Wong in my Chinese dress).

I lay back on the plump, feather pillows and high thread count sheets, and considered the question. Would the answer affect what happened next? Had his business interests infected him with some obsessive health-and-fitness ethic which precluded having a girlfriend with a history of substance abuse? Hoping I wasn't shooting myself in the foot, I decided to continue with my earlier resolve to tell the truth, the whole truth and nothing but the truth.

'For a little while. More to keep Jay company than anything. But I looked in the mirror one day and came to my senses – heroin chic didn't suit me.'

All this had been fairly well-documented in the tabloids at the time, with pictures and suggestive captions. Common knowledge, really, so no point in lying.

He continued his cross-examination.

'What about hash? Did you try that first?'

'Yeah. Didn't everybody?' I turned to him. 'Didn't you?'

'Nah. Too hard to get hold of where I hung out. Not my thing anyway. It was always booze for me.'

When he said that, our thoughts must have flown to the same thing. To the night all those years ago when he drank too much and crashed his car.

His grip on my hand tightened, and he said, in a hoarse voice, 'I wish I could go back and change what happened. It's always been the biggest regret of my life.'

He rolled closer and I cradled his head on my chest. It was lovely. Like having a child to soothe to sleep. I kissed the tears from his cheeks and told him how much I loved him. Then I started to cry too, but mine weren't tears of regret like his. They were of pure happiness because I was sure we wouldn't be parted again.

After a little while I thought of how he must be used to sleeping on his own. What with all the nights in hotel rooms when he was travelling on business, and with being divorced. 'You don't have to stay here, you know,' I told him softly, 'if you'd get a better sleep in your own room...'

'Don't you want me to stay?'

I detected a hint of alarm in his voice.

'Of course I do. I've been waiting thirty years for our second date and I don't want it to end.'

We kissed and fell asleep. And from that moment we spent every night together. Apart from when he was taken to hospital after his first heart attack. And, of course, when he died.

* * *

I was the first to wake the next morning, and made us both tea, thinking how strange it was that I didn't know whether he took sugar. He opened his eyes at the sound of the kettle boiling and read my mind.

'No sugar, thanks.'

I gave him his tea and observed his right elbow rising forty-five degrees as he put the cup to his lips. I'd noticed it last night in the restaurant.

'You could have someone's eye out with that arm action,' I laughed.

'It's the one I broke in the accident. Didn't set right.' He smiled wryly. 'A lasting souvenir of where my temper got me.'

'I'll have to make sure I stay on your left side.' I said, glibly, half of me wanting to cover him with kisses of compassion, the other half thinking it had served him right.

Mike and I spent the rest of the morning mostly in bed, catching up with as much of our lives as we could. It was like a crash course in each other. We both heard things that we didn't really want to hear.

Over breakfast, eaten in bed on a tray, Mike asked me what caused Jay and me to split up.

'At first we lived the high life,' I began.

'With the emphasis on high,' Mike grinned.

'We weren't that bad,' I protested, 'Jay didn't touch drugs before we got married. But once the group got famous, it was part of the job description. Anyway, we liked parties. Liked a drink. Our social scene was good, we enjoyed being with the other group members. Why not? We always said we'd have fun until the babies came along, then we'd calm down and live in the country permanently.'

'How big was your pop-star mansion?' Mike teased.

'Quite big. And Jay wasn't pop,' I said reprovingly. 'He started off rhythm and blues. In fact, you probably saw him at the Green Oak – when they were called James Jay and the Blue Jays.'

Mike thought hard and made the connection. 'Yeah, I remember him. Tall, dark, skinny bloke. They weren't bad. Is that where you met him?'

'No. It was the Blue Parakeet in Wardour Street.'

'When was that?'

'Oh, must have been 1974.'

Mike looked reflective. 'Danny would've been three. I'd just got my second shop.' He paused. 'My uncle left me the first one.'

I nodded, remembering what Cece had told me a couple of nights before.

'And I was working six days a week. He only saw me on Sundays, poor little beggar.' He lowered his eyes to disguise his guilt and when he looked up, they were misty. 'All ancient history now.'

I took his hand and kissed it, and he said softly, 'Tell me about the mansion.'

I struggled to continue. I was finding talking about Jay to Mike unexpectedly painful.

'We bought a place in Great Marlow – big enough for a football team. I stopped taking the pill as soon as we got married, so we expected to fill it with kids. But that didn't happen. So we filled it with livestock instead. We had dogs, chickens, a couple of cats, even a goat.'

I must have looked sad, because Mike stroked the back of my neck and then patted my tummy. 'Look on the bright side, Suze, at least you've still got your figure.' He drained his cup and continued the interrogation. 'So how much time did you spend there?'

'Usually the weekends. We'd get down to see the animals when we could. We had a married couple living in. They kept it ticking over. Jay needed to be in London when he wasn't touring, so we stayed at our flat in Fulham in the week. Actually I still live there. I kept that and Jay got the house.'

Mike looked serious. 'What happened to the animals?'

'I never saw them again.'

'So,' Mike said, with a hard edge to his voice. 'You just got the flat?'

I rushed to clear Jay's name. I could tell that Mike was more than ready to hate him.

'No, no. I got a good settlement. They were still big in the States, so he could afford it.' I smiled, trying to lighten the atmosphere. 'I was lucky it didn't happen a year later, when they'd gone off the boil.'

'Yeah,' grinned Mike, as if he was enjoying the thought of James Jay and the Jaylers plunging down the charts, 'Wham! came along.'

'Along with a few others,' I chided. 'You can't let George Michael take all the blame.'

I appreciated Mike's protective attitude, but part of me was slightly wounded at his eagerness to wallow in Jay's musical demise.

Mike didn't seem to notice anything and continued, 'So what did you do when he was away strumming and you were waiting to get pregnant?'

There were some memories of that time that made me fidgety, so I slipped out of bed and put my breakfast tray on the table. Then I sat down on a chair facing him.

'I did get bored sometimes, especially when Jay was on tour. But I tried to keep myself busy. I got friendly with Clive's girlfriend, Patti. Clive was the drummer. She had a stall in Camden market selling vintage clothing and I used to help her out. Then we moved on to designing more modern stuff. We even had our own shop in Covent Garden. We were in vogue. Did quite well in the early eighties.'

Mike nodded, 'Come to think of it I might have seen you in the papers once or twice.'

I brightened. 'Did you? I'm surprised you recognised me.' I quailed at the memory of the gauche schoolgirl I'd been when Mike had met me. But I liked the idea of him looking at my picture and kicking himself for losing such a tasty bird.

'I think it was the name that gave it away,' he drawled sardonically. 'Are you the Pandora Fry who got married in Fulham register office in a mini dress, fur jacket and white leather boots, by any chance?'

I caught my breath. I'd become so used to erasing Mike from my mind that I'd imagined he'd done the same with me. It was a surprise to find that when I'd featured occasionally in the tabloids, he'd been monitoring my progress. And that he'd remembered in such detail.

Seeing that I was lost for words, he continued gently, 'When did you know you couldn't have children?'

I braced myself to admit the unpleasant truth, 'We never had any tests. But we knew it was me when a girl who worked for the management company got pregnant.'

Mike raised his eyebrows. 'It was his?'

'*They* were his,' I replied. 'She had twin boys.'

Mike whistled and shook his head. 'Double whammy.'

I felt that he wasn't just referring to double babies.

'Yes,' I said, going down the flippant route, 'That's twice I've lost out to fertile women. First Val, then Debbie.'

'So is that why you split up?' Mike was looking concerned, probably because he could see a few tears in my eyes.

'Yes. Although he didn't want to. He wanted us all to live together.'

'Mad bastard.' Mike spat out the words and moved as if to get out of bed and comfort me but I put up my hand to stop him.

'Wait. Don't feel sorry for me until I tell you something. Something I'm ashamed of. Something I shouldn't have done to Jay.'

Mike stayed where he was and I continued.

'I got interested in PR and this guy Alvie, who worked freelance for the group, took me under his wing. He was dark, like Jay.' My voice broke into a croak as my throat constricted in shame at the thought of it. 'We started sleeping together. I didn't even really fancy him – I just wanted to get pregnant and pretend it was Jay's.'

Mike let me have a little sob and then asked quietly, 'So what happened to Alvie?'

'I dropped him like a hot brick once I knew I couldn't conceive,' I sniffed.

'So was it a friendly split with Jay-boy? Do you still see him?'

'No, I don't—' I paused, making the decision not to tell him about our occasional postal correspondence. '—When I first found out I told him to leave, but after that we had to meet, to discuss the divorce. I suppose you could say it was as amicable as it could have been in the circumstances. And how could I blame him for wanting children – the one thing I couldn't give him?'

'Come back to bed,' said Mike tenderly. We lay and cuddled and Mike whispered, 'I've done worse than that. I went a bit mad once I sold the shops.'

I rested my head on Mike's chest, while he told me he'd behaved like a typical travelling man. His gyms and leisure centres had been teeming with fit young females ever eager to please the big boss. And he hadn't been backward when they'd been forward.

'But did Val know about the flings?' I demanded.

His face reddened. 'Well, I never admitted anything, but she had an idea. I don't blame her for leaving me.'

I thought of eighteen-year-old me cradling Mike in my arms when he'd cried at the thought of telling his mother and Val about us, being so sure that he was fine and decent, and not by nature a two-timer. How wrong I'd been.

'I never thought I'd say this, but I'm beginning to feel quite sorry for Val,' I sighed.

Mike shifted uncomfortably, looking guilty. 'I know I wasn't a good husband. But, believe me, she didn't want for anything. And she can afford to keep her bloke in Ferraris with what she got from me when we divorced.' His face saddened. 'The problem was, I didn't love her. But she always was,' he corrected himself, 'is, a good mother to Danny.'

I kissed his chest, feeling glad that he hadn't put all the blame on Val for his behaviour. And at the same time I felt pleased that he'd told me he hadn't loved her, even though I already knew that.

'So did you have a relationship with any of them, or were they all one night stands?' I asked, trying not to sound as keenly interested as I was.

He stretched back and looked at the ceiling. 'While I was married, I was only looking for casual sex. But once Val left, I did meet someone. We got serious. She even moved in. But it only lasted a few months.'

He'd stopped speaking. 'Why?' I asked.

'Because I found it impossible to be faithful,' he admitted.

I felt shocked at his candour. Was he pathologically incapable of being true to one woman? I couldn't bring myself to ask him that question in case the answer was yes, so instead I moved to a position where I could see his eyes, and asked, 'Are you involved with anyone at the moment?'

He turned towards me, and as his lips met mine, breathed, 'I hope so.'

* * *

A bit later on, I asked him about the Ray and Cece plot and he told me how it all came about.

Ray hadn't had enough money to buy The Glasshouse and renovate it as well. He was roughly £250,000 short, so he'd sent a business plan to Mike, asking him to invest. Mike had come down with Ray to Brighton and thought it seemed like a good proposition. He was happy to be back in touch and once they'd bought the property, he came down to stay occasionally, at first to see how the work on the hotel was going, and then socially. Sometimes he'd bring a lady friend. It was always someone different, and Cece had started lecturing him about his lifestyle.

One time when he'd come to see them on his own, they were talking about the old days, and Cece asked why he'd got drunk just before he'd had his accident. He opened up and spoke about what had been going on with me and him. And about what a shock it had been when Val announced she was pregnant. Mike said he'd never been able to get me out of his head, so she suggested trying to trace me. When he heard I wasn't married or living with anyone, he said if she could get me down here, he'd come and try his luck.

After a morning of revelations and passion, and feeling more than a bit wrung out, we thought we could both do with some physical activity of a less amorous kind. So Mike rang Ray and arranged to go to the yacht club for some diving, and Cece managed to get us girls into the swimming pool of one of the large seafront hotels.

We had a lovely last evening together. With the subterfuge and subtext out of the way, and ancient history revealed, and possibly rewritten in places, we were free to rediscover why we all chose each other as friends and lovers in the first place.

I'd like to be able to say that we all lived happily ever after, but actually, while Ray and Cece are still going strong, Mike and I lived happily for only three short years, which flew by at the speed of light.

* * *

From Brighton, Mike and I went straight to my flat in Fulham, and, at his suggestion, started house-hunting for a place I could let out for events, finding the properties in Chace Standen almost immediately. He never went back to Southampton to live. Danny didn't raise any objections – he was pleased for us when he heard our story and saw how happy we were together. And it wasn't as if they were out of contact, as they saw each other regularly at work.

Mike insisted on commuting, first from Fulham, then from Chace Standen. Danny and Mei kept his rooms free in case he ever wanted to stay there, but he never did. Neither did he ever stay anywhere overnight on business. I used to wonder whether that was because he was afraid that if he was on his own at night, he might be tempted to stray, although he said he just wanted to get home. I soon saw for myself how much of a workaholic he was, but when he had his first heart attack, two and a half years after we got married, I managed to persuade him to cut his working week to just two days. I'd expected resistance when I'd first suggested it, but he'd been surprisingly compliant. Looking back, he probably felt worse than he ever let on. I should have read the signs – as Frankie says, coming events cast shadows – but I wasn't seeing clearly then.

We got married in The Glasshouse Hotel, which by then had got its licence for weddings. Mike and Ray wore pale blue linen jackets and straw hats, looking very seasidey. They were in complete contrast to us girls, with me in the red and gold Suzy Wong dress, to ensure 'brissful married life', and Cece as bridesmaid, wearing a similar emerald-green one she'd found online, its larger-than-life dragon and phoenix pattern lending a cheeky Disney vibe to the proceedings.

Ray had too much champagne and, as Mike told me afterwards, whispered to him, 'Lucky bastard. You've got the hot bird, I've got the dragon.' But I'm sure he didn't mean it really.

As it turned out, the cherry blossom was the truest symbol of all. Our married life was sweet, but oh so short.

Chapter 21 – SUMMER 1970

Much to my relief, my mother was waiting in Arrivals at Girona Airport. She was wearing a yellow and green tie-dyed t-shirt and paint-spattered jeans, so not easy to miss. Her long, dark hair was tied back in a low ponytail which made her look Spanish. She wasn't as tanned as I'd expected.

The heat was unexpectedly intense, but welcome – so far, the British summer had been disappointingly cool. The airport smelled quite pleasantly of insect spray and I loved being somewhere that was so utterly different.

Although I'd strapped some wheels to the bottom of my large, expanding suitcase, getting it to roll in a straight line was a struggle. This case didn't just contain my clothes, but also delicacies such as English cheese, bacon, tea bags, baked beans and sausages that Frankie and Toby had been craving. Frankie hugged me and took over the case-lugging.

'It's so good to see you, darling. Were you okay travelling by yourself?'

'It was fine, Mum. I just wish Cece could have come with me.'

The master plan that Cece and I had cooked up for her to come out to Spain for a couple of weeks, had fallen at the first hurdle. Mrs Byrne had got herself a job as a machinist and needed Cece to be at home in the summer holidays to look after her younger sisters.

Mrs Byrne was quite good about it at first and suggested she could send the girls off to stay with her cousin in Camden Town, but then Mr Byrne had come home from work and put the kibosh on it. His reaction to the news went along the lines of, 'Why do you want to go gallivanting off to Spain when you've just met a nice boy here?' (He was referring to golden boy Ray who had a job with prospects and lived in a nice house in Oak Green, of course.) 'If you're not careful, you'll lose him...' etc, etc.

Cece had phoned me in tears to tell me all this, though I suspected she wasn't giving me the whole story. Her parents had probably added in a few comments about my mum and her untoward living arrangements with a fellow Bob Dylan fan. Although if Cece's father had seen the splendour of Toby's Chelsea town house, he might have changed his mind about him, predisposed as he was to residents of superior housing.

I told her I was sorry, but didn't try to persuade her. Mr Byrne was a friend of my dad's, and I didn't want to risk my own chances of getting away, so I thought I'd better head off any ideas she might have about defying him.

'Do you think your dad may have a point about Ray? He might not like you disappearing for two weeks.'

'Well he told me he was going on a cycling tour of France in August, so I don't see how he could object. If I have to trust him, then he'll have to trust me.'

I restrained myself from pointing out that the occasions of sin, as Sister Joseph would have put it, were probably more plentiful in Spanish bars and discos than on the highways and byways of Gaul.

I was in a sort of limbo for the next couple of weeks – revising, sitting exams and waiting for my mother to get in touch. Finally, one Saturday morning she called.

'Hi, Pan. Sorry I haven't rung before, but we've been so busy. And it's hard to find a phone. I'm ringing from Señor Capella's office. He's the owner of the club. I'll be quick. Can you tell me when you and Cece are coming?'

I poured out my disappointment to her as briefly as I could, explaining that Cece couldn't come. She consoled me, but I detected a hint of relief. I'd bought a ticket for the end of June so she took down the details. Then came the list of essential items to bring, mostly comestibles. She sounded happy and relaxed as she said goodbye – only she didn't say goodbye. Instead she said, '*Hasta la vista, chica*'.

I understood this as 'Be seeing you, girl', having endured O-level Spanish with Sister Eulalia – what fun we'd had with that name. My mother must have picked it up in the way ex-pats do, pronouncing the Spanish in an exaggerated English accent. I hoped she wasn't going to converse in Spanglish. I'd had enough of that as a twelve-year-old when I'd first engaged with the subject.

Frankie was alone when she picked me up from the airport, Toby being hard at work on the wall paintings. As we hoisted my case into the boot of Toby's jag, she brought me up to speed with the work schedule.

'Señor Capella wants to open the night club before the end of the season. He's thinking of August the fifteenth, so we've only got six weeks to complete. That's why it's all hands to the pumps. Hope you don't mind starting work tomorrow, darling.'

I shook my head. My fantasy of leisurely days spent building up a decent tan on the beach, punctuated by a couple of hours here and there playing with some paints and a paintbrush, was rapidly vanishing into the wide blue yonder. It became clear why my mother had been relieved that Cece wasn't coming. We got into the car, and Frankie continued, 'Toby's got this great system – he draws enormous outlines on the main walls and does the complicated bits and then I fill in the easy bits, like the skin and clothing.'

I could see now why my mother wasn't very brown. She'd been spending every day engaged in a giant painting-by-numbers project.

Aigua Blau, the place we were making for, was on the Costa Brava, about fifty kilometres north of Girona. After about forty minutes, we turned off a main road on to a minor one. Frankie was giving me a running commentary on the area.

'It used to be just a fishing village but it's a resort now. Luckily the sailing club saved it from getting like Tossa or Lloret.'

I knew next to nothing about the Spanish tourist industry, having only once left the British Isles, on a school trip to visit the shrine of Our Lady of Lourdes, in the French Pyrenees.

'What's wrong with Tossa and Lloret, Mum?'

'Tourists on cheap package holidays go there for the cheap booze. Aigua Blau's a bit more upmarket. It's popular with French families and with people who want villa holidays.'

'So what's the nightlife like, or do they all go to bed early?' I was beginning to think that Tossa de Mar might have been my preferred destination.

My mother smiled. 'Don't worry, there's a few good bars and a couple of clubs. We haven't been to many, but they definitely exist.'

By now we'd reached the outskirts of the town, a mixture of tourist villas and the odd bar. As we drove down the main street, we passed jewellers, food shops, and several tourist shops, their shelves packed with straw donkeys, wooden bulls and plastic flamenco dancers. There were also a couple of signs for spit-roasted *pollo y patatas fritas* (chicken and chips) which made my mouth water.

Frankie slowed down to point out some lettering on one of the café windows: TEA AND CAKES LIKE MOTHER MAKES.

'Don't worry,' she laughed, 'They're not all like that. We're taking you to a real Spanish restaurant tonight.'

At the bottom of the main street, we joined a narrower road running parallel to the coast. The sea looked beautiful – a clear blue-green, the sun glinting on waves frilled with white spray. The beach was still populated, not bad for five o'clock in the afternoon. Frankie seemed very much at home, as if she'd lived here for ages, rather than a few weeks.

'The apartments are a kilometre or so away from the main town,' she told me. 'It's okay if you've got transport, but most of the vacationers don't have any. They're complaining that it's too far and too dark to walk back from the town in the evening. Señor Capella was worried he'd have the same problem getting people to and from the club.'

'Can't he lay on transport?' I said.

Frankie nodded.

'Actually, that's just what we suggested. So he got hold of an old minibus and Toby's painted it for him. Looks great. It's covered in rainbows and flowers with its name on the back. It's called the Beastie Bus.'

I must have looked blank.

'Don't you remember, Pan? Toby's christened the club the Inner Beast.'

At that moment we drew up next to a newly-built apartment block. Frankie parked in a reserved bay and together we heaved my case out of the boot and took the lift, which she called the *'ascensor'*, up to the top floor. She put the emphasis on the middle syllable instead of the last, but who was I to correct Spanglish? Opposite the lift was a door with the word 'office' written in English, Spanish, French and German.

'This is where Carlos Capella, works,' she winked, 'and sometimes sleeps. He's in his fifties. And single. He has a girlfriend he entertains here sometimes.'

Too much information, Mother, I thought, hoping she wasn't going to make a habit of it. She led me to an apartment at the other end of the corridor.

'This is us. Are you thirsty? We've got Fanta, coffee, vino.'

I was busy taking it all in so I said, 'Whatever you're having.'

The apartment was clean and bright with a small kitchen, two double bedrooms, a bathroom and fairly large living room with glass doors leading to a small balcony. Beneath us I could see a restaurant patio, set with tables and chairs which overlooked the beach and the Mediterranean Sea beyond.

My mother joined me on the balcony, bringing two glasses and a bottle of red wine. She placed them on the table and we both sat down on the hard, metal chairs. Her features assumed a coaxing expression and I wondered what was coming.

'Darling, would you mind calling me Frankie while we're here? You see, Carlos saw my wedding ring and assumed Toby and I were married. He started calling me Señora Packwood-Jones so we went along with it.'

I nodded.

'And if I introduce you as my daughter, it just complicates things. Because...'

I finished the sentence that she was struggling with.

'Because obviously Toby isn't old enough to be my dad.'

I stopped there, not wanting to twist the knife further. Frankie certainly didn't look her forty-two years, but Toby was only about twenty-five or so. If I turned up as a daughter it would draw unwanted attention to the gap in their ages.

'So who am I, Mum?'

She poured us each a glass of wine. I took a sip and nearly spat it out. She laughed.

'You'll get used to it. It's *vino tinto,* otherwise known as gut-rot.'

I raised my eyebrows, waiting for my mother to answer my question, and she spoke quickly, as if it was already decided.

'My niece.'

Thank goodness she hadn't said little sister. That would have felt really weird.

'Okay, but don't ask me to call you Aunty.'

'Good God, no. Frankie's fine. That's settled then. Come on, I'll take you down and show you the work in progress.'

The shell that was being transformed into the Inner Beast night club occupied the basement of the apartment block. Frankie explained that there was a primitive form of ventilation but, of course, no windows, so she and Toby had been sweltering in the heat. Señor Capella had promised to have a modern system installed as soon as possible but in the meantime they roasted.

When we got down there, we found some Spanish workmen putting finishing touches to the toilets, but otherwise Toby was the only person working in the vast L-shaped area. The place smelled of paint and turpentine. And putty. There was dust on the floor from the building work, which no one had bothered to clear up.

Toby put down his brush, got off his step ladder, and came over to us. He was dressed in dungarees with no shirt underneath, giving him the appearance of a hill-billy. The trouser legs had been cut off at the knees and the garment was so spattered with paint that the original colour was indiscernible. He took off his dust mask and looked from one of us to the other, appearing unsure whether to kiss me. I'd only met him once before, when Frankie had been angry with him for giving the game away about my dad asking for a divorce, and I wasn't sure what to do either. He was sweating, and he dabbed his face and hands with a paint rag before he shook my hand tentatively.

'Good to see you. Did you have a good flight?'

Frankie answered for me, putting her arm round his waist.

'Everything went like clockwork. Didn't it Pan?' I nodded.'I told Pandora that as far as Carlos and anyone else is concerned, she's my niece. To keep things simple.'

Toby looked blank. The shrug of his shoulders implied there were things that women said and did that he found impossible to fathom.

We all sat down on one of the long, black, concrete banks set round the edge of the club. We'd taken Toby a cold lemonade and he drank it greedily. He waved the bottle towards the walls.

'What do you think of it?'

'It's super,' I answered, emphasising and elongating the first syllable. As soon as I heard myself, I blushed, aware that I was already taking on the cadences of my mother's remodelled accent. Since she'd been living with Toby, I'd noticed she'd acquired a bit of a Chelsea bray. Which was odd, because Toby was doing just the opposite – toning down his accent to sound less posh. Trouble was, neither of them was getting it quite right.

I got up and had a look round, absolutely loving what they'd done so far. John, Paul, George and Ringo were already finished and dominated a large wall opposite the dance floor. Einstein and Che Guevara were sketched out, waiting for Frankie to colour them in, and Bob Dylan was in the process of being fine-tuned. Adjacent to the dance floor, stood a tall glass box in which a disc jockey would eventually preside over the dancers. A large bar snaked round a corner, mimicking the L-shape of the room.

I noticed a self-portrait of Toby on a minor wall, beyond the bar. Unlike the Beatles, who were gigantic, Toby had painted himself as less than life size, complete with dungarees and paint brush. It reminded me of the children's puppet, Andy Pandy – all he needed was a stripy hat and a teddy bear.

Decorating one of the larger walls, was a portrait of Frankie, which could only have been painted by someone in love. She was naked, her long dark tresses partially concealing her generous breasts. Her enormous green eyes stared out, Mona Lisa like, and her lower torso curved in a way any mermaid would be proud of. I could indeed have passed for this woman's sister. Without the voluptuousness, of course. And the fishy tail.

Toby had a clever way of painting with solid lines in a deceptively naive technique which looked wonderful from a distance. The size of this basement was the perfect canvas for his style. He used colour boldly, especially in the alcove paintings, which were more truly psychedelic than the rest – surreal and full of fantastic imagery.

Frankie had explained to me briefly on the day I'd delivered her passport, that a psychedelic artist gets his inspiration on acid trips, or similar mind-enhancing drugs. But I wasn't to worry because he wasn't an addict and only took drugs for inspiration. And he'd be completely clean while we were away because everyone knew it was too dangerous to take drugs in Spain. If you were caught they could put you in prison and throw away the key, so Toby would be working from sketches.

While this was going through my mind, Toby was explaining that the sound systems and strobe lighting had been installed by a specialist company based in Barcelona and he was very excited about the total effect when everything was finished. The artwork was about half done. As he and Frankie had started painting halfway through May, I calculated that with me helping them, they might just be able to meet the deadline.

'Look at this, Pan,' called Frankie from an alcove in the smaller part of the L-shape. 'I love this one.'

She was showing me the image of a turbaned man sitting cross-legged, his eyes closed. An aura of golden light surrounded his body on which there shone a vertical row of star-like flowers, starting with red at the base going up to orange, yellow, green, blue, and indigo at his brow. Above his head was an enormous amethyst-coloured lotus flower and beneath him, a coiled serpent.

'What gave you the idea for this one?' I asked.

Toby looked a bit bashful and embarrassed.

'Oh, it's someone I met in India when I was a student. A yogi. He said something I've always remembered: "An artist has to close his eyes to see clearly".'

'What do you think he meant?'

Toby hesitated. 'I assumed he was talking about getting inspiration through meditation.'

I looked more closely at the coloured flowers. Each one had a different symbol in the centre. 'What do these represent?' I asked.

'The body's energy points. It's part of their religion.' Toby looked slightly wistful. 'He was a nice old guy. He tried to show me how to sit properly – he called it sukhasana – but my knees always came up to my ears. Not very bendy, I'm afraid.'

Frankie had been listening with an adoring ear.

'I haven't got any complaints.'

They clutched hands, exchanging an intimate glance, and I screamed inwardly, covering my ears with invisible hands. Toby was perceptive enough to see I was dying inside, so he retrieved his hand and continued.

'I scaled up a sketch of him I had. That's what I've done for most of the paintings in this part of the club. If you're any good at painting you could copy from my sketches.'

I brightened up. This was more like it. Tons better than just filling in.

'Okay. I'll have a go. Can I have a look at your drawings and choose one?'

It was getting on for seven o'clock by that time, and Frankie was panicking about the food still in my suitcase, so the lovebirds and I ascended back up to the apartment to unpack it into the fridge – which was empty except for some bottles of water, beer and soft drinks. Frankie and Toby ooed and aahed over the bacon and sausages.

'We can have a super-duper breakfast tomorrow, can't wait.'

And they danced around like happy children.

We were going out to a restaurant called *La Mariposa* so I changed into pink trousers and a white cheesecloth top. After their showers, the lovebirds transformed themselves from jobbing painters into trendy artists. Toby sported a long brocade jacket in magenta with a mandarin collar, which suited his height. Under this he wore a flowered shirt and slightly flared trousers. Frankie had also gone for the tunic look but hers was a diaphanous, pale lilac creation, teemed with plum velvet bell bottoms. I felt a bit of a sparrow beside these birds of paradise, but Frankie promised to take me to a boutique she'd found in the next resort up the coast to kit me out more appropriately.

It was a short drive to the restaurant. As we entered, the head waiter greeted us warmly.

'*Buenas tardes, señores*.' He paused his smile, his eyebrows aloft. '*Y señorita, también*?'

Frankie tossed her head in what she probably saw as a girlish manner and proceeded to perjure herself. '*Mi sobrina*.'

Frankie must have looked up 'niece' in her pocket Spanish dictionary proving that this crime was definitely premeditated. It was lucky for her I'd agreed to it. The waiter beckoned us forward. '*Bienvenido*. Your table is ready. Come.'

He seated us, took our drinks order, and returned with the menus. Frankie was just explaining to me which dishes were delicious and which not, when a portly man approached our table.

'Good evening.' He bared his teeth in a smile which he directed at Frankie. 'And you have a free-end with you, this evening?'

I suppressed a smirk. Frankie was looking puzzled, but Toby had caught on.

'More than a friend, señor, this is Frankie's...niece.'

It was the man's turn to look bemused, so Toby translated.

'*Su sobrina*. Pandora, this is Jordi. It's his restaurant.'

Jordi bowed in my direction, keeping a discreet eye on my mother's curves, accentuated by the tightness and semi-transparency of her tunic.

'Señorita Pandora. A pretty name. I hope you enjoy your stay here.'

I thanked him in English. It was too soon for Spanglish. I'd only just got off the plane. He squared his shoulders and moved on to the reason for his attention.

'I have *especial* dish tonight. *Especial paella.* You would like to order that? Is very good.'

I noticed Frankie and Toby didn't jump at the offer.

'What's in it?' I asked.

'Oh, rice and, um, seafood,' said Frankie.

'Chicken,' chimed in Toby.

'Loss of good things, señorita,' beamed Jordi, making a circle of his right finger and thumb and kissing it delicately, but with panache.

By now I was beginning to sense there was no way out of the *paella*.

'It sounds okay.'

Like me, Frankie buckled under pressure and surrendered.

'Well, if we're all agreed...'

After Jordi had gone, Frankie told me that they had a running tab with the restaurant, giving them a discount – which was why she'd felt obliged to go along with Jordi's suggestion.

The place was gradually getting busier. From where I was sitting, I had a good view of the door and had observed that the diners had so far been a mixture of locals and well-heeled tourists, rather than the *pollo* and chips brigade.

My eyes widened when an attractive, fair-haired man on his own came in and looked around. I noticed what a lovely complexion he had. He was tanned, but not deeply bronzed in the way of Spanish or French skin. It was a fresher, healthier colour as if mixed with a touch of rose. Toby followed my gaze and called him over.

'Hey. Collins. Come and join us.'

The man sauntered over and made a small bow, 'Ah. The beautiful people.'

A waiter immediately appeared with a chair. Toby was visibly enlivened at the appearance of another male. It started to dawn on me what a strain my arrival probably was for him. Having to share his love nest with a third person wasn't every red-blooded male's dream. I made a mental note to keep Frankie as happy as possible, for his sake. It wasn't fair to burden him with any of my how-could-you-have-left stuff.

Toby presented his friend, almost proudly.

'Pandora, this is Collins. He works at Club Calypso. The best disco in town.'

I said 'hi' and he answered in kind, surveying me with amused, blue-green eyes, and addressing his next words to Toby.

'But we have some competition soon, I think.' His accent was hard to identify, but it didn't belong to any Romance language I recognised.

'You on holiday?' he asked.

'No, I'm helping Frankie and Toby with the painting.'

How good it felt to say that. Yesterday I'd been fresh out of school and unemployed. And today I was an artist.

A waiter appeared with an enormous pan of *paella* full of saffron rice, red peppers, mussels, prawns, inky chicken and various other unidentifiable components. The alien aroma arising with the steam did nothing to excite my taste buds. Oh, for some chicken and chips. Or even tea and cakes.

Having duly persuaded Collins of the benefits of the *paella*, the waiter left us to help ourselves. Frankie piled a generous portion on to my plate.

'Eat up. You must be starving.'

I tried my best but the rice was rich and cloying, attaching itself to my soft palate as well as my ribs. The flavour was totally unlike anything I'd ever eaten before. I was struggling with some rubbery bits which Collins gleefully identified as squid, at which point I put down my fork and gave up. Frankie opened her mouth to protest, but then checked herself. I could see she was torn between getting some food down me and appearing unduly maternal. The four of us could only manage about half of what was in the pan and Collins made a joke about the restaurant serving it up again later that evening, to Toby's great amusement.

I chose something called flan for dessert, which turned out to be *crème caramel*, a slippery pudding covered with a dark brown syrup. Ugh. So far Spanish cuisine was not impressing me.

After some very good coffee – the best part of the meal – Collins invited us to his club, which was a ten-minute walk away. Night clubs didn't seem to open much before ten, so it was pretty empty when we arrived. Our host took his place behind the bar and we sat on bar stools, sipping white rum and cokes, called Cuba Libres, listening to the disco music. The dance floor was empty. There was a larger bar and dance floor upstairs but it wasn't busy either, so the staff came down and chatted to Collins from time to time. Only one or two of them were Spanish. Toby explained that the owner was Swiss and the staff were mostly Swiss French except for Collins, who was Swedish.

'Swedish? Then why's he called Collins? Doesn't sound very Swedish,' I puzzled.

'It's a nickname. No one can pronounce his real name and he likes Tom Collins cocktails, so that's what everyone calls him.'

Collins must have been alerted at the sound of his name and came over to us.

'You giving all my secrets away, Toby?'

The music had been turned up, to attract passing tourists, so he had to lean over the bar to make himself heard.

I felt a little tingle of excitement as his lips touched my ear. 'Would you like me to make you one?'

Frankie must have heard what he'd said – maybe he'd even asked her the same thing on a previous occasion. She shook her head meaningfully, looking at her watch. 'Pan. We'd better get going. Lots to do tomorrow and we start at eight, while it's still cool.'

Collins placed his hand on his heart in pretend regret, then said in a low voice, 'Why don't you come in to see me on your own one night. You can have as many cocktails as you like.'

I didn't know what to say. There were all kinds of logistical reasons why not. Like how I'd get there and back, what I'd do all night if he was working behind the bar, what I'd tell the lovebirds. I hadn't even been given a key to the apartment yet. I decided to keep all this to myself and smiled as if it was a possibility.

On the drive back, Frankie told me that Collins was typical of the young men who worked in clubs. Very charming but with a different girl every week. They loved the tourists because there was always a fresh supply on the next plane. I listened and nodded, but the pleasure centre in my brain was overriding her words as it relived the evening, especially the last part.

* * *

The next morning I couldn't face the cooked breakfast that Toby was lovingly creating from the bacon, sausages, and baked beans I'd smuggled into the country. A cup of coffee was just about all I could manage.

'You have to watch the drinks they serve,' said Frankie, 'All the spirits are double measures and the ice disguises how strong they are.' She added, a touch disapprovingly. 'And you *were* drinking on a mostly empty stomach.'

Downstairs in the club, Toby gave me a trial with a small section of painting that was part of a larger mural of San Francisco, where all the flower-power thing had started. My job was to paint two hippies with flowers in their hair who were hanging off the rail of a cable car, which was careering down a hill.

He was happy with the result and he gave me his portfolio of sketches so I could select one of them to paint on one side of a large rectangular retaining pillar. He suggested that a full-length figure would be a good choice because the pillar was so tall.

When I saw the area to be covered, I had serious doubts about my ability to transfer the image successfully. I'd dropped Art at the end of fifth form and hadn't picked up a brush since.

'What happens if I mess up, Toby? I'm a bit out of practice. And I've never painted anything so big.'

'Don't worry. I'll chalk a grid on the sketch and on the pillar, so your perspective should be okay. I'm on hand anyway. Don't be afraid to ask.'

The one I picked was of a woman dressed in a sheer robe with long, flowing, red hair holding an open casket. Toby had finished his preliminary chalking and had wandered over to see which of the sketches I'd picked out.

'I thought you might choose that one. You know who it's supposed to be, don't you?'

I couldn't think who he meant, not being particularly familiar with ancient redheads. The only one I knew of was Mary Magdalene. He laughed when I suggested this.

'No. Someone less biblical, more mythical. It's Pandora. Your namesake.'

I groaned in disbelief. 'Not her, please. How could my mother have named me after a woman who'd opened a box against orders, and unleashed all the evils on the world? Some role model.'

As soon as I'd said it, I felt awful. So much for my resolution to go easy on Frankie in front of Toby. Frankie was over the other side of the room dressed in a red and white polka dot bikini, balancing on a plank of wood resting on two step ladders, humming to herself while she painted, and mercifully oblivious to my slander. Toby laughed. He was chalking a grid on the Pandora sketch and he paused to scrutinise me.

'Don't you like your name?'

'No. Anyway, no one ever uses it. It's always Pan. I might just as well be called saucepan lid. And frequently was.'

He looked thoughtful.

'My name wasn't much better. It was always Toby jug or jug ears.'

He lifted his hair at the sides to reveal long sideburns and two quite large ears which stuck out slightly. 'Why do you think I wear my hair like this?'

We were interrupted by a wolf whistle directed at Frankie, delivered by a Spanish workman emerging from the toilets, where he'd presumably been doing some plumbing. It was clear that he hadn't seen us, tucked away as we were behind the pillar. Frankie turned towards the man, shaking her head in rebuke but with a smile playing round her lips.

'Muy guapa,' the man shouted as he exited the club. I recognised this as meaning 'very pretty'.

I glanced at Toby and caught a fleeting expression. He looked like I felt today, overwhelmed and out of my depth. I raised my eyebrows in a what-an-idiot expression, and Toby responded, looking relieved when the man disappeared. He handed me the sketch and I began to outline my picture on the pillar, while Toby crossed the dance floor to join Frankie.

Soon it was lunch time which, being Spain, was two hours long. To make the most of the sun, the lovebirds were in the habit of dashing upstairs to *El Delfín,* the restaurant I'd seen from the balcony, where they'd grab a drink and a toasted sandwich, then sunbathe on the beach until half past two. So that was what we did.

We walked rather sleepily back to resume work, Frankie disappearing up to the apartment to get some water. While we were alone, Toby took the opportunity of putting the finishing touch to our earlier conversation.

'By the way, Pandora. There was one thing your namesake kept in her casket.'

I vaguely recalled that part of the story, but wasn't sure.

'What was that, Toby?'

'Hope.'

Chapter 22 – SUMMER 1970

I lost my virginity to Collins a couple of weeks after I first met him. We'd bumped into him again at *La Mariposa* restaurant and this time he'd persuaded Frankie to let me spend the evening at the Calypso, promising I'd be back before one o'clock at the latest. I think Frankie said yes because she knew he didn't finish work till about three in the morning, so she assumed no hanky panky could therefore take place. Plus, of course, she couldn't appear to be overprotective because she was pretending not to be my mother.

The day before, she and I had managed to get to the boutique she liked, and I was wearing one of the outfits she'd bought me – a yellow silk wrap-around blouse with green silk harem trousers. If there'd been a fancy dress party, I could have gone as a daffodil. As it was, I was feeling a bit all dressed up and nowhere to go, until Collins turned up with his invitation. So you could say it was meant to be.

As he and I walked from the restaurant to the club, he draped his arm around my shoulders, being tall enough to do so without sustaining undue arm strain. I'd seen French couples walking like that, and it felt agreeably cosmopolitan. I'd soon realised that it wasn't hip to be a pale Brit of the unsophisticated variety. Toby, Frankie and I passed muster because we were in Aigua Blau to work. But if I'd been with a friend of my own age, on a package holiday, my status would have been quite different. And, from what Frankie had said, Collins wouldn't have viewed me as any more than a passing fancy.

It was 9.30 – early in Spanish time, still thirty minutes before the Calypso opened.

'What shall we do now?' he asked winningly. 'We could have a drink.' He motioned to a bar we were passing, but he didn't stop. 'Or come to my room. I've got a drink there.'

I laughed. The easy way he'd slipped into his role of seducer amused me.

'Don't tell me. You'll make me a Tom Collins.'

He tutted in mock indignation.

'I'm supposed to say that.'

We were just approaching his club. I knew from what he'd said before, that he and most of the bartenders lived in a large villa on the side of a hill, just outside the town. But often, after their shifts, they slept in one of the rooms the club rented in the building next door.

He pulled me into the shadows and kissed me. It was very enjoyable. His breath was fresh and he smelled good. His body was lean and strong. And he didn't thrust his tongue down my throat the way one or two of the St Vincent boys had.

'Are you coming up for a drink, then?'

What could I say? I knew what would happen next, but it had to happen some time. And what better setting – a balmy night, a foreign land, a handsome Swede – it felt perfect.

When I saw the room, however, the perfect quotient dropped like a stone. It was pretty basic. From the ceiling hung a light bulb barely covered by a cheap, discoloured shade. The bulb threw its dingy light on to a single bed with sheets that had presumably once been white, but were now the colour of pale sand. Beside the bed stood an ancient wooden chair, reminiscent of one in a Van Gogh painting,on top of which sat a black ashtray featuring a red bull. From the only other piece of furniture in the room, a small wardrobe, Collins took a bottle of brandy and two small glasses.

'Drink?'

'Are those glasses clean?'

He shrugged, grinning, 'Don't worry. Alcohol kills all germs.'

He sat on the bed and I perched on the edge of the chair. We both sipped the warm liquid. It was rough and almost made me retch. The squalid room rendered me awkward and tongue-tied so I welcomed his taking my glass and pulling me on to the bed with him. He unwrapped my blouse and kissed my breasts. It was so hot in Spain that I was, as usual, bra-less.

'I'm sorry it's not so nice here,' he whispered. 'Next time I'll take you to the villa.'

He seemed to be having some trouble undoing my harem trousers.

'Do you want to take your clothes off yourself or should I keep trying?'

We both giggled. I stood up and took off my trousers and briefs.

'We'll be here all night if I leave it to you,' I said, meaning to be humorous but realising, from the pained expression on his face, that Collins took it as a criticism. I was again consumed with shyness. It occurred to me that it must be past ten by now. Maybe I could get out of it that way.

'Have we got time? Aren't you supposed to be at work by now?'

'I'm the manager. I can be late if there's a good enough reason.' He patted the bed. 'Come. I can't reach you from there.'

His blue-green eyes were smiling again. He really was very attractive. The brandy had begun to anaesthetise me, so I let him make love to me. I was happy to lie back and let him do all the work. After all, he was the expert. I was the novice.

I felt no real pain when he entered me, just a bit of discomfort. When I gasped, he said, 'Sorry. I'm clumsy with this johnny.'

I assumed he meant the condom. He didn't take long to come. He kissed me, then got up quickly and left the room. When he came back, he grinned at me.

'Are you ready to taste my Tom Collins?'

Everything he said sounded slightly ironic to my ear, possibly because English wasn't his mother tongue, and it was usually accompanied by a grin. I suppressed the desire to say, 'I thought I already had,' and asked if he'd show me where the bathroom was. He handed me a toilet roll he got out of the wardrobe, and directed me to a room with a stained shower and toilet. A grubby-looking hand towel hung on a rail and there was no soap. I did the best I could with cold water and toilet paper. This wasn't exactly how I'd imagined my first experience of sex. I think my fantasy had involved a warm bath, a feather bed and a nice cuddle directly after. Added to that, I was slightly anxious about the evening ahead, wondering if I'd be sitting on my own at the bar with no one to talk to.

I needn't have worried on that score. Collins settled me down on a bar stool and made me his famous Tom Collins, which turned out to be gin and lemon with ice, slices of orange, and something else he called his secret ingredient. It was okay, but I stayed on Cuba Libres after that, which were much more to my taste. He chatted to me in between serving drinks, and even danced a couple of slow dances with me. During one of them he asked if I was having a good time. I kissed him in reply, feeling much more relaxed after the drinks.

'And making love? You liked it?'

I wondered what he'd say if I told him it had been a bit of a disappointment. I'd expected the earth to move, but the only motion had been the ashtray flying through the air when Collins had struck it in the heat of the moment. Luckily it had been empty.

'It was lovely,' I lied. Putting my lips close to his ear, I admitted, 'It was my first time.'

He pulled away as if stung, and said something under his breath in Swedish.

'No. It can't be. You're joking.'

I shook my head.

'But,' he searched for the right words, 'it wasn't difficult. And there was no blood.'

I couldn't explain that either. All I knew was, I was telling the truth. But I didn't want to make a big thing of it, as I could sense his twitchiness about the situation. So I said casually, 'I felt a bit, you know, uncomfortable, but it was much easier than I expected. That's good, isn't it?'

Seeing I was apparently unconcerned about the loss of my maidenhead, he slipped back into suave Swede mode.

'Maybe your body's made for love.'

I burst out laughing then, otherwise he might have continued down that road and oiled his way out of my favour. His face slipped into a rueful expression.

'I forgot. You English girls don't go for the romantic approach.'

He seemed genuinely downcast. Feeling sorry for him, I put my arms round his neck and continued dancing, my head on his shoulder. At the end of the track, he released his hold so he could see my face.

'Seriously, how old are you, Pandora?'

It was the first time he'd used my name all evening. Up to then, he'd been calling me Cinderella because of the curfew.

'Eighteen. How old are you?'

He looked a little uncomfortable. 'Twenty-five.'

I kept my face impassive. He'd told Toby a little about his past – his conscription, different jobs he'd had, etc, and Toby had worked out that Collins must have been around thirty, although he didn't look it.

He led me off the dance floor to a stained, red velvet *banquette*. I wondered for a nervous moment if he was going to send me home early for being a closet virgin, and for laughing at him, but he just wanted to interrogate me further.

'Have you got a boyfriend at home?'

I thought of Mike and suffered a pang of wondering what it would have been like with him.

'No. No boyfriend.' But I didn't want to seem as if no one wanted me, so I added, 'We split up just before I came away.

'Why didn't you have sex with him?' Collins was nothing if not direct. This annoyed me a bit because he wouldn't have asked an eighteen-year-old Spanish girl that question. English girls, it seemed, had a reputation for casual promiscuity.

'Because we hadn't being going out long. And I've only just left school.'

Collins nodded. That explanation seemed to satisfy him and he pulled me closer.

'So you're my own little virgin. I'll have to take special care of you, Pippi Longstrump.'

'Who?' I enquired.

'Pippi Longstocking. A little girl in a book. She's quite naughty.'

An image of James Mason as Humbert Humbert lusting after Lolita invaded my brain. Ironic or not, Collins needed to rewrite his chat-up lines or risk creeping me out.

After that he was almost proprietorial. If anyone asked me to dance he'd lean across the bar and ask if I was all right, so they would know I was with him. A couple of times I accepted the invitation, just to keep him on his toes, but if they wanted to buy me a drink I told them my boyfriend worked behind the bar, which was enough to prompt them to try their luck elsewhere.

All too soon it was the moment for Collins to walk me to the taxi office. I wanted to stay longer, gambling on the lovebirds Toby and Frankie being asleep and not knowing what time I'd come in, but he said it was important he kept his word to Frankie. I swayed a bit as we walked down the street, giving him an excuse to hold me tighter.

'You a little bit drunk, or what, Pippi? I'll have to ration you next time.'

He kissed me goodbye before we got to the taxis. Public snogging wasn't viewed very kindly by the locals, and Collins was savvy enough to want to keep his and the club's reputation as unsullied as possible.

'I'd like to see what you're painting,' he said, as I was getting into the taxi. 'How about I come by tomorrow, in the afternoon?'

I wasn't quite sure if such a junior on the painting scene as me, was allowed to have interested parties popping by. But I knew Toby liked him, so why not?

'Yeah. That's fine. You know that Toby does most of it though, don't you? Mum and I just do the minor stuff.'

He nodded and waved as the taxi drew away. Through my alcoholic haze, it dawned on me slowly that I'd blown Frankie's cover. I'd just have to hope he hadn't heard or understood the word 'Mum'.

I crept in quietly and went straight to the bathroom and showered. My body didn't look or feel any different. I don't know what I'd expected, but this particular rite of passage had been remarkably unspectacular.

* * *

Toby and Frankie had realised that Collins and I had something going on when he appeared at the club with some bottles of beer the following day. I hadn't mentioned he was coming, in case he didn't turn up. And then when he did, at about four o'clock, I couldn't think of how to explain his presence. Collins seemed a little sheepish at first, when they looked so surprised to see him.

'Hi. Just thought I'd come see the paintings. You don't mind, do you?'

Toby got down from the platform and shook his hand, taking the bottle of beer that Collins was offering. Frankie joined them and I let them chat for a bit before I emerged from behind the pillar I was working on. When he saw me, Collins looked relieved and turned to Frankie.

'You see I got her home on time last night?'

Frankie looked thoughtfully at me. 'Yes. Thanks. But she's tired out. She's been a bit droopy all day.'

Collins looked puzzled. Heaven knows what he was guessing 'droopy' meant.

'I'm fine, M...' I nearly said 'Mum' because we were used to being just the three of us in the club and it didn't matter if I forgot to call her Frankie. I saw her give a slight start and reasoned this would be a good time to wangle an early end to my working day.

Toby had just started showing Collins around the place, so I whispered to Frankie, 'Is it okay if I go with Collins if he asks me? I know it's a bit early, but...'

She finished my sentence, 'But you like him.'

I nodded, even though a more accurate rendition would have been, 'I'm shattered.'

'Just make it a couple of hours on the beach, then.' Frankie scrutinised me like an Irish grandmother. 'You look tired. Don't go out with him again tonight, darling. Promise.'

Before I had a chance to reply, Collins had appeared by my side, and Frankie said, 'If you two want to get some sun, Pandora's finished her painting. We'll see you back here for dinner, Pan,' she said pointedly, as she waved us out of the basement and into the sunlight.

I got back from my outing with Collins about three hours later. Frankie and Toby were waiting for me and the three of us went straight down to El Delfín to have dinner. Señor Capella was there as well and invited us to stay for a drink, but Frankie and I returned to the apartment, where she proceeded to give me the third degree. First she wanted to know more about the night before. I'd already given her the authorised version at breakfast, but since Collins had turned up, obviously keen, she seemed to want reassurance that he'd behaved himself. Which I gave her, lying through my teeth. So then she asked about the afternoon.

Luckily, I was able to tell her, quite truthfully, that we'd gone to a small ski beach where I watched Collins water ski. The instructors, regulars at the club, let him take a turn at piloting the boat, with me beside him. And how I'd loved it. It was like being in a film. Sun, sparkling sea, the wind in our hair, people watching us from the beach.

After that, we'd sat outside a bar café where Collins had devoured an omelette between a baton of bread and I'd drunk hot chocolate laced with Cointreau which tasted like orange Smarties. Then he'd walked me back to the apartments.

When I finished telling her all this, she put her arm round me.

'Pandora, I've got to say this. I think Collins likes you, otherwise he wouldn't have turned up today. But you're only eighteen and he's...' She searched my face, 'Did he tell you how old he was?'

'He said twenty-five.'

'And the rest.' We both laughed. I wondered if she could see any parallels between me and Collins and herself and Toby. She must have had the same thought.

'It's different when the man's older, Pan. Don't let him pressure you if you don't feel you're ready. If Collins asks you to sleep with him – I'm not saying you can't – but you know he has to take precautions. You're not on the pill, so it's his responsibility.'

I must have gone red from the roots of my hair to the tips of my toes. If she'd known the truth – that I'd wandered into his bed the evening before without a thought of the consequences, and if it hadn't been for him, I could even have been pregnant by now, she wouldn't have been sitting there so calmly.

'Mum. Don't worry. If it happens, I'll make sure he does.'

Frankie didn't look convinced. 'Do you want Toby to have a word with him?'

The prospect of this conversation caused chaos in my vitals.

'No, no. Honestly, there's no need. Don't spoil it, please Mum. I thought you didn't want it to look as if I was a kid.'

This seemed to bring Frankie to her senses, so she kissed me and left to rejoin Toby in the restaurant bar. Collins had asked me to meet him the next day so he could take me to the villa where he stayed. This was ostensibly to use the swimming pool, but I knew I'd be inspecting his bedroom at some point. And I was really looking forward to it.

Last night I hadn't been quite sure how I felt about him, but today he'd been lively, good fun, attentive. He'd made me feel attractive and special.

And thus our love affair had blossomed. That is, up until my unexpectedly hasty departure from Aigua Blau.

Chapter 23 – SUMMER 1970

It was the day before the grand opening of the Inner Beast and Toby, Frankie and I were putting the final touches to our artwork. The space we'd come to think of as our exclusive territory, had now been invaded by workers burnishing the dance floor, stocking the bar, unpacking bar stools. The DJ, a refugee from Radio Caroline, was practising with his new deck, providing the workforce with backing music for its various routines. We were quite sorry to put down our brushes for the last time and finally surrender our space to the bar staff and cleaners.

Just as we were leaving, Señor Capella came in to show his girlfriend Montsi the finished product. Her family owned a large hotel in Aigua Blau and they had invested in the club, so he needed to keep her sweet. But it was plain from the look on her face that wall art and functional seating were not her usual taste. Luckily Señor Capella had a trick up his sleeve. He beckoned us over, beaming.

'Toby. I think you have something to show us?'

Toby led them to a pillar where he'd painted the goddess Venus in the style of Botticelli, flanked by angels, standing on a large sea shell. So far, so mythological. But closer inspection revealed her face and hair to be that of Montsi's, her figure swathed in filmy gauze to preserve her modesty. The contrast of such a heavenly body with the head of a woman in her forties with short, dark hair highlighted with implausibly blonde streaks could have been disastrous, but Toby had managed to render the likeness both attractive and recognisable. Montsi studied the fresco closely, delight suffusing her features.

'Is wonderful. I love it. But I think,' she simpered at Toby, 'you make me a little more tall and slim.'

Toby shook his head shyly, not sure what to say. Señor Capella saved the day.

'I gave him the only photograph I had, *mi amor*.

She nodded. From that I deduced the photo in question must have been taken on a good day. A tall, slim day in fact. She kissed each of us in turn while Señor Capella looked on, grinning from ear to ear.

'Happy, Montsi?'

'Very happy, Carlos.'

She wandered around scrutinising the rest of the images, pausing to admire a detail here, some colours there. 'I love it. Is like an art gallery.'

Toby explained that the large murals of popular musicians and famous people, living and dead, were designed to please lovers of contemporary culture, but the art on the pillars and alcoves evoked the neoclassical and the transcendental. Montsi's eyes softened. When Toby spoke about his work he was transformed – he became passionate and articulate. I noticed that Frankie moved closer to him, protecting her property. Toby seemed quite willing to keep chatting, but Frankie excused us all on the grounds of getting something to eat.

Over lunch, we talked about what we would do next, now we were unemployed. Or now we were free, whichever way you looked at it. For me it was free, but for Toby it wasn't. As for Frankie, she was somewhere in between.

'There's a couple of options,' said Toby. 'We've got the apartment till the end of August. So we could relax, sunbathe a bit, maybe see a bit more of the Costa Brava.'

Toby was a fan of Salvador Dali, so we knew he'd want to be heading for Port Lligat to see if he could catch sight of his hero. Frankie didn't look too keen and put forward her own suggestion.

'Or there's the option of driving a bit further south, to the Costa Dorada. We could see Barcelona on the way.'

Toby looked a little hurt.

'But I thought we could take it easy, have a leisurely look at Port Lligat and Cadaqués. I'd like to see Dali's house. And there's a Romanesque monastery not far away. And the remains of a medieval town. You could sunbathe while I made some sketches.'

Frankie turned to me for support. I'd already asked Collins about Port Lligat and he'd said the area was quiet with nothing much going on. I'd told my mother, figuring it would give me an excuse to stay in Aigua Blau and spend time with him while they were away, but unfortunately it had put her off going.

'We'll have to vote on it,' said Frankie, sending me furtive eye signals.

'Wait,' said Toby, seeing there wasn't much enthusiasm for his suggestion. 'There's a third option. We could top up our tans here for a couple of days and then head home.'

Frankie looked horrified.

Toby persisted. 'Hands up who wants to do that.'

Frankie and I sat motionless. Toby half put up his hand, then let it drop.

'Sorry. Don't want to be a party pooper. But I need to get back to the studio. See if any work's come in. If I can't go to Port Lligat, I'm not really interested in staying.'

* * *

The following evening, Frankie, Toby and I were sitting in the Inner Beast watching Señor Capella and Montsi entertaining their friends and business contacts at a pre-opening drinks reception. All the local hoteliers, tour guides and tourist agents were buzzing around like mosquitoes, inspecting the murals and generally giving the place a good once over.

Toby had spent part of the morning being photographed and interviewed by a reporter from the regional newspaper. Frankie had initially gone down to the club with Toby, but when she was excluded from both the interview and the photographs, she took the hint and left. She could put up with Montsi monopolising Toby for a couple of hours as long as the promised bonus for completing on time was forthcoming.

When he returned to the apartment he had the imprint of two scarlet lips on the corner of his mouth, which indicated that Montsi had targeted his lips and he'd taken avoiding action. He saw us staring at his face, rushed to the bathroom mirror, and groaned.

'I was lucky to get out alive. Why did you leave me with her?' he moaned.

Frankie went to their bedroom and returned with some cleansing cream.

'Because she made it obvious that she didn't want me around.'

Toby looked worried. 'I didn't encourage her, you know.'

Frankie rubbed hard at the scarlet lipstick and Toby winced slightly. The atmosphere had been uncharacteristically cool between them since yesterday, when there'd been stalemate on where we were all going next. In the end, they'd decided to wait and see if Toby got paid on time before making a decision.

Frankie shook her head and spoke as if talking to a child.

'Of course you didn't encourage her. I know my Toby jug too well for that.'

Frankie's words took me back to what Toby had said about his jug ears and the teasing he'd suffered. And I wondered if she had any idea he might not like being called that. Frankie stopped rubbing, and got to the crux of the matter.

'Did you get paid, darling?'

'Yes. No problem there. The money's been transferred. It'll be in the bank by the time I get home.'

'And did you get your bonus?'

Toby smiled and produced an envelope bulging with banknotes from his pocket which he presented to Frankie with a flourish.

Whooping with joy, Frankie ran to Toby and kissed him several times. I didn't join in the whooping, as I thought it'd be presumptuous of me to act as if I were getting a cut. They might think that the bed and board I'd been given was sufficient.

When she'd calmed down, Frankie counted the money.

'It's forty thousand pesetas, Toby,' she said in disbelief. 'We're rich!'

Toby picked Frankie up and twirled her round, which gladdened my heart even further. There'd been more than enough cold spells between Frankie and my dad in the last few years. On balance, I found warm, embarrassing lovey-dovey to be preferable.

'It sounds more than it is, darling,' Toby said gently, 'But it's still very generous. I think it was the Botticelli Venus that swung it.'

'So does that mean we can go to Barcelona?' said Frankie, her eyes shining, choosing to ignore his reference to his painting of Montsi.

Toby pulled her down on to the sofa and took her hand. 'Bad news, pumpkin. Carlos told me last night that Steve had been trying to get in touch with me, so I rang him this morning. He's got a commission he needs help with urgently and I have to go back right away.'

'Oh no. I can't believe it.' Frankie groaned and put her head in her hands. 'We've worked so hard, day after day. And now we can't even have a break before we go back. I just can't bear it.'

Toby got up and paced the room.

'I've been thinking. Just because I have to go, it doesn't mean you do. Why don't I fly back tomorrow and you two drive home in a couple of weeks or so? The bonus money's all yours. You deserve it. There's enough there for you to do all the sightseeing you like.'

Frankie's shoulders lifted. But she made sure she still looked a little sorrowful. 'Are you sure you don't mind, honey bear? I'll miss you so much. But it would be the perfect solution.'

They went into another clinch and finally asked me what I thought. Naturally, I agreed with what Frankie wanted, but inside I had mixed feelings.

If it hadn't been for Collins, I'd probably have been more than happy to have my mother to myself on an extended tour. But he and I had been seeing quite a bit of each other in the last few weeks – in the late afternoon on the beach, after I'd finished the day's painting. And up at the villa, at weekends, where we'd swim in the pool, alongside whoever else was living, or staying there, at the time.

I'd actually got quite friendly with the bar staff. So much so that whenever I was in the Calypso, I'd help them out by collecting empty glasses. It was more involving than sitting at the bar all night. One evening, when one of the bartenders was sick, Collins gave me a bit of training so I could lend a hand behind the bar. It was easy. And as a lot of the clientele were British, I could understand what they wanted, and have a joke with them as well.

After that I helped out occasionally when they were busy. One night I noticed Collins watching me more than usual. At first I thought he was jealous but later, when he was putting me in a taxi, he said, 'You're okay behind the bar, Pippi. You talk to the customers. They like that.'

I laughed. That evening I'd had to help the Swiss boys in the upper bar with a group of northern rugby players who were drunkenly demanding Newcastle Brown Ale.

'What they like, Collins, is that I understand what they're saying.'

As he closed the taxi door, he said, 'If you want a job here next season, it's yours. Think about it.'

* * *

So there we were, spending our first and last night at the Inner Beast when it was finally operating as a night club, waiting for Collins to come and join us. Some of the specially invited guests had left before the public were admitted at ten o'clock, preferring to avoid the Saturday night crowd – a mixture of Spanish youths on the pull, who tended to hit the town at the weekend, and tourists, also on the pull.

Everything seemed to be going like clockwork. The Beastie Bus had been besieged with eager first-nighters. The music was pounding, the dance floor filling up, and the bar staff dispensing alcohol in large quantities. When Collins finally arrived, the place was packed.

He kissed me and Frankie on the cheek and greeted Toby. His

eyes narrowed as he looked around. 'Now I know where all my customers are,' he said in mock despair.

A waiter brought us over a complimentary bottle of champagne and we toasted the Inner Beast. Then Frankie raised her glass to Toby, saying, '*Bon voyage* for tomorrow, darling.'

Collins looked mildly surprised and Toby began to explain why and how our plans had changed. As it began to sink in that we were all leaving the next day, albeit in two different directions, his expression became serious. When he spoke, he directed an accusing gaze at me, his voice sharp.

'So you are leaving tomorrow? And you tell me now.'

I could feel my face redden. Surely he didn't think this was what I wanted. I couldn't bear it if we parted with him believing that the last few weeks had meant nothing to me. Frankie was watching me so I tried not to sound too unhappy.

'Yes. We're dropping Toby off at Girona airport then driving on to Barcelona. Frankie wants...' I corrected myself hastily, 'We want to see as much as possible before we go home.'

'You're not coming back here, then?' said Collins, looking thoroughly dejected.

I nodded towards the dance floor and he took the hint. At least we could have some privacy there.

'I'm so sorry,' I breathed in his ear, wishing the Carpenters song we were dancing to wasn't so sad. 'This all happened today and I couldn't refuse. I couldn't just say to her, you go on your own and I'll stay here.'

Collins held me tight and leant his head next to mine. Finally, he said, 'Go with her for two weeks then come back to the villa. You can stay with me till the end of the season.'

I was so naive that I didn't realise what an enormous commitment this was for a man like him.

'I really want to, but I can't expect her to drop me back here and drive home on her own. I'm sorry.'

'Why can't you? You're old enough to know what you want.'

I began to cry and he stroked my hair. After a while, he said, 'Is she your mother?' I nodded. I think it made a bit more sense to him then. 'At the end of September I go back to Sweden. I give you my address and if you want to work here next year, write to me. And if you like, maybe I visit you in London.'

At the thought of that, I felt a whole lot better and by the time we joined Frankie and Toby, I was quite composed. Collins stayed for another hour or so until we had to leave. We had an early start the next day and packing to do, so there was no prospect of me going back to the Calypso with him for a proper goodbye. In my pocket I had the piece of paper he'd written his address on. When he'd asked for mine, I'd hesitated over which one to give him. Frankie and Toby had said I could come and live with them if I wanted.

It was that moment, when I wrote down Toby's address, that I made the choice between my mother and my father.

Chapter 24 – SPRING 1971

It was the beginning of April and I was sitting in the function room of The Marlborough Arms, listening to my dad giving thanks to the former Mrs Browning, now Mrs Fry, for plighting him her troth. Or for anyone who doesn't speak Middle English, promising to be true.

I was still close enough to my religious roots to wonder what happens when marriages break down and the promises are broken. Does any form of retribution ever come back on the promise breakers? Is that why my dad had been so keen for my mum to be named as the 'guilty party', and would it haunt Frankie for the rest of her life, casting bad vibes on any subsequent unions?

The ceremony had taken place a couple of hours earlier in the register office at our local town hall. Dad had looked tall and handsome in a new grey suit. Joan, inexpertly teetering on bright red high heels, was wearing a navy blue dress with white piping and matching jacket. She'd lost a bit of weight and looked more attractive than I'd ever seen her. Her daughters must have had a hand in her choice of outfit, as even her red wide-brimmed straw hat was in fashion. Joan was four years older than my dad, but you'd never have known it. With all the stress connected to my mother's leaving, Frank's hair had turned greyer and his lines deeper. But today he was smiling, which made all the difference.

I've still got a wedding photo taken outside on the steps with Dad's brothers, Dave and Anthony, and their wives and children, smiling broadly at the camera. The photographer had probably just told a rude joke.

Among the guests I can just make out Mr and Mrs Byrne, Cece's parents. I'd said hello to them outside the register office, but from then on had been dodging them because of my embarrassment at not keeping in touch with Cece.

I'd been sticking pretty close to the Fry family table, but nevertheless, in the lull after the meal and before the dancing, Mrs Byrne cornered me on my way back from the loo.

'Pandora, love. You're looking well. How are you?'

'Fine, thanks, Mrs Byrne. How are you?'

'Fantastic. Everything's great with us. And Cecilia's going great guns at teacher training college.'

At the mention of her name I suddenly really wanted to know how Cece was, and whether she and Ray were planning to get engaged. Maybe I'd been wrong to lose touch with her. Now I'd met Collins I could probably even bear to hear how Mike was doing. His baby must have arrived by now. But before I had a chance to get underway on the subject of Cece, Mrs Byrne unexpectedly changed tack. 'And how about you? Your father said you'd been working in London.'

I blushed, not sure what my dad had told them – to save having to admit that his only daughter had spent the winter as an office temp and was now about to flee the country again, without once applying for a 'decent' job.

'It was a temporary job, actually, Mrs Byrne. I was planning to look for a permanent one, but then I got offered a job in Spain, so I'm off next week for a few months. I 'm hoping to improve my languages.'

This was baloney of course, as Collins had employed me specifically to be the one native English person in his club. And I already had all the rudimentary Spanish I needed to serve drinks and take money from the locals. But this was what I'd told my father because I could hardly say I was going out to live and work with my Swedish lover, could I? So instead, I pretended I was doing it to become fluent in Spanish.

I hadn't told him it was bar work. Because, when you think about it, that was what had started all the trouble in the first place – him believing that living in a pub wasn't the right life for me, therefore giving up the pub, and making my mother unhappy in the process. So I told him I'd be working in a travel agency. He'd still looked terribly disappointed, though.

'Shouldn't you be thinking about a proper career, Dora?' he'd said, sorrowfully. 'You could be an Executive Officer in the civil service with the A-levels you've got.'

I had no intention of going anywhere near a stuffy government office but I didn't have the heart to tell him that. I'd been pretty chuffed at getting good grades for all three exams, though. At least I had them to fall back on – if, or when, I had to knuckle down and get a permanent job. So I'd reassured my Dad that I'd be back at the end of September, and would start looking in earnest then.

Mrs Byrne had been ruminating on what I'd said about going away in a few days to improve my language skills.

'You're going back to work in Spain? Is it more painting and decorating, dear?'

Damn. My cover story last year had been that I was involved in the interior design and decorating of the apartments, and my dad must have leaked this to Mr Byrne.

'No, that job's finished. I'll be a trainee in the tourist industry. It'll give me a chance to see if I like it or not.'

Mrs Byrne looked genuinely pleased. 'That sounds nice. I'm glad for you, love. Your dad would be upset if he thought you were wasting your education.' She looked around to see if anyone could hear her and lowered her voice. 'How's your mam? Is she upset at all, at your dad getting married?' She gestured at the wedding reception room where people were drinking and smoking, waiting for the disco to start.

I shook my head.

'You're feeling all right about it, though, aren't you, dear?'

I nodded my head.

'And you've been living up in Chelsea. Is the place lovely? Do you get on with him? Is your mam happy?'

I nodded again. I found these questions strangely comforting. I suppose it was because they suggested that she genuinely cared about my wellbeing. And Frankie's too.

It hit me then, how I'd become almost as excluded from my former life as Frankie had, since I'd left Manor Wood and moved in with her and Toby.

Mrs Byrne was waiting for me to speak.

'I get on well with Mum's...with Toby. And Joan's nice too. But it's different when they're not your mum and dad. I feel a bit in the way sometimes. But that's me – they don't do anything deliberately to make me feel like that.'

Mrs Byrne gave me a quick hug.

'Sure, you were great to come through it all the way you did. And to do so well in your exams, with all that was going on.'

By this she meant my mother having left home, but my thoughts flew to Mike and all the turmoil that meeting him had created.

'So when you come back from this next trip, Pandora, where will you be living? Would you ever come back to your dad's?'

I knew in my heart this was unlikely, but I didn't want her to think I looked down on this part of north London which she and her husband had happily inhabited for twenty years or so. 'I'm not sure. Dad said I was always welcome to live with them, but Mum's place would be more convenient for jobs in central London.'

There was a pause and I felt the implicit enquiry which hung in the air. What she really wanted to know was if I'd be in touch with Cece when I came back.

I was on the point of saying that I would be in contact, when one of Mrs Byrne's younger daughters appeared and tugged at her sleeve, complaining of feeling sick, completely disrupting our conversation before I'd had a chance. All I could do was call out, 'Give my love to Cece,' at her retreating figure as she hurried the girl into the ladies.

* * *

A few days later, on the plane to Girona, I thought about the last time I'd seen Collins. It had been just after Christmas when he'd come to stay with us for a couple of weeks. There'd been no embarrassment about where he'd sleep. My bedroom in Toby's house contained a bed large enough for both of us, and its own bathroom.

Frankie didn't mind us sleeping together as long as we took precautions. In fact, she'd made an appointment with her doctor for me to go on the pill. She'd lent me her old engagement ring so I could pretend I was getting married, just in case he raised any objections to prescribing it for me. He gave me a cursory examination and asked when the wedding was, to which I replied, 'Easter'.

'That's a few months away, so it'll give you a chance to see if this one suits you. Come back if you experience any side effects, and we'll try you on another.'

Then I sailed out of the surgery, prescription in hand.

I imagined what the scenario might have been like with Dr O'Brien, our family doctor in Manor Wood. His reaction would have been rather different if I'd asked for the contraceptive pill, I do believe. And would definitely have involved a quiet word with my father.

How impatient I'd been for Christmas to be over and to see Collins again. Our parting in August had seemed an age away. It hadn't been easy keeping in touch, as from October to December he'd been working on, of all things, an Icelandic fishing trawler.

When he arrived in London, it was almost like meeting a different man. We'd said goodbye with golden tans, in bright summer clothes. We met again in winter, our pale skins concealed by dark sweaters. We'd missed each other's autumns, which would have eased the way.

Even his fair hair seemed mousey without the benefit of the lightening sun. In Aigua Blau he'd been at ease in the landscape of Club Calypso and the town. But here in Toby's house, he was as much an outsider as I had been there. London was my landscape, not his.

After our initial hungry passion had subsided, and each had said how much they'd missed the other, I found myself worryingly lost for words. In Spain we'd chatted and laughed about the people who were working the season, the customers in the club, local gossip. But here we lacked a familiar cast of characters to discuss – apart from the four of us.

So I started to tell him a bit more about our situation. He'd already guessed that Frankie was my mother, and I filled him in on the last couple of years – how Toby and my mum had got together and why I was living with them. I thought if he knew a bit more of our background, he might open up about himself.

And that's how I gradually found out about his life. At least, the bits he decided to tell me. But I suppose we're all like that to some extent, reinventing ourselves, editing our lives for public consumption.

He was a real jack of all trades. Before becoming manager of Club Calypso, he'd worked on fitting it out. He also talked about meetings he'd had with his bosses in Geneva and how he'd acquired a property for them in Playa d'Oro, thirty kilometres down the coast from Aigua Blau, which they were going to open as a second club. And of how he'd been given a generous number of shares in their property company as part of his salary. He told me he'd grown up on a small farm, and had worked on that until he'd been conscripted into the army.

When I asked him why he'd left Sweden, he said, vehemently,'I hate it there. In Sweden, if you would do anything, everyone would know.' I didn't press him further, but I think it was safe to assume that he'd rattled the neighbours with his exploits a few times.

Frankie and Toby left us alone for the first couple of days, which was great to begin with, but I soon found my small pool of recreational activities almost drained. Collins had been to London before so didn't want to do the sightseeing thing. Neither did the cinema or theatre hold much appeal. He seemed to need a lot of exercise, but a girl can only take so much trekking round Kensington Gardens on cold, dank January days. So I was delighted when Toby took Collins off my hands to a football match. It was while they were out that I confided in Frankie that I didn't know how I was going to keep him amused for the rest of the time. She promised to have a word with

Toby and after that, much to my relief, he stepped in as joint entertainments officer.

Collins had told Toby that he wouldn't mind seeing some clubs, to get ideas for the new place in Spain. Frankie was working at The Unicorn most nights, so Toby, Collins and I spent those evenings trawling round sleazy joints in Soho, which were hopeless as models for Collins, but great fun. As a result of staying out till the early hours, we spent our mornings in bed, thus solving the problem of what to do before lunch.

In the afternoons, at Frankie's suggestion, we went swimming at the local baths or took the tube to green places like Hampstead Heath, as an antidote to the smoke and must of the Soho dives, and to burn off some of Collins' excess energy.

At the other end of the nightlife scale, we actually managed to get into a smart Mayfair nightclub, signed in by one of Toby's old school friends who could afford the membership fees. Toby had to lend Collins a suit and tie that evening. When he emerged from the bedroom, my first thought was that he looked as if he was going to a funeral.

'I feel like I'm getting married,' he'd joked.

Toby had laughed. 'So that's why you're wearing black?'

For the first time I wondered if Frankie ever harboured any thoughts of marrying Toby. I hoped not, as from the sound of it, it wasn't high on his list of must-dos. I watched fascinated as Collins preened himself in front of us. This man in a suit and tie seemed to be a completely different variety from the one I'd known in Aigua Blau.

On the day he left, I kissed him goodbye at Victoria station where he was taking the train to the airport. It was an awkward parting. I sensed that he'd already detached himself from me, and from London, and was well on the way to his next destination.

We'd performed a suitably passionate goodbye the night before. He was a considerate lover, who I still found physically attractive, but it bugged me when he spoke to me as if I were a little girl. And there was the language thing. I was constantly having to explain words, expressions, that he didn't understand. His lack of fluency limited our intimacy. When we made love he'd say 'I love you', but always in the heat of passion and never outside of the bedroom.

I travelled back home by bus and, paradoxically, immediately began to miss him. Tomorrow my life would revert to temping and the occasional visit to the cinema or a club with someone from work. I'd be mostly spending evenings in, watching TV or reading. Toby wasn't around much. He often went to see Frankie in The Unicorn, or played music upstairs in his studio while he worked.

It was good to hang out with them at weekends – shopping, exhibitions, concerts and stuff. But I had to be careful not to monopolise Frankie, otherwise Toby got a bit jealous.

Sometimes I'd get invitations to parties but I usually said no, using the excuse that I had a boyfriend. I wasn't quite sure if Collins thought of me as his girlfriend, but it suited me to behave as if I was. I didn't want to complicate matters by dating anyone else while he was still in the picture.

* * *

When she heard my key in the door, Frankie came running downstairs. There was a patio garden at the back of the house, and she led me to the small sunroom which overlooked it. She'd recently joined a psychic awareness group, and had placed several quartz crystals in the room, suspended to catch the light. The winter sun was almost at its zenith and the crystals were twinkling their rainbow reflections all around.

She brought us coffee and cake, most of which I devoured. Collins and I had left without breakfast, as we'd slept through the alarm, and had rushed out so he wouldn't miss the train.

I glanced up and found my mother scanning my face. I guessed she was trying to gauge my reaction to the parting.

'How do you feel, Pan? Sad that he's gone?'

'I'm not sure, Mum. I still like him, but it's not the same...' I was going to say 'as I felt with Mike', but I'd never told her that sorry tale, so I finished, 'as it was in the summer.'

Frankie nodded.

'I know, darling. Toby and I have talked about this, and our theory is that being in love with someone can work, and last, in a certain environment but not necessarily in another. Your dad and I were fine when we were working as a team in the pub. But once that was taken away, it was as if we didn't have our right place to be happy in. Toby calls it the canvas. He says if the background of the picture is repainted, there's a greater chance one of the figures will be painted out as well.'

I had to admit that Collins and I hadn't blended quite so easily in London as we had in Spain, but I was loath to write us off completely.

'Don't forget, Mum, we'll be back in the same place at Easter.'

'I know, Pan. It'll probably be fine. But it won't be quite the same as last year because you'll be working and living together. You'll either get closer. Or...'

Frankie didn't finish, probably because I'd started to cry. Her eyes glowed with compassion.

'Look, if you get out there and find it doesn't work out, or you're homesick, just come straight back. You don't have to stay till the end of the season if you're unhappy.'

I must still have looked glum because she asked me something she never had before. 'Darling, was there someone before Collins you were keen on?'

I started to cry again and found myself nodding.

'He was a boy I met at the Green Oak. But I don't want to talk about him, Mummy.'

* * *

The plane was preparing to land and I pictured Collins waiting for me as my mother had waited nine months earlier. I had six months' supply of the pill, and an abundance of lotions and potions which were cheaper to buy at home than in Spain. I also had a suitcase full of great clothes which Frankie had helped me choose.

I was going to be staying at the Swiss villa and living the good life. What could go wrong?

Chapter 25 – SUMMER 1973

When I rang my father to tell him that I'd handed in my notice at work to tour round Australia for six months with one of my colleagues, Fiona, he went ballistic.

'For God's sake, girl. What's wrong with you? What in hell's name are you throwing away a good job for? There's people'd give their eye teeth to work for that company.'

I could hear Joan in the background asking what on earth was wrong, and hoped she'd be able to calm him down. I hadn't realised how much my career shifts still affected him.

When I'd got back from Spain the second time, I'd done as he wanted and duly registered with agencies for permanent employment – which was a first for me. My good exam grades had got me a job as a management trainee with an oil company the following January. In my opinion, staying in a job I didn't much like for a year and a half, should have been enough to satisfy him. But obviously not. I could hear him ranting and raving to Joan about me, so I butted in.

'Dad. My friend Fiona's in the same section as me. We started on the same day. And she doesn't like it there either. Our supervisor's horrible. She gets us to do her job when we should be shadowing other people in the company. We'd both decided to leave, so what's the difference if we look for new jobs now or in six months' time?'

My dad snorted. 'I wash my hands of you. You have no loyalty to your employer. No loyalty to your friends. You've cut yourself off from everyone round here. When I think of the high hopes we had for you. And how you've turned out. Look at Cecilia Byrne. She's just graduated as a teacher. She'll be set up for the rest of her life. And what will you have? Bugger all.'

I listened in astonishment. My father had never before sworn in a direct conversation with me. I'd heard him swear in the distance – when he'd hammered his thumb instead of a nail – that sort of thing. Or, under his breath, when he was driving and someone cut him up.

But he'd always moderated his language in my presence. Just as I was about to put the phone down, there were a couple of clicks and Joan came on the line.

'Hello. Pandora. Are you still there, love?'

'Yes. I'm still here.'

She lowered her voice. 'Your dad's upset. I'm sorry he shouted at you. He's gone into the garden now to cool off. Don't take any notice of what he said. He's been a bit under the weather lately, and it's made him irritable.'

My stomach churned the way it does when you think something might be wrong with your parent. He'd looked all right the last time I'd seen him. But that was how long ago? It must have been around the time of his birthday in February. It was the end of June now.

'Is he ill, Joan? It's nothing serious, is it?'

'He's been suffering a bit with his stomach. Dr O'Brien thinks he may have an ulcer and he's made him cut down on rich foods and alcohol, and he isn't taking kindly to the new diet.'

I felt a warm surge of gratitude for Mrs B. She was technically Mrs F now but I'd always think of her as Mrs B. If it wasn't for her, who would be looking after my dad? Certainly not my mother. Nor me.

'Thanks, Joan. I don't know what he'd do without you. I'm so glad he's got you.'

There was a sharp intake of breath from her and a sort of gulp, and then we both started to cry. She was the first to recover and said, in a thick voice, 'When are you leaving? Will you be able to pop round and see us before you go?'

I must say that I hadn't thought about bidding anyone a special farewell. It wasn't as if I was emigrating. And then there was the business of my dad's disapproval. Would he really want to see me?

'If you think it won't upset him, I'll come.'

So we arranged I'd have Sunday lunch with them, and my father, usually the most undemonstrative of men, actually hugged me when I arrived on their doorstep with pink roses for Joan and half a bottle of Irish whiskey for him. Joan had sworn me to secrecy on the subject of his bad stomach, so I had to take him his usual present or he'd have smelt a rat. Joan cooked a roast pork dinner, but there was no crackling for him, and for pudding just a small piece of apple pie with no cream.

After lunch, we sat in the front room, to which Joan had added personal touches like flowery curtains, lace doilies and reproduction side tables with tooled leather insets. These were the remnants of the disposal of her house and its contents on her marriage to my dad. My mother's taste had been more contemporary, but I found the revamped room warm and inviting.

A picture of the Lady of Shalott, hanging above the fireplace, made me think of the Tennyson poem. And of how the only way she was allowed to see the world was as a reflection in a mirror. Until one day the handsome Lancelot passed by and she couldn't resist looking at him directly from her window. Then the curse caused the mirror to crack so she left her tower, and floated down the river towards Camelot to find him, but died in the boat before she got there, never attaining her new life, her love unrequited. It was a sad story, but part of me thought she'd probably been spared a great disappointment, as who could say whether Lancelot would have returned her love?

Over coffee, I told them about the horrible Mrs Drake who'd made Fiona's life and mine a misery, and in the end even my dad was nodding in sympathy along with Joan. They couldn't wait to show me their new colour television. They switched it on and Joan and I watched the black and white Sunday afternoon film together while my dad read the paper. Then Joan produced sandwiches and cakes for tea. I must have put on a couple of pounds at least that day.

At seven o'clock my Dad gave me a lift to the tube station, and on the journey there he said, 'How's your mum, Dora?'

'She's fine, Dad. Still working at The Unicorn in the King's Road.'

I sensed my dad's surprise that I'd told him where she worked, but I really didn't see any need to conceal that fact now they were divorced.

'The Unicorn. Who's running that, do you know?'

'He's called Richard. Can't remember his last name.'

My dad's attention must have wandered because we narrowly missed hitting the car in front, which had stopped at the traffic lights.

'Would it be Tait? Richard Tait?'

It sounded familiar. I pictured the name of the licensee over the pub door and I saw that very name. 'I think so. Do you know him, Dad?'

'Oh, I know him all right. He and his wife were trainees with us but he couldn't keep his eyes off your mother.'

I felt almost as shocked to hear these words from him, as I had been to hear him say 'bugger' on the phone.

'I've never seen his wife. I thought he was single.'

My dad shook his head. 'Wouldn't be surprised if he ditched her years ago.'

We were nearly at the station, so he slowed down and instead of dropping me off quickly, he parked in a bus lay-by so he could finish what he wanted to say.

'Is your mother still with the Toby bloke?'

I was surprised at this question, considering that my dad knew very well that Toby was providing me with living quarters.

'Of course she is, Dad.'

My dad's face reddened. 'But she's forty-five. And he's, what? Thirty?'

'I think he's twenty-eight.'

'Well how long will that last? As soon as she starts to lose her looks he'll be on to the next one. A young bloke like him. Big house, plenty of money. He could probably get any woman he wanted.'

He glowered at the dashboard and went on.

'Look, Dora. You'd tell me if he ever...'

The look of horror on my face stopped my dad in his tracks. We both sat in silence for a moment to regain our composure.

'Dad. Don't worry. Toby's always been like a big brother to me. And as for Richard, Mum only ever talks about him as her boss.'

My dad looked relieved, but when he spoke, his voice sounded faintly strangled.

'I just wanted to make sure that you weren't going to Australia to get away from anything. Or anyone. You know you've always got a home with us, don't you, love?'

I looked at my dad and I loved him so much it hurt. And yet no matter how much I loved him I knew I'd never be able to make his home my home again. I leaned over and kissed him softly goodbye on the cheek.

'Thanks, Dad. But believe me, the only person I want to get away from is horrible old Mrs Drake.'

* * *

When I got back to Mulberry Walk, Frankie and Toby were in the drawing room with some of their friends, playing records and drinking cocktails. I waved to them as I passed the open door and Frankie came out and walked me to a smaller room, with book cases and a comfortable old sofa, where we tended to go if we wanted to read.

'Come on then, tell me all about it,' she said. I gave her a highly edited version, but I did tell her that Frank had been ill.

'That's strange,' she brooded. 'Your dad could always eat and drink anything. I hope it's just a passing thing.'

'What are you girls up to?' Toby had put his head round the door and was waving an empty glass. 'Anyone for a Tom Collins?'

We said that we'd love a drink and soon Toby reappeared with three full glasses of pale liquid bubbled over ice, topped with slices of orange and a glacé cherry. He raised his glass as if he was celebrating something.

'By the way, Frankie, have you told Pandora that Collins phoned earlier?'

Frankie shook her head. 'Haven't had a chance. Why don't you tell her? You took the call.'

'Well,' went on Toby enthusiastically, 'he's getting married in France in September, and he wanted to know if we'd all like to go to the wedding. I told him you'd be in Australia. But how would you feel if Frankie and I went? I wouldn't mind seeing him again. Or *la belle France*, for that matter.'

This news wasn't unexpected, but it still grabbed my insides like a vice. Frankie took my hand and shot Toby a disapproving stare. Toby was often in trouble for dropping clangers. For an artist, it was amazing how much he saw in black and white.

'Sorry, Pan. Was that thoughtless? Didn't know you still cared. Thought you'd been the one to chuck him.'

Frankie spoke quickly and spontaneously. 'That doesn't mean you stop loving the memory of what you once had with that person. People don't just stop feeling, once they part.'

Her words hung in the air and each of us was silent for a little while. I imagined she was thinking about my father. I didn't know what Toby's romantic history had been – only that he'd dumped his previous girlfriend in favour of Frankie. But he was probably thinking of Frankie's earlier, happy years with my dad and wondering how often she thought about him. As for my thoughts, well, as always, they flew to Mike. But I'd locked that box, so they fluttered back to Collins.

Our parting had been hard for both of us in the end. Our relationship had started easily enough, then stuttered a bit when he came to stay. We'd revived it in Spain, then it had stuttered again, and climaxed with a passion which surprised us both. But by that time I'd lost faith in him, and there was no going back.

'It's okay. It would never have worked out with us.' I managed a weak smile for Toby. I always felt sorry for him when he was in trouble with Frankie. 'Go to the wedding and give him my love.' Keeping my face deadpan, I continued, 'But if you get a chance to trip up the bride, stand on her train or push her downstairs, be my guest.'

That evening I joined the party and drank copiously of the various cocktails that kept appearing. But when they brought out the LSD I decided to call it a day and so did Frankie, leaving Toby and his friends to party till dawn.

* * *

The next day, I dragged myself to work despite having a colossal hangover. There was only this week to get through, and then freedom. Fiona and I usually lunched in the large, subsidised restaurant, but it was such a lovely day that we bought sandwiches instead and sat on a bench in a nearby square. She asked me about my weekend and I blurted out that I'd missed a phone call from my ex.

'Can you believe, he was ringing to ask me to his wedding. And my mum and her boyfriend are actually thinking of going. Fi, I'm so glad I'll be thousands of miles away.'

Fiona looked intrigued. I'd only briefly mentioned Collins to her, because by the time I'd joined the company, he was history.

'Tell me what happened, Pan. Who's he marrying?'

'A French girl. I don't know her, but I've seen her once. I walked in on them when they were in bed together.'

Fiona gasped. 'My God. What a nightmare. Go on.'

'He was working in a new club down the coast, getting it ready, and four of us from the Calypso decided to go and see how it was coming along. We drove over in the daytime and some workmen let us in. We asked where he was and they told us he was upstairs.

'There was no one on the first level, so we went up to the top. There were some rooms being converted into staff quarters. One of the guys, Jean-Claude, pushed open the doors expecting to find him working in one of them, but instead he was in bed with this French girl. Actually, it was an old mattress on the floor. You could see she was French. It was the Bardot pout and underarm hair.'

Fi was listening open-mouthed. 'What did you do? I hope you lamped him one.'

I laughed. I wasn't familiar with the expression but I assumed she meant slapped his face.

'I just stood there feeling as if I wanted the floor to open up and swallow me. It was bad enough being cheated on. But in front of three guys I worked with...'

Fi was eager to get to the nitty gritty. 'So what did he do?'

'He jumped up and grabbed some jeans. Then he just stood there, sort of half grinning and shrugging his shoulders. I was so shocked I couldn't move. Finally, he came over and kissed me on the cheek and said, "Pippi, you didn't tell me you were coming".'

'Why did he call you Pippi?' asked Fiona.

'I blushed slightly. 'Oh, it's a character from a Swedish book. A little girl.'

Fiona's nose wrinkled, so I hurried on.

'I think he was betting on me not being the type to make a scene. He was the boss, so none of the boys was going to challenge him. Except Jean-Claude, who'd been managing the Calypso while he was away. He looked daggers at Collins and said something in French to the girl.'

'Was she embarrassed?'

'Not at all. She even had the cheek to tell us to get out while she got dressed. Anyway, we all went down to have a look at the club, Collins included. It was about two weeks away from opening, so it looked pretty impressive. The dance floor was enormous. And there were doves in massive cages. Normally, we'd have had a drink and he'd have played some music, but the atmosphere was so awkward that we didn't stay long. I saw the French girl leaving a few minutes after we came downstairs. She tried to get his attention, but he looked away.'

'Cheeky cow. I'd have killed her. So did he at least have the decency to apologise?'

Fiona was showing herself to be deficient in her understanding of the alpha male.

'Not really. He would never have said sorry in front of the boys, anyway.'

'So was that it?'

'Not quite. He walked us to the car, told them to wait, and took me back into the club. Then he kissed me and I could feel his whole body shaking. All he could say was that sometimes he needed a woman and if I wasn't there, and someone else was, he couldn't help himself.'

Fiona shook her head in disapproval. 'Yeah, yeah, yeah, usual story. Complete lack of self-control so they blame it on biology—'

I closed my eyes, trying to erase the memory of Collins and the girl together in that room.

'—So did you give him the elbow, or what?'

I sighed. Nothing was ever that simple.

'It was tricky. I'd told everyone at home I'd be in Spain until the end of the season. And I'd never been completely sure I was going to be his exclusive girlfriend, anyway.

'It'd been great at first. After the Easter crowd, the Calypso was quiet, so we both went to Playa d'Oro and worked on the new club. Collins got me to do some artwork in the powder room. It was easy compared to what I'd done the year before.

'But then the season got going, I went back to the Calypso, and he stayed in Playa d'Oro all week. We just saw each other when he came back to Aigua Blau at weekends. The fact is, sleeping around had been a way of life for him. And he was gorgeous-looking, so girls were always throwing themselves at him. It would've been unrealistic to expect him to be faithful when he was living away.

'The last thing I wanted was to come home halfway through the summer, so I stuck it out. The villa I was staying in was lovely. The maid did everything, even my washing. I just decided to enjoy myself and play it cool.'

'So did you sleep with him again?'

I looked at my watch. It was ten to two and time to walk back to the office, so we left the square and talked as we walked.

'When I felt like it. But, at first, I refused him more often than not.'

Fiona nodded in agreement. 'Treat 'em mean, keep 'em keen.'

That was a mantra we often repeated to each other. The sexual revolution didn't have to mean total availability. If we didn't use our power to say no, what power was left to us?

'Yeah,' I went on, 'I thought two could play at that game, so when he came back at the weekends I made sure he saw me chatting up some of the best-looking blokes. He didn't like it but I said he couldn't expect me to be faithful to him if he hadn't been to me. I even took one of them back to the villa when he wasn't there.'

'Pandora! It's all coming out now. You're a dark horse. I thought you didn't sleep around.'

'I don't. It only happened once. But the funny thing was, Collins found out about it and it really got to him.'

'So did you ever see him again after you went home?'

'No. I told him it was over just before I left. Although it was hard because he was back at the Calypso full time at the end of the season and we'd got close again, just like we'd been the summer before. You know, really into each other.'

We were in the lift and Fi delivered her question quickly while she had a chance.

'So why did he decide to marry the French girl?'

I happened to know the answer to this, as Jean-Claude had written to me earlier in the year with news of their engagement.

'Her family are loaded. Collins worked most of last season at Playa. Her people spend every August there at their villa, and she spent all her time in the club. Wouldn't let any other girl near him.'

'Mercenary stalked by spoilt little rich girl,' said Fiona, with a cynical curl of the lip. 'Say no more.'

The lift pinged and deposited us opposite the glass doors leading to our office. Mrs Drake was frowning and looking at her watch as we sat down. I reached into my bag for a tissue to dab away the tears that had sprung up against my will, and briefly touched the note that Collins had sent me a week or two before Jean-Claude's letter had arrived. And to which I hadn't responded.

It simply said:

Pippi, I'd like to talk to you. Ring me at this number before the end of the month. This is your last chance to change your mind.

Collins xx

Chapter 26 – 2003

It was the Thursday following the Cakes For All Occasions weekend, or what I'd come to think of as 'the Zac Weekend' and I was wondering when, if ever, he would ring, when the postman knocked, bearing gifts.

They were gifts in the form of letters. A padded envelope from The Enoch Society and a slimmer one from Oven Ready Productions, which read as follows:

Dear Mrs Armstrong,

Many thanks for your recent hospitality in allowing our company to observe and film the workshop presented by Olivier Dubois. We are pleased to report that the location was more than satisfactory.

I am therefore delighted to be able to offer you a contract for exclusive use of The Cedars during the months of October and November this year. If you accept, it will be necessary to make some adjustments and additions to the kitchen and the dining room. With your permission, these will be made, at our expense, as soon as possible.

In addition, I understand that you can offer accommodation for those members of our team who might need it. We will have a catering wagon on site, so all catering will be provided by us. If you could submit an invoice for full occupancy for the entire period, I would be obliged.

I have enclosed details of our standard location payments. I hope very much that you will find our terms acceptable.

Please don't hesitate to contact me to discuss it further.

Yours sincerely,

Zachary Willoughby

My eager fingers opened the document in search of the location payment, which was generous enough to make me gasp, there being several noughts involved. I closed my eyes and felt an enormous wave of relief, picturing The Cedars with a spanking new roof. I found myself saying, 'Oh thank you, thank you,' over and over again.

Oscar came to see what all the excitement was about and joined in, tearing round and round the garden. So I decided to go for a run with him in tow, to get the adrenalin out of our systems. I wanted to be calm and relaxed when I rang Zac.

It occurred to me, as I ran through the woods, that I should ring Olivier beforehand, to check he'd been hired. So when we got home, that's the first thing I did.

'Ello, yes. Pandora?'

'Hi Olly. Can you talk?'

'Yes, I can. You sound excited. 'Ave you heard from the delicious Zac, by any chance?'

'Yes, I've had a letter. You got the job, I hope.'

'Of course, *ma chère*. I had no doubt.'

'Great. Did you know Oven Ready were going to ask for The Cedars as a location?'

'Yes, yes. They were planning to use a studio but when they saw your 'ouse, they said they prefer that. I drop you a hint on Monday, *non*? When I said there might be a nice surprise? I couldn't say too much because Zac had to consult with his partners. I'm so 'appy for you, darling. It's time something good 'appen to you.'

I swallowed down the lump in my throat which always arose when somebody gave me some sympathy.

'Thanks, Olly. So are you pleased with it as a location?'

'Of course. The kitchen just needs one more oven, a bigger fridge, bit more equipment. It won't take them long. And big bonus for you – they leave it all there when they go.'

'Sounds good to me. I'll get on to Zac right away and give him the go ahead.'

'That's my girl. Your place is perfect, because Zac want to show people learning to make the recipes and eating them afterwards. So it'll be a sort of repetition of the workshop scenario. I think you find they make the dining room, 'ow you say – hup to scratch, as well.'

The dining room was a large room but sparsely furnished with two oak refectory tables pushed together, surrounded by an assortment of dining chairs. A dresser in a darker wood had been acquired at auction on the same day. Mike and I had reckoned that if the stuff was second-hand, we wouldn't worry if people left rings from damp-bottomed coffee mugs on the tables.

I tried to picture how the kitchen and dining room would look, after the refurbishing. It'd be a waste if they stayed unused once the production company moved out. But I was never going to throw any banquets, was I? My family consisted of me, Oscar, and my mother, who rarely ventured up from Somerset these days.

'Well, the dining room could certainly do with it,' I responded. 'I'll have to make more use of it once it's tarted up. It'd be a shame not to.' There was a slight pause. 'Olly. Are you still there?'

'Yes, I'm here. I may be able to help you with that, *chérie*. We'll see. *A tout à l'heure*.'

I had no idea what he meant and I'd just remembered something I'd wanted to ask him, so it hardly registered.

'Okay. By the way, Olly, what about the shop? Can you be spared for that long?'

'*Mais oui*. My filming only takes two weeks, and I've found a good *chef pâtissier* who's coming in to cover. I'm filming for the first 'alf of October, that's all.'

'Wow. I've just realised. That's only a couple of weeks away. So who's going to be there for the rest of the time?'

Olly laughed indulgently.

'The other chefs in the programme. I'm the cakes and puddings man. There'll be someone for starters, main courses and supper snacks.' He then named three quite-well-known chefs.

'Who knows, you may even be entertaining them in your guest rooms.'

'Would you mind rephrasing that, *m'sieu*.'

'I'm joking, of course. Although I'm sure if the gorgeous Zac arrived again on your doorstep, you'd be the 'ostest with the mostest. *C'est vrai*? See you tomorrow.'

Olly's teasing about Zac had made me even more nervous about calling him. The very idea of it was causing my heart to race. The letter had sounded pretty official. Maybe he'd had second thoughts and that's how he wanted our relationship to continue.

I poured myself a sweet sherry for Dutch courage and waited a couple of minutes for it to take effect before I dialled the number. A woman's voice answered. I kept my tone formal.

'Could I speak to Mr Willoughby, please? It's Pandora Armstrong.'

'What is it in connection with?'

'It's a location offer. I'm calling in response to his letter.'

'Hold on, please, I'll just see if he's available.'

This was the moment when she'd ring his extension and see if he wanted to speak to the caller. And if he wanted to avoid the call, he'd tell her to say he was in a meeting.

I finished the contents of my glass and tried to rehearse what I might say. Probably just hello, I'm fine, I'd like to accept the offer, thanks, goodbye.

'Hello.' It was his voice.

'Hello.' My mind went quite blank and silence ensued.

'Pandora. It's me. How are you?'

'Fine.' Then I found my voice. I thanked him, told him of course I'd jump at the chance, asked him when the fitters would come to install the oven, etc, until he gently interrupted me.

'Great. I'm so glad you're pleased. We'll give them your number so they can speak to you directly. And the interior designer for the other room. We'll need the contract signed first, though. Any chance I could pop by this evening and get it done?'

I felt as if all my birthdays had come at once. Although at my age I refuse to have any more, so change that to Christmases. I felt all warm and flushed, but that could have been the second schooner of sherry. I was refusing the menopause, so it definitely wasn't that.

'This evening's fine. Would you like me to pick you up from the station?'

'Yes. Thanks. I'll probably be on the train by about five. I'll give you a ring then.'

Oh bliss. What a wonderful day. To hear I'd be making real money from The Cedars at last and also meeting up with Zac again. I could hardly wait.

* * *

Later that day, there I was, all dolled up, hanging around for Zac's call to say he was on the train, when I remembered the other letter. I'd left it in the hall and forgotten all about it in my rush to prepare for the evening. I'd spent my time tidying the house, beautifying myself, and raiding the delicatessen in town for a selection of appetisers that could be conflated into a salad of sorts. Keep it simple, I thought. No point in slaving over a hot stove and then him saying, thanks for the contract, I'm off now. My initial euphoria had worn off at the same rate as the sherry, and I was now in a state of being almost certain it was just a business call.

I picked up the padded envelope and opened it with trepidation, hoping that Cass wasn't into letter bombs. Inside was a letter and a cardboard box containing a small alabaster pot and some written instructions. I quickly read the letter which contained comments on my Level One essay and details of Levels Two and Three. It read as follows:

Dear Pandora,

Thank you for completing Level One, when you described the happiest time of your life. The purpose of this exercise was for you to re-engage with the feelings you experienced at that time. The memories you wrote of were full of love. Your heart, and the heart of your loved one, Mike, opened to give and receive love. But Mike was also the cause of much sorrow and he remains so because of his physical absence in death.

In life there is always the prospect of joy leading to sorrow, for it is part of the human experience to lose dear ones. For every positive there exists an opposite. You cannot experience the summer sun without the ice of winter; the light without the shade. The Society is concerned that your unexpressed grief in this and other areas has forced your life out of balance. These matters must be addressed if you are to bring harmony into your life and live without anxiety and fear.

The key to happiness is to bring balance into the way you view the ups and downs of life. Choose to see the positive in every situation as it arises. Seek peace and harmony. Do not torment yourself by dwelling on painful thoughts of the past. Bring them into the air, into the light, and release them. In the words of the Buddha, 'Peace comes from within. Do not seek it without.'

Above all, ensure that your heart is fully open to giving and receiving love. This is the state the heart should naturally be in at all times. Please strive to feel compassion for others. Feel gratitude for the blessings you have. Forgive others for perceived transgressions.

There was a bit more along the same lines but I got the message. Less of the Poor Me and more of the Pollyanna. Smarting slightly, I turned my attention to the next sheet.

Level Two – Assaying Your Life

'The unexamined human life is not worth living.' – Socrates

We have seen from Level One how you have experienced separation and sorrow, resulting in periods of distress and anxiety.

A conscious examination of any life will reveal patterns of behaviour which are impediments to spiritual growth and happiness. If a person remains blind to these patterns, much of their life will consist of unconscious repetition – going through life repeating the same mistakes as though they are hypnotised. It is the constant mental replaying of unhappy events caused by this repetition of adverse patterns of behaviour which saps the energy.

It is clear that your depression and anxiety are in need of remedial action. To assist you to wake up and break out of any harmful patterns, The Enoch Society strongly suggests that you write more of your life and times with the loved one, Mike, and of any others with whom you have had loving relationships. You will be writing with the intention of examining the events leading up to, and following, the peaks and troughs of your life so far, and looking for any unhelpful behavioural patterns which led to similar conditions recurring.

In addition, you must also state your intention, before you start each session, that you are writing the sad thoughts out of your system. Think of it as a sort of healing.

This assignment is for your personal development; there is no need to send your manuscript to the Society. But perhaps, one day, you can share it with others.

Please start your writing as soon as possible, as it is advisable to finish this before starting the final part of the course, Level Three.

I felt quite persuaded by this analysis, although I wasn't sure about the Society's suggestion that I should write what amounted to my romantic memoirs. But if this was the way to smooth out my ups and downs – to silence the poor me-me-me monotone inside my head – could I afford not to?

I was curious to see what Level Three was all about, so I consulted the third sheet of paper.

Level Three – Renewal

This unit aims to connect you to higher planes of awareness, enabling you to complete the release from despair and depression suffered by those who are shackled to negative memories of the past.

To help you free yourself from this cycle, we have enclosed some sacred ointment containing oils distilled from bark, resin, rhizome and roots. These elements: cinnamon, myrrh and spikenard, were used by the ancient phoenix to create the fire in which she was reborn.

If you anoint yourself with this chrism as directed, your sadness will be replaced by hope. Your old, programmed ways of thinking and behaving will die and your new paradigm – your pattern of seeing the world – will emerge. You will have reached the position of an anointed one, anointed with chrism, from which the word 'Christ' comes.

The process must start at the time of a new moon and culminate two weeks later at full moon. More detailed instructions are within the box.

Finally, before you make the decision to finish the course and proceed into a state of spiritual rebirth, please consider what you are taking on, for there comes with it a responsibility to help and heal others.

This does not mean you have to give up your life and go to work among the poor and suffering of the world. Although some have. No, there is no need to change your life radically. But you will be expected to consciously maintain your enlightened way of thinking and behaving by meditating regularly, eating healthily, exercising your physical body and avoiding alcohol and other addictive habits. Otherwise you risk sinking back into unhealthy ways of thinking and your newly achieved, ideal paradigm, will be compromised.

Know that once you have become spiritually awakened, you must make a conscious effort to transform any difficult situations by your very presence. You will have the power to do this because you will be filled with light (en-lightened). Your function will be to raise the energy of any person or situation that crosses your path simply by focusing on your Oneness with All That Is. In this way, you will help others with their soul evolution.

All this will become clearer to you once the process has been accomplished.

I hope our correspondence has been, and will be, of help to you in your hour of need. It only remains for me to wish you Godspeed in your endeavours to bring harmony and balance into your life and into the lives of others.

Cassiel.

This was heavy stuff indeed, and before I had a chance to absorb it, the phone started ringing. It was Zac. He was on the train and would arrive at the station in twenty minutes, so I put everything back into the envelope and tucked it into the bureau drawer.

The journey to the station to pick up Zac gave me a chance to reflect on the matter. I decided that I'd contact Enoch as soon as I could and ask his advice. We hadn't been in touch since that day last week when Olly had phoned and interrupted us. I'd been so busy with the workshop and then, falling in love – or lust – with Zac, that I'd neglected to get back to him.

Drawing into the pick-up area of the station forecourt, I felt weak at the knees when I saw Zac waiting there, in all his Viking glory. He opened the car door, ducked his head, and folded himself into the passenger seat, his long legs clutching his briefcase in a pincer grip.

'Not much room in these toy cars.'

I laughed. 'Oscar never complains. You're in his seat.'

He patted my left leg. 'Come on, old girl. To a suitable hostelry. And don't spare the horses.'

Chapter 27 – 2003

Seeing that Zac had ordered me to a 'hostelry' for a drink, I didn't suggest we went back to my place. It was primarily a contract signing meeting, so best not to assume he'd be wanting to take up where we'd left off, romantically speaking. Anyway, for all I knew he might have a string of women on the go. He was good-looking and charming enough, that was for sure.

As he didn't know the area, there was no point in asking him to choose a place. Judging it still prudent to avoid the Lamb and Flag, I headed for the best hotel in the vicinity. When we got there, Zac looked impressed.

'Really, Pandora. No need for you to go to this expense. Will there be champagne and chocolates on the pillow?'

My heart gave a little leap at this. Pillow talk. So he must have bed on his mind. Yippee.

'Now, now, Zachary. This is a business meeting. We're just having a drink at the bar. Anyway, I'd need a bank loan to spend a night here.'

We got out of the car and he took my hand. 'Only my mother called me Zachary. You remind me of her sometimes.'

I immediately felt as if I was holding hands with a little boy. Deflated wasn't the word. Our feet crunched the gravel of the car park in the direction of the main entrance. This might be a good time to broach the subject of my age.

'I hope I don't remind you of her because I'm so ancient.'

He stopped and took my other hand so we were facing each other.

'Actually she died when I was a teenager. She was only forty-two.'

I felt a rush of sympathy. The mood had changed. Zac looked solemn.

'How old *are* you, Pandora?'

'Fifty-one.'

I don't know why I was so honest. Must have been the influence of that pesky pair, Enoch and Cass. It was still light enough for me to detect a flicker of surprise in his eyes, but his reply was faultless and it reset the scale, from major to minor.

'The perfect age for someone like me, who prefers a woman in her prime.'

'What, like Miss Jean Brodie?'

'I was thinking more along the lines of prime steak.'

'Are you saying I sizzle, Mr Willoughby?'

He laughed, then kissed me for quite a long time. As our lips parted, I took the plunge. Not lingually, of course – I didn't stick my tongue down his throat – but verbally.

'So how old are *you,* Zac?'

'Forty-five.'

I felt a glimmer of surprise myself at this news. He was older than I'd thought, and six years' difference between us wasn't too bad. But I'd still have preferred it in the other direction. We hadn't yet continued walking. He seemed to be waiting for my reaction. I decided to flatter him as a thank-you for my Oven Ready contract.

'You certainly don't look it.'

He grinned. 'Neither do you. Shall we call it a draw, then?'

He took my hand and cantered onward, pulling me and my high heels behind him.

'Come on, old lady, I'm dying for a drink.'

Over champagne cocktails in the hotel bar, which Zac had insisted on, I duly signed the contracts, one for me and one for him, which he countersigned, putting his copy into his briefcase. My clutch bag wasn't really big enough for my copy, so he smiled and took it from me.

'I'll look after it for the time being.'

This was another good sign. It could mean he intended to come home with me. My pulse had started to pound at the prospect, and then I remembered the Buddhist precept I'd read recently. Craving is the cause of suffering. And how I craved him. Mercifully, Zac's urbane drawl interrupted my train of thought.

'So what are you planning to do with the money?' he asked playfully. 'A world tour?'

I made a wistful face. 'I wish.'

There were so many things we didn't know about each other. Maybe he thought I was rolling in cash just because I owned a big house and had been married to a rich man. Two rich men, actually. But the fact was, that when we made new wills after we got married, I'd insisted on Mike leaving his whole estate to Danny and his family, even though he'd wanted to leave me half of it.

I already had the flat in Fulham, which gave me a steady rental income, so I told him I was happy with The Cedars and Phoenix Cottage. It was my way of saying that I loved him for himself.

But the truth was, that these three properties were quite expensive to run. What remained of the settlement I'd got from Jay, had gone towards buying The Cedars. I had no savings left. My only regular income was the rent from the London flat, and my wage from Olivier, so the Oven Ready contract was very welcome indeed.

The champagne had loosened my tongue, so I merrily revealed all this to Zac, although I thought it best to keep the bit about the roof to myself. I didn't want him thinking he was hiring a faulty property.

He seemed quite interested when I mentioned Jay.

'Really? You were married to James Jay. He was quite big in his day. Why'd you split up? Was it the usual – sex, drugs, 'n rock 'n roll?'

'Kind of. I wanted to get pregnant and couldn't. But he got there in the end. With someone else.'

Zac looked slightly surprised. 'Didn't you have any tests done? Maybe you could have got some treatment.'

I always felt uncomfortable when people asked me this, because it made me feel as if I was complaining about a condition I could have had corrected. The fact was, we didn't want to rock the boat. I suppose it was a sort of defence mechanism – best not to know which of us it was, because then the other one might have a reason to leave. What cowards we'd been. And for some reason I'd been convinced it was Jay who was firing blanks. And I was nervous that if it was established as a fact that he was, it would make him feel less of a man.

This was a touch too Freudian to admit, so I just replied, 'I sort of lost interest after that.'

But the memory of how I'd felt when I'd found out about Debbie had wounded me, so I excused myself to the powder room to cover the tracks the tears had forged through my make-up.

* * *

While I was in there, my mind replayed the scene of finding out about Debbie. An anonymous letter arrived at the flat a few days after Jay and the band had played at the Live Aid Concert, which he'd said was one of the best days of his life. Anyway, this letter arrived, telling me that I 'had a right to know' that Jay had been having an affair with Debbie, and she'd given birth to his twins. I thought it was just one of the nutty letters that wafted in from time to time, but when I showed it to Jay he went white and started shaking. It was then I knew it was true. The shock made me feel faint and I half-slumped to the floor.

All I remember is Jay saying over and over that he was sorry. I just sat on the floor. Like a rag doll. Numb. Unable to speak.

I could see him now, pleading with me, tears streaming down his face.

'We can do it, Pan. We can work it out. I can be here with you, and with them as well. They're just babies. They're part of me. I can't turn my back on them. I want you to be part of their lives too.'

He got me a glass of water and cradled me like a child, holding it to my lips as I sipped.

'Or we could all live together if you like. Us, the dogs. The twins, Debbie.'

At the mention of her name, I knocked the glass of water out of his hand and made for the bedroom where I could finally unleash my grief in all its muscle-wracking ferocity.

He didn't follow me and I lay there sobbing, waiting for him to go out.

When I heard him leave the flat, I packed as much of his stuff into two suitcases as I could, and had them couriered round to the studio where he was recording that day. The courier also carried my letter telling him not to come back, that I would send the rest of his things to our house in Great Marlow, and that he'd be hearing from my solicitor. I followed that by getting a locksmith to change the locks – in case he did come back and I weakened, and let him stay.

Then I smoked a spliff and rang my favourite neighbour, Peter, from the basement flat, to see if he fancied a drink. Never one to refuse, he was at the door within five minutes. We consumed three bottles of Cristal between us, the last glass of which I raised to Jay.

'I propose a toast to James Jay. For proving himself to be a real man after all.' Then I collapsed and had to be put to bed.

In a funny sort of way, it was a relief finally to know which one of us it was. And when I met up again with Mike I found myself actually feeling glad he'd got Val pregnant and had Danny, because if he'd married barren old me, he wouldn't have had a lovely son and two beautiful grandchildren, would he?

When I got back to the bar, I found Zac was peering at his smart-phone. Oh no. Please don't let him be a texting fiend, reporting to someone somewhere of his progress into an old bird's bed. He looked up as I sat down. Happy to see a second champagne cocktail on the counter, I lifted the glass.

'Cheers. This is lovely – you should have let me buy these. I'm the one celebrating.' I nodded towards his phone. 'Anything interesting?'

'I was just googling James Jay. Thought I'd see what he's doing now.'

I was a bit taken aback. All this instant information access was disconcerting.

'Did you find anything?'

'Loads of old stuff. But there is something recent. His partner died this year in a car crash. Says here he's got five children. The youngest's only eleven.'

He studied me for a reaction. I could feel the blood draining from my cheeks but I needed to wait till I was on my own to process this disturbing piece of news, so I went all out for pokerfaced and diversionary tactics.

'How sad. I didn't know.' I paused for a moment as a mark of respect, then continued. 'Listen, Zac. Are you hungry? We should eat. I can't keep drinking on an empty stomach. Would you like to come back to the cottage for something? Or do you have to get back...?'

My voice trailed away of its own accord. I so wanted him to come back. For some reason even more so after hearing about Debbie's death.

He put the phone away and grinned. 'A light bite at your place sounds just the thing, Mrs Armstrong. Soon as you've polished off your champers, we can be on our way.'

* * *

Later, having survived the drive home – those two cocktails had gone straight to my head – and wined and dined on Cabernet Sauvignon and tapas, Zac and I found ourselves in bed together. Actually, there were three people in the bed – until I hauled Oscar out of it and imprisoned him in the kitchen. How he howled. But a gal's's gotta do what a gal's gotta do.

Our love-making was eager and more fervent than before. In fact, as soon as we'd got through the front door we'd headed for the kitchen, crammed some food into our mouths, glugged some wine and taken the rest upstairs with us.

I put it down to the highly charged memories the evening had stirred up. There was Zac's of his mother, and mine of Jay. Plus, of course, Debbie's death. That had shaken me. She'd been younger than me, for God's sake. Shades of mortality or what?

Zac was now lying beside me with his eyes closed. The way his lips fell into a smile, even at rest, was very like Collins had looked when he slept. The first time I'd met Zac, I'd thought of Collins. Had that been a sign to steer clear of him? Maybe the similarity wasn't just physical. Maybe Zac was a rover as well. Unwilling to commit to one job, one country, one woman.

The wine bottle, which was round Zac's side of the bed, was empty now. I took a sip of water instead and wondered what would happen next. Would he stay? I thought he might have fallen asleep for the night, but his drowsy voice broke the silence.

'I should be getting back really, hon. Got an eight-thirty breakfast meeting tomorrow. Can you believe it? I think Ben and Greig do it on purpose so they've got an excuse to get off early for the weekend. And now your contract's signed, I'd better get the ball rolling.'

I presumed Ben and Greig were his partners. I don't know what I'd expected to hear, but I felt a little used. You'd never have known it, though, from my tone of voice.

'No probs,' I piped brightly. 'Do you mind if I call you a taxi? Don't want to get done for drink driving.'

'Indeed not,' he smiled. 'Couldn't have that on my conscience.'

I put on a wrap and made for the door. He called me back.

'Pandora. I've promised to see my sister and her family this weekend, so I'll be in touch next week. Is that okay?'

I turned and flashed the most brilliant smile I could muster.

'Of course it is.'

Twenty minutes later the taxi hooted, Zac pecked my cheek, and disappeared into the dusk.

This was Oscar's cue to beg for a treat. The smell of the tapas had been driving him crazy. I was so glad he was here with me – a constant presence I could rely on. I settled down on the sofa and he jumped up beside me, forgiving me for the low-fat healthy dog chew I'd fobbed him off with. He always came closer when I was feeling down. I was finding it hard to suppress the longing for someone who, like Oscar, would be by my side and not forever popping in and out of my life when they felt like it. And who had two legs, not four.

Oscar and I had started watching a programme on endangered species, but so many big cats unsettled both of us, so I turned it off and made myself some strong black coffee so I wouldn't fall asleep too early and wake up at the crack of dawn with a hangover.

Now that Zac had gone I allowed myself to take in the news of Debbie's death. But it wasn't Debbie who kept invading my head space. It was Jay.

Chapter 28 – 1974

I suppose after travelling round Australia with Fiona, the next big thing in my life was meeting James Jay. I rang Fiona a couple of weeks after we got back and she suggested going to the Blue Parakeet. She was living at home and dying for a night out in London. I jumped at the chance, as life in a bedsit was pretty disagreeable. Particularly when the creepy bloke in the next room kept knocking at my door on one pretext or another. He played music at top volume and I'd been daft enough to ask him to turn it down when I first moved in. Since then, he'd kept the volume up, on the off chance I'd knock again, presumably.

I trudged through Soho, past the strip joints and the seedy pubs, into Wardour Street. Fi was waiting outside the club at eight o'clock, as agreed. It was cold and our teeth were chattering. Acclimatising to the dankness and gloom of the northern hemisphere after the glorious sunshine of Oz was hard for both of us. I just couldn't keep warm in this bleak February weather, despite my layering of tights, long boots and black woollen midi dress, which was scratching like mad.

Like me, Fi was temping, but she was commuting from the comfort of her parents' home in Forest Hill, whereas I'd been forced into bedsit-land because my mother Frankie had split up from Toby, resulting in my room being no longer available. This had come as quite a blow when I received her letter just a week before we were flying back.

Dear Pan,

Hope you're having a lovely time. I'm looking forward to seeing you soon, so we can have a good catch up. As you can see, I'm writing this from The Unicorn, where Richard's letting me stay at the moment. I'm not living at Mulberry Walk any more because Toby and I have split up.

It's awful for you, I know, not having your usual room to come back to. Aunt Maggie says you're welcome to stay with her, but Chelmsford probably isn't much good to you. The only other place I can suggest is your dad's. You always got on well with Joan, didn't you?

It all happened quite suddenly. Toby locked himself out one evening and popped into the pub to get my key and found I wasn't there. One of the regulars spilled the beans that I was out with Richard. When I got home that night, my worldly goods were on the doorstep in two suitcases, plus the things you'd left in your room, in a black bin bag. I had to get a taxi back to The Unicorn and throw myself on Richard's mercy.

I wrote to Toby explaining that Richard had come with me to a film – one that Toby hadn't wanted to go to – but he never replied. So I think that's it.

To be honest, Toby and I had probably reached the end of the road anyway. We bumped into one of his art school friends in Portobello Road one day and the friend thought I was his mother! Toby said it didn't bother him but I cried for hours when we got home.

Please ring the pub as soon as you get back and let me know where you are.

All my love,
Mum xxxx

Fi had been very sympathetic, offering me the spare room at her parents' house, but I was too embarrassed to take her up on it. What would I say to them? I haven't got anywhere to go because my mum's homeless and my dad's remarried?

I felt I'd left England an independent young woman and returned a waif and stray. Although, in truth, that was an illusion. I'd never really been independent because I'd been reliant on Toby's generosity for a roof over my head.

I knew I wanted to be in London, where there was plenty of temporary work, so I decided to be sensible, and rang my dad's house as soon as the plane landed. I was surprised when I heard his voice answering the phone on a weekday.

'Hello, Dad. How are you?'

'Dora. We thought you'd be back soon. I'm fine. Where are you?'

'I'm at the airport. I wanted to ask you and Joan a favour.'

His voice softened. 'You want me to come and get you?'

The favour I wanted was more along the lines of board and lodging, but if he wanted to pick me up, all the better.

'Yes please. And would it be all right if I stayed for a few days?'

He muttered a few hurried words to Joan and I heard her say, 'Of course it is.'

After we'd arranged where to meet, I remarked, 'You're not at work, then, Dad?'

'I'm on a three-day week,' he huffed. 'It's that buffoon Heath's idea – it started with the miners' strike and now we're all on short time to conserve electricity. This country's a shambles. If I was your age, I'd be off to Australia myself.'

I hadn't really bothered about keeping up with British news while I was away, but my father gave me a crash course in the parlous state of the economy on the drive home from the airport. Once we arrived, Joan gave me the third degree about why I couldn't go back to Chelsea.

I watered down the reason for the split between Toby and Frankie, hinting at a clash of personalities. I suppose preserving Frankie's reputation was a form of self-protection, because I never wanted my dad to think too badly of my mum in case he thought I'd turn out like her. And then there was that remark my dad had made about Richard fancying Frankie. If he knew she'd gone to the cinema with him – like Toby, he might jump to the wrong conclusion. At least, I assumed it was the wrong conclusion.

So that's how I'd ended up back in my old room in Nightingale Road. But, alas, the treat of free lodgings and Joan's home cooking was diluted by recollections of the anguish my eighteen-year-old self had suffered in that room. Memories of Mike returned in vivid detail and I dreaded the nights when I'd be wide awake, going over what had happened, what hadn't happened, and what could have happened.

All this prompted me to register without delay with employment and accommodation agencies, which produced a temping job at an insurance company in the City. There wasn't a great choice of bedsits for my limited budget, but I managed to find a fairly clean one in Earls Court, which, being known as 'Kangaroo Valley', seemed oddly appropriate considering my recent return from the Antipodes.

* * *

Fiona and I showed our membership cards to the cashier at the Blue Parakeet as we paid, but they'd expired, so we had to wait for her to make out some new ones. While we were waiting, I became aware of a tall, slightly hunched figure at the other side of the lobby, smoking a cigarette. Slim to the point of skinny, he was wearing a white ruffled shirt and leather waistcoat with tight black jeans and ankle boots.

Taking a cigarette from my pack, I walked over to him. As I got closer, I could see how black his hair was and how it curled slightly at the nape. His face, with its deep brown eyes and olive skin, was framed with the requisite longish sideburns. He looked slightly foreign. When he saw me approaching, he reached into his pocket and took out a Zippo lighter, adorned with a maple leaf.

'Light?'

'Thanks.' My hand shook a little as I put the tip of my cigarette to the flame. I wasn't sure why. I'd only wanted to get a closer look at him.

'Thanks.' Embarrassed at my shaking hand, I blamed it on the weather. 'I'm freezing.'

He looked me up and down as if wondering how anyone could be cold dressed in as many layers as an Eskimo.

'Don't worry. One dance and you'll soon warm up.' There was nothing in his accent to suggest anything more exotic than a Greater London Borough. 'You come far?'

I felt myself blush, hoping he didn't think I was a country bumpkin, 'up London' on a rare night out.

'We've just come back from Australia, so we're feeling the cold.'

'Yeah,' he said, laughing, 'that's quite far.'

I blushed again. 'No,' I replied, emphasising the word as if talking to a stupid person. 'Tonight I've come from Earls Court.'

He was beginning to look interested. 'That's a place I've always wanted to go. Australia, that is. Earls Court – I can take it or leave it.' He paused to check I was smiling, which I was. 'You'll have to tell me about it.'

This sounded promising. But first there was something I wanted to ask him.

'Did you ever play at the Green Oak?'

His eyes gleamed with surprise.

'Yeah. We used to play there now and again.'

'I remember you and the Blue Jays. You're James Jay, aren't you?'

He still looked a little taken aback.

'Yeah. We had to change the name, 'cos there was another group called the Blue Jays.'

I'd seen the poster by the door as we'd come in – James Jay and the Jaylers. It was a terrible name. He must have read my mind.

'Rubbish name, but people remember it. And we get a few laughs when we do our last number. I come on wearing a prison outfit with a ball and chain and the lads wear prison-warder caps. Then we sing Chain Gang.'

'Really? This I must see.'

'We're not doing it tonight. It's not that sort of gig. This is a bit more mainstream. You know?'

'How disappointing.' I made a sad face and he laughed.

'How come you recognised me, anyway? We've smartened up a bit. It was jeans and t-shirts back then.'

'Don't you remember? We went out a couple of times.'

The look on his face was priceless. It wasn't true, of course. The words had slipped out almost unconsciously, but I was enjoying the effect it was having. He was scratching his head trying to remember me. 'When was this, exactly?'

Fi appeared with our new membership cards and stood waiting to be introduced. It was a welcome diversion.

'This is my friend Fiona.'

He nodded his head in greeting and looked back at me. 'Remind me. What's *your* name?'

'Pandora.'

'Christ. I think I'd have remembered a name like that. What's your last name?'

'Fry.'

'Pan-fry. What d'you get called at school? Frying pan? Andy Pandy?'

I smiled thinly, trying to look as if I hadn't heard it a million times before. 'Something like that.'

Our discussion was cut short by the arrival of a tall lad with long hair, telling him it was nearly time to go on. James Jay said he'd be there in a minute, and his friend shouted okay and went back into the club. He walked nearer to the street door to get rid of his cigarette butt, and paused, staring out. I wasn't sure if our dialogue was over.

Taking Fi's arm, I headed for the door leading into the club. I certainly wasn't hanging around like a groupie to see if any more crumbs of conversation would fall from the table. He was extremely good-looking, so I had to follow my rule and treat him cool, letting him make the running. If there was running to be made.

Oddly enough, I'd always found the opposite to be true of the not-so-good-looking ones, who could be attractive for different reasons – quirky personality, good sense of humour. Make a fuss of *them* and they were putty in your hands. But James was definitely in the top ten per cent on the phwoar scale and had to be treated accordingly. This category, by virtue of physical superiority, had no lack of female attention so were much more intrigued by a girl who didn't fawn all over them.

We'd just reached the entrance when he called out to us, 'I'll buy you a drink when we finish our set. See you at the bar, then. Yeah?'

Scarcely turning my head, I answered, 'Yeah, see you then,' and Fi and I disappeared through the door.

* * *

Later, sitting at the bar, James and I resumed our conversation.

'It's a wind-up, isn't it? We didn't really go out, did we?'

I performed a Gallic shrug, which involved pursing my lips and hunching my shoulders up to my ears. 'How can you be sure?'

'Well, this may surprise you, but girls didn't hang round us in those days. The Green Oak wasn't the sort of place you'd get anyone waiting at the stage door, if you know what I mean. I honestly don't remember pulling anyone at the Green Oak.'

I held my hands up in a gesture of surrender. 'You win. I was having you on. But I like the answer.'

He looked serious. 'What is it, some sort of test? Have I passed it?'

'Yep. Flying colours.'

'Nice one. I'm glad.'

He grasped my hand in a sort of mock handshake. His hand felt strong but surprisingly soft. I felt a tingle of electricity when we touched. My feet were perched on the rungs of the bar stool, so I couldn't blame the nylon carpet. James looked as if he'd felt it too, because he didn't let go, and held my gaze for quite a few seconds. A couple of girls over the other side of the bar were watching us and whispering. James released his grasp but immediately flipped my hand over and looked at my palm.

'I can see a long life ahead and seven children...'

I wasn't quite sure what was going on. The move from flippant to intense and back again had confused me. But I could play that game.

'Don't tell me, I'm going to meet a tall, dark, handsome stranger. And sometimes I like to be on my own, and sometimes I crave company.'

He laughed, letting go of my hand, tossing his head and pushing his fringe away from his eyes, the way he did when he was singing. 'We've got another set later, then I've got to drive the van back to Hammersmith. What you doing tomorrow?'

'Nothing.'

'It's my birthday. Do you wanna meet for lunch?'

'I'm working. I thought you meant in the evening.'

'No. We're playing here every night this week. We can't talk here. Take the day off.'

'I can't. I get paid by the hour. And my agency wouldn't be too pleased.'

I badly wanted to see him, just the two of us, but my finances were too precarious to gamble with.

'What about Saturday?' I suggested. It was Tuesday and the weekend felt like an age away, but I couldn't see any alternative.

'That's when we rehearse. The rest of the boys've got jobs. It's the only time we can all get together.'

'Haven't you got a job, then?'

He smiled indulgently, and shook his head. 'I write the songs, Andy. I'm the main man. I manage the group, liaise with the bookings agency, do the publicity, make sure the van's okay. Make the tea. It's my living. Has been for a couple of years.'

'Andy?' I was indignant. 'That's a man's name.' Who did he think I was, one of his mates?

'Well, it's better than Pandy. But if you don't like it...'

He looked genuinely sorry. I told myself I had to stop overreacting where my name was concerned. Either that or get therapy. Or change it.

'No, it's okay.' After all, it was marginally better than Pan. Or Dora. Or Pippi. And I quite liked the fact that nobody else had ever called me that before. My rebranding was interrupted by one of the band tapping James on the shoulder.

'Jay. What you having? The usual?' James nodded.

'Yeah, cheers, Clive.'

The Jayler peered at me through his long fringe. 'And for you, little lady?'

I said 'no thanks' because I knew if I accepted he might get the wrong idea. And it wasn't a Jayler I wanted. Not when I could have the main man.

Fifteen minutes later and Clive was still deep in conversation with James. I'd hoped that he'd go back and talk to the others but Fi had disappeared with the keyboard player and the other two Jaylers were talking and laughing with a group of girls they seemed to know. James intermittently rubbed my leg gently while Clive was holding forth. I was sitting to his right, facing the bar and Clive was on his left, so no one could see.

The interval was over and a group playing traditional jazz, which Fi loved, had just come on. Appearing out of nowhere, she pulled me off my seat and dragged me on to the dance floor. She'd taught me how to do a weird, skippy, jazz jive – certainly not what a dolly bird like me wanted to be seen doing, especially in front of a really tasty bloke.

As we performed this ridiculous routine, every so often I'd glance at James from the dance floor to see if he was watching. A couple of times I saw him grinning, so in response I made a mad face and exaggerated my moves.

Fi was enjoying herself and wanted to natter about the boys.

'Donny's a great laugh. He's asked me out.'

'Don't tell me. It'll have to be Sunday.'

'How do you know?'

'James. He said they're here until the end of the week and rehearsing on Saturday afternoon. He wants me to take tomorrow off. But I can't afford to.'

'Can't you pull a sickie? One day won't hurt, surely. You could always do an extra couple of hours the rest of the week.'

The music ended and Fi went in search of Donny. I looked towards the bar expecting to see James, but he wasn't there. My heart sank. I hoped I hadn't blown it by saying I couldn't get the day off. We hadn't even exchanged numbers – although the only phone I had access to was a communal one in the hallway. So a bit of a waste of time for incoming calls.

I felt someone touch me on the arm.

'Who taught you to dance like that? I'd get my money back if I was you.'

Shaking his head in mock dismay, James put his arm round my shoulder and walked me to one of the booths at the far end of the club. I was so pleased to see him that my heart felt about to burst.

'It was Fiona,' I laughed, 'She made me do it.'

We sat down and I cuddled in as close as I could to him. He nuzzled my cheek.

'You smell nice.'

'James, about tomorrow...'

'Don't worry, Andy, we'll work something out. Call me Jay, by the way. Everybody does.' He looked at his watch. 'We're on next. I think I'd better take your number, if we're ever gonna meet up.'

'It's okay. I've decided to have the day off tomorrow—' I kissed him full on the lips to give him something to remember me by, '—Damn the expense.'

Chapter 29 – 1974

Jay lived in a rented terrace house in Hammersmith. He'd given me the address and told me to be there at one o'clock. As it was his birthday, I'd assumed we were going out, but when I turned up he took my coat, ushered me into the front room, plonked a glass of red wine in my hand and removed himself to the kitchen to put the finishing touches to a spaghetti Bolognese. He was wearing a sort of butcher's apron over old jeans and a maroon and brown patterned shirt. Quite a contrast to his leather waistcoat and ruffled shirt combo of the night before, but in spite of the pinny I found him even more appealing in daylight.

He'd told me last night that he shared the house with two of the Jaylers, Clive and Donny, and it was as grotty as I'd expected it to be. There was dust on every surface. A couple of plates with the remains of takeaways lay abandoned on the floor, and some empty beer bottles lolled on top of an ancient piano. Jay came in to tell me lunch was ready, looked around, and swore under his breath.

'I told Clive to do his washing-up.'

I picked up the dirty plates and took them into the kitchen, intending to wash them. But the sink was already full of saucepans and crockery floundering in scummy grey water. As I hesitated, I noticed Jay giving my short, pink, corduroy shirtdress an approving once-over.

'Glad to see you're out of mourning,' he said – this being a reference to my mostly black outfit of the previous evening. I'm afraid I couldn't think of a smart riposte as I was experiencing such a tsunami of shyness, I could barely string two words together. So I just smiled inanely.

He took the dirty plates and motioned his head towards a chair.

'Don't worry, Andy. They'll get done. Sit down.'

I did as I was told. Jay started piling a slick of orange-brown sauce over two mounds of spaghetti and placed them on the table. How could I tell him that I didn't like spaghetti Bolognese, after all the trouble he'd gone to?

'Thanks,' I smiled, floundering for something to say. 'So Clive and Donny are at work?'

What an idiot I must sound, I thought. Talk about stating the flaming obvious.

'Yeah. They'll be back about six. Then we're out again at seven fifteen. They're not too keen on this gig. Tuesday to Saturday's a bit much for 'em. That's why I do 'em a dinner.' Jay indicated another saucepan full of the oily sauce.

In an effort to delay the moment when I'd be expected to consume the pasta from hell, I raised my glass and said, 'Happy birthday.'

Jay raised his glass in reply, adding shiftily, 'For last Thursday.'

'You said it was today!' I exclaimed.

'I thought if I said that, you'd be more likely to come. Anyway, what's a few days between friends?'

I shook my head in mock disapproval, secretly pleased that he'd lied to get me round his house. When he saw I didn't mind, he began attacking the steaming heap on his plate with gusto.

But I could only pick at the pasta before me. I felt I should be telling him how much I was enjoying it, but that plainly wasn't true. Five minutes later, he'd nearly finished his, but I'd barely touched mine. I looked up from my plate and caught him watching me.

He smiled wryly, 'You don't like it, do you?'

'It's not that. I'm not very hungry. Sorry.'

I could feel my cheeks flaming. What was wrong with me? He must have thought I was the dumb twin of the girl he'd laughed and joked with last night.

Jay poured us more wine.

'Cheers. Drink up. Here's to me having my wicked way with you as soon as you've cleared your plate.'

His directness took my breath away, causing me to inhale the wine I was sipping. This triggered a choking fit, at which Jay leapt up and started thumping my back. Once I'd got my breath, he fetched me a glass of water. Then one thing led to another and before

I knew it I was upstairs in his bedroom and we were both getting undressed. We dived under the covers, as the room was freezing. To my relief, the sheets and pillow cases smelled fresh, and the room was surprisingly spick and span. There were no piles of discarded clothes, no dirty underwear. Everything must have been tidied away in anticipation of my visit.

What followed was tender and passionate. In fact it was everything I would have liked my first time to have been.

I'd had no other lover since Collins. When I'd returned from Spain I'd sworn off dating and stopped taking the pill, feeling too crushed by my experiences with Mike and Collins to risk another fiasco. So I became a born-again virgin. Occasionally I relented and accepted invitations to go out, but after a couple of dates they usually wanted sex, which I didn't, so it always fizzled out in the end. I think I got the reputation of being frigid at work, which had been another reason I'd been glad to leave.

* * *

Before we set off on our travels round Australia, Fiona and I had agreed we wouldn't entangle ourselves with any vacation flings. But we almost weakened when we met a couple of young New Zealanders on a group trek in the Blue Mountains National Park. They were a bit younger than us, both of them clean-cut and good looking. I fancied Bob, the dark one, and Fiona fancied Richie, his red-haired friend. They were full of high spirits and insisted on giving us piggy-backs, with us hanging on for dear life, screaming and pretending to be scared. But we enjoyed the physical contact as much as they did.

'Can we tag along with you girls for a coupla weeks?' Richie had asked, as we sat around the camp fire on the last evening with the other trekkers. 'Seems we kinda got the same itinerary.'

Later, settling down for the night in our tent, Fiona and I had discussed what we should do. We couldn't make up our minds, so the next morning we told the guys that if we were going to team up with them as 'travelling companions' (except we all knew it would be more than that) we'd be at The Diggers' Rest Bar that evening. But when we got back to our hostel, we were so exhausted that we fell asleep, not waking till the early hours.

Fiona was consumed with disappointment and guilt, thinking of them sitting there waiting for us, but I found myself feeling relieved. So I figured I couldn't have been ready to thaw out, even under the baking hot Australian sun.

But meeting Jay last night had started the melting process. And today saw any remaining icicles dissolve dramatically.

'Steady on, kid,' Jay said at one point. 'You're wearing me out. I'm gonna make a sandwich. Stay there.' And he'd brought back a tray with two mugs of builders' tea and two enormous cheese sandwiches. I polished mine off in no time because by then I was starving.

We stayed in bed for a couple of hours, talking and making love, my powers of speech having returned along with my libido. Finally, we reluctantly got up and between us took care of the pile of washing-up. In fact, we even blitzed the whole of the downstairs.

'I'll clean the bathroom tomorrow,' he said. 'It'll all be shipshape by Friday. I'll pick you and your stuff up at nine on Saturday morning.'

* * *

When I'd got back from Oz, my instinct had been to contact Frankie straight away, but I waited until I'd moved into the bedsit. It just didn't seem right to do it before. I didn't want to relapse into the old blueprint of living in my Dad's house and being in contact with my mum behind his back.

I rang The Unicorn the Saturday after I'd moved to Earls Court, to be told that Frankie was out but she'd be around that evening. So I got to the pub about six, taking an empty suitcase to carry the things that Toby had dumped on the doorstep. I was running out of warm clothes and couldn't afford to buy new ones.

As I entered the saloon bar, I caught sight of my mother and Richard, chatting and laughing together. He was behind the bar and she was the other side, her stiletto heels perched on the foot rest of a bar stool, her uncharacteristically manicured fingers clasping a cigarette. She was wearing a figure-hugging, royal blue dress with a scooped neckline and narrow sleeves, sipping what looked like a martini. Her hair had been cut into a sleek bob. She no longer resembled a hippy chick. What, I wondered, had brought about this transformation?

'Mum,' I called out, eager now to see her after our seven-month separation. She turned round in surprise, a broad smile lighting up her slightly flushed face.

'Pan, darling. Come to momma.' So saying, she got to her feet, swayed across the carpet, and enveloped me in her arms. As she kissed me, I detected a significant scent of alcohol on her breath.

'Let me introduce you to Richard. I know you've already met. But I want to introduce Richard as... ' She waggled her left hand at me, on the ring finger of which dazzled a diamond solitaire, '... my fiancé. Richard took me to buy the ring today and we had a lovely lunch afterwards to celebrate.'

She kissed me again, 'I hope you're happy for me darling.'

To say I was flabbergasted would have been an understatement. Just where in Frankie's letter had she said anything about Richard being her boyfriend? I'd had a picture of him as a sympathetic buddy, giving her shelter in her hour of need. Now it seemed I had to rearrange his portrait into that of prospective stepfather. I was trying to conceal my uneasiness at this news when Richard chipped in.

'Your mother and I have known each other for a long time, but while she was with Toby, trust me, nothing was going on.' His voice was as persuasive as that of a used car salesman. He came out from behind the bar and put his arm around Frankie's waist. The pub had only just opened but was filling up quite rapidly. 'Why don't you and your mum go upstairs for a little chat. She'll fill you in.'

The look he and my mother exchanged seemed genuinely loving. But then the last time I'd seen her with Toby they'd still seemed besotted with each other, so what did I know?

I hadn't really paid much attention to Richard before. On the few occasions I'd come to the pub, he'd been pretty much a shadowy figure, at times working behind the bar, at others appearing at closing time. I viewed him now with fresh eyes. He was tall and well-built, in his late forties at least. His well-cut, dark hair was going grey, but his fresh pink complexion gave him a youthful air. He had clear blue eyes which reminded me of my dad's. I noticed he was wearing an expensive watch and well cut clothes. I was looking at a man of means.

Once upstairs, I brewed coffee, toasted bread and scrambled eggs, feeling that Frankie needed sobering up. We took this into the small living room on trays and she started telling me her version of events, which was more or less what she'd written in her letter. With the added information that once she'd started living here, a romance had sprung up between her and Richard.

I felt this was all very well, but what about poor Toby? I couldn't put it like that, so I just said, 'Didn't Toby ever contact you, Mum?'

Frankie at least had the grace to look remorseful. 'No, darling. I wrote to him early on – I think I told you. And I rang him, but he put the phone down.'

'But didn't you ever get a chance to talk? His reaction seems a bit extreme...' I was going to add, 'if you'd only been to the pictures', but some instinct stopped me.

So instead, I said, 'When I left for Australia you were fine. What happened?'

Frankie dissolved into tears which immediately made me full of guilt for casting a cloud over her engagement day, but at least what she had to say clarified the situation for me.

'Things began to go wrong almost as soon as you left. I really missed you. I'd got used to having someone around to chat to. And Toby had some big projects to work on, so he was out a lot. He even cancelled the trip to France – so we never did get to Collins' wedding. And I'd been really looking forward to it.'

My heart gave a little skip of gratitude. The gory details of the Swedish-French nuptials was one of the conversations I'd been dreading.

'Then there was the drugs thing. I don't mind the odd joint but I'm not into their scene. Sometimes they'd be up all night in the studio and then Toby would sleep half the day. I think that was the real reason he came back early from Spain, because he was missing all that so much. To tell the truth, Pan, I started feeling lonely. Toby even stopped coming here to see me. You know how he always used to be here two or three times a week? Richard noticed me crying one night when Toby hadn't turned up. He suggesting an evening out together to cheer me up, and I suppose that's how it started. But I do love Richard, so please be happy for me.'

I kissed her and told her I understood now why she'd broken up with Toby.

'By the way, Mum. I like the new look. What's brought that on?'

Frankie beamed, quite back to her earlier happy self.

'That's Richard's influence. He booked me into Vidal Sassoon's for a restyle. And I've got my own credit card. Honestly, Pan, he can't do enough for me.'

The only thing I found incongruous in all this, was the shabby furnishings in the living quarters. The kitchen was small and dingy and the room we were in was equally scruffy. The carpet was threadbare in places, the curtains lacked sufficient hooks, and the orange moquette suite looked dated and grubby.

'Do you like living here, Mum? It's a bit different from Mulberry Walk.'

'Oh we don't live here, darling. Richard's got an apartment on the embankment. This is just used for meal breaks, or staying overnight in an emergency.' She stopped suddenly, aware that she'd told me a slightly different story. 'But I did stay here at first. I was glad to have somewhere to go.'

I didn't press her as to how long she'd stayed here before moving into Richard's Chelsea Embankment pad, but I suspected not very long. He must be rolling in it. But it baffled me how he could afford his lifestyle as the tenant of a public house. The Chelsea folk must put away a lot of pints.

My thoughts returned to Toby. I still couldn't quite get my head round the finality of it all. I suppose now I'd never get to say a proper goodbye to him. I'd been thinking of ringing him, but after what Frankie had said about him putting the phone down, I wasn't too sure. I had a bit of a phobia about people putting the phone down on me. Ever since Mike's mum had done it.

When I got back to Earls Court, bearing my belongings, which luckily my mother had stored upstairs in The Unicorn, I wrote quite a long letter to him. In it I thanked him for giving me a roof over my head, for a great experience in Spain, and for lots of hospitality and good times.

A week later I got a lovely hand-painted card back – a miniature of the mural of Pandora and her casket that I'd copied on to a pillar in the Inner Beast. Inside the card, Toby had scrawled,

Never give up hope. Keep in touch. love, Toby xx

I'm so glad he replied when he did, or I might have missed it, as the following weekend Jay came and carried me and my personal effects off to Hammersmith.

Chapter 30 – 1974-1975

I loved living with Jay. From the moment he'd picked me up on that Saturday morning, I was in seventh heaven, especially when I saw that he'd bought a wardrobe just for me. When we took my cases up, he opened the wardrobe door to show me it was empty, and said, 'It's all yours.' Then, smiling, 'But when we get to know each other a bit better, maybe we can mix our stuff up a bit and you can put some of yours in mine and vice versa.'

I laughed and said, 'You'll be lucky, I don't want your moths,' but when his expression turned serious I kissed him, whispering, 'Thanks. I love it that you thought of it.'

There were two living rooms downstairs. The front room had a TV and a piano and the back room a record player, so the four of us could choose whether to hang out together or separately. When Jay was in the mood, he'd try out some chords on the piano, and he'd ask me to sing along. I could just about carry a tune, though it wasn't my singing voice he was interested in, just the lyrics I made up. We got quite good at writing together. Some of the songs he composed after that named me as co-writer, which was a gross exaggeration, but it was sweet of him to give me a mention.

There were plenty of gigs available for the group if they wanted them, but they didn't accept everything they were offered because they didn't always feel like playing after a day's work. Clive had a job in a recording studio in Denmark Street and Donny was a graphic designer. He and Jay had met at art school. The other two, Eddie the bassist, and Ian the guitarist, were painters and decorators. Jay was the only one at that time who made a living out of music. He took a greater share of the money, but then he acted as manager, roadie and songwriter, so it was only fair and nobody complained.

It took a couple of weeks for Donny and Clive to get used to having a girl around the place. Jay was fierce in his insistence that the bathroom was left clean and nobody wandered around in their underwear while I was in the house. As a result, there were raised voices behind closed doors and threats to leave. It must have been even worse when I wasn't there.

Anyway, I hit on a plan which worked like a dream. I got Jay to buy a washing machine, then I waited till they were all out rehearsing one Saturday and stripped all the beds and washed the bedding. There was a long washing line in the quaint little garden and soon it was full of clean laundry blowing in the wind. I wasn't sure where they kept the fresh bedding, so I speed-ironed it and put it all back on the beds.

When they got home I casually announced, 'I've washed your sheets.'

There was a stunned silence and Clive said, 'But we take our washing to the launderette,' to which Donny responded, 'Once a month, whether it needs it or not.'

'Look,' I said. 'Now we've got a washing machine I don't mind doing the washing. Call it my contribution to the house. But I draw the line at ironing.'

So from that moment on, I was the best thing since sliced bread. I had to field a few jokes from Clive and Donny about being their 'resident scrubber', but I didn't really mind, because it meant Jay no longer had the hassle of them moaning about me being there. And of course I did *his* ironing. Because I loved him.

A few months after Jay and I got together, he was approached by Lou Green, a top music-artist manager, offering to manage the group, and steer them away from more traditional rhythm and blues into blues rock. He guaranteed them a record contract, which meant having to give up their day jobs, something they'd resisted up to now.

Most people would have been overjoyed at this rocket boost to their career, but Jay was strangely reluctant to climb aboard. Maybe it was because he didn't want to surrender his position as group captain. Or because he didn't like being told what kind of songs to write. Maybe he had a premonition about how things would change.

'They'll be calling the shots, Andy. If the records take off, we'll be touring up and down the country all the time. Maybe even the States. At the moment we've all got our feet on the ground. But you take the lads away from their jobs, their friends, their families, and the boredom sets it. Then it's boozing, birds and substance abuse. I've seen it happen. You get stir crazy on the road, and it all goes haywire.'

'I think you're just worried he'll take your mouth organ away,' I laughed, but he didn't join in. Anyway, the lads got wind of the offer and called a meeting to talk it through. They were all in their twenties and ready to take a chance. What did they have to lose? With the country in recession, if there was any hope of making better money, how could they let it pass by?

And that was how James Jay and the Jaylers became one of the top British blues rock groups, evolving into more commercial rock as time went on, and even breaking into the US Billboard charts.

* * *

Jay proposed to me as soon as he'd made enough to put a deposit down on a place of our own. We got married in Fulham register office on his twenty-seventh birthday, almost exactly a year after we'd met in the Blue Parakeet. We had a small reception at a very expensive Italian restaurant – I couldn't refuse Jay that, given his addiction to pasta – attended by a select few.

My dad and Joan were there, and Frankie. But not Richard, who was otherwise detained at Her Majesty's pleasure, for operating some sort of bogus property investment company. When the case had got to court and been reported in the papers, we found out why he'd been so flush. Apparently he'd been persuading some of his rich old regulars to hand over large sums of money, promising them great dividends, but counting on them kicking the bucket or forgetting all about it before he had to cough up. It turned out the only property he'd actually bought, had been the apartment in which he and Frankie had been living. The rest of the money had been siphoned into an offshore account.

So my mother was single again. Luckily, the new publican had kept her on, and she was now occupying the dingy flat above the pub, but on the look-out for another job and a better place to live. I wasn't worried. Knowing Frankie, it wouldn't be long before an eligible male appeared and carried her off to his cave. Or his castle. You never knew with her.

The last of my guests was Fiona, who'd agreed to come even though she knew Donny would be there. They'd had an on-off relationship for a few months until the group had got 'discovered', when, true to Jay's prediction, Donny had gone wild and proceeded to sow his wild oats all over the country. Maybe she'd been hoping for a second chance, but she was out of luck because he had a sexy starlet on his arm that day. Fiona was intelligent and good fun, but a trophy girlfriend she was not.

As for Jay's guests, there were the four Jaylers, Donny's starlet, and another girl Ian brought along. Lou Green hadn't made it to the marriage vows but turned up at the restaurant. There'd been quite a crowd outside the register office, and he said he didn't fancy fighting his way through.

Jay had never known his father, but both his mothers were there. Luckily, Jay had warned me about his family history before the big day. We were lying in bed one night and I'd just told him about my mother leaving me and my dad. I got a bit upset in the telling and Jay tried to soothe me.

'I feel for you, baby. But you're marrying me now and it's my job to look after you. I won't let you down. Promise.' And then he added, 'Nobody will ever love you like I do, Andy.'

I stroked his dark, silky hair. 'What about you? You never talk about your parents.'

'That's because I've never seen my dad and I thought my mum was my sister until I was about fifteen. Then I found my birth certificate and I worked it out for myself.

'My birth mum got pregnant when she was sixteen, went away somewhere to have me, stayed around for a couple of years, then emigrated to Canada, leaving me with my gran. I suppose my gran was trying to protect me, but she let me think she was my mum. She always talked about my "sister" in Canada.'

I was stunned and intrigued by this story. 'And did you have a granddad?'

'Yeah, I remember him. He was nice. Kicked a ball around with me in the garden. But he died when I was three.'

'Does it give the name of your father on your birth certificate?'

I was thinking that maybe we could pay a private detective to find Jay's father so he could make it to the wedding.

'That's the embarrassing bit. It says "father unknown".'

Jay's body suddenly convulsed, and he got up and stumbled to the bathroom. I thought he was being sick but when I put my ear to the door I heard gut-wrenching sobs. I went back to bed and waited for him. After about ten minutes he crept in beside me.

'Are you all right, Jay?' I whispered, cradling him.

'Yeah, babe. Don't worry. I'll be all right. I've got you now.'

I felt so sad for him. It must have scarred him – growing up in a house with such a secret. I felt indignant on behalf of the child he'd been.

'Did you ask them who your father was? Your mother must have known who she slept with.'

'Course I did. My gran didn't want to say, but I kept on until she told me. She was a daily housekeeper for a doctor who lived in a big house down the road. He had a friend from Kashmir staying with him. He'd come to England to give some lectures or something. Anyway, my gran wasn't very well and she sent Sharon round there to do some of the cleaning for her. Then she started, you know, putting on weight. She told my gran who the father was, but she didn't believe her until I was born. Then it was obvious.'

'So all we've got to do is trace the doctor your gran worked for, find out the address of his Indian friend, and send him a wedding invitation.'

I was being serious but Jay assumed I was joking and laughed, in that shuddering way of someone who'd been crying a lot.

'Yeah. He'd come running, wouldn't he?'

'Where's your mum now?' I asked, reversing from the father cul de sac.

'Which one?'

'Your real one.'

'She's still in Canada. She comes back every couple of years. Always remembers my birthday. Funny, she never had any more kids. But my gran feels like my real mum. She's always been there for me.'

'Send Sharon an invitation. I'd like to meet her.'

'Okay.' I kissed him and we clung together.

Jay sighed, '"They fuck you up, your mum and dad."' This was a quote from a Philip Larkin poem we'd read together, when we'd been trying to get inspiration for lyrics.

'We won't do that to our kids.' I said. I knew that Jay and I would be great parents. We'd avoid all the pitfalls and give our kids so much love.

'Too right we won't. We'll be the best mum and dad ever,' he said, stroking my face.

'How many shall we have, Jay?' I was nearly twenty-three, and ready to start nesting.

'As many as we can knock out, baby. As far as I'm concerned, you can stop taking that pill tomorrow.'

Later that night he had one of his nightmares and woke, as he usually did, drenched in sweat. It was always the same dream. He could never remember the exact details but he'd tried to murder somebody and he was running away from his pursuers who were gaining on him. He'd even written a song about it: *If you pull out the dagger he'll bleed to death.* But it didn't stop him having the nightmares. He was still having them when we split up, ten years later.

* * *

I met Jay's two mothers for the first time on the day we got married. Mrs Jay had retired to Eastbourne and it was from there that they both travelled up to west London. It was strange to hear them calling him Jim. I'd almost forgotten his name was James until I heard the registrar saying it.

After the ceremony, when Jay was chatting and laughing with his mates, Mrs Jay kissed my cheek, then stepped back and stood regarding me shyly, her eyes carrying an almost pleading expression.

'I'm glad to see him settled, love. You can give him what he needs, a close family of his own. That's what he's always wanted. I did my best, but...' She stopped, not sure what Jay had told me.

I hugged her gently. 'I understand. He's in safe hands, don't worry.'

Sharon, his real mum, was only forty-three and very attractive. She spoke with a Canadian accent unless she was speaking to her mother, when she fell back into the language patterns of her youth. In colouring, Sharon and Mrs Jay were quite fair, with English rose complexions and blue eyes. I wondered what Mrs Jay's employer had thought when baby James had appeared with his jet black hair and liquid brown eyes, closely resembling one of his house guests from nine months previously. Whatever anyone had thought, it would probably have been swept under the carpet, as so much was in those days.

Sharon and Frankie hit it off and ended up sitting together, alternately flirting with the Italian waiters, the Jaylers, and Lou Green. Although I think their efforts with Lou fell on stony ground, as he seemed more interested in the Italian waiters.

Frankie had by then forsaken her soignée image – financed by Richard – and was in boho-chic mode, in long flowing dress with batwing sleeves, and Pre-Raphaelite curls. Her presence didn't seem to faze my father too much. I think his delight in the downfall of the detested Richard Tait temporarily outstripped any feelings of bitterness he still held towards her.

I spotted him popping indigestion tablets between courses and surreptitiously asked Joan how he was. She said he wasn't too bad. 'And all the better for Maggie seeing Ted Heath off,' she added, gleefully. This was a reference to the battle for the Conservative Party leadership. It baffled me why my father, a lifelong socialist, would have a soft spot for Margaret Thatcher. Maybe because she was proof that a girl from humble beginnings could crash through the glass ceiling.

At one end of the table, Lou Green kept himself busy holding forth to Clive and Ian on the importance of keeping the fans happy, and of not falling prey to temptations which might sully the group's image, while at the other end, Donny couldn't keep his hands of his luscious starlet. Fiona triumphed in the end, however, as Eddie made a distinct play for her, jumping into the seat beside her in the restaurant, and telling her jokes almost non-stop. He wasn't a bad-looking guy, a bit of a rough diamond, but Fiona didn't seem to be bothered by that. So everyone left the restaurant in high spirits.

And I do mean high. As in high as a kite, since it transpired afterwards that the cook who'd supplied the cake, paid for by the Jaylers, had made a hash cake of it. (Which is very different from making a hash of it.) By the time they told us this, the remaining layer had already been carved up, put in little boxes and sent off to various relations and music-business contacts. Oh well, ignorance is bliss. Quite literally, in this case.

At the close of play, Jay and I were happy to make straight for our comfortable new pad in Fulham, where we immediately got out of our wedding gear, put our feet up, and exchanged intelligence on who'd said what to whom and who we thought fancied each other.

The wedding dress I took off was a simple white silk shift with a softly pleated skirt. Mini, of course. And because it was February, a white fur jacket with matching hat (fake fur, naturally, but still cost a bomb) and white leather boots. I'd carried a 'fair maids of February bouquet', the fair maids being snowdrops. Jay had been dressed in a blue pinstriped suit with wide lapels and a pink Mr Fish shirt and kipper tie.

Our pictures were in the paper the next day and that's the only record I've got of the event, as we forgot to engage a photographer and nobody had a camera with them – the older guests thinking they could order prints from a professional, and the younger guests being too cool to carry cameras.

My dad got in touch with *The Daily Mirror* to ask if they'd supply two photos, one for us and one for him, which they did. In it, he and Joan are standing next to us, beaming. It's the last one I've got of him. Joan still displays hers on the sideboard in Nightingale Road. And I've recently dug mine out from an old storage chest, reframed it, and put it in pride of place on the Steinway.

Chapter 31 – 2003

I was still sitting in Mike's armchair, thinking about Jay, when I glimpsed a couple of sparks out of the corner of my eye and Enoch flashed into my mind.

After the contract signing and our subsequent bedroom activities, earlier that evening, I'd been left high and dry by Zac, who'd hightailed it to the station in a taxi. The evening, like me, was still comparatively young, so I decided to get in touch with my antediluvian friend.

I went into the study, lit a candle and took out the file with my Enoch notes inside. I sat at my desk and went into meditation by speaking Enoch's name and imagining a column of white light entering my crown and extending down through my body deep into the centre of the Earth. I remained like this for twenty minutes or so, concentrating on my breathing and emptying my mind. When the time seemed right, I opened my eyes and picked up my pen.

Although up to then I'd written most of my questions down, it had become evident that Enoch could often read my thoughts. I had a lot to talk to him about, what with the letter from Cassiel and everything, and didn't want to be writing unnecessarily. So this time I experimented and spoke the question out loud.

'Enoch. Greetings.' (My words were still coming out as if I were in a history play.) 'Do I still need to write my questions down for you, or can I just speak them out loud?'

The pen moved into action, taking my hand with it.

Greetings to you, scribe. I am glad you have resumed contact. Our last conversation was interrupted. The answer is yes, our communication has developed enough for your questions to be spoken out loud.

His mention of our last conversation prompted me to examine what I'd written just before Olivier's phone call had broken our contact. The sentence, *I have reached a point in my life when I don't want to continue with this pattern,* leapt out at me. And I remembered my fear at the time that subconsciously I felt tempted to end my life. It had been followed by the phrase: *I can break out of this paradigm and choose my own reality.*

'Can you explain the information you gave me about breaking out of the paradigm, please, Great One?' (There I go again).

It simply means to let go of the harmful patterns of behaviour you have accumulated in this, your life, and to consciously choose to see yourself and the world in a different way. Do you remember what you had been reading before you wrote those words?

I reflected for a moment. It was the Buddhist notes about escaping the cycle of karma and reincarnation.

'Is it like seeing the world with clear sight and deciding not to buy into the illusion of what we think we must have? Like the Buddhist teachings about putting an end to craving and stepping off the wheel of karma.'

Enoch's reply appeared as quickly as the pen could touch the page.

Yes. But stepping off the wheel of karma does not mean leaving your physical body. You will still live in the same world, dear one, but your outlook and understanding will be different. Some may describe the process as a spiritual awakening, an ascension, nirvana, or a change in your energy vibration...but words do not convey the experience. If you choose this path, only then will you know what it means and how it feels.

I felt little the wiser, but was relieved that I didn't have to shuffle off my mortal coil to be still in the game, so I thanked the old boy for setting my mind at rest. Then I remembered that Cassiel had written something similar in his description of the third, and final, level of The Enoch Society Correspondence Course.

'Enoch, was it right for me to answer The Enoch Society advertisement?'

Most certainly. Prince Cassiel has given you information about how you can achieve a more joyful life, in the service of others.

The pen hesitated for a few seconds, as if unsure whether to encourage me, or remain neutral, allowing me to make up my own mind. I was curious about Cassiel's title, so I continued talking.

'Tell me about Cassiel. I wasn't sure if he was male or female. But if he's a prince he must be male. And where is he prince of?'

Cassiel is an Archangel, prince of the seventh heaven. Angels do not separate into gender as humans do, for they are a perfect balance of male and female. For the purpose of communication, we can use the masculine gender. His duty is to help souls create their own good fortune and to get into positive habits of thinking, so their lives become balanced and harmonious. He also enables the release of unexpressed grief.

I dimly remembered that my Enoch research had shown him ending up in the seventh heaven, taking dictation from God. That must have been where he and Cassiel had been introduced. I was still a bit puzzled about the seeming randomness of my encounter with Cassiel, though.

'So does he work independently from you? Was it a coincidence that I saw the advertisement and contacted him?'

His manifestation was no coincidence, dear one. Cassiel and I work to the same end. We are available to any souls who seek to raise themselves up and to rid themselves of the destructive thoughts which babble in their troubled minds. He is closer to the earth element than I, so he is able to make contact in a more material way. I understand you received some sacred chrism from him.

'Yes. But I haven't had time yet to read the instructions. And he said I should start the process when I've finished Level Two, which is writing more of my life and examining any unhealthy patterns of behaviour.'

Exactly so. Now is too soon. Follow his direction. Begin to transcribe your story, and learn from it. Then make your decision whether to advance to the final level. But remember, you have the free will not to undertake the process if you so decide.

Think of it as emerging from an egg. The egg is the paradigm in which you have been trapped. Once you break the shell there is no going back, as you'll see the infinite possibilities of a new reality.

I had a vision of a bedraggled chick pecking at its shell from the inside.

'So you want me to get cracking, then?'

My pen drew a smiley face. Enoch was almost texting – whatever next? But he continued in a more serious tone.

Taking on the mantle of an ascended one brings with it responsibilities, as Cassiel has explained. You would have to devote your life to helping others. Often in ways that would go unrecognised. But the benefit is the fulfilment of your life purpose at last.

While I reflected on this, my pen rested. After a little while, it began to move across the paper again.

Have you any other anxieties? I sense your spirits are low this evening.

I mulled over Enoch's question. Would it be frivolous to ask him about Zac? Would it be a misuse of my gift to treat my pet patriarch as an agony uncle? My pen started to move. There he was, reading my mind again.

You are troubled about your new love. I can only say that as long as love opens your hearts equally, you will both benefit. But it is vital to remember that where such encounters between two souls are concerned, always resist any possessiveness or excess of need. Your energy exchange will be beneficial if it flows in equal measure from one to the other. Any imbalance in this, when one or other of you is giving or taking too much, will be detrimental to you both.

My heart sank at the truth of this. I had to admit I couldn't get enough of Zac, but I still wasn't sure how smitten he was with me, if at all. I made a mental note to heed Enoch's 'excess of need' warning in any future dealings with him. The pen skipped and Enoch continued.

You feel lonely at the moment without a companion. But look not for salvation in others. Recognise the difference between a healthy and an unhealthy union. Focus on becoming whole and complete yourself. Like attracts like, so if you attain this state, you will attract a similar soul. Take care not to feed off the energy of others by being hungry for them. And if the object of your affections is one who feeds off your energy, advise him how to change so he does not drain you. If he cannot learn, then let him go.

These words took me back to how Jay and I had become.

Restless, addictive and, in my case, unfulfilled – yet clingy and possessive.

* * *

A couple of years into our marriage, I'd caught a girl slipping her phone number into Jay's jacket pocket. He'd left it lying on a seat on a pile of others and gone off to the club casino with Donny. It was a heavily studded aviator jacket, so you couldn't mistake it. Even though I was on the dance floor with Clive, I saw exactly what she was up to.

We were in a club in a large group. She was Ronnie's girlfriend. Ronnie was a guitarist with The Blue Roosters. She'd been flirting with Jay all night. Anyway, I followed her to the loo, drink in hand, and asked her what she thought she was doing. I could feel my insides shaking with rage when she just laughed it off and said she'd only been trying to make Ronnie jealous.

I pretended to accept her explanation but as I turned to leave I 'accidentally' slipped, and my mint julep flew all over her strapless white catsuit and platinum blonde perm. A sprig of mint flew through the air and landed right between her cleavage. I said sorry but seasoned it with a sardonic smirk. She was fuming. So I left her dabbing at the damage, hurried back to the group, found her boyfriend, and dragged him on to the dance floor. I raised my voice to be heard over the music and looked deep into his eyes.

'Ronnie. I've got a confession.'

His crafty little eyes, already glazed by illegal substances, glinted excitedly. He leered at me as he executed some fancy footwork.

'Go on, doll. Don't tell me. You fancy me.'

I laughed, but not too much. I didn't want to offend him. 'Everyone fancies you, Ron.' I twisted my face into a mask of remorse. 'Had a bit too much.' I mimed putting a drink to my lips, up and down a few times, so he'd get the gist of it. 'Spilt my drink. Went all over Evie's outfit. Don't think she's too pleased. Feel terrible.'

Ronnie looked even shiftier. Maybe that was his sympathetic expression. Anyway, he shrugged his shoulders and resumed leering.

'It's only money, darlin'. Don't worry. She'll be raiding 'arvey Nicks tomorrer. Any excuse.'

The music had slowed and, just as he moved in for a clinch, I saw Evie approaching. Her catsuit, skin-tight at the best of times, seemed to have shrunk in her effort to soak the stain out, and was barely clinging to her large breasts. Limp, seaweed strands of hair framed her full face. Following my startled gaze, Ronnie turned, and seeing the state she was in, burst out laughing.

'Blimey, Evie. You look like summing outa fucking Star Trek, the porn movie. Do somefin' about yourself, for chrissake.'

Over Ronnie's shoulder, I reprised my sardonic smirk.

Evie glared at me with murder in her eyes. 'What's she told you, Won?'

Ronnie looked a little bemused. Jay was the most successful member of our party and as such, he and his wife were due a little more respect than Evie was showing. The people near us had stopped dancing and were observing the scene with interest.

'She said she spilled her drink over you. Calm down, girl. It was an accident, wonnit?'

Evie and I stared at each other with equal venom. But she was the first to lower her eyes. She must have figured out, that with her note as incriminating evidence, I had the trump card if it came to a showdown. But she couldn't resist a final whine.

'This cost me a fortune. It's exclusive. And it's ruined now. Who's gonna pay for it?'

I wasn't having this, so I smiled a sweet smile for the audience and let rip.

'Are you sure it's exclusive? Only I've seen one down Shepherd Market.'

Ronnie was eager to bring this exchange to a close. 'That's all right, then, Eve. You can go down the market, get a new one.'

My claws were fully extended as I addressed my words to the crowd. 'One of the regulars was wearing one exactly like it. She's on the corner every evening.'

Shepherd Market was a notorious location for all manner of ladies of the night. At the mention of this venue, a few of the onlookers had started tittering. Evie moved forward as if to strike me, but Ronnie's lightness of foot saved the day as he glided between us to block her.

Like the useful flyweight he'd once been, he locked her in an embrace, at the same time pinning her arms by her side. When he was satisfied that she'd calmed down, he pushed her gently in the direction of our table. 'It's all right, girl. Why don't you go and sit down ? You'll soon dry out.'

Evie gave me the dirtiest of looks, then pouted, gazing up at Ronnie from beneath a double layer of false eyelashes. 'Can we go home now, Wonniekins. Baby wants a nice shower and beddibyes.'

At the mention of the 'b' word, Ronnie perked up. 'Count me in, darlin'. That's just what I fancy.' He winked at the small crowd which had gathered and gave them all a wave, as if they were his personal fans instead of strangers in a nightclub. 'Hope you enjoyed the show, folks. Ta ta.'

And off they went into the night. As far as I know, Jay had no idea of any of this, as I made sure I retrieved her phone number from his jacket before he got back. Her name and number were printed on a piece of pink notepaper and she'd scrawled a message underneath it: *Give me a ring if you want to see what a real woman's like.* Cheeky cow. My face burned when I read that. Who says you have to have enormous mammary glands and child-bearing hips to qualify as a 'real woman'. But a small nagging voice tormented me. Maybe if I was built like an Earth mother, I'd have more chance of becoming one.

It's funny. At the time, I revelled in my victory. But I don't feel the same any more. My soul must have taken Enoch's advice and forgiven Evie her trespasses. And my old self, for ridiculing her in public.

* * *

The French wall-clock chimed the hour, bringing me out of my reverie and back to the moment.

'So what you're saying, Enoch, is that if a person is happy with herself—' the expression *bien dans sa peau* flashed into my mind, '—then she'll attract someone who's happy too. And that some people are like vampires, except they drain people's energy instead of their blood. And if we can't teach them to become radiators instead of drains, it's best to kick them into touch.'

The pen sketched a tick and continued.

Those who experience depression and are low in spirit have lost their passion for life. So they often seek the passion they lack by becoming obsessed by another being, looking to them for rescue from their unhappiness. But I must ***emphasise*** *the importance of recognising that this is a false salvation. Because in the search for a saviour, seekers cast themselves in the role of helpless victims. A passionate union always has more chance of success when underpinned by a passion for life. For if your loved one departs, your passion for life will sustain you.*

I could see the truth of that now. No wonder I'd been so depressed after Mike died. He and I had been so happy in each other's company, that we hadn't really needed anyone else. I'd put all my eggs in one basket, as it were, and had felt life wasn't worth living without him. That is, until Zac had come along. But if I took Enoch's advice, I'd have to learn not to see Zac as my knight in shining armour, come to unlock my chastity belt and rescue me from my loneliness.

The pen stayed where it was, but I felt that a yes to the last bit was implied. Like the pen, I was beginning to fade. This channelling...automatic writing...whatever it was called, needed a steady focus. Memories of Mike and Jay, which kept crowding in, were distracting me. But there was one last thing on my mind.

'Enoch, I heard something sad today. My first husband's wife died recently. He must be feeling awful, just like I did after losing Mike. Do you think I should contact him?'

I was going to say something more about not wanting to give him the impression I was still holding a torch for him, when the pen started up.

Your instinct to comfort another soul is in keeping with the role we believe you will, at some time in the future, be ready to play. Your conversations with me and your work with Cassiel have already set you on the path to awakening. As your radiance increases, you will be able to help yourself and others by transforming heavy energies such as grief and despair into hope and anticipation of good things. The connection of Pandora, your mythic namesake, to the virtue of Hope is very apt. This is a quality you should nurture in yourself and others. By all means contact this soul. For he is, indeed, in need of solace.

The pen came to rest quietly on the desk, rather than on the paper, and I understood that our communication was at an end. I packed away my file and went up to bed, where I lay thinking about what a conversation with Jay, after all these years, would be like.

Chapter 32 – 2003

It was Friday afternoon, the day after my heart to heart with Enoch. I'd just returned from a busy stint at Cool Cakes and I was staring down at my address book, contemplating the entry beside Jay's name. Should I write or ring? If I wrote and he ignored it, I'd feel bad. And if I rang and there was just an answering machine – or, worse, if one of his children answered – I'd probably ring off in embarrassment.

I hadn't spoken to him since our divorce, but contact had been maintained by his habit of sending me postcards from improbable places.

If you look hard enough in perfectly ordinary towns without a scrap of sea or decent landscape, you'll nonetheless find postcards of local views. These are often artists' impressions of historic buildings before the bulldozer intervened. Or canals. Who on earth ever bought them apart from me and Jay is anybody's guess. He started it shortly after we got divorced, and I thought it only polite to send him one back occasionally. We always wrote the same first line: *Wish you were here*. I suppose it was a kind of code. A hint at what might have been, had I been in possession of Debbie's reproductive system.

Besides this, he regularly sent me a Christmas card with one of those printed letters with every detail of his children's achievements. How avidly I tore open the envelope (not) to read about the twins and their siblings – discovering who'd won the class chess prize, made the first eleven, etc. I assumed it was sent to me ironically. God help him if he was serious.

From time to time I sent him a Christmas card back, signed from myself and a man. Always a different name – and all invented. He never referred to this. But it made me feel better.

In the early years he used to enclose a handwritten note keeping me up to speed with the pets he'd accused me of abandoning, and inviting me down to see them. He even sent me invitations to his children's birthday parties a couple of times. But I never went, as the sight of the dogs would have killed me. Time solved the problem in the end, as eventually Django, Marley and Lulu gave up the ghost, along with the handwritten enclosure.

We hadn't exchanged any bizarre postcards since I'd married Mike. Which wasn't surprising, as I'd mailed him a change of address card when we'd moved to Chace Standen and he'd have been blind not to have noticed that Pandora Jay had become Pandora Armstrong.

The first Christmas after that, I'd sent him a card, signing it from Andy, Mike, and Oscar. For once it was the truth, unlike the fictitious names I'd included in the past – never really knowing if he'd got the joke. I didn't get a card back, making it the first Christmas he'd missed since we'd split up, a snub which had upset me more than I'd expected. So there'd been no communication between us for almost four years, which made it all the harder to make a sympathy call out of the blue, especially as I'd never liked the husband-rustling, deceased anyway.

My hand hovered over the phone, but I still couldn't bring myself to dial Jay's number. Oscar decided matters by running to the door and whining for a walk. So I buttoned on his red mac and we both trotted out into the showery afternoon.

When we got back I felt invigorated and raring to go. But go where? Once Mike had come on the scene and we'd moved here, I'd mostly lost touch with the friends I used to knock about with in London. I'd even neglected Fiona.

I suppose there was always Brighton. But it was Cece's turn to come to me. And with her home being her workplace, I couldn't just descend on her at short notice expecting to be entertained.

As I tried to dry Oscar's wet feet – a process he disliked, and which involved me placing a second towel over his head so he wouldn't know what was going on – I found myself thinking alternately of Jay and Zac. I tried to imagine where they were and what they were doing, and I wondered how I was going to spend the coming weekend, which stretched out before me like a wasteland, with no sign of an oasis.

And then the phone rang. It was my mother, Frankie.

'Hi darling. How are you? I wondered what you were doing this weekend. Do you fancy coming down to see us? There's a Harvest Moon celebration tomorrow. It'll be outside, so bring suitable clothing. But you don't have to take part if you don't want to. You can just sit and watch if you like. We haven't seen you in ages...'

When I could get a word in edgeways, I said I'd be happy to come. I think my mother was rather surprised at how little persuasion I needed. Not that I didn't love seeing her, but she and Charles were so absorbed in each other, sometimes I felt like an intruder. And their friends, like them, were such old hippies. It was all crystals and joss sticks, and everyone sounding wise and other worldly. A day or two of this could get a bit much, and I was usually glad to leave. But this time I had an ulterior motive. This particular visit would be a lifeline. To keep me from brooding and dithering at home.

* * *

Just before Oscar and I left on Saturday morning, I deliberately put my mobile phone in a drawer so I wouldn't be tempted to do anything silly while I was away. Frankie and Charles always had plenty of booze around the place, and I didn't want to engage in any drunken dialling that I'd regret my whole life thereafter.

I settled Oscar in his basket in the footwell of the passenger seat, and we hit the road in the little red sports car Mike had entrusted to me when we got married. Up to then, it had spent half its life in his garage while he used his turbo charged monster. My old Mini Cooper had bitten the dust just after we got together, so the timing had been perfect.

Luckily the rain had cleared and the weather forecast was good. I had no idea what this harvest ceremony was going to be like, but knowing Frankie and her friends, it probably involved dancing by the light of the moon and some cymbal clashing.

Charles was going to be in their crystal shop all day today, which would give me a chance to catch up with Frankie at their home. This was a typical olde English, roses round the door, white-washed, thatched cottage. Its chocolate-box image was shattered, however, when you got through the front door and caught sight of the clutter. Years of accumulated trinkets and mementoes of their individual and combined travels lay on every surface, vying for space with crystals of all shapes and sizes, the spookiest being in the shape of a skull.

My mother had developed a Quentin Crisp attitude to dust and used to say, 'When you dust, it creates electricity, which attracts new dust immediately, so it's a complete waste of time.'

I'd told Frankie ages ago about the effectiveness of damp dusting, and of vacuum cleaners which picked up animal hair, but it went in one ear and out the other. Luckily, Charles was more scrupulous than Frankie, and every so often would roll up his sleeves and give the old place 'a good bottoming', as he called it. Otherwise, Oscar and I would never have set foot in the place.

We arrived at midday and Frankie ushered us in and proceeded to scrutinise me. She seemed to have shortened and widened as she got older, and had to stand on tiptoe to kiss me. She was dressed in a voluminous kaftan, her once dark hair now almost pure silver. But her face was wonderfully unlined for someone in her seventies. Her black cat, Anubis, took one look at Oscar and fled through the flap in the back door.

'We won't see her again till Sunday,' said Frankie. 'She'll be all right. She has places she goes to for food when we have visitors she doesn't get on with.'

'Gee, thanks Mum. Nice to feel wanted.'

Frankie patted me on the back and led me to the small dining room next to the kitchen.

'You know I mean Oscar. Now I'm going to make you some

relaxing camomile tea and a devilled tofu sandwich and you can tell me what you've been up to. You've got the look of a woman with something on her mind.'

Luckily the sandwich was much tastier than it sounded, so between bites I unburdened myself, trying hard not to whinge too much in the process. I told her how lonely I'd been without Mike, and how Zac had come on the scene. When I fretted about the age difference, my mother was reassuringly sympathetic, having herself had a penchant for younger men. Her sympathy evaporated, however, when I told her the news that Jay's wife had been killed. At the mention of his name, her mouth tightened.

'Serves him jolly well right after the way he treated you. His karma's come home to roost, and about time too.'

'Mum, how can you say that?' I was deeply shocked. I could understand her objecting to his drug habit, and getting Debbie pregnant. But not caring about his children becoming motherless? That was taking loyalty to me too far.

'I'm just stating the obvious, Pan. Nobody gets away with anything. It always comes back and bites them in the butt eventually. It wasn't your fault you couldn't conceive. And you could have adopted. If he'd been faithful to you, none of this would have happened.'

That's a bit rich, I thought. Coming from someone who'd run away from my dad with a man she'd met at a music festival.

I wanted to know if she agreed with Enoch, about Jay being in need of solace, so I ventured, 'Don't you think I should ring him to say I was sorry to hear about Debbie?'

Her face turned pink, as she attacked the items on the draining board, clattering them away as she dried them.

'Absolutely not. He's bad news. All that business about not knowing his father, and thinking his mother was his sister. If he wasn't permanently screwed up, it'd be a miracle. Take my advice and steer well clear. Don't get involved.'

'I never said anything about getting involved. It'd be a simple phone call.'

'After what he put you through...' she snorted, then shut the cabinet door with a bang, as if she'd said all she was going to say on the matter.

'I thought your spiritual books recommended as much forgiving and forgetting as possible,' I persisted. 'Isn't forgiveness supposed to be healing? Anyway, I wasn't exactly an angel, either.'

She had the grace to look reflective for a moment, before she stormed on. 'I think you'd be mad to get in touch with him, especially now this new chap's in the picture. It'd just complicate matters. And if you want to forgive him, you can always do that from a distance. It works just as well.'

I hesitated. Pointing out one's parents' shortcomings to them was always difficult. 'Couldn't *you* forgive him from a distance, then, Mum?'

Frankie put down her tea towel, choosing to disregard my last remark completely.

'Do you think some of my crystal healing might help you get your head together? We'd have to go to the shop, though. You know I don't like doing it here.'

Frankie had a treatment room above the shop which she also let out to other healers. She'd told me once, when she'd been a bit tipsy, that she'd never do healing at home because of the negative energy the clients might release. Her actual words had been, 'I don't want their crap in my house.'

The thought of my mother placing crystals on my body and possibly reading my future with angel cards, or whatever she did, unnerved me. It was time to put the lid on Zac and Jay, otherwise the weekend ahead could be tricky.

'No, don't worry, Mum. It's lovely of you to offer, but it's your day off.'

Frankie nodded. 'Okay, darling. But I think I know someone who might be able to help you at short notice.'

She put her glasses on and moved into the living room where she began searching for something under a stack of papers piled haphazardly on a mahogany tallboy.

'Here it is. Rosemary's card. She's conducting the ceremony tonight. She does energy healing. I could see if she'd fit you in for a session before you go back.' Her luminous green eyes surveyed me over her glasses. 'Truly, darling, I think you need something more than camomile tea to calm you down.'

Frankie handed me the card and I read the words: *Rosemary Austen, Practical Alchemist and Energy Healer,* followed by her address and telephone number.

'Practical Alchemist? Mum, does this mean she's a witch?'

'Good lord, no. She's a sort of herbalist, that's all. She concocts herbal remedies.'

'But I'm not ill.'

Frankie raised her eyebrows quizzically. 'Well, maybe not physically...'

'Do I come across as nutty, then? Oh God!'

'Well,' she retorted, 'when you start talking about getting back in touch with that adulterous, alcoholic, drug addict, what do you expect me to think?'

I flung myself down on the sofa, to be immediately joined by Oscar, thinking it was some sort of game. I jumped up quickly because, paradoxically, even though it was encased in a purple velvet throw, no dogs were allowed on it. Tracking my mother's gaze, I saw that the throw had discharged a trail of black cat hairs on to the back of each leg of my white jeans.

Frankie ordered Oscar into his doggy bed, knelt down, and proceeded to brush the hairs off my trouser legs with a clothes brush. Rather more harshly, I thought, than was warranted.

'Pan, you should know by now not to wear pale clothing in the moulting season. I hope you've brought something more suitable to change into.'

I had no idea when the cat-moulting season was. What did I know about cats? I was a dog person through and through. My mother finished beating my legs and stood up.

'Now do you want me to get in touch with Rosemary or not?'

The irritation in Frankie's tone wasn't lost on me.

'Well, I suppose it wouldn't hurt to have some energy healing, whatever that is.'

I was used to therapies with more definite names like shiatsu, reiki, reflexology. Even crystal healing I understood. This energy healing sounded a bit vague.

'Have you had it, Mum?'

'Once or twice. She works on the head quite a lot. I always ask for a demo before I let a therapist advertise, or rent the therapy room. Then every so often they give me a free session so I'll keep recommending them. That way I keep nicely topped up without having to pay a penny.'

Yes, I thought, that sounds like Frankie, remembering the crystal workshop she'd held at The Cedars when she'd contributed nothing towards the food and lodging I'd provided. What with all the crystal sales she made on top of the course fees, and what she'd charged for distance healing after that, she'd raked it in. Mike had said, 'So what, we can afford it.' But I'd felt a bit as if I was being ripped off by my own mother.

Frankie was waiting for me to make a decision.

'Okay. But she won't be doing it tonight, will she?'

I didn't think I could cope with the Harvest Moon shenanigans and the laying on of hands all in one go.

'Let's ring her and see.'

So Frankie rang Rosemary and we arranged for a session on Sunday morning. And I went upstairs and changed out of my good cashmere sweater and white Levis into a grey fleece and a pair of old denims in readiness for the Harvest Moon ceremony at Apple Blossom Cottage.

Chapter 33 – 2003

Rosemary, a tall, middle-aged woman with short, fair hair, dressed in a white robe which reached her feet, stood facing a stone altar in her garden. Circled around her, several Glastonbury residents, including Frankie and Charles, watched while she conducted the Harvest Moon Ceremony. The altar was dressed with sheaves of wheat, small pumpkins, and overflowing baskets of russet apples picked from the ancient apple tree which stood directly behind the altar.

Four people were holding different coloured candles: green, yellow, red and blue and were positioned at the four points of the compass. They each in turn lit their candles, when directed by Rosemary, but the light wind kept blowing them out. The large, fat white candle in the middle of the altar was protected by a candle sleeve, so it flickered on regardless. But it was nothing in comparison to the size and splendour of the pink harvest moon, which hung low and vast in the sky. It was so low it almost seemed to touch St Michael's Tower, which could be seen clearly from the garden, silhouetted against the night sky, sitting on the tall mound they call the Tor.

I was resting in the conservatory observing the scene behind glass, huddled in a blanket, having excused myself from the great outdoors on the grounds of period pains. The cramps had come on that afternoon, and no amount of whisky, lemon and honey, liberally prepared by Frankie and Charles, had eased them. Frankie had been convinced it was the effect of the full moon and it was evidence of my 'divine feminine' aspect synchronising with nature. I suppose someone of my age should have been glad to see evidence that my oestrogen was still pumping. But actually, only just, as it'd been three months since the last menses.

Snuggling down in my blanket, I couldn't help sniggering as first the drumming, then the dancing, got going. To begin with, the dancing was quite sedate, in single formation, moving round the circle. Then the Great Mother Goddess, whom Rosemary had earlier invoked and now seemed to be channelling, encouraged them to go freestyle, whereupon a couple of them started bounding about like mountain goats, their silver-grey ponytails tossing as they leapt. I'd noticed a chalice of cider being passed round the group earlier, which was regularly refilled, and I think this might have contributed to their gay abandon.

I must have dropped off, because the next I knew, Frankie was shaking me.

'Wake up, Pan. We've finished now. Do you want any curry before we go?'

Whenever Frankie's friends got together for communal suppers, they always seemed to end up with a selection of disparate curries. Not for them finger rolls and quiches with a jacket potato and salad on the side, which would have gone down a treat. My stomach was growling with hunger but it wasn't tempted by what was on the table.

'How about some apple pie and custard, made with Apple Blossom apples?'

Rosemary had appeared, divested of her white robe, and was offering me a steaming bowl which spoke of cloves and vanilla. I took it, and found it to be so delicious I willingly accepted a second portion.

It'd been quite a surprise at the beginning of the evening, to find that Rosemary wasn't the witchy crone I'd imagined her to be, but a tall, slim, attractive woman who dressed well and whose house was immaculate. Wherever her paraphernalia was – she must have had a cache of crystals, candles, joss sticks, reference books and the odd crystal bowl and drum somewhere – she certainly kept it well out of sight, unlike my disorganised parent and her paramour. The only obvious sign of New Agery in this room, was a large picture of a beautiful woman in a long, violet robe, holding a bough of flowering hawthorn, who appeared to be walking on the surface of a lake with a swan beside her and the Tor in the background. Inscribed on the golden frame, were the words: 'Lady of Avalon – Mother of Transformation'.

Rosemary sat down beside me.

'How are you feeling now? Are you sure you don't want anything for the pain?'

She'd offered me one of her herbal concoctions earlier, but I'd declined, as I'd just had some aspirin. This time I decided to give it a try. She went away and returned within five minutes carrying a lurid green brew in a small glass which she told me to drink quickly all in one go. I saw the reason for this when I narrowly escaped regurgitating it halfway through. It left a taste in my mouth like old vase water which forced me to grab a barley sugar from the dish on the table and stuff it in my mouth.

By this time, Charles was hovering in the doorway with his scarf and gloves on, ready for the short walk back home.

'Coming, Charles,' trilled my mother.

They almost looked like members of the same tribe tonight. Charles's shoulder length, wiry grey bob was swept straight back from his large pink face into a ponytail and my mother had done the same with her silver mane. Yes. I'm ashamed to admit that they were the goat dancers. Thank heaven I'd been half dozing under glass, and therefore spared the embarrassment of witnessing their performance in its entirety.

As we said our goodbyes, Frankie went through her toy-boy routine, a theme on which I'd heard variations on several occasions. Frankie was seventy-five and Charles sixty-nine, but she had the energy of a woman of my age, whereas Charles would nod off at the drop of a hat.

Despite this, or maybe because of it, she would link her arm in his and lean on him like an old lady. Then she'd say, 'Thank goodness I've got a toyboy to look after me in my old age.'

And Charles would chuckle and say something along the lines of, 'Come on, old girl. I'll get you home, give you your cocoa and tuck you in.'

So there they were, performing their shtick in Rosemary's hallway, when I had an epiphany. That could be me and Zac in twenty-four years' time. The age difference was the same. And really, what did it matter? Because they didn't look odd together at all. Well, no more than any old ponytailed couple would.

We were back home in fifteen minutes. Charles kindly took Oscar for a lap around the paddock which adjoined their back garden, then the dog and I turned in while the lovebirds cracked open a bottle of wine and watched an episode of a mafia mobster series they'd recorded. Oscar was quite happy in his basket and it wasn't long before he was on his back, legs aloft, gently snoring. But it was slightly more difficult for me. I wasn't used to sleeping in a single bed and my toes were overhanging the mattress.

I got up to rearrange the bedding, automatically putting my hand on my tummy, when I realised it didn't ache any more. Rosemary's vile potion had actually done the trick. Pulling the covers as far up as I could without exposing my feet, I fell asleep and didn't open my eyes until nine o'clock when Frankie brought me a cup of tea.

'Wake up, sleepy head. You didn't even stir when Oscar scratched to come out. That was an hour ago. You'd better get up soon, you've got your appointment with Rosemary at eleven.'

In honour of Rosemary's clean house, I put on my white jeans and soft blue cashmere sweater. Charles had offered to walk with me in case I got lost, but I navigated by keeping my eye on St Michael's Tower, having observed, the day before, roughly where it should be on the skyline when I reached Apple Blossom Cottage.

In response to my knock, a teenage boy opened the door. He looked a little surprised to see me.

'Hi. Rosemary's expecting me.'

He let me in, shouting up the stairs, 'Mum. It's someone for you.'

The boy left me standing in the hall and disappeared. After a couple of minutes, Rosemary came down the stairs. She had on dark trousers and a short white tunic – the sort that health professionals wear.

'Please come up,' she smiled. 'I'm sorry Max left you in the hall. He's not usually here when I see clients, so he was probably a bit unsure.'

I followed her up the stairs and she led me into a spacious room with white walls. A sturdy therapy table stood in the centre of the room, covered with a spotless white sheet. There was an apothecary chest at one end – presumably where the herbs were kept. On the wall hung some framed certificates and a large chart depicting and naming the thirty-two adult teeth. There were two chairs and a table at the other end of the room and that's where she took me.

'Sit down. I just want to tell you a little about myself. I'm actually a dentist three days a week – I think of it as my 'civilian' job – and an alternative therapist and herbalist the other two. My husband always used to say I put the 'dental' into transcendental.'

I suppressed a titter, but she didn't seem to notice, and went on, 'I usually like to keep weekends free for Max.' A shadow crossed her face.

'Sadly, his father isn't with us anymore, so I'm all he's got. And he's at an age when he needs a father figure.'

I uttered some words of sympathy, assuming he'd died, but she blushed.

'No. He met someone else and they went off to an ashram in India.'

While she was talking, I tried to work out why this woman was confiding in me. Whenever I'd had therapy treatments before, we'd gone straight to the table, I'd stretched out, and they'd done what they had to do, which usually involved the laying of hands on different parts of the body, to the accompaniment of tinkly music or an assortment of nature noises: usually ocean waves or a light shower in the rainforest. When they finished, they would leave me for a few minutes, bring me some water, and I would pay and take my leave. Unless I was a guinea pig and it was a freebie, of course.

Rosemary had by now finished her emotional offloading, and had moved on to outlining the treatment itself, explaining what might happen if the energy she was channelling got too strong. Apparently on occasions in the past, the lights had fused and people had been moved sideways with the force of whatever it was. I was beginning to feel a flutter of apprehension, hoping she'd hurry up and get on with it.

'So, if you'll just come over to the treatment table.'

I climbed on and relaxed immediately. There was nothing like being the passive recipient of a therapeutic treatment. I don't know why I'd left it so long since the last one. Probably because when The Cedars was thriving, we'd regularly had workshops for complementary therapies. And they often used me as a practice body to work on. So I didn't have to pay a penny.

I instantly heard the echo of Frankie saying those same words yesterday, and my blood ran cold. Had I inherited her freeloader gene without even realising it?

Rosemary asked if I was warm enough and then added, 'By the way, Pandora, how are you? Did the tincture help?'

'Yes. It was marvellous. And the pain hasn't come back.'

'Good. If you have any trouble with your perimenopause, just let me know. There's a lot we can do to regulate your hormones.'

My plan for regulating my hormones had been to go straight on to HRT. But it was probably prudent not to mention that to a practical alchemist.

'Thanks,' I muttered, willing her to get on with it.

'Okay, so I'm going to work mainly on your head and spine. I might need to stretch your neck a little bit, but I'll warn you first. Okay?'

Rosemary started to stroke my head, then asked me to turn over, and she worked on the back of my neck and my spine. The white sheet was pulled back so I could put my face into a circular aperture in the treatment table.

I had been half waiting for the lights to fuse, which wouldn't have mattered, as we didn't really need artificial light anyway, but nothing like that happened. What happened instead was that the room itself suddenly seemed to be full of electricity. And Rosemary's voice changed. It became lighter, very feminine, running up and down the scale. She was talking in a language I didn't understand and it was only towards the end that I got a clearer idea of what the voice was trying to tell me.

After that, Rosemary's voice altered again. This time it was deeper and I began to understand snatches of it, even though it was still in a foreign tongue. This second voice was talking about the physical body, and how it is the instrument which allows human beings to operate on Earth. And how all human souls are multidimensional but when they come to Earth and acquire the necessary carapace to allow them to live and breathe on this planet, they tend to forget about their supernatural natures and operate simply on the physical and mental levels.

The speaker said it was important for us to consciously connect with Beings of Light, like himself, because they need humans to be channels, so their messages can be heard.

He explained that those humans who are awake, and aware that the human role is to evolve spiritually and to help others develop in the same way, should always be joyful and compassionate. And loving. By doing this, they will help the people on our planet to move on from wars and bloodshed. The more compassion, love and joy that is expressed in the world, the less likely human beings will be to commit violence against each other, and the more advanced they will become.

He said human beings are all linked and every one of us who raises himself or herself up spiritually, contributes towards raising the others up as well. And even if their connection with their spiritual origins goes unrecognised by their physical brains, it is still there. And it will respond to kindness from others on some level. He said this applies to even the seemingly blackest of hearts. So no good wish directed towards another ever falls on stony ground, no matter what outward appearances may suggest.

There was a bit more in the same vein and then Rosemary

stopped talking and I opened my eyes. I was now lying on my back and she was standing at the end of the table with her eyes closed, nodding every now and then as if she was listening to someone. After a little while, she made some sweeping movements over my body, and drew up a chair beside me.

'What did you think of that, then? We had quite an important visitor, you know.'

I blinked, to disguise the tears which had unexpectedly started flowing when the voice had stopped speaking. Rosemary wasn't fooled and handed me a man-sized tissue. I consulted my watch and saw it was past noon. We'd been in the room for over an hour, but it felt like half that time.

'I feel sort of...' I searched for the words but could only come up with, 'wiser than I was before. What language were you speaking, by the way? I understood some of it.'

Rosemary looked surprised.

'Good for you. I was channelling what people call the Language of Light. It only comes through sometimes. But I don't always understand it word for word. I often just get a general impression of what the speaker's saying.'

The term 'Language of Light' sounded a bit vague to me.

'Is it the lost language of Atlantis or something?'

Rosemary grinned. 'Well I suppose it could be. Your guess is as good as mine. I 'm not sure where it comes from. Some say it was the first language. Or the language of the angels. I call it the Language of Light because channelled speech is generally known as that.'

'So who was the important visitor then? There were two of them, weren't there?'

'Yes. First Quan Yin came in. She specialises in opening the heart chakra to unconditional love and compassion. She's associated with fertility.'

(Ah, I thought, that explains why she told me I could still be a mother. But in view of the menopause conversation we'd just had, I decided not to share that with Rosemary.)

'I got an impression of a pinky-purple-coloured flower,' I said, quite surprising myself, as I'd almost given up hope of ever 'seeing' anything, apart from the occasional dancing flame.

Rosemary smiled. 'That's her. I have no memory of what she said, but I can tell you a bit about her. Quan Yin is the Buddhist equivalent of Mother Mary. She represents the Divine Feminine and her task is to help living souls complete their enlightenment—'

A little light bulb went on in my head. It sounded as if she was in cahoots with Enoch and Cassiel on that one.

'—What you saw was her symbol, a lotus flower. Her invocation is *Om Mani Padme Hum* which means, "Hail to the jewel in the lotus". It's good practice to say that every day with the intention of invoking her protection. She's also involved with the process of releasing feelings of resentment and sadness. Holding on to them harms us and prevents us being at peace.'

Om Mani Padme Hum rang a bell, but I couldn't quite remember where I'd heard it before.

'So, I suppose her message boils down to: "forgive and forget".'

Rosemary smiled, 'More or less.'

'So who was the second speaker, Rosemary?'

'One of the big cheeses. Metatron. He's in charge of the Ascension of the entire planet.'

My heart gave a start. How thrilling that Metatron had stopped by to say hello. Another link with Enoch. I loved these synchronicities – they made me feel that my celestial contacts weren't figments of my imagination. So he was in charge of Ascension.

'Does that mean we're all going to leave planet Earth and fly up to heaven at some point, Rosemary?'

She smiled ruefully. 'Afraid not. But it would be much simpler to explain, wouldn't it?'

'Is it so hard, then?' I groaned, thinking that if I did decide to go for it, I could be faced with explaining the complexities of the process to friends and family. And – my heart sank at the thought – to any sceptical lover who might be around at the time.

Rosemary's expression became impish. 'He said Ascension is when humanity rises into a higher, crystalline dimension. For many thousands of years this has been unavailable because of the dense physicality of life on Earth, but is soon becoming possible. The process transforms the cells of the body from being carbon-based to crystalline-based to allow us to ascend from our third-dimensional paradigm to the fifth dimension. From there we can work our way up to the twelfth.'

Seeing my horrified expression, she laughed and patted my hand.

'Don't worry. There's no need to get too technical. I just like to think that he encourages us to be nice to each other.'

I liked Rosemary's attitude. It saved me from being overawed. My views on the mysteries of the metaphysical were similar to those I held on computers – that I'd never totally grasp them. She was telling me it didn't really matter.

'So you don't think it's necessary to understand this Ascension thing completely, because I'm still not really sure what it means or how it would change a person...'

She shook her head. 'Don't worry about it. You can feel something's right without having to intellectualise it. I suppose it's like driving a car – just because we don't know what's going on under the bonnet, it doesn't stop us getting to our destination.'

I smiled in agreement and Rosemary continued, 'So you understood the gist of what Metatron said, did you?'

'Yes, it was about what we had to do to improve the world. I've been hearing something similar from someone else recently, so I think I've got the message now.'

'Great. I don't need to give you the standard Metatron pep talk then. By the way, I'm sorry if I bent your ear earlier on. I don't usually spill my troubles out to clients. I asked Metatron about it at the end of the session and he said it was because you were in the process of developing your divine mission, which is to listen to others and give them hope. So I was a sort of guinea pig for you to practise on. Thanks, by the way. I felt better after our heart-to-heart.'

I felt as if she and I had been in different realities.

'But, Rosemary, I didn't say anything to you.'

'Don't you see? That's the point. You're a listener and a transmuter. You don't need to say anything. It's all done at an energetic level, through your heart chakra. You're an energy alchemist.'

Rosemary glanced at the watch pinned to her tunic. I took the cue and lifted my unwilling legs over the side of the treatment table. They could have stayed there all day.

I offered to pay more than the £50 fee because we'd overrun by half an hour, but she wouldn't hear of it. As I was walking to her gate, she called me back.

'Pandora, I've just remembered. He said something about a book. Does that mean anything to you?'

The hairs on the back of my neck stood up.

'Um. Well. The only book I'm sort of being encouraged to write would be a semi-autobiography, concentrating on my love life.'

I made a face when I said this in case she thought I was being self-important. She paused a moment and closed her eyes.

'He says that's the one. And to hurry up and get on with it.'

She smiled and waved me goodbye. As she closed the door I could hear her son asking what was for lunch.

Chapter 34 – 2003

When I arrived back, the lovebirds were eager to hear how I'd got on. I told them all about it over the cauliflower and lentil curry that Charles had created, preceded by tomato and apple soup, courtesy of Rosemary's windfalls. Not quite my idea of Sunday fare, but at least Oscar hadn't been tormented by the smell of roasting meat.

They didn't turn a hair when I described how Rosemary had channelled Quan Yin and Metatron. All this was as normal as breathing to them, just part of everyday Avalon. At the end of the meal, when I mentioned being prompted by Metatron to write a book, they wanted to know more, so I found myself telling them about Enoch, and even Cassiel.

Charles got to his feet. 'I might have something on Enoch from when I was making notes on Ascended Masters.'

He led me into his den, where he kept all his reference books and notebooks. He took a large leather-bound volume, one of many, from a high shelf, and found the relevant passage. Then he laid the book on a table so we could sit down and read it together. His notes were written on parchment in beautiful, slanted copperplate writing, which corresponded to the antiquity of the material.

Notes On The Book of Enoch

The legend of Enoch's adventures was passed on by word of mouth over thousands of years and written down in Aramaic in the first and second century BC, probably by the Essenes, a Jewish sect with a colony at Qumran. Several fragments of Enochian writings were found at Qumran among The Dead Sea Scrolls. These fragments were evidence that The Book of Enoch was included in the Essene canon of sacred scriptures.

The book was considered apocryphal (with hidden or secret meaning) and is in five parts.

Here Charles listed the parts, with a short summary of their contents. My attention was drawn to the description of Part Five of the book –

The Epistle of Enoch – which stated that God would reward the good, but that sinners would be punished.

The punishing thing was the complete opposite of what he'd told me. No wonder he hadn't wanted his name attached to this book. The notes continued.

The Book of Enoch is part of a collection of Apocrypha, originally included in the Bible but banned by the Council of Laodicea in 364 BC as being heretical. It was labelled as Pseudepigrapha, meaning the writings are not by the attributed author. This was a time when Church theologians were also selecting the politically correct scriptures which would make up the New Testament. They settled on twenty-seven texts including the gospels of Matthew, Mark, Luke and John but excluded the gospels of other apostles like that of St Peter.

Charles pointed to this part of the notes and exclaimed, 'Extraordinary considering Jesus had made Peter the first pope. Apparently, the Council objected to his account of Jesus feeling no pain at the crucifixion. And the suggestion that he was pure spirit and not really human.'

He smiled wryly, 'They judged Peter's gospel to be pseudepigraphic. Whatever the truth of the matter, they threw a lot of babies out with the bathwater in 364 BC, that's for sure.'

I'd had enough ancient history by that time and made to close the book but Charles urged me to read on.

Up to the period when this Council of church elders decreed against it, The Book of Enoch had been esteemed by Christians. Jesus had certainly studied it because some of his sermons bore the influence of Enochian scripture. It had also been a popular text with the Jews, until the second century when some rabbis objected to the stories of the fallen angels and were also afraid the book might encourage more revolutionaries like Jesus.

Once The Book of Enoch was no longer being copied by Christian scribes and the extant copies had been destroyed (or used as firelighters), it disappeared from general use until 1773 when a copy was brought to Europe from Ethiopia and interest in it was reignited.

'No pun intended?' I smirked, and we both giggled.

'I know about Enoch's book,' I said, smugly. Then, pausing for effect, 'He said he'd been misquoted.'

'Oh well,' smiled Charles, 'it's probably all down to Chinese whispers.'

Wondering what the Chinese had to do with it, I raised my eyebrows, and Charles explained, 'You know, "Send reinforcements, we're going to advance" whispered along the line, becomes: "Send three and fourpence, we're going to a dance". So Enoch's words would have been mangled over the centuries. And certain scribes would have been putting their own spin on them anyway.'

To my relief, he closed his book of notes. 'Now let's see if I can find anything on the other one. What was his name? Cassiel?'

He unearthed an old compendium in which there were just a few lines about Cassiel, which he began reading aloud. Enoch had already told me most of it, but there was an extra bit of information I hadn't heard before.

'...He can transmute listlessness into purpose. And he holds the power to help people bring works into being.

Charles snapped the book shut, creating a little puff of dust. 'Now if that doesn't encourage you to start writing, I don't know what will.'

I did, indeed, feel encouraged when I heard that. Life is so much easier when you feel someone's rooting for you. And with Cassiel's special powers to draw on, maybe I could knuckle down and complete Level Two of the Correspondence Course by writing that book. But it still seemed a daunting task.

'Just because I was good at writing essays at school, doesn't mean I can knock out a whole book,' I fretted.

'You're afraid that your reach exceeds your grasp, my dear.' Charles patted my hand in encouragement. 'Don't you think that's how every writer feels before they start? You owe it to yourself —' he raised his eyes to the ceiling, '— and to them upstairs, to at least have a go.'

I nodded. 'You're right. Thanks, Charles. I feel a bit more motivated now.'

I made a move to return to the kitchen, but he gestured to me to sit down.

'Pandora, can I just say something? The menstrual pains you had yesterday...' He blushed slightly, but went on. 'When the body's going through changes, it's even more important to keep balanced, otherwise other areas of one's life can go skew-whiff.'

I was wondering where this was going. Maybe he and Rosemary offered a joint menopause package, him on the crystals and her on the herbs. Charles took a slim magazine from a pile on the floor and handed it to me.

'With my compliments,' he smiled. 'I'm on page ten—'

Then I remembered that Charles wrote a weekly column for a Glastonbury magazine.

'—Why don't you read the article while your mother and I do the washing-up? It won't take you long.'

So I did. And the article was entitled:

Balancing Yin and Yang by Charles Lockwood

The physical differences between men and women can be traced directly to our primeval roles as male hunters and female child-bearers. This also extends to the brain – women are designed to be more sociable and nurturing because they are the ones taking care of the children, whereas men are encouraged to switch off emotionally, so they can overcome fear and protect the women and children when fighting off sabre-toothed tigers or males from other clans. The male brain is wired to be logical and analytical while female brains are better attuned to emotions.

In cosmic terms, the Divine Mind is seen as the masculine principle, and the Divine Heart, the feminine. So not only do we need to balance our minds, but also our hearts. Both male and female, God and Goddess, were necessary for the act of Creation, although humanity, in its pursuit of power, has erred towards the worship of the patriarchal God, without tempering it with the love and compassion of the sacred heart of the Goddess, the Divine Mother.

The unification of the feminine and masculine elements of one's being is the key to the survival of the planet. The balance of the yin and yang energies is important because individuals who are out of balance cause imbalance around them. The right, creative, holistic side of the brain has traditionally been seen as representing the feminine and the left, logical, sequential side, the masculine. But creative endeavours and logical problem-solving call on both sides of the brain. So left needs right and vice versa. The thinking mind and the feeling heart need to be brought together. It would benefit each of us to balance both hemispheres and practise whole brain thinking because, according to the microcosm/macrocosm theory, not only do we balance ourselves, but we enable a greater, planetary, balancing to take place.

Then there was some stuff about earlier civilisations, and whether they'd been dominated by men or women. And a chakra-balancing meditation, all of which I skipped through. But towards the end of the article there was a paragraph about the Holy Spirit which I found really surprising.

In Christianity, the first two persons of the Holy Trinity, God the Father and God the Son, have been seen as strong masculine energies, with the Holy Spirit as a more ephemeral presence. But the word for the Holy Spirit in Hebrew is 'Shekinah' – the god who dwells within – which is a feminine noun, leading to speculation, and in some people, certainty, that the Holy Spirit represents the feminine attributes of God. So perhaps a more accurate description of the Holy Trinity would be: God the Father, God the Son, and God the Holy Mum!

I thought of all the times in my youth when I'd begun my prayers by crossing myself and chanting, 'In the name of the Father, and of the

Son, and of the Holy Ghost. Amen,' first visualising a white-haired patriarch on a cloud, then His son, Jesus Christ, with a sorrowful expression. And, finally, the Holy Spirit as a white dove. But never as a smiling Mother Goddess.

I put the magazine in my bag and joined Frankie and Charles in the kitchen where I caught them canoodling, which was really embarrassing. For me. But not for them. They were quite shameless.

'Thanks, Charles,' I said, as he reluctantly let go of my mother, 'It's good to be reminded that men are from Mars and women are from Venus – and that it's time for the twain to meet. So I will be doing the yin-yang balancing meditation.'

As soon as I said that, I heard the strains of the Ying Tong Song from The Goon Show in my head. Maybe Spike Milligan had been downloading the Language of Light without even knowing it.

Frankie hugged and kissed me, whispering, 'Don't feel bad about what's happening in your body. The change of life isn't just an ending, Pan, think of it as a new beginning as well.'

They were being so kind, that I felt sorry to leave them. That is, until Frankie said, 'I hope you've put all that nonsense about phoning Jay out of your head.' Which was my cue to ignore her words, as she had mine the day before when I'd asked her to forgive him.

That's karma, Mother, I thought. Quid pro quo. Tit for tat.

Needless to say, another reason I wasn't eager to go home was that once there, I'd have to make some decisions about men and telephone calls.

Chapter 35 – 2003

As soon as Oscar and I were settled back in Phoenix Cottage, I checked the phones for messages. There were two on the house phone, both regarding The Cedars. One from a kitchen fitter who wanted to know when he could start work, and another from a room designer who needed to inspect the dining room. There were no messages at all on my mobile phone. I don't know why I'd expected to hear from Zac, really, as he'd said he was spending the weekend with his sister, wherever that was, but I felt disappointed nonetheless.

I decided to focus on making a decision about ringing Jay. I took my Enoch file out of the drawer and turned to the most recent page, when I'd mentioned Jay and he'd said: *By all means contact this soul. For I see he is in need of solace.*

Just before then, Enoch had said that I needed to give others hope. Which was ironic, as that was a quality I felt sorely in need of myself, much of the time. Unless you counted *hoping* that Zac would get in touch. Of that sort of hope I had a shed load, unfortunately.

The bald truth was, that while I appreciated the danger of what Enoch called 'an excess of need' in a relationship, it was hard to stop longing for someone you wanted. I imagined myself sinking my fangs into Zac's neck the next time we met, extracting his life blood to feed my thirst for him. I found this thought disturbingly compelling, but managed to force myself away from my vampire movie to matters pending.

The problem was, I didn't really want to make the call to Jay now. Much as I tried to erase them from my mind, my mother's words had brought back all the hurt I'd suffered when our marriage had ended.

What had seemed like a human gesture of sympathy on Thursday, had, in the space of a weekend, become a niggling obligation – a bit like my duty visits to Joan. She was over eighty now, still living in Nightingale Road, with an enormous tabby cat for company. Actually, it wasn't Joan I had to steel myself for, but the house itself, and all the memories it stirred up. The sharpest of these was my father's early death from a perforated ulcer, along with my profound regret at not having spent enough time with him.

On the way home from Glastonbury, it had come to me where I'd seen Quan Yin's mantra before – it'd been in the book that I'd found in the suitcase under the bed, in my dad's house, all those years ago. I didn't have it now, never having reclaimed it from Sister Joseph. I wondered if she'd carried out her threat to destroy it. I imagined her taking it out of her desk intending to burn it, but reading it instead. Then undergoing a miraculous conversion, leaping over the convent walls, and hot-footing it to Tibet to become a Buddhist nun.

Rosemary had written the mantra down for me, so I sat quietly and recited *Om mani padme hum* over and over until I felt a little better.

I returned to my address book and checked the phone number. This house had been our country retreat when we were married, but it'd been so long since I'd lived there, I'd forgotten the number. I hadn't heard from Jay since I'd left Fulham, so for all I knew, he could even have moved.

I found that my hands were shaking. So much so, that I was forced to pour myself a sherry, which I downed in two gulps, waiting a couple of minutes for it to have an effect. As soon as I felt a warm glow, I dialled the number.

As I'd feared, it wasn't Jay who answered. It was a girl's voice. But I had no intention of giving up now I'd started.

'Hello,' I said. Thinking it was safe to assume this was one of Jay's children, I continued, as confidently as I could, 'May I speak to your father, please?'

'Hold on,' she replied, in a polite tone, and disappeared. I strained my ears for what she might be saying to him, but could hear nothing. After a couple of minutes, a man's voice came on the line.

'Hello. Hello' The voice was his. And I hadn't prepared anything to say.

'Hello Jay. It's Pandora.' I stopped, not sure whether to wade right in with my condolences or open with small talk. But Jay got in first.

'Pandora who?'

I laughed, because I was pretty sure he was joking.

'How many do you know?'

'I only ever knew one. But she dumped me and married someone else.'

'Yeah,' I replied, 'The same thing happened to me.'

'*Touché*.' Then came an awkward pause with neither of us knowing quite how to continue. In the end, he spoke first. 'What can I do for you, Andy?'

'Someone told me that Debbie had died and I wanted to say...' What did I want to say? '...that I know what you're going through.'

'Who told you?' His voice had risen in surprise. 'I didn't think you kept in contact with anyone we knew.'

'I don't. A friend of mine happened to see it on the internet.' I pictured Zac telling me the news and then us coming back here and making love. When Jay spoke, his voice was harsh.

'So it took Debbie dying for you to ring me. How many years is it? Eighteen? The times I wrote and asked you down here and you never answered. You never even rang to see how the dogs were.'

He was angry and I couldn't blame him, but I could at least defend myself.

'Ask yourself who started it, Jay. I didn't get someone pregnant and install them in our house.' The absurdity of what I'd said slipped past both of us.

'Not for lack of trying from what I heard.'

A band of fear tightened my chest and I gasped out the next question.

'What do you mean?'

'Alvie spilled the beans after we took our business to a bigger agency. He told Clive all about your cosy little PR training sessions. I think that makes us pretty even, don't you?'

And do you know what, I had to admit he was right. I wasn't the innocent party. I hadn't divorced Jay because his behaviour was worse than mine, but because I couldn't bear him having a child with another woman.

But what was harder to understand was why, knowing about Alvie, he'd kept inviting me down to see the dogs and meet his kids. And kept sending me all those postcards and Christmas cards over the years. Until I'd married Mike. When it all stopped.

Jay was waiting for a response. He'd exposed me as being disloyal and deceitful, so what could I do but apologise?

'I'm sorry. It was complicated. I didn't even like him that much.'

Jay gave a deep sigh. 'I assumed you did it to see if you could get pregnant by somebody else.'

'I think we both did, didn't we?

'Yeah. And I hit the jackpot and you didn't.'

Recalling the crippling pain I'd felt every time a new baby Jay wunderkind had been born, I thought this rather cruel. But I was determined to steer clear of a slanging match, so I attempted a joke. 'You didn't have to rub it in by having five of them.'

'Oh well, all tadpoles under the bridge now.'

He paused, and I willed him to go on. Now I'd heard his voice, I didn't want the call to end. Talking to him was bringing back memories of how close we'd been. I felt a rush of relief when he continued speaking.

'How about you? All those names you put on the cards – how many blokes did you live with?'

This stung me. 'Didn't you get the joke? I made them up. All except the last one.'

'Why?'

'I dunno. I had to do something to compete with the annual boast-fest from you. Which mountains you'd all climbed, who'd been scuba-diving champion of the world that year.'

Jay snorted as if he was suppressing a laugh. 'You're speaking of the people I love.'

'But admit it, Jay. You used to make fun of that sort of thing.

Seriously, what were you thinking, sending me their annual progress reports?'

'You got me there. Actually, you weren't the only one who complained about the Christmas letters. They were Debbie's idea. She used to spend hours on 'em.' He sighed. 'I don't know why I sent you one. Maybe you're right. Maybe I was saying – look at me, I can do it, but you can't.'

At this, the spasm of sorrow that had been threatening to grab my throat, took hold, and I let out an involuntary yelp. I leaned across the desk to pour myself some more sherry and as I picked up the glass, which had been resting on my Enoch notes, I saw its base had left a circular, brown imprint around the words *in need of solace.* Jay wasn't the only one.

I'd momentarily placed the phone on the desk while I did this, and I could hear Jay's voice calling, 'Andy. Andy. You still there?'

I picked up the phone. 'Yes. It's okay. I'm all right now,' I said. 'I've been a bit over-emotional since Mike died.'

'Mike?' Jay sounded puzzled.

'My husband. He died in March this year. His heart...gave out.'

'Debbie died in April.'

'So we're both in the same boat. That's what I meant when I said I know what you're going through.'

Jay started to speak when he was interrupted by someone shouting his name. It was a woman's voice and she was calling out that dinner was ready. 'Andy, I gotta go. They're all waiting for me. I'll be in touch. Bye.'

And then he was gone.

* * *

Zac finally rang me on Monday afternoon. First of all he asked me if the contractors had been in touch, and when I told him a trio of silver vans had turned up bright and early, he got down to more personal matters.

'Sorry I had to rush off last week. Thursday and Friday were manic. It's calmed down a bit now. How's everything with you?'

I matched his tone, which was friendly rather than intimate.

'Fine. I spent the weekend with my mother in Glastonbury. She dragged me along to a Harvest Festival.'

'What, in a church? Is it the Church of the God Who Doesn't Punish?'

The yellow post-it note with the words GOD DOES NOT PUNISH which Zac had discovered on the inside of my wardrobe door flashed before my eyes. I could see the funny side now, and giggled.

'Those were words of wisdom which were given me by a very venerable old individual and I wrote them down so I wouldn't forget them. I didn't expect anyone else to see them. Anyway, it was a Harvest Moon festival and it was in somebody's garden.'

Zac sniggered, 'Oh, one of those where you conduct fertility rituals *au naturel*. What do you call it, sky clad? Mrs Armstrong, I do believe you might be a practising pagan.'

'Actually I let my mother and her boyfriend do the dancing. I sat in the conservatory and watched. And nobody was sky clad. Quite the reverse – predominantly long skirts and corduroy trousers. And thermal underwear, no doubt, given the average age of the happy band. I think you're letting your imagination run away with you, Mr Willoughby.'

He was chuckling now. 'Don't spoil my fun, Pandora. I was savouring the image of you dancing naked round a bonfire giving thanks for the fruits of the harvest.'

His enthusiastic tone made me think this might be a good time to suggest meeting up, but because he was younger than me and very good-looking, I held myself in check. I was glad I did, because that's just what he went on to propose.

'Look, I'm still at my sister's and I have to more or less pass your place. What say I peel off the motorway and come and say hello on my way home this evening?'

I agreed, with the eagerness of a woman half my age, and immediately began planning a fashion campaign that would knock his eyes out.

Oscar and I were in the middle of performing a little salsa of happiness around the room, when we were interrupted by the room designer at the door with some proposals for his revamp of the dining room in the main house. It looked truly wonderful to me, all the more so because I wasn't paying for it. So I gave him the go ahead and then proceeded to primp and pamper myself in readiness for my toyboy to make an appearance.

Chapter 36 – 2003

And there I was, eagerly awaiting Zac, all made up and dressed to the nines, in a skin-tight, low-cut Armani dress, sipping a gin and tonic, when the knock came on the door. Oscar did his usual trick of barking continuously until he could see who the caller was.

'It's all right, Oscar. It's only Zac,' I cooed, as I tottered into the hall on skyscraper heels.

Except the man standing on the doorstep wasn't Zac. He didn't resemble him in any way. He was a tall, rangy man in his fifties, with dark hair, greying at the temples. His large, brown, sorrowful eyes blinked slightly at the racket Oscar was making.

'Hi, Andy,' he said. 'I was passing and I thought I'd pop in and say hello.' He looked me up and down, making no move to cross the threshold. 'But if you're expecting someone, no sweat.'

'Jay!' Surprise at seeing him made my heart beat like a drum. My nervous system had moved into fight or flight response, but I didn't want to do either.

'Come in, come in. Oscar, be quiet! Would you like a drink?'

Jay ambled in and followed me into the living room.

'Yeah, why not? I'll have what you've got.'

He sat down and patted Oscar, who immediately exhibited his undercarriage for a tickle and became his friend for life. 'Nice dog.'

Remembering something we used to say, I automatically said it.

'In dogs we trust.'

Jay smiled and stroked Oscar some more. 'Yeah, they never let you down.'

He raised his eyes and gave me a searching look. I wasn't quite sure what was going on – why he was here – so I looked away and poured his drink. Jay continued speaking in his laconic drawl. 'I nearly didn't find you. Came by about four and tried the big house, but some bloke opened the door and said he was fitting an oven or something and he thought you lived in the cottage. I knocked here. Heard the dog bark...'

That must have been when I was at the hairdresser's, I thought.

'Yes, I did pop out this afternoon. I'm glad you came back.'

I wondered what he'd been doing for the last couple of hours.

I gave him the gin and tonic, and we both said, 'Cheers.' And he added, 'Good to see you again.'

My thoughts turned to Zac. He'd said he expected to reach my house by about seven. I couldn't begin to think what would happen if my unexpected visitor was still here when he arrived. But now that Jay was sitting a few feet away from me, I knew one thing for certain. I liked him being here.

'How did you find me, by the way?' I asked.

'You sent me that change-of-address card. Three, four years ago?'

'So you knew my address but you stopped writing.'

'Well, you got married, didn't you?'

'But that didn't stop you when *you* were married.'

Jay shrugged wearily. He'd given the impression of being relaxed and laid back when I'd known him, but now he gave off an air of lassitude. His slumped shoulders and face etched with lines, spoke of a man whom life had beaten, somehow.

He didn't answer me directly, just asked, 'Who was this Mike geezer, anyway?'

How long have you got, I thought. But I merely said, 'No one you know. Someone I met when I was eighteen. Then we met up again.'

That was when I made a conscious decision not to bang on about Mike. To stop resurrecting him and to let him rest in peace.

'Tell me about you. And your children.'

And then he talked. And talked. He told me about the group breaking up when they fell out of fashion, not long after we'd split up. How he'd started writing songs for other artists, and had turned his hand to composing music for film soundtracks. He'd even written a few jingles for radio and TV commercials. Anything to put food on the table for his family. Not just food, of course – private schools, holidays abroad. Everything that Debbie expected for herself and their brood.

The twins were now boys of eighteen, about to start university, then there were two girls of fifteen and thirteen, and a boy of eleven. He never mentioned anyone else. No reference to a girlfriend. So it still left me wondering whose was the female voice I'd heard last night.

'Have you got a housekeeper?' I asked.

'No.' He looked at me quizzically. 'Why?'

'Yesterday. Someone was calling you to dinner.'

He smiled a little lopsidedly. He was on his second gin and tonic.

'That was Sharon. She came back from Canada a couple of years ago. Moved in to help me out.'

I had to think who Sharon was. 'You mean your mum?'

'Yeah. My sister-mum.'

There was a knock at the door which set Oscar off again. I hadn't mentioned Zac to Jay but with me all done up like a dog's dinner, he'd sussed out that I was expecting someone.

'Is that your date? I should go.' He got up, but I waved him back down again.

'Where were you this afternoon, Jay?'

'Some pub down the road. Lamb and Flag?'

That explained why he was so heavy-eyed. He must have been drinking for two hours. There was another, more impatient, knock. By this time, Oscar was almost hysterical.

'It's okay. It's only Zac,' I said, as I opened the door. And this time it *was* Zac, standing before me with a huge bunch of flowers.

'Come in, come in,' I urged. 'Oscar, shut up! What lovely flowers.'

Zac leaned forward to kiss me but the bouquet got in the way. I took it and backed into the living room, so he could see that someone else was in the house. He stared past me and I turned to see Jay asleep on the sofa, still cradling his glass.

'You've got company, I see,' said Zac, his eyes wide and wary.

I don't know whether it was surprise at seeing a man sprawled on my sofa, or super surprise because it was James Jay, but he seemed fixed to the spot. All he could do was stare dazedly at the figure on the sofa.

I took the glass out of Jay's hands and he barely stirred, then I motioned to Zac to follow me into the kitchen, where I found a vase and started to arrange the dozen perfect, long-stemmed red roses and their accompanying foliage.

'It's Jay. He just turned up out of the blue.'

'Does that make him a blue jay?' laughed Zac nervously.

'It's not funny,' I hissed. 'He's been drinking since four o'clock. He's had two here and he's been in the Lamb and Flag for a couple of hours. There's no way he can get home tonight unless I take him. Or call a taxi, which would cost a fortune.'

Zac's face fell. 'How many have you had?'

'About three, I suppose. I didn't expect to be driving.'

'You're over the limit then. What's he doing here anyway? I thought you said you weren't in touch.'

I paused, trying to remember what my line had been on the topic of Jay's wife dying. I seem to remember I'd changed the subject. But I had to offer some explanation, and, courtesy of three stiff gin and tonics, it slipped out. 'Enoch told me to ring him to offer my condolences.'

Zac was sitting at the kitchen table, not sure whether to drink the beer I'd offered him. I followed his train of thought. At the moment he was the only sober driver.

'Who's Enoch?' Zac was beginning to sound uncharacteristically tense.

I tried to make light of it. 'He's the one who told me to love myself. He appears from time to time. Well, I don't see him, but I write down what he dictates. I'm his amanuensis.'

'His what?' Zac shifted uncomfortably in his seat. 'I'm beginning to get seriously worried about you, Pandora. Are you saying this house really is haunted? And some sort of ghost has taken possession of you?'

'Don't be ridiculous!' My voice was rising now. 'All I've done is make contact with an ascended master and he's been helping me get over Mike's death.'

'How?' Zac's tone had become more sympathetic at the mention of Mike's death, so I thought I might as well come clean about the whole thing.

'Well I have to be positive and help other people by being positive. And I have to try not to repeat old patterns of behaviour. And I've got to write a book. But it was Cassiel who told me to do that in the correspondence course.'

'Cassiel?' Zac's brow furrowed. Incomprehensionhad certainly been the theme of his evening at Phoenix Cottage so far.

'He's an archangel who's closer to Earth than Enoch, so he sent me some ointment for an enlightenment ceremony. That's the third and last step – after I complete the book.'

'And have you spoken to this Cassiel?'

Zac had still failed to open the bottle of beer, a hint, perhaps, of his readiness for a quick getaway from a lunatic who spoke to ghosts.

'Yes. We spoke on the phone briefly.'

At that moment a tall figure loomed in the kitchen doorway.

'Everything all right in here?' Jay mooched over to the kitchen table and sat down. He turned to me for an introduction and I realised he didn't know who Zac was.

'Jay, this is Zac. His company's leasing the house for a couple of months. They're making a TV programme. I'll tell you about it later.'

I stopped, because I didn't know why I'd assumed that he'd be here later.

Zac shook hands awkwardly across the kitchen table and waited for Jay to speak, but he sat in silence, so Zac said, 'Pleased to meet you. You're a legend. My big sister was a great fan of yours. Sorry to hear about your wife.'

When Zac said 'wife' Jay looked across at me. I felt myself blush, aware that he thought Zac was referring to me.

Zac elaborated. 'The car crash.'

Jay shook his head as if to clear it, 'Yeah. Sorry, man. Debbie. We never did get married. In fact for the last couple of years, she was living with someone else. Still came as a shock, though. The kids were devastated.'

This piece of information cheered me up enormously. Not the bit about the kids – but all the rest.

'So were you the friend who told Andy about it?' Jay had always been astute and he'd put two and two together quite successfully.

'I suppose I was. Yes. She's the only person I know without a computer.'

Jay nodded in approval. 'That's okay. From what I heard just now, she's plugged into something a bit higher-tech than that.'

I gasped. 'We thought you were completely out of it. You've been drinking all afternoon.'

Jay gazed at me with soft eyes and drawled, 'You assumed too much, Andy. I was on lemon and lime in the pub. I'm dog tired, that's why I flaked out.'

I'd finished arranging the flowers, and placed the vase in the middle of the kitchen table. The scent was divine and I took a deep breath and sat down, whereupon Jay took my hand and gave it a little kiss, as if it was the most natural thing in the world.

'I couldn't get what you said out of my head, last night, Andy. Didn't like you being so upset. Never slept a wink. Had to see you.'

I glanced at Zac to see what his reaction was. He was staring at me reproachfully, clearly hoping I would snatch my hand away and ask Jay to leave. I think I might just have been able to hang on to him – if I'd been prepared never again to mention Enoch and probably never again to see Jay. For a split second I wavered. Zac was looking exceptionally fit in jeans and a fine knit sweater, that hugged his long, muscular body. He exuded an energy, a vitality. Beside him, Jay seemed drained and worn out, his shirt hanging loosely on his bony frame, his once-handsome face now set into a mournful mask.

But then, tossing his head and pushing his fringe away from his eyes, Jay delivered the *coup de grâce.*

'I once promised to love and cherish you as long as we both should live, Andy. I'm still willing to keep my pledge. Maybe I'll get it right this time.'

He pulled me to my feet and kissed me in a way that proved there was plenty of life in the old dog yet. Giving myself up wholeheartedly to the kiss, I played a line from one of our songs in my head, 'Since you came I feel so happy I could die.'

In the distance I heard a door slam. I turned towards the sound and Jay softly touched my cheek to bring us back face to face.

'He's history now.' A mixture of pain and passion simmered in his deep brown eyes. 'I'm back. And I'm all yours, if you'll have me.'

Chapter 37 – 2003

I finally set eyes on Jay's children, or 'saplings', as he called them, the weekend after he stayed the night at Phoenix Cottage, when he took me home to meet them.

After reading of their superhuman exploits in Debbie's Christmas letters, year after year, I was relieved to see how normal they were. The boys were called Ashley, Linden, and Rowan, and the two girls, Cherry and Willow. From these names, I'd deduced that Debbie must have liked hugging trees.

Without exception, the five of them had inherited Jay's dark eyes, but their hair ranged from raven black for the twins, through shades of cappuccino for the girls, to dark caramel for the youngest boy. They'd inherited Jay's long, loose limbs and formed an attractive tribe.

All of them, especially the two girls, were suspicious of me at first, but they thawed out a bit when Jay's birth mother, Sharon, greeted me warmly. At lunch that first day, they seemed to enjoy listening to the three of us reminiscing about old times.

Willow came and sat down beside me afterwards and said, 'I like your dress. Is it true that you and Daddy used to be married? That's what Ashley said.'

I felt I wanted to hug her, but I knew it was far too soon for that, so I just answered, 'Yes. It was before he met your mummy.'

Rowan, the youngest, had been listening in and piped up, 'Does that mean we've got more brothers and sisters?'

I laughed. 'I think you've got enough already, haven't you? No. I wasn't able to have any babies.'After a pause I added, 'And I'm too old now.'

There, I'd said it. For most women, being past child-bearing age would have meant a lament for lost youth, but for me it was a welcome release from an urge to reproduce with a body which couldn't deliver.

I expect, dear reader, that you're wondering about Quan Yin

telling me, when I was lying on Rosemary's treatment table, that I could still be a mother. It was the unlikelihood of the accuracy of this piece of information, that had prompted me to keep it to myself. But a few tiny brain cells had been secretly hoping that after sleeping with Jay, perhaps a little miracle would take place. A miraculous conception. But of course it didn't.

I eventually told him about it, more as a joke than anything, and he replied, quite seriously, 'Would you do me the honour of being a mother to my children? I don't mean stepmother. I want them to look on you as their mum.'

And then everything fell into place. I knew at last what Quan Yin had meant. And of course I said yes, as long as that was what they wanted.

I mentioned this to Enoch the next evening and he approved of my future role as tribe mother. But being Enoch – the person who'd first invented books and writing – he put his own spin on it.

Those who anchor new paradigms of information are known as Mothers of the Way. It is the destiny of these to access the new energies that are coming through and be the harbingers of the truth. If you proceed along the path, dear one, your task will be to bring this knowledge into a clearer form of expression for the benefit of your readers. You will show others the way forward.

I took this to mean that I'd be expected to continue writing even after I'd finished Level Two. I couldn't see how I'd have much time for that, now I'd acquired five children, but decided to cross that bridge when I came to it. Presumably all would become clear if I took the giant step for womankind that was Level Three.

* * *

After Zac left, on the night when they'd both turned up, Jay hadn't carried me upstairs and ravished me, as you might have expected, even though I was all for it. Seeing the tears in his eyes after he'd told me he was all mine if I wanted him, I'd experienced a surge of longing for him. But when I took his hand and said, 'Come to bed,' he'd simply answered, 'I think we need to talk first, baby.' Then he'd led me back into the living room and sat me down on to the sofa where we cuddled like two kids.

We stayed up till two in the morning, telling each other our life stories since we'd parted. He told me that, first of all, life with Debbie had been good, although she'd insisted he stopped attending the all-night studio sessions he and the Jaylers were partial to.

'I could understand where she was coming from, but at least those sessions kept the booze, drugs and birds on neutral ground.'

He'd said this matter-of-factly, as if it was the most normal thing in the world.

I bridled at that. I'd known about the drugs and the booze, but not the birds. I'd naively assumed that Debbie was the first.

'Did you go with any of the girls when we were together, Jay?'

I couldn't see the expression on his face because I was lying with the back of my head on his chest, but I heard his voice shake slightly when he answered.

'Fraid so, baby. But I never did it in cold blood. It was always under the influence of something or other. You know, wide-eyed and legless.' He stroked my hair as if soothing a child. 'Didn't mean anything. That's what I meant by neutral ground. None of us let it affect our home lives. Except for Donny, maybe.'

He clasped me closer. I kept my head still so he couldn't tell I was crying, but he sensed it anyway.

'I'm sorry,' he whispered, 'Sorry it hurts you. I wanted you to know before you...' He moved position so we were face to face, and started wiping my damp face with a spotless white handkerchief he produced from his pocket, '... made up your mind.'

I had already made up my mind, but I wasn't going to let him off the hook that easily.

'I suppose it happened when you were on tour as well?'

He half shook his head. I think he'd been hoping one confession would be enough.

'Are you saying that Donny and the others were at it, but not you?' I chided.

He paused, as if weighing up the pros and cons of complete honesty. 'No one breaks the code of the road, Andy. What goes on tour, stays on tour.'

I took that to mean that he had been at it as well, and I instantly wanted to interrogate him for more details. Had I known any of the women he'd slept with? How many had there been? Or were they too numerous to mention? Had the awful Evie been one of them? If there'd been a powerful spotlight handy, I'd have shone it straight in his eyes.

But then my better part – the part that had been meditating and communing with the celestial set, refused to picture Jay in hotel rooms with other women. That part told me that the people we'd been then were a different Jay and a different Pandora. It was time to live in the present. So I tried really hard to extinguish my jealousy, and smouldered in silence.

Looking relieved that I hadn't cross-examined him further, Jay told me that the all-night sessions didn't go on much longer anyway, because soon after that the record company chose not to renew their contract. The hits had dried up and it seemed the right time for the group to disband.

So they all parted amicably with a party to end all parties in the Tangerine Lounge. Everyone present got smashed, even the glasses, as they ended the night by hurling them on to the dance floor.

'A few of 'em were so off their heads they kept dancing.' Jay smiled ruefully at the memory. 'Ended up in Casualty, having glass picked out of their feet. Anyway, that marked the end of James Jay and the Jaylers.'

'What happened to the others? Did they stay in the business?'

'Only me and Clive. He joined a New Age band, would you believe? Donny went into the fashion business with his wife. She was stunning – an ex-supermodel.' He shook his head. 'Now she's his ex-wife, but you know what Donny's like. Eddie bought a trout farm. Ian got married and settled in Wales. I see 'em all occasionally.'

Jay went on to tell me about his recent experiment with a short opera. This intrigued me, but interested as I was in his music, I wanted very badly to hear more about Debbie's reasons for leaving him. I bided my time, however, and waited for him to ask about Mike first. Finally the question came.

'So how did you meet this Mike, then?'

'At the Green Oak club, when I was eighteen. Then I bumped into him again, three and a half years ago. We were both divorced so we got together and moved here. He thought The Cedars would give me something to do. He was right. I enjoyed running it. We had some good stuff going on.'

Jay contemplated what I'd said. 'That's what I should have done for you, Andy. Given you something to do. Bought you a place like that. You were always searching for something. You never really found your purpose in life, did you, kid?'

This observation disheartened me. Is that how people had seen me – an aimless hedonist?

'I probably wouldn't have appreciated it then, Jay. I just wanted children. At least, that's what my body was telling me.'

'The creative impulse, Andy. It was strong in both of us. I had my music. And eventually,' his voice softened, 'five fruits of my loins.'

I smirked. 'You wait until I write my book. That'll be my baby.'

He grinned. 'You'll need a ton of biros and exercise books if you haven't got a computer.'

Jay went outside into the night air for a smoke, and when he came back he continued with his creation theory.

'You know, Andy, having children wouldn't necessarily have fulfilled you to the extent you thought it would. You and me used to talk about having a big family, but after the twins I would've said that's enough if it hadn't been for Debbie. Wouldn't be without any of 'em now, but I never knew why she kept wanting more kids. We had to get a cook because she didn't have a clue. And the number of nannies we had, you wouldn't believe.'

I was surprised. 'I thought she was the Earth-mother type. I always imagined her with a baby on each hip, breastfeeding, the whole works.'

Jay laughed. 'Not a chance. No, she loved 'em all right, don't get me wrong. But she didn't have a practical bone in her body. Couldn't cope. I think she reckoned giving me kids would keep a hold of me.'

Now was my chance. 'So what happened? You said *she* left *you*.'

I'd expected Jay to be bitter about this, but he sounded quite detached. 'My fault, I'm afraid. She caught me playing away with the girl who used to help with the ponies.' He looked suitably shamefaced at my shocked expression. 'I say girl, but she was twenty-eight. It was no big deal. Just boredom really. The combination of too much time on my hands, and opportunity. Many a man's downfall.'

I examined myself for any jealousy I might feel towards the pony girl, but there was none. I could only conclude that, as it had been Debbie he'd been cheating on, and not me, it left me cold.

Jay was still talking. 'Debbie packed her bags and took the youngest three to her mother's. There wasn't room for all five. We sorted it out in the end. I bought her a place a couple of miles away and the kids came to me at weekends. That's when my mum moved in.'

'And the accident?'

'Thank Christ she was on her own. She'd had a drink and collided with a tree. I went to the funeral. Took the kids. Saw her bloke there – he was pretty cut up.' Without a pause, he rasped, 'Did you love him, by the way?'

'Did I love…?'

'This Mike?'

'Yes. Very much.'

Jay looked stricken.

'Have you let go yet?'

'I think I might be in the process of doing that.'

'Good. Because I don't love any other woman, nor am I in the process of letting go. Just so we've got that clear before we proceed.'

We did share the same bed that night, but were so exhausted we fell straight asleep. The next morning I woke first and took him up a cup of coffee. That was when I saw that he wasn't quite as bony as I'd thought. In fact his bones were very satisfactorily covered with the flawless, honey-coloured skin I'd adored when we were married. His body was that of a much younger man, unlike his face.

'How do you keep your skin looking so young?' I'd murmured, as I pressed the special place on his back that had always turned him on.

'I use all-over moisturiser,' he'd gasped. 'Because I'm worth it.'

Both of us shook with laughter. 'Shame you didn't use it on your face,' I responded wickedly, proving that I hadn't quite mastered the feat of rising above his disclosure of infidelity on a grand scale.

He must have guessed what was bugging me because he slowed right down, kissed my breasts gently, and said, 'Think of my lined old mug as proof that I never stopped caring about you. It was always you, Andy. The others were just sex.'

In reply, I traced with my finger the heart tattoo bearing my name on the inside of his left arm, a few inches above the wrist. 'I'm surprised Debbie didn't force you to have my name lasered off.'

'She tried.' His beautiful eyes locked mine. 'I never kept the appointment – told her they said the ink was too deep to erase. But it wasn't the ink that was too deep.'

So in a funny sort of way he *had* been faithful. And then I felt a surge of love for him that took my breath away. I kissed every one of the precious lines on his face, and after that turned my attention to the rest of him, to demonstrate just how much I'd forgiven him.

Later on, it was his turn to bring me coffee. He placed it on the bedside table and, kneeling beside the bed, said simply, 'So what's it to be, Andy? Yes or no?'

You should have seen the look on his face when I leapt out of bed in a bunny girl outfit – minus the ears, which would have given the game away. Mike had bought it for our first wedding anniversary. It hadn't taken a minute to put on when Jay was downstairs in the kitchen.

I ran past him, avoiding the lunge he made for me, and met Oscar on the landing, who decided to have a go at my fluffy tail. I thought about Reg the medium who'd told me that Mike was 'always with me', and wondered if he was watching. It was a sobering thought, but I was determined to carry on anyway.

'What are you like? Mad woman,' laughed Jay as he watched me gather Oscar up in my arms and croon one of our songs to him. When I got to, 'My heart called to you, and you came to me', I thought of Enoch.

And when I reached the last line, 'We'll leave our fears behind us, and let our love take wing', Jay joined in, shortly followed by Oscar, who yodelled along in harmony.

'I never dreamt I'd wear this outfit again,' I said, when we'd sung the last note.

'I'll take that as a yes, then,' said Jay, planting a kiss first on Oscar's head, then mine.

Chapter 38 – 2003-2004

In the weeks following Jay's reappearance, events had progressed just as planned. Olivier had performed his part of TV chef to perfection and the production company had finished on time at the end of November.

After Zac's abrupt departure from Phoenix Cottage, we hadn't been back in contact, even though he was regularly on site for filming. I'd seen his car a few times, but I kept away from the house on purpose, as bumping into him would have been too embarrassing for both of us. Margery changed the linen and cleaned the bedrooms. Everything else was organised by Oven Ready Productions.

Then one day, in the final week of shooting, there was a knock on the door. When I opened it I was surprised to see Zac and a member of the production team, both looking solemn. I asked them in and the man, who Zac introduced as Sam, got straight to the point.

'Mrs Armstrong. A couple of us were exploring—'

The contract had given them the run of the house for two months, so I wondered why he was looking so guilty.

'—And we got into the cellar.'

'Oh, I thought I'd locked it,' I said. 'I didn't realise you'd want to use it. It's full of old sports stuff anyway.'

His tone was contrite. 'No, we didn't want to use it, we were just being curious. Actually, we didn't realise it was locked. Thought it was stuck. We gave the door a bit of a push. Some of the wood's splintered, I'm afraid.'

He glanced at Zac, a touch sullenly. 'Just thought we should let you know.'

Zac was looking on like a teacher who'd marched a naughty schoolboy to the headmistress's office.

'Naturally, Pandora, we'll be making good the damage and fixing a new lock immediately,' he said, adding stiffly, 'I can't apologise enough.'

My heart gave a little stir when he said that. I wanted to say: no, it's me who should apologise to you for being too cowardly to say a proper goodbye. A goodbye to our special relationship. But I knew it was too late to have that conversation, so I just answered him as sweetly as I could.

'Please don't worry, Zac. There's no hurry. I don't suppose the stuff's worth much, anyway. I keep it for the children. They like to play with the bats and balls.'

Sam looked relieved and Zac looked quizzical.

'Mike's grandchildren,' I explained. 'They visit occasionally.'

There was a pause while Zac's eyes and mine locked in a highly charged gaze, which was interrupted by Sam.

'You know, you might be surprised if you got that collection valued. There's quite a market for that sort of thing.'

'Oh, really?'

His words didn't properly sink in, because all I could think of was how attracted I still was to Zac.

The two men got up to go. Zac let Sam walk ahead and paused at the front door. His lips were smiling but his eyes were sorrowful.

'Are you happy, Mrs Armstrong?'

I lowered my eyes, to conceal the pangs of yearning which had gripped me. The last time I'd felt this way was when I'd got Collins' note, saying: *This is your last chance to change your mind.* I gave myself a mental shake and came to my senses.

'Mrs Armstrong, but soon to be Mrs Jay again.'

I think that answered his question.

'What about you? Are you happy Mr Willoughby?'

Zac kissed my cheek and we hugged gently. 'I'm happy if you're happy. And don't forget my invitation to the wedding. You're not getting rid of me that easily.'

* * *

Once Jay and I had decided to renew our vows – neither of us could see the point of getting legally married again – we had to make decisions about where to live and what to sell. He wanted me to join him and the children in the house at Great Marlow. And once they'd accepted me as tribe mother, how could I live anywhere else? I could hardly uproot them and replant them in The Cedars just because I wanted to keep Phoenix Cottage. Mike and I had bought both properties as one lot, so I assumed that's how they'd have to be sold.

We both wanted to keep the flat in Fulham for when we needed to stay over in London. Something had to give, as I was still struggling to pay all the bills. And Jay had enough on his plate keeping the saplings fed and watered.

In the end, Olivier solved the problem for me. I'd handed in my notice at the Cool Cake Boutique when I hooked up with Jay, but he hadn't minded.

'You were sent from 'eaven for me, Pandora, since without you and your 'ouse, I would still be making wedding cakes for *la bourgeoisie*. Don't worry about leaving Cool Cakes. The whole system's going on computer, anyway.'

A couple of weeks later he rang.

'Pandora,' he cooed, 'Justin and I are bursting out of our apartment and I 'ave a little proposition for you. Now you are reunited with your ancient rocker, we wondered if you wanted to sell us The Cedars. There'd be plenty of room for us and all our stuff. We can give workshops there – maybe even do weddings – and we can make location income on it, like you. Is it a possibility?'

'Um, Olly. When I talk about Jay as my ancient rocker, it's a term of affection, but you won't ever tell him I call him that, will you?'

'*Non, non, non*. But I still think you turn your back on a very delectable morsel in the shape of young Zachary. His mouth was very down when he talk about you. I 'ope you don't regret your decision, *chérie*. Anyway, what do you say to my little proposal?'

His timing was impeccable, as the roofing company had just dismantled their scaffolding, leaving The Cedars crowned with a beautiful new grey slate roof. So what I said, was *oui, oui, oui*, with the proviso that however quickly the sale went through, Jay and I could hold our ceremony at The Cedars on his birthday, February 14th. He'd particularly requested this, as we'd originally got married on that day in 1975.

'You don't think that's tempting fate, Jay?' I'd worried, when he'd suggested it. 'It wasn't very lucky the first time, was it?'

'It's not a question of luck, Andy. Call it my way of revisiting the day of the promise. Kind of setting the record straight.'

* * *

Getting The Cedars ready to hand over to Olivier was easy, given his request that all the furniture was to be included in the sale. The only thing I had to do was clear the cellar, so I arranged for a valuer from a specialist auction house to come and inspect the collection. When I received his valuation I whistled with surprise at how large the sum was.

I began to imagine how differently events could have gone, had I initiated the cellar sale eight months' earlier. I could have got the roof done in the spring, and I'd probably have gone back to running the house as I had before. Which meant I wouldn't have applied for a job with Olivier, and thus never met Zac. And possibly never have got in touch with Jay.

I'd been sitting on a golden egg without knowing it, yet had I discovered it earlier, my life would have taken a completely different turn. Having recently read an article on parallel realities, I had a mental picture of several versions of me living parallel lives which diverged in different ways at various times, according to which decisions they'd made. Maybe one of me had chosen Zac over Jay; maybe another me had married Mike when I was twenty and led an ordinary life like Ray and Cece. Finding the latter notion oddly unappealing, I distracted myself by ringing Danny to tell him the good news about the valuation. I felt he had just as much right to the profits as I had.

But Danny was adamant that I should keep all the money. 'Of

course you should have it. You made Dad happier than I've ever seen him. And kept him on the straight and narrow for the last three years of his life. For that alone you deserve a medal.'

This was very generous of him, but it wouldn't have felt right using Mike's money while living with Jay – the words 'spinning' and 'grave' leaping to mind at the thought. And it wasn't as if I was hard up now, having accepted Olivier's offer on the house. So, between us, Danny and I chose a range of organisations to donate the considerable proceeds of the auction to. Naturally, these included heart, animal, and children's charities. As I wrote the cheques, I whispered to Mike, 'I'm doing this in your name, in the hope you'll get a boost up to a higher astral plane. Or the seventh heaven. Or the fifth dimension – whatever it's called.'

* * *

During the house-purchase negotiations, it had come to light that Phoenix Cottage was actually registered as a separate property with its own boundaries.

'Does that mean I could keep it, and just sell The Cedars?' I'd asked my solicitor.

'Certainly, but your buyer will want to revise his offer if he's been under the impression that the price included both properties,' he'd replied. 'And he might well want to withdraw from the sale completely.'

I'd got straight on to Olivier, who at first had ummed and aahed. But after speaking to his partner Justin, he'd agreed, as long as I reduced the original asking price and gave him first refusal if I ever decided to sell the cottage.

'Thank you, Olly. You don't know what this means to me. I was having such regrets about losing it.'

'*De rien, chérie.* A smaller mortgage makes Justin more 'appy. He worries what 'appen if people stop getting married and his business close down. Silly boy.'

So, thanks to Justin's pessimism, I held on to my favourite property and pleased my mother at the same time. After her experiences with Toby and Richard Tait, she used to say, 'No matter how close you are to someone, it's best to keep a property of your own, Pan. Just in case it all goes belly up.' And ever since Jay and I had arranged to re-plight our troth, she'd taken to repeating this advice on an almost daily basis.

Of course, there was another reason I wanted to keep Phoenix Cottage. This was the place I'd established contact with Enoch, and there was still one vital ceremony I had to perform before I decamped to the country with Jay.

* * *

I had been staying on my own at Phoenix Cottage for a couple of days ahead of the Handfasting ceremony, a ritual which Frankie had persuaded us to sign up to. And Jay was to join me the night before the big day.

I was sitting in my study, a lighted candle on my desk, absorbed in what I was doing. On the shelf above my desk, among my other photographs, Mike's photo was on display – the one taken the Christmas before he died, with him in his lilac sweater and paper hat. I'd finally had the courage to liberate it from the bedroom chest of drawers. And when I looked at it I felt happy. Not sad, as I had before.

'Hey, baby. How you doing?' Jay had come in so quietly that I almost jumped a foot in the air when he put his hand on my shoulder. 'Sorry, didn't mean to scare you.'

I patted his hand and continued typing. 'I'm on the last chapter. Then I'll have to go back to the beginning and finesse it endlessly, according to the *How To Write A Book* manual.'

Jay kissed my left ear. 'In the words of the great Leonardo, "Art is never finished, only abandoned". So don't knock yourself out, sugar.'

'Try telling them upstairs that.'

Jay chuckled. He liked it when I talked other-worldly. 'So have you thought of a title yet?'

'Apart from *Level Two of the Enoch Society Correspondence Course*, no. There's so many things it could be. But none of them quite covers it all.'

'What about *Memoirs of a Born-Again Woman*? Or *The Only Way Is Up*?'

I smiled indulgently. 'Very funny. If all else fails, maybe you could turn it into a musical.' As I spoke, my fingers were moving over the keyboard as quickly as my pen had, when I'd been communicating with Enoch via pen and paper.

'It's writing itself really. Enoch's adapted very well to the keyboard.'

I loved being able to talk to Jay freely about Enoch, without feeling like a freak. His positive reaction when he'd overheard me telling Zac about Enoch, had surprised me at the time, but what he'd told me subsequently had explained why he'd been so accepting.

* * *

One day, soon after we got back together, I'd asked him if he still suffered from the same bad dream, where he'd murdered someone and was being pursued by shadowy figures. He told me that he'd consulted a hypnotherapist some years before, to see if he could get rid of it. 'The therapist said that the dream related to the father I'd never known. I wasn't acknowledging my feelings of abandonment, so I was trying to destroy those feelings. The people who were running after me represented parts of myself I didn't want to recognise – the parts that desperately wanted a father. Because deep down I felt guilty about that. Felt I was being disloyal to the woman who brought me up. My gran-mother.'

'So it wasn't about you wanting to murder your father?' I'd said.

'No. And I was relieved about that, I can tell you. Sometimes I used to panic that the dream was predictive, and I'd end up killing someone. No, it wasn't my father I was trying to kill, but the feelings of abandonment I was having. I talked it all through with the guy and pretty soon I stopped having the dream.'

I knew a little bit about hypnotherapy, that having been one of the correspondence courses I'd taken, but never taken any further. For any cynics reading this, if enlightenment can be a distance-learning experience, why not hypnotherapy?

'So, Jay,' I said, trying to wear my distance learning lightly, 'Did you notice any difference in your behaviour after that?'

'I certainly did, my flower. Why do you ask that?'

'Well, I remember reading that the only way to stop a recurring dream successfully is to break out of the pattern in your life that's causing it. This is what you did, when you acknowledged the feelings you had, and stopped trying to suppress them.'

Jay nodded. 'Yeah, that's pretty much what he said.'

'But,' I went on, 'there's also another aspect. The pattern doesn't only cause the dream, it can cause damaging behaviour as well. Did you recognise your recurring patterns of destructive behaviour?'

Jay looked abashed. 'You lived with me for eleven years, what do *you* think they were?'

I tried not to sound disapproving. 'I witnessed the booze and the drugs. And you've recently admitted to the women...'

Jay held up his hands, 'Guilty as charged. Yeah. Once I stopped having the dreams, I gradually came off the drugs. No more uppers, no more downers. Plus I cut down on the booze.' He hesitated, no doubt thinking it was still a sore subject with me. 'And I even knocked the birds on the head as well.'

I had a vision of Jay murdering chickens, which I thrust promptly from my mind.

'What about the pony girl?'

'She just slipped through the net, Andy. You've gotta allow a guy an occasional lapse. Remember the genetic imperative.'

This expression had been a joke in the band ever since one of them read an article about why men's instinct was to have sex with lots of women, while women tended to look for one partner. It was something along the lines of women only being able to have one child a year, while men were continuously able to father more children, and so were just following their basic impulses to keep the human race going. I always felt rather excluded from this joke. If it had been up to my body, the human race would have died out.

Jay kissed me then and muttered something about being sorry for all the shit I'd had to put up with when we were married. But that's not how I remembered it. Probably because I hadn't been aware of half of it.

'Yeah, but whether you knew it or not, it happened,' he whispered. 'I just want you to know I'm sorry. And I'm a reformed character now.'

Calling to mind the article about balancing yin and yang that Charles had written, I joked, 'Sounds like you had a yang overload.'

He looked puzzled, so I elaborated. 'You know, the Chinese symbol. The male and female tadpoles. Too much testosterone.'

He smiled, 'I get it. Now I'm in touch with my feminine side, I'm a more balanced human being. And my pendulum's swung the other way.'

'Yeah,' I taunted, 'As long as it hasn't swung too far.' Whereupon Jay proceeded to prove that he was in a very poised place indeed.

Jay told me a little later the same evening, that once he'd got himself clean of all his addictions, he'd joined a local reading group, which focused on spiritual subject matter. He'd also been on retreat a couple of times, to the temple that George Harrison had bought for his Hare Krishna friends. Like me, he hadn't been much of a joiner, but read the books and cherry-picked the parts he empathised with. So that was why we were on the same wavelength, and why I could speak to him about Enoch and not worry that he thought I was weird.

As we talked, he smoked one of the three roll-ups he permitted himself every day. 'Allow me one small vice, Andy,' he'd said when

I'd first looked doubtful, 'It's only Old Holborn, don't worry.'

'Okay,' I'd agreed. I actually loved the smell of it as it reminded me of my dad. 'You can make me one if you like.'

So every now and then we smoked a roll-up together and chanted our new mantra – 'moderation in all things'. Except, of course, in our love for each other and the children. And Oscar.

Chapter 39 – 2004

So here we all are, at the climax of the Handfasting ceremony when the priest, Charles, and the priestess, Frankie, are about to tie our hands together with two cords.

'All things of the material world eventually return to the Earth. This bond and the connection your spirits share is destined to ascend to the heavens. May you be forever as one in the passion and fire of you,' intones Charles.

He places a silken cord around my right hand and then loops it over Jay's left hand, in a figure of eight, tying the ends together. Frankie does the same, looping and tying a second cord round Jay's hand and then mine. As she does so, she murmurs in an undertone, so only we can hear, 'And if you ever break my daughter's heart again, this'll be round your neck, my lad. And that's a promise.'

Some lad, I think, as I scan Jay's lived-in face to check that he isn't taking Frankie too seriously, even though I know she means every word. He looks mortified and I mouth 'sorry'. But mortified isn't such a bad thing. And I feel almost proud of Frankie, for speaking up for me.

Having trussed us up, she continues her discourse. 'Thus are your hands fasted for infinity, and two are now made one, in the eyes of the gods, goddesses, your family and friends.'

She turns to where Hannah has been standing since the beginning of the ceremony, holding a white silk cushion on which two gold rings lie sparkling. They sparkle because Jay had them cleaned. They're actually the originals he kept from our first wedding. This came as a pleasant surprise to me. When I sent mine back to him, I never dreamt I'd ever see it again, let alone wear it.

Frankie fails to catch Hannah's eye, so demands loudly, 'Who holds the rings?'

Hannah returns with a jerk from wherever her daydream had taken her, the rings swaying alarmingly. But she manages to deliver them safely to our side. Jay winks at her and she blushes. This is a sign she really likes him.

I'm not sure what Jay and I are going to say next. Charles suggested that at this point we could declare that we'd never stopped loving each other, but we thought this would be tactless in view of the circumstances. Jay didn't want the children thinking he hadn't loved their mother, and I didn't want Danny thinking the same about my feelings for his father.

In any case, proclaiming our undying love till death us do part the first time round, hadn't kept us together, had it? Although we'd meant it when we said it. We'd been innocent, then, untainted by experience.

Jay takes my ring from the cushion with his free right hand and puts it on the ring finger of my left hand. As he does so, he whispers, 'I promise I'll try and be faithful this time,' which causes me to frown in a very unbridely way, until he adds, 'If I do, you have my permission to kill me.'

'If my mother doesn't get there first,' I reply, out of the corner of my mouth, and he widens his eyes in mock horror.

I take his ring from the cushion with my free left hand and put it on the ring finger of his bound left hand. Jay's eyes, serious now, stare at me intently, waiting for me to speak. So I just say the first thing that comes into my head, loudly enough for all to hear.

'I promise to love and support you and the children. For ever. With all my heart and soul.'

There's a small ripple of applause followed by a few whoops, and Charles hurries on with his next line, before the congregation gets too raucous.

'These rings are circles. They have no beginning and no end. They symbolise unity. May the love you have for each other be as eternal as these rings. Pandora and James, you are now as your hearts have always known you to be. Husband and wife.'

Jay and I kiss, and everybody cheers. We're standing on a raised dais at one end of the main meeting room, which is unrecognisable, being decked out as a Midsummer Night's Dream garden, its bowers heavy with gauzy drapes, strewn with woodbine, violets, roses and eglantine, resting on a carpet of artificial grass. We'd set a medieval theme, with me in an ivory organza wedding gown complete with a long v-shaped girdle belt and a train. My hair's all plaited and coiled, encircled by a garland of snowdrops. Jay's dressed in a gold doublet with an enormous buckle and brown leggings. Outrageously kitsch, but that's the idea.

I look out at the assembled company, resplendent in their costumes. There's Clive, who's come as a court jester: vertically half red, half yellow, topped off with a jester's cap complete with bells. Donny and his beautiful third wife pose in impeccable creations, woven and tailored, no doubt, by rude mechanicals.

Olivier and Justin are grinning at the back, maybe contemplating a similar ceremony sometime soon. We planned to bring in outside caterers so they could sit down and be waited on for once, but they wouldn't hear of it. Though I'm sure their decision had a lot to do with wanting to dress up as medieval chefs in enormous blouson tops, baggy trousers, floppy hats and suede boots.

Mr and Mrs Grove have strategically placed themselves beside Olly and Justin, desperate as they are to be kept on by the new owners, chatting and laughing with them as if they're old friends.

In front of them stands Fiona, in a floor-length, low-cut, pink-satin number with leg of lamb sleeves, chatting to a very attentive Eddie. Who, as I remember, showed a similar interest in her at our last wedding.

Ian's sitting on a chair the other side of Fiona, having sprained his ankle jumping off a table at Jay's stag do a couple of nights earlier in the Tangerine Lounge.

My old friend Peter, our neighbour in Fulham, is smiling and giving us the thumbs up. He told me he was looking forward to seeing us both again, once the tenants have gone and we start using the place as our *pied-à-terre*.

Beside him is Rosemary, in a robe of plush plum velvet over a white peasant blouse with drawstring neck and sleeves – her short, neat, dentist's hair incongruous as ever. Her son Max is in jeans and a hoodie, having refused to dress up fancy. He seems to be eyeing up Cherry and Willow, our two girls. Cherry, being fifteen, will probably ignore him completely, but thirteen-year-old Willow may well give him a run for his money. I'll hear all about it tomorrow – Willow tells me everything now.

Next to them is Zac, accompanied by a svelte young woman, who, according to Olivier, has recently joined Oven Ready. They haven't come in fancy dress, but Zac's wearing a token Henry VIII hat, at a fetching angle. I wave at him with my bound hand, which means that Jay's hand waves as well.Zac grins and doffs his hat with an impressive flourish.

Toby is standing next to Zac. Haven't seen him in ages. He's a couple of years older than Jay but still looks quite boyish. Frankie was visibly shaken when she caught sight of him earlier on. I hope they get to resolve their historic differences later, over a drink. That was part of the reason I invited him.

Cece and Ray are in a group with Danny and Mei, who's trying to stop William playing hide and seek underneath the chairs with Oscar. Hannah, who couldn't wait to escape from the bridal dais, has just joined William. She's managed to transfer her floral headband to Oscar's neck and now he's trying like mad to shake it off.

My thoughts float back to Christmas, when my worries about whether I was a pity-nana had been finally dispelled. Dan had suggested we all spent the day together – the four of them and the ten of us, including Sharon, Frankie and Charles. They all came up to The Cedars and stayed the night, so at least the newly refurbished kitchen and dining-room hosted one good family banquet before being handed over to Olivier. Everyone got on fine. And I'm pretty sure they'll always be in our lives.

I wave at Cece, this time with my free hand, and she curtseys, which looks really good, as she seems to have come as a scullery maid, and a well-endowed one at that. Ray seems to be channelling Robin Hood – got up in a green jerkin, boots, and feathered cap.

Joan is sitting next to them, her hair beehived for the occasion, face powdered, lips a slash of scarlet, sporting a ginger fur coat. I'm not sure what species of animal it's come from, but an undernourished one by the look of it. She's a bit deaf, so with any luck missed the worst of the neo-pagan incantations performed by Charles and Frankie, featuring Aphrodite and Eros along with Beings of Earth, Air, Fire, and Water. I almost expected Bottom and Puck to make a guest appearance. Thank heaven for small mercies.

Sharon is beaming, positioned right at the front, with the saplings. They've all been to Angels Costumiers and are medievally dressed to perfection.

Jay and I try to look suitably serious, as Frankie and Charles remove the cords from our hands and give one to each of us.

'I've got a proper one that you can tie me up with later,' whispers Jay. I laugh and then stop in wonder. Above everyone's head, a tiny flame is dancing. I didn't know Enoch could be in so many places at once. I haven't forgotten, I tell him silently. It won't be long.

EPILOGUE

I'm standing outside my study. The enlightenment kit is waiting for me on my desk. There's a white candle, an incense stick, some typed pages comprising the first guided meditation, and the alabaster pot of chrism. It's six days after our Handfasting, and tonight there's a new moon.

Jay is standing next to me, willing me on. 'Go on, babe. If anyone can super-spin into Wonder Woman you can.' His voice mutates into mock lecherous, 'Do they supply a costume as well, my pretty?'

I'm too nervous for levity, so I'm afraid I snap at him a bit.

'For goodness' sake, it's only the first night. There's still two weeks till the full moon. It probably won't even work. I don't know why I'm bothering really.'

I'm having a wobble now about whether I'm really ready for enlightenment and the duties and responsibilities that come with it. It seemed feasible when I was single, but now I've got Jay and the children to think about, it might not be so easy.

Jay's looking a bit worried but carries on anyway. 'Well, if they give you the option, I quite fancy Lara Croft. Or Batgirl. She's quite tasty.'

I pretend to punch him in the shoulder and he catches my hand and kisses it.

'You know you're already my perfect woman, Andy. But remember what you said about having a purpose.' He tilts my chin to engage eye contact. 'Do you really want to pull up at the last hurdle?'

I take Jay's hand, blinking back some tears which have started to well.

'But starting it tonight means we have to spend the rest of our honeymoon here. It's not much fun for you. Why don't I postpone it?'

'No worries, baby. I'll be writing. Got an idea for a song already. It's called Phoenix Woman.'

I laugh feebly, not sure whether he's joking.

'You're exploiting the superwoman trope with a vengeance tonight, Jay. I feel more like the Lady of Shalott, going to my doom.'

He laughs and his arms encircle me. 'Well, if you feel like your boat's sinking I'll be your lifeguard.'

I cuddle into him, taking comfort from his embrace. He smells faintly of roll-ups and wine. What was it Cassiel wrote? After the rebirth process, I'll have to meditate regularly, eat healthily, exercise regularly and avoid alcohol. I didn't mind the first three but the last one's a big ask.

'I'm supposed to give up drinking,' I moan, 'I'm going to miss my glass of wine with dinner.'

Jay steps back in mock indignation. 'What! You mean they want you to save the world and they won't even let you have a glass of sauvignon blanc?'

'I'm not saving the world. You're bigging it up out of all proportion. They just said something about me bringing myself and other people hope and—' I scan my memory banks for their exact words, '—that I had to make a conscious effort to transform any difficult situations. Rosemary said it's like being an energy alchemist.' Under my breath, I add, 'Whatever the fuck that is.'

Jay looks pained and I feel ashamed for being such a foul-mouthed prima donna.

'That sounds like a pretty crucial mission to me. For starters, there's the kids. They could definitely do with a bit of transforming.'

An image of Rosemary's picture of the Lady of Avalon appears in my mind and, beneath it, the words 'mother of transformation'. Maybe my fate had been sealed as soon as I'd drunk the green potion Rosemary had given me. Like a character in a fairy tale, I'd become enchanted.

Jay can see my mind has wandered, so he waves his hand in front of my face to bring me back. 'The magic worked for me, so why not for other people?'

He's right. Jay and I had already opened our eyes to what little satisfaction there was to be found in the self-indulgent life. And discovered that a healthy relationship, built on truth and keeping promises, was a million times more satisfying than one tainted by deceit, neediness and jealousy.

I wipe away the tears and kiss Jay tenderly, as if saying goodbye. I feel like the phoenix, about to start building its nest of cinnamon, myrrh and spikenard, in preparation for the burning away of the old life and my rebirth into the new at the coming full moon.

'I think it'll take between one and two hours,' I whisper. 'I'll see you then.'

I open the study door and walk into the room. The door closes behind me. I sit down at my desk, light the candle and the incense stick, and, following the instructions carefully, anoint the palms of my hands and my brow with Cassiel's pungent chrism. I close my eyes and feel them roll back, as I visualise light flooding into my crown, down my body to the Earth. I imagine Enoch and Cassiel, my two sentinels, with me in the room. Like centurions. On guard.

After a few minutes, I focus on the first page of the first stage of my journey, and start to read.